WILL TO LIVE

William Seckington

ISBN: 1494461455
ISBN-13: 9781494461454
Library of Congress Control Number: 2013923507
CreateSpace Independent Publishing Platform
North Charleston, South Carolina

For John Allison:

A true friend of Kingswood School and to all who met him.

PROLOGUE

Germany, 1934

Marie's lungs were bursting and her face was as red as the dark bricks of the schoolhouse walls. She was out of breath but also out in front by more than twenty meters. Franz, however, was closing fast. One last obstacle lay ahead. Marie dove for the ground and easily squeezed through the pipe's opening. Just as she extricated herself from the pipe, she heard Franz dive inside. Franz was not as agile and yelled as his head struck the top of the pipe. Marie could not help but laugh to herself, *silly Franz. You think that you can beat me. My father has helped me to train for months just for this moment. I am the best. As the Führer has said, "We are the future of Germany".*

The entire school was crowding around the finish line. As she rounded the last obstacle, Marie saw her friends had moved closer, arms high above their heads, making a tunnel for her triumphant finale. She heard them screaming and beamed because she knew they were right. She was the strongest. She was the lioness, the queen of the jungle.

It was all over now. After a week of games, challenges and races, she had emerged the victor. She had beaten everyone in her grade, even the boys. The winners of each grade level competition were called to the platform and the school director handed them two papers. The first paper proclaimed each of them as a champion of the Third Reich and the second gave instructions regarding attendance at a future rally. Marie was just too excited to read the second piece. She would give the second letter to her father because he liked to read any information coming from the new government.

After shaking hands with the director, she was led to a higher position on the platform. On the top level stood Hauptmann Heinrich Froer, the district head of the Nazi Youth program. He was dressed in the neat, crisp military uniform of the Third Reich, complete with shiny black shoes and sparkling gold buttons. Marie stared at him as she moved closer.

He looked so proud, she thought. I want to be like him, a proud German. At that moment Marie lifted her head higher, smiled brighter, and pushed out her chest. Just a slight bit of embarrassment showed on her face because, at thirteen, Marie still did not have much of a chest to push out. Heinrich Froer stuck out his hand and said, "Congratulations! So you are the little girl that beat all of these boys. You must be very good." Froer then bent down and pinned a medal on Marie's dress lapel. She wanted to look down at it but she could not take her eyes off of the handsome Heinrich Froer.

Marie confidently returned the handshake and said, "Yes. I worked very hard and I am the best!"

Froer smiled and said, "Today you were the best and the strongest. The Führer will need strong women to help achieve his dreams for Germany, you know. Would you like to have an opportunity to see him one day?"

"Oh yes!"

"You take the paper home that your director gave you and let your father read it. You may have a chance to see the Führer very soon," Froer said.

"Yes, I will immediately! Thank you again for this day. I will never forget it."

Froer finished the conversation with, "Oh young lady, I think that there may be many more unforgettable days in your future."

Marie couldn't wait to get home and tell her father all about the day. For the past eight years it had just been Marie and her father, Herman Monin. Monin, a former decorated officer in the *Imperial*

German Army, was wounded twice along the Eastern Front. He had thought of making the military his career but returned home in 1918 disillusioned with the German government and the military blunders made by those safely out of the fight. Herman Monin married Helene shortly after his return to Frankfurt. Helene was not a healthy woman and most of Marie's memories of her mother revolved around moans and cries, dumping bedpans, and the horrid odors lingering in her parents' bedroom. Herman never remarried, so Marie was running home to the only family she had really ever known.

"Daddy, Daddy," Marie yelled, as she swung the front door open. Just as Marie was closing the door, her father entered the parlor room.

"Marie, what is all the excitement?" her father countered.

"Oh Daddy, I won today!"

"The race?"

"Yes Daddy, I won the race! But more than that, I won the entire competition. All three days. Daddy, I am the very best. Hauptmann Froer even said I was the best and he gave me this." Marie pushed her lapel up toward her father. Smiling, he looked down and saw a shiny gold eagle sitting on top of a white ceramic circle. Inside the circle was a blue swastika. "Oh Daddy, the director also gave me these papers."

"Well, let's take a look at these." Her father saw that the first was a certificate for Outstanding Physical Achievement and the second paper was from the Nazi Youth Division. "It looks like the Party is inviting all the youth champions from across Germany to the party rally in Nuremberg next week." He reached down and grabbed Marie hoisting her into the air. He could feel the moisture on her blouse and when he gave her a kiss on the cheek, he could taste the salt that remained from the perspiration.

Marie squeezed her father's neck as tightly as she could and kissed him back. "Do I get to go?"

Her father beamed with pride and said, "How could I stop such a strong champion and how could I say no to Hauptmann Froer or to our Führer? Of course you can go!"

On September 5, Marie sat in the great Luitpold Hall in Nuremberg, along with seventy-five other children. Marie noticed that each child wore a medal just like hers, openly displayed on his or her lapel. And like Marie, everyone touched and played with their pin, as though it was transmitting some magical powers. Marie quickly counted only seven girls in the group and felt proud to be in such an elite group. Music began playing. She recognized Strauss and knew his music was the Führer's favorite. Her eyes darted everywhere. There were so many people; some were in military uniform but most were dressed in evening clothes. To Marie the people looked similar to audiences she had seen at the opera house with her father. Approximately an hour after the children were seated, the band began to play Beethoven's *Egmont Overture*. The crowd became quiet and all eyes were focused on the dais. The curtains behind the dais parted ever so slightly and out from behind came the Führer, Adolph Hitler. Following close behind Hitler were Goring, Goebbles, Hess, and Himmler, each a close advisor in the new government.

When the orchestra stopped playing, all 30,000 people stood with their right arm erect and shouted, "Heil!, Heil!" The Führer raised his arm and acknowledged the crowd. Then Hitler turned toward the young champions, smiled widely and raised his arm again. Each champion could see the pride in Hitler's face and each thought he was looking directly at them. Marie was sure the Führer made eye contact with her. It was at that moment Marie said to herself quietly, "*My Führer, my Germany. I will love you and serve you forever.*"

PART I

PATRIOTS

CHAPTER ONE

Germany, 1940

Marie arrived at the train station early. Central Station was busy with cars honking, moving slowly in and out of traffic and dropping or loading passengers near the large entrance. Without the good fortune of a ride, Marie had packed her two small suitcases and walked to the bus stop. The bus sojourned across the city like a worm crawling across garden soil. It traversed the one-way streets, picking up passengers along the way. Some men and women dressed surely for work and a few children dressed smartly in the uniforms of local prep schools had come and gone by the time the bus made its stop at the Central Station, the end of the line.

The curbside bustled with men. Many appeared excited as they juggled their bags to their shoulders and waved goodbye to the women who had driven them to the station. Since Germany's annexation of Austria and the invasion into Czechoslovakia, thousands of men had been called into the service and were now heading toward Berlin or other military locations.

It was almost one year since Germany invaded Poland, protecting the security of the country. The Führer had addressed the people regarding the new Reich and the right of the true German people. The Führer said that it was Germany's time to take its place on the center of the world stage. True Germans should never again have to prostrate themselves in front of other Europeans. He said that Germany was forced into signing the Versailles Treaty and France and England

3

to blame for the economic problems currently facing Germany. ⌐ it was time for Germans to take control of their destiny. Every ⌐zen would be called on to sacrifice for the good of the German ⌐e. The most current news out of Berlin informed citizens that the ⌐erman army had opened a Western front, moving toward Holland ⌐nd Belgium.

Once inside the station, Marie pulled out the second-class ticket sent to her by Heinrich Froer. She received the ticket and a letter three days ago. Froer opened the letter reminiscing about Marie's physical conquests within the Youth Sports Program. He continued by stating how impressed he was with her dedication to Germany and to the Führer and that he was saddened when he had to leave his post with the youth program and move to Berlin. She was most surprised by Froer's last comments. He asked her to use the ticket and to come see him in Berlin. He said there was a special job for her within the new government. The job would require all of her physical and intellectual capabilities. He concluded with, "Tell no one of this letter or the reason for your travels to Berlin."

The train pulled slowly into the station and passengers moved from their leisurely positions toward the cars. Marie walked over to one of the conductors. He was tall and thin, almost sickly thin. His face was ashen gray with stubble from a day's growth of beard. His uniform fell over him in a wrinkled heap and Marie was reminded of the difficult financial times for all of Germany. He paused for a moment, reading the ticket, and then said, "Why is such a lovely young Fräulein going off to Berlin all alone? Have you not heard about the new fighting?"

Marie lied and said, "My aunt has asked me to come and help her. She is about to give birth to her third child and her husband has been called back into military service. A neighbor of hers will be waiting for me at the Zoo Station in Berlin. Thank you for your concern." Hoisting her two small suitcases off the ground, Marie made her way through the herd of passengers toward her car.

The train was a dented, rusty, old steamer in need of some new color. Upon entering her car, Marie was overcome by the suffocating heat. There were several other passengers in the car each already lowering windows in an attempt to get some ventilation. Marie quickly placed her luggage under her seat and joined in.

"The Führer must be using all the quality trains for his military," said a young male passenger as they both reached for the same window. "My name is Hans von Schroedder," he continued.

"Hello, it's nice to meet you. My name is Marie Monin," Marie said as she stuck out her hand.

Hans smiled and inquired, "Are you traveling alone today, and if so, would you mind if I joined you?"

Marie took some time before answering. She thought of the Froer's comment about secrecy but decided it would be charming to have some company for the twelve-hour trip. She had to admit that Hans was certainly much better to look at than some of the others in the car. "That would be fine. It doesn't look like there will be too much competition for seats or for the little oxygen we may find in this oven."

Hans laughed saying, "It is stifling, but things should improve once we are underway. Let me get my things and I will be right back."

Hans disappeared out the front of the car for just a moment and returned with two bottles of lemonade. Handing one of the bottles to Marie he said, "This might help cool you for a short time." As Marie took the bottle, their fingers touched slightly. It was the second time their fingers had touched. The first time was when they both reached for the window and Marie felt a surprise of excitement pass over her body. Earlier, Marie had looked at boys only as competitors, but Hans was a handsome, polite gentleman. Considering other ways to inadvertently touch him, Marie slowly sipped on the lemonade.

Looking back at the city and the mountains, Marie saw fall beginning to awaken among the trees, turning them from summer greens to fiery colors of yellow and orange. These would be the last hot days. There were always a few weeks in September when the weather was fickle, with hot, humid days and nights cooling considerably.

Marie spent all of her life living just outside of Frankfurt, along the Rhine River Valley. This place was the only home she had ever known.

Her father's sudden death had robbed her home of its magic. After her mother's death, her father's love increased and took up the void left by her absence. Her father never remarried. It was just the two of them, loving and caring for each other. For the first time in her life she was alone. She knew it was time to find another place to call home.

"So where are you off to?" asked Hans.

"Berlin, and you?"

"I have been called to an enlistment center in Hannover and from there I will join a navy training group in Hamburg. Have you ever been to Berlin?" asked Hans, just as Marie was taking a drink.

Marie nodded her head and when finished said, "I was there only once for the Olympics. I was involved in the Youth Sports Program and our team won the Frankfurt track championships. Our team of ten received tickets to the track and field finals."

"That must have been exciting. Have you always been interested in track and field?"

"Yes. I have always loved to run. My father called me the little lioness because he said that I ran down my competition. He said that I had the eyes of a wild cat waiting to pounce on my prey and devour them. I loved to compete and more importantly, I loved to win! Boxing would have been my chosen sport, but my father said that boxing was not for young girls and so track became a more civilized way to defeat my foes."

"When did you get interested in track competition?"

"I guess it would have been in October of 1934. My father had just brought home a poster advertising the Nazi League of German Girls and I remember seeing a picture showing a female runner bursting through the finish line tape. Her stride was powerful, her body erect, and she was looking toward the heavens. I could hear the shouts of adulation for her. Hans, you know all I could think was that she looked so proud to be a champion German woman. The Youth Athletic Festival was going to begin in two weeks and I told my father that I was going be just like the runner on the poster. I hung the poster on my bedroom door and each day I looked at it before leaving for school or track practice. I won my division, beating both boys and girls for the overall title. How about you? Did you ever compete in any athletic competitions?"

"Never at your level. I like to get outdoors and exercise, but my competition has been limited to a few shooting contests and a weekly game of chess with my uncle."

Marie laughed, "Chess?"

"Don't laugh. Chess is mental competition and just as strenuous as your track. Have you ever played?"

"No, but I doubt that you ever left a chess game with your uncle in a full sweat."

"All I am saying is that chess teaches you discipline, patience, strategy, and you do get to destroy the enemy. Your mind needs exercise too. You shouldn't condemn it until you at least give it a try. I'm sorry that I don't have a board with me now or I would show you. Maybe some other time. So why are you off to Berlin now?"

Marie was so relaxed and enjoying the conversation that she almost spoke without thinking of Froer's admonishment. "Oh, I'm out to visit my aunt. Her first child is due next month and her husband is away with the military. She asked if I wouldn't come and help with some of the house duties for a while."

"It seems like such a long way for you to travel. Doesn't she have anyone closer that could help out? Where in Berlin does she live?"

Marie had to think quickly. "They just moved from Frankfurt two years ago and don't have any relatives around to help them. She will be picking me up at the station, so I don't know just where in the city they live." Marie remembered she had just earlier told a different story to the conductor. If she was going to lie, she thought, she had better use the same story. Now Marie had to find a way of diverting Hans' questioning. "Are all of these questions part of your chess game mental gymnastics?"

Hans retreated and looked saddened. "Oh I am sorry. Please forgive me. I didn't mean to offend you or to pry. I was just trying to make conversation. I'll stop the inquisition."

7

Marie felt somewhat relieved but reached over and touched Hans' hand and said, "That's okay. Tell me about yourself. Why the navy?"

"I am not sure really. I come from the mountains around Heidelberg and have never seen the ocean. I didn't even learn to swim until I was thirteen. Anyway, my grandfather served in the navy during the last war and I loved to listen to his stories. He made the underwater world of the navy seem so exciting and adventurous. That's why I am off to Hannover. I am going through testing to see if I qualify for the navy's program. If I don't qualify, then I guess it's the infantry and off to the Eastern front. Maybe I should have been doing more of the physical fitness training like you."

"I think you will do just fine," Marie said, relieved that the conversation had been diverted from her trip to Berlin. "If you don't mind, I think I will just try to close my eyes and rest some." Marie took a sweater out of her bag, folded it and made a small pillow. She leaned against the wall and felt the air as it brushed through the window, across her face. As she began to fall off to sleep, Hans looked over at her, smiled and whispered, "Okay for now."

Marie awoke to find Hans gone. She stretched to get the stiffness out of her legs and arms and decided to walk to the next car and use the lavatory. As she approached the door, Marie saw Hans through the door's window. He was standing in the aisle having a conversation with two other men in German military uniforms. She stood at the door and watched. He was short, compared to the other men, but he had more legs than upper body. His waist was thin and with his sleeves rolled up she could see that his forearms were certainly muscular. His hair was black and combed back in a very sophisticated way. He looked dark and mysterious and for just a moment she wished that he was not getting off at Hannover. Hans turned as Marie opened the car door. Their eyes met just before Marie ducked into the lavatory. Marie found Hans back at the seats, just opening a bag holding two sandwiches. "I was hungry so I went to the café car. I picked you up a sandwich too, if you would like it," Hans said.

"Thanks, I am rather hungry," Marie said as she slid in beside him. "Who were those soldiers you were talking to?"

"One of them was a friend from my school days. Franz is his name. He joined the army maybe four months ago. He just returned home for a few days of leave before his unit ships out to Poland."

Marie was excited. "What does he say the army is like?"

"He said that the training has been tough. He also said his whole unit was consumed with the anticipation of finding and fighting the enemy. Franz actually seems to be looking forward to battle. I think that's crazy, don't you?"

"Not at all! We are Germans! We all have jobs to do for the good of the country. The Nazis have finally brought strong leadership to Germany. Now we can take back the land that belongs to us and be able to unite all of Europe. Hans, this is our chance to drive out all of those opposed to a greater Germany and to rid ourselves of the Jewish demons that have been parasites for far too long."

"I know Germany needs a strong leader like Hitler and unifying all Germans is a good idea, but don't you think invading other countries might be provoking a war that will lead to the deaths of innocent thousands? Aren't you afraid that maybe your aunt's husband will not return from his military duties? What about your cousin? Will he or she be left with only pictures of a father? I am just not sure if this is right."

Marie wanted to tell him about her true reasons for going to Berlin. She wanted to hold him and say that all would be well, but deep inside she was unsure. She was certain that Germany should fight, but unsure of whom would survive. In the end Marie said nothing. She just took another bite of her sandwich.

It was just about 3:00 p.m. when the train pulled into the station at Hannover. Hans stood and began to get his things together. Marie also stood and said, "Hans, be careful and stay well. Neither of us knows just where we will be located but know that I will think of you." Marie put her arms around his neck and gave him a kiss on the cheek.

Hans dropped his bags and placed his arms around Marie's waist. "Thanks for putting up with my inane questions. Maybe we will run into each other again on the train, next time heading south. Take care, Marie, and good luck with your aunt and new baby cousin." Hans then picked up his bags and started toward the front of the car. Just as he got to the door, he turned around and looked back at Marie. She threw him a kiss and mouthed, "For luck." Hans nodded and walked away.

As the train began its final leg toward Berlin, Marie once again pulled out the letter from Heinrich Froer. *Please accept my sincere condolences on your father's passing. He was a fine man and loving father. This must be a lonely time for you and thus the reason for my letter. I remember, and hope you do as well, the wonderful times that you and your father had at the Party festivals. He was the proud parent of the champion daughter. Knowing how much your father believed in the Führer's program makes me comfortable in asking a favor of you at this time. The Party needs some women to become involved in a special project. It will require all of your strength, both physical and mental. If you still have the same dreams and desires to help our new Germany, please use this ticket and arrive in Berlin on 27, September. I will be at the Zoo Station awaiting your arrival and at that time we can discuss your involvement with the new government. Please do not mention this letter to anyone. I look forward to seeing the little lioness once again.*

My condolences,

Heinrich

Marie sat back and thought. *What does Froer mean ' the same dreams and desires'?*

CHAPTER TWO

The announcement came overhead that Zoo Station was only min-utes away. Marie had been alone in the two seats since Hans left the train in Hannover. She was now filled with anticipation; she had not seen Heinrich Froer since her visit to Berlin in 1936. During that time there were many changes in her life: her father's death, the na-tional movement in Germany and the strange invitation from Froer.

For the summer Olympics, Berlin had been alive with a feeling of nationalistic pride. Everywhere she went there were flags waving and cheery vendors ready to sell their wares to tourists. Nazi posters show-ing proud German men and women were readily plastered to poles, walls and windows. Everyone was so helpful to her group of young Nazi sports members. Marie remembered seeing the photographers pushing and shoving trying to snap pictures of the athletes. She also recalled some of the foreign photographers taking pictures of German soldiers, standing guard on the street corners. Her final thoughts were of dreams of becoming an Olympic athlete representing Germany. She had returned to Frankfurt and continued to train, but after her father's sudden death, she was forced to leave school and find a job to support herself.

When Froer's letter arrived and she decided to go to Berlin, Marie told Mr. Schnotz, the bakery owner, that she needed to take leave for one week. Mr. Schnotz, knowing of Marie's single solitude, agreed she could take some time to visit a sick aunt in Berlin. Marie hoped that one week would be enough time for her to see Froer and maybe find a better paying job in Berlin. There was nothing really left for her back in Frankfurt as she had moved from the house her father had rented for them and now lived in a small furnished flat near the outer section of the city.

As the train slowly ground to a stop, Marie reached down and picked up one of the two suitcases, placing it on the vacant seat. The second case was in the compartment just above her seat. She moved out into the aisle and bent slightly forward rubbing her hands up and down the front portion of her dress, attempting to press out the wrinkles. Reaching into her case, she found some lipstick and applied a bit of bright red to her lips. She shook her head and pushed at her hair; the hair was always the easiest part. Her hair was a light chestnut in color and extremely full. Whether it was down around her shoulders, pulled back and pinned, or full of curls, people noticed it. On more than one occasion men had reached out to slowly caress it.

The exit was at the front of the car and most of the other passengers had already made their way out the doors. Marie reached up for the second bag and saw a piece of paper attached to the handle. She dislodged the paper and opened it. Inside was a note from Hans. *Marie, I very much enjoyed the time spent with you. May we find each other's company once again. Stay safe. Your Friend, Hans.* Marie smiled warmly, folded the note and placed it into the pocket of her sweater. Pulling the second suitcase down, she headed for the door.

Out on the platform, Marie craned her neck looking for any sign of Froer. Other passengers were milling around, looking for familiar faces as well. The lucky ones found friends or loved ones and were already departing. While searching, Marie took in the surroundings of Zoo Station. Nazi Party flags were flying from each pole in the station. The walls and floor were vanilla-colored marble but looked as though they had not been cleaned for some time, showing the signs of the fuel residue and heavy foot traffic. Marie also became aware of the amplification of sound as patrons pulled carriages of luggage across the floor.

Not seeing Froer, Marie decided to join the exodus of passengers to the end of the platform and up the stairs to the main hall. When she was just about to take her first step up, she spotted him at the top of the stairway. Heinrich Froer was in the uniform of the SS and when he saw Marie, he removed his officer's hat and bowed gracefully. Quickly he moved down the stairs and, with hat in hand, hugged her and issued a respectful kiss to both cheeks. "It is so good that you are here," he whispered in her left ear.

"Thank you. It is so very good to see you again as well," Marie answered.

Froer reached down to take up her bags. "Let me get these for you. I have my car just outside. You must be drained from the long train ride. I will take you to your hotel and you can freshen up. I have made reservations for dinner tonight, if that meets with your pleasure."

"Oh yes! Your letter was so vague. I have been awaiting the chance to talk with you," Marie replied.

"Not tonight, Marie. Tonight we will just reminisce about the old days of the Youth Sports Program. You were just a young girl the last time we saw each other and today I see a beautiful woman," Froer said as he placed his hand on Marie's back and gently moved her up the stairs.

Froer's car was parked directly in front of the station. People were busily passing by, while three soldiers stood near the car in guard posture. As Froer approached, each soldier snapped to attention and raised his right hand in salute. Froer paid little attention to the soldiers but raised his hand saying, "Heil" and then moved Marie toward his car. The car was a 1936 Mercedes Towncar, black in color, clean and polished. Froer placed the luggage in the trunk and opened the door for Marie. "We are only a few minutes from your hotel, my dear," he assured the young woman.

Marie smiled, sweeping the back of her dress with her right hand, and slid into the front seat. They left the station and proceeded out through Zoologischer Garten and over toward the Grober Stern roundabout. They drove through Tiergarten and Marie saw the long stretches of the park dotted with numerous trees. The center of Berlin reminded her of the great forests of her Southern Germany. At the edge of the park sat the Bueder Haus where Froer had made reservations.

As they entered the lobby, the attendant at the desk raised his hand in salute to Froer, or at least to his uniform. Froer nodded and said, "This is Marie Monin, my dear friend. Please take good care of her."

The attendant snapped his hands and a young boy appeared. "Take Fräulein Monin's bags to room 3. Make sure she has fresh towels and flowers in the room."

The attendant turned to Froer and said, "Everything will be taken care of. I will treat her as my own daughter. Be assured that she will want for nothing."

Froer smiled and again kissed Marie's cheeks. "I will be back for you in two hours. Please take your time freshening up." With that, Froer turned and left. Marie followed the boy up the stairs to her room. Using the key, the young boy opened the door and let Marie enter. He quickly moved the bags over to the side of the bed, checked to see that there were fresh flowers on the dresser and looked into the bathroom for towels. "Everything is as it should be," he said as he bowed forward.

"Thank you," she replied, as the young boy slipped out the door. Marie gazed at the room. It was small but beautifully decorated in soft lavender. The bed quilt was done in a wedding ring pattern. Lace curtains framed the window and from it she could see out onto Tiergarten. Marie moved to the bathroom and turned on the hot water. She thought, *How long has it been since I have soaked in a warm tub?* She did not know exactly what Froer had in mind when he wrote the letter, but she was more than willing to have the secret last for another day. For the next hour she would simply soak out the aches of the train ride while she closed her eyes and recalled the mysteriously handsome Hans von Schroedder.

CHAPTER THREE

Marie awoke the next morning with the sun just beginning to trickle across the hard wooden floor toward her bed. She rolled over once; her dry mouth and slight headache indicated that she had enjoyed the evening. She and Froer had a wonderful supper at the Mendole Haus, a converted wine cellar dating back to the early eighteenth century. They had spent the evening sitting at a back table sipping wine and feasting on various schnitzels. Although Marie was still curious about the letter and the job Froer wanted her to accept, they kept the conversation to events of the past.

"Marie, do you remember the day I pinned the medal to your dress?" asked Froer.

"Yes, very much so. I was never completely accepted by my classmates. The girls didn't like me because I hated playing girls' games or just sitting talking about the best way to tease the boys. Well, and the boys never wanted me to play with them because. . ."

"Because you were better than they were," Froer finished.

Marie smiled and whispered, "Well, not every time."

Froer then abruptly changed the conversation, "Tell me about your father's death. How did it happen?"

Marie replied pensively, "I don't really know for sure. I was at school and the headmistress came into my class and asked me to come with her. When we reached her office she told me to please sit. Then she said the school had received a call that my father had been taken to the hospital and for me to come quickly. The head mistress had one of the custodians drive me there in a school truck."

"Did she say what had happened?"

"No. When I arrived at the hospital the nurse told me my father was gone. He had been taken to a funeral home. She asked me about reaching my mother and I told her that my mother died many years ago. When I asked what happened to him the nurse just said that it was his heart."

"With no family around it must have been difficult for you," Froer said sympathetically.

"We had wonderful neighbors that helped, but after mother's death it was only my father and me. Without my father, I was depressed and my home and life seemed less important. Your letter gave me cause to move forward from the darkness that surrounded me."

***

Marie moved from the bed to the dresser. She chose a soft gray skirt and white blouse for the meeting this morning. Bringing the clothes into the bathroom, she stopped and stood for just a moment thinking how wonderful it was to have a private bath. Since she had moved to her small flat, she had to share a bathroom with two other girls on her floor and, although it was not a major problem, it was not her bathroom exclusively.

When she finished in the bathroom, Marie walked back over to her suitcase. In a jewelry pouch tucked inside the case, Marie pulled out the pin Froer talked about last night. She looked in the mirror and pinned the medal on her lapel, taking one last complete look at herself.

There was a driver downstairs just as Heinrich Froer had said there would be. He nodded to Marie, opened the door, and said, "Good morning, Fräulein."

"Good morning," she returned with a smile.

The driver made his way through the streets in quick fashion. Their route took them through the Brandenburger Tor, down Unter Den Linden and over toward Alexanderplatz, where they stopped in front of a building that housed Froer's office. Standing on the street were two guards in the uniform of the SS; each was checking papers of those wishing to going inside. The building itself was gothic, made of dark brick and reminded her of hardened mud. The first floor was solid and stairs rose from the street up to the second floor. The doors were black oak and on either side were two enormous paned window panels. Above the door was another window; two Nazi Party flags hung limply below their poles.

The driver escorted Marie to the door and handed papers to the guards. Marie noticed that both guards looked as young as she was. The one holding the papers looked at Marie and said, "Just inside the door and to your right." The second guard opened the door and Marie moved inside.

Just inside, she spotted Heinrich Froer coming toward her. "Marie, good morning. Last night was pleasant, but today we have business to attend to. Please come this way." Froer placed his hand on her back and escorted Marie to the room on the right. As they stepped inside, Froer said, "Please have a seat here." The room was magnificent, with solid black oak panels similar to the front door. The floor was also dark oak and Marie would have thought that she was in a cave but for the two beautiful crystal chandeliers that illuminated the room. Centered on the wall at the far end was a picture of the Führer standing at a podium. Also scattered around the room were smaller pictures of Hitler opening the Olympics, at the Nuremburg rallies and a few casual photos of him sitting among children.

Just as Marie was taking her seat, another officer joined her and Froer. Hauptmann Froer immediately snapped to attention, "Heil Hitler."

"Heil Hitler," the other man echoed in return. He was about the size of Froer, but his hair was lighter and much shorter. His uniform was starched and crisp, fitting perfectly to his body. Marie could not help but notice that he walked in with a swagger, one not of arrogance but rather one of tremendous pride.

"Marie, let me introduce to you SS-Obergruppenführer Reinhard Heydrich, head of the Sicherheitsdienst." Then looking at Heydrich, "Marie Monin."

Reinhard Heydrich took Marie's hand in both of his and kissed the backside. "Marie, you look startled. I have heard much about you. It is my pleasure to finally meet you."

Marie withdrew her hand and said, "Well, thank you sir. I hope my expression did not offend you, but I did not know that there would be others at the meeting this morning."

"Oh I know, Marie. I made sure that Hauptmann Froer kept my attendance private. However, Marie, I am the reason that you are here. Let me explain. Before I go on can I get you anything, water perhaps?"

"No, I'm fine. Please continue."

Heydrich began, "I am sure that you have read of Germany's great triumphs on its Eastern borders. The Führer is hard at work uniting true Germans everywhere. We are taking back land that belongs to Germany and to Germans. We are finally gaining the respect that we deserve. How do you feel about the events of the past year?"

"Oh Obergruppenführer Heydrich, I support my Führer's program. Germany must make the first strike or continue to be suffocated by the industrialists in France and Great Britain. We have suffered greatly since Versailles and now we are strong."

"Yes, Marie. Have you always felt this way or are you just making these statements to impress Hauptmann Froer and me?"

Sitting more upright and forward, Marie showed a bit of anger at being questioned about her allegiance. "I have always supported a strong Germany! I even argued with my father when he thought that Hindenburg was correct in forcing the Nazi Party to subjugate to his power. My father warned me that the Führer was no longer looking out for the good of Germany. He said Hitler was a ruffian ready to steal everything from Germans. I did not believe it then and I do not believe it now. My Führer is right and what is happening now is good for the German people."

Heydrich turned toward Froer and smiled. "You are right Hauptmann Froer. She is strong, maybe even a bit contemptuous, but perfect for the job at hand."

Turning back to Marie he continued, "Not all the battles fought by Germany have been with soldiers in uniform. I have been given the task of developing an intelligence operation for the Führer. My men and women are specially trained and seek to assist our troops by working not on the battlefield, but instead by working undercover wherever that may take them. I am looking for strong, cunning individuals with no ties to families that might compromise their endeavors. Hauptmann Froer says that you are a fiery competitor. You love to win. You love to see defeat in your opponent's eyes. Marie, I am offering you a chance to serve Germany."

Before he could finish, Marie stood, offered her hand and said, "Obergruppenführer Heydrich, I am exactly who you have been searching for."

CHAPTER FOUR

The next ten weeks were strenuous and stressful for Marie. Directly after the meeting with Reinhard Heydrich and Heinrich Froer, Marie was taken by her driver back to the Bueder Haus. Froer had told Marie to gather her belongings and to go with her driver, Alex, to a location outside of Berlin.

Alex weaved his way through the Western part of the city and out into the hills and pastures beyond Lake Wannsee. As the car slowed on the circular driveway, Marie saw a vast display of 18th Century architecture in front of her. As a schoolgirl, Marie had seen pictures of the building now in front of her. "Is that Schloss Sanssouci up ahead?"

"Very good," said Alex as he glanced over to take in Marie's profile. "You must have paid close attention to your history instructors. What can you tell me about it?"

Marie was a bit embarrassed because she actually could not remember much about the palace. "I know that it was built during the mid 1700's by the Prussian King, Friedrich II. Sanssouci and the newer palace of Neues Palais were some of the last castles built by Prussian kings. Beyond that, I am sorry to say my knowledge is limited."

"That was more information than I could remember and I have lived in Berlin all of my life. I must confess that I was never much of a student of history, or any other subject for that matter," Alex said while pulling the Mercedes to a stop just beyond the palace steps.

An older woman, dressed in a very smart black skirt and white blouse, came quickly up to the car door and opened it for Marie. "Good morning, Fräulein Monin. Obergruppenführer Heydrich notified me of your arrival. My name is Frau Schafer. I am the house mother to the young women staying here."

Marie exited the car, smiled and said, "Good morning, Frau Schafer. I am so excited to be here. Please call me Marie."

Frau Schafer gave Marie a very disturbing look saying, "Marie, this is not a place for wondrous excitement and insouciant behavior. This is a training ground for important members of the Reich. Your training will be tense, strenuous and quite demanding. You will be expected to learn a great deal in a very short period of time and your survival will depend on the mastery of every lesson."

Shocked by the tone of Frau Schafer's voice, Marie's entire demeanor abruptly changed. "I apologize if you took my words to mean that I did not take my work seriously. I am a gracious and deter-mined servant of the Reich. Have no worry, Frau Schafer. I will take my studies seriously and become the best at what I am asked to do for Germany."

Frau Schafer finished and smiled, "Very good. Take your bags and follow me to your room." Marie's room was in a large brick building built behind the palace. Her room was situated on the second floor, at the far end of the hall. As she walked down the hall Frau Schafer said, "These rooms belong to other young women training here. In the cen-ter you will find a lavatory and showers." The hallway was barren and the sound of their shoes striking the hard wood floor echoed off the walls. Marie was suddenly reminded of the visit to her mother in the hospital years ago; she hoped this place was a place of new beginnings and not the waiting lounge for death.

When they reached the room, Frau Schafer opened the door. "Make yourself comfortable. You will need to write to the baker Schnotz. Tell him that you will be staying in Berlin and to please gather the remainder of your things and send them to this address." Frau Schafer handed Marie a piece of paper with a Berlin address written on it.

Frau Schafer then handed Marie some German marks saying, "Place these with the letter. There should be enough to cover his expense with some left over for his troubles. Please assemble down-stairs in the center hall for the noon meal in two hours." Before Marie could ask how she knew about Marie's work at the bakery, Frau Schafer turned and walked out.

Marie spent the hours putting things away, making the room feel comfortable and composing the letter to Herr Schnotz. He had been so kind to take her in and give her a job after her father's death. Marie knew she needed to continue with the fabricated story of helping her aunt but really wanted to tell him the truth. Marie also wondered just how Frau Schafer knew about Herr Schnotz. Had Froer told her or had Heydrich found out and passed on the information? However the information was obtained, one thing was certain. Frau Schafer knew a great deal more than Marie was comfortable with right now.

***

Marie arrived in the center hall and found it empty. She took in the view of the room and quickly made mental notes. First, there were three doors leading into the hall. She was standing in the doorway that originated from the hallway. Directly across was a set of double doors that opened out onto a grassy lawn and through the side windows she could see walking paths. To her left, the third door she guessed led into a kitchen used to service the room. She also saw three heavy wooden tables, each with four chairs. The interior walls were paneled in a deep red mahogany and on the west side of the room there was a large stone fireplace. The Nazi flag was drawn across the stonework above the mantle and on either side were pictures of Adolph Hitler speaking at various locations across Germany. Marie noticed that one of the pictures was taken at Luitpold Hall. Just as Marie was beginning to get caught in the reverie of the moment, she heard the outside doors open and women began entering.

Frau Schafer walked into the room and immediately stepped beside Marie. "Ladies, please take your seats. I would like to introduce you to the final member of the Führer's elite women's society, Marie Monin."

Then pointing to an empty chair Frau Schafer said, "Marie, please take a seat at this table."

Frau Schafer continued speaking to the assembled women, "Ladies, enjoy your meal and please continue to get familiar with each other and the surrounding areas. You will all return here at 5:00 p.m. At that time you will all be told of the great plans the Führer has for each of you and for all good German people."

One of the women excitedly asked, "Will the Führer be here to speak to us this evening?" Others fidgeted in their seats and whispered to those seated at their table.

"No," Frau Schafer said. "I am sorry. The Führer is sending Obergruppenführer Heydrich to address you." Marie noticed that two of the women at her table frowned and looked bemused as though the name was unfamiliar to them. Marie wondered if she was one of the few assembled that had already met Heydrich and if so, why. Just as Frau Schafer was finishing her words, the door to the kitchen area opened and the staff brought in large serving bowls and pitchers, placing them at each table. As the women ate, introductions were made at Marie's table. The talk turned to Frau Schafer's comments. The women wondered just how they were going to help the Führer and Germany. One of the women curiously looked at Marie and said, "Marie, tell us about yourself."

Marie smiled and told the women briefly about her mother dying when she was young and about her trip to the Nuremburg rally. She also mentioned that just after her father died, she had received a letter from Heinrich Froer asking her to come to Berlin. Froer had said that the Führer was looking for young women to help with a special project.

One of the others, Lisa, leaned in toward the middle of table and whispered, "I received a letter too from a Nazi official about a special project. My first thought was that the Führer had chosen me to become the *mother* of the new Germany."

Another girl nervously responded, "Oh no! I hope that we are not here to become the mistresses or the entertainment for Nazi officials."

Marie quickly responded, "I met Obergruppenführer Heydrich just a few days ago. His demeanor was very professional. He was polite and focused. He told me that Germany needed women to become involved in rooting out the enemy from the civilian population."

"He wants us to become spies?" asked Lisa.

"I am not sure just what he has in mind, but I know it is not to become social prostitutes for the Nazi Party," Marie responded. "Now let's just relax, eat and wait until we hear more tonight. Lisa, would you please pass the bowl of soup? I haven't eaten since early this morning and I am starved." The focused discussion abruptly ended and the table turned quickly to idle female chatter.

***

In the early evening, the women reassembled in the central hall, each taking the same chair that they had used earlier. The flames in the fireplace were silently ascending and the room had a warm comforting feel. Marie recognized the man that entered with Frau Schafer as Obergruppenführer Reinhard Heydrich. Frau Schafer made the complementary introduction and then took a seat near the back of the hall. Heydrich looked around the room and smiled. He was aroused by the sheer power that he possessed over all of these women. They all had arrived here because of his labor and they were ready to give everything for the Reich and for Germany. He was the man behind the Sicherheitsdienst, the Nazi's own secret intelligence organization. Hitler had created the organization to be the eyes and ears of the Nazi Party. The Sicherheitsdienst would rival the Abwehr, the military's intelligence agency. Heydrich was in charge and enjoyed the prevailing power.

"Ladies, I welcome you on behalf of the Führer himself. Tomorrow you will begin training in the area of intelligence gathering, defense and covert tactics. Germany has many enemies. Some still live and work in Germany while others are plotting against us from other countries. As you each become proficient in the tasks assigned, you will be given details of your assignments. Some of you will work together while others will be assigned male partners. The men are currently being trained in another location so as to confuse those who would try to destroy our plans. I wish you all well on the great work each of you will be doing for all of Germany." Heydrich proceeded to walk slowly around the room, softly taking each woman's hand in his and kissing the backside. He passed in and out of each group with the graceful motions of a dancer moving to a Strauss waltz. As Heydrich reached for Marie's hand he said, "Fräulein Monin, Froer's little lioness, a pleasure to see you once again. Are you ready for the dangerous tasks ahead?"

"I am ready to do my part for the German cause," Marie replied.

"Very good, Marie."

Frau Schafer spoke up over the buzz of inquisitive discussions taking place among the women. "It is time to retreat to your rooms. The staff has placed a small tray of meats and cheeses in each of your rooms. There is also a glass of wine on each tray. Eat a small meal this evening, get a good night's rest and be ready to begin work tomorrow morning. Good night."

Marie and the others picked up their things and retired to their rooms. Quietly, Marie closed the door to her room. She suddenly realized she was alone, completely alone, again. First, there was the isolation brought on by caring for her mother. Throughout her life, her competitive nature also had created more enemies than it had friends. Since her father's death, Herr Schnotz had been a good friend and had seemed to care about Marie, but he was also now gone from her. Even Hans, the young man on the train, seemed to be someone that cared about her. She certainly enjoyed his company, but he was also gone. Marie said to herself, "I am strong. I will be the best and will make Herr Heydrich and Froer proud of me. I will make you, Papa, also proud of me." She was not hungry. She set the meat and cheese aside, drank the glass of wine and fell off to sleep.

CHAPTER FIVE

The training was intense. There were early morning runs and self-defense classes. The girls learned how to fight and to neutralize men much larger in size. Marie was learning to kill in close combat using her hands and feet. She took classes on anatomy. Learning the pressure points and the soft points on a human body and how to use weapons against each point for quick and quiet control of her adversary made Marie feel powerful. Each day the girls trained and competed against each other. Their trainers said, "We do not hand out medals or ribbons here. You train to be a winner because to be a loser means torture and death at the hands of the enemy." Marie believed those words completely. Early in her life she had been the lioness. But now she was also becoming the fox.

Marie grew up speaking French along with German and was proficient in both. She only knew a bit of broken English, most of it learned from listening to Billie Holiday sing with Benny Goodman or Count Basie's bands. Marie and her father sat in the evenings listening to this new American music. Then when the Nazi Party outlawed the music of impure "kikes" and "niggers", Marie's father bundled the records and hid them in an old steamer trunk. The trunk now sat in the basement of the Schnotz Bakery.

Marie spent three hours each day with English studies. The trainers told the girls they needed to learn English just in case Chamberlain or Roosevelt grew vengeful of Germany's prestige and honor and decided to use their respective countries' military to stop the rightful advance of the German people.

One evening after dinner near the end of the training, while Marie was readying for bed, there was a light knock on her door. Opening it, she found Frau Schafer. "Good evening, Marie, may I come in for a moment? I have an important issue to discuss with you."

"Why of course, Frau Schafer. What sort of issue do you have?" Marie asked inquisitively.

Marie knew her trainers had given her high marks in every aspect of training. Even Oberleutnant Hoster had said on more than one occasion that she was an exceptional opponent. Quickly, she recalled an incident that had taken place just yesterday morning. Marie was in the library reading through a letter she had received from Herr Schnotz when Captain Hoster quietly approached Marie and grabbed her arm. Hoster said, "You are good, but if need be can you kill?"

With one quick move, Marie used her free arm to slam into Hoster's rib. At the same time, Marie stood slamming the chair back at Hoster while grabbing the letter opener on the table in front of her. She spun quickly around to the backside of Hoster and brought the opener up under his jaw. With the opener pressed against Captain Hoster's throat, Marie whispered, "Oh, I think I can, Herr Hoster. You certainly don't want a demonstration now, do you?"

Frau Schafer sat in the chair at Marie's reading desk. Gesturing to the larger stuffed chair in the corner of the room, she said, "Please Marie, I won't be long." Frau Schafer continued, "Marie, you are the most talented woman in our group. You are a strong fighter and have mastered every training technique that we introduced you to."

"But what?" Marie cut in. "You certainly did not come here this evening just to give me compliments on my work. What is it, Frau Schafer?"

Frau Schafer looked deeply at Marie and said, "There is one part of you that has not come out and it is causing us to worry about your success. Marie, you have not learned the art of being a woman. There are times to be strong and powerful, which you so proudly display everyday. Sometimes, Marie, you need to be delicate. Maybe it was the early death of your mother that caused your feminine side to be wanting. All

I know is that for you to perform your duties, you will need to learn at times to be soft and persuasive."

Marie was hurt. She slumped in the chair and dropped her head, visualizing her mother on her deathbed. Marie's whole body ached with the pain of years without her mother. She didn't know just how long she had been looking down, but when she lifted her head, tears slid down her face like the first drops of water forcing their way out of a bursting dam. Frau Schafer rose and walked over to Marie. Kneeling beside Marie, Frau Schafer put her arms around her and said, "My dear, this is a good start. These are true feelings that you need to be able to control and to use to your advantage. There is something that I now need for you to do."

Looking up at Frau Schafer, Marie asked, "What is it you would like?"

Frau Schafer explained that Marie was going to be spending the weekend with two 'social women' in Berlin. "I want you to watch how these women work with men, tease men, seduce men and," she paused for a moment, "ultimately control men with their femininity. Tomorrow after lunch you will pack a light bag and meet me in the library." Handing Marie a piece of paper, Frau Schafer continued, "A driver will take you to this address. There you will meet Fräuleins Inga Schoff and Helena Trolt. Watch them. Listen to them. Learn from them."

***

Marie arrived at the apartment just after three and rang the bell. The door opened and a beautiful redheaded woman smiled and reached her hand out saying, "Good afternoon, Marie. I was expecting you. My name is Helena Trolt."

As Marie reached for Helena's hand she was, for the first time, overwhelmed by the sensation that she had always been a tomboy. Helena was unlike any woman Marie had ever seen. Helena's skin was like soft cream and the red lipstick accented her red hair. Her blue eyes sparkled and her makeup was perfectly applied. Helena was wearing a dark blue silk gown. The gown had spaghetti straps and was fit tightly against her body, showing off her voluptuous breasts, thin hips and long legs. The smell of Helena's perfume triggered a sense that had been dormant since Marie was a very young girl nestled close to her mother during cold, wintry German nights. Marie closed her eyes, just briefly, and drew in as much of the air around her as possible. She thought just how similar Helena's name was to her own mother Helene. "Oh, I am so sorry. I am rude. Please forgive me."

"Nonsense!" said Helena. "Come in and have a seat. Let me get you something to drink. Inga will be back soon. Frau Schafer sent over your dress size and Inga is out shopping for some things for you to wear this weekend." Helena returned with some tea and said, "I was somewhat surprised when my Aunt, Frau Schafer, called and asked a favor. She has not always understood or accepted my way of life." Marie sat and listened as Helena explained just what the weekend held for the three women.

An hour later the door to the apartment swung open and in walked Inga Schoff, clutching a number of boxes and bags. Inga was shorter than Helena, but with immaculate Arian features. Her blond hair was pulled back so that her strong, high cheekbones defined her face. Inga's eyes were dark blue and looked as deep as a Bavarian lake in springtime. She had on a purple skirt and a ruffled chiffon blouse. The skirt was pulled tightly around her small waist and muscular buttocks. The blouse revealed small round breasts, more like Marie's. She saw herself more in Inga than in Helena. Inga, setting down the packages, swung a look toward Marie and said, "This must be our ménage à trois guest." Blushing, Marie stood. Before Marie could speak, Inga continued, "Don't worry. Not today, sweetie. You must be Marie. I'm Inga."

Marie shook Inga's hand. "Nice to meet you, Inga. Thank you for letting me share the weekend with Helena and you."

Inga, noticing Marie's red complexion, finally said, "Nice meeting you as well, Marie. By the way, I was just kidding about the ménage à trois. I don't care for sharing." Inga then gave Marie a wink and said, "Let's just see what goodies I have for you to wear tonight."

CHAPTER SIX

The three women left around 8:00 p.m. for the Hotel Adlon Kempinski. The Adlon was one of Berlin's five-star hotels. Even the Kaiser had spent many a night there when the palace was being refurbished. As Inga pulled up to the valet, Marie could see just down the Unter Den Linden toward the lighted Brandenburg Gate. The Brandenburg Gate was a triumphal arch commissioned by Friedich Whilhelm II and built in the late 1700's. Tonight it was awash in lights. Red panel banners with a Nazi swastika centered in a white circle hung from the arches. Once again, Marie felt an electric charge flow through her body as she thought about the greatness of Germany and the German people. Helena and Inga told Marie that they would be meeting two industrialists from Frankfurt tonight. The men were in Berlin to meet with some military officials regarding steel manufacturing. The women told her that they cared little about the politics of it all. They were hired by the Reich to be friendly with the men and in the process they made a great deal of money. There would be dinner, music and dancing, and some social time later in the evening. Helena told Marie she was going to be introduced as their cousin, visiting Berlin for a short time. As they left the car for the hotel, Inga whispered to Marie, "Watch, enjoy, and learn."

As the three women entered the hotel's dining room, Raul, the hotel's concierge, quickly approached and reached first for Helena's hand. Lightly taking her hand in his and slowly bringing the hand to his lips, Raul said, "Buenos Nochas Señorita Trolt." As Raul reached for Inga's hand, he looked up to see Marie standing next to Inga. Raul stopped short. "Inga, who is this lovely young friend of ours?" Raul took Marie's hand and caressed it within his. He bent forward, raised her hand to his lips saying, "I am not worthy to be in your presence. How may I be of service to you?"

Inga quickly replied, "Relax Raul. This is my cousin Señorita Monin. She is just in Berlin for a few days." Inga then leaned in toward Raul, letting him have just a whiff of her fragrance and a quick glance at the diamond suspended above the plunging top to her satin dress. Raul's eyes grew wide as Inga whispered in his ear, "You stay away from my cousin and I might just come back later tonight to see if you are the man that I suspect you are. Can you wait for me?"

Raul fumbled for the words but finally stammered, "Señorita Schoff, you are an angel on earth. I will be waiting to hear from you at your earliest convenience."

Helena said, "Raul dear, if we are through with these pleasantries, could you point us in the direction of Herr Schroeder's party?"

"Why of course, señoritas. Please pardon my momentary infatuation. This way. Please follow me."

Raul stuck his arm out for Helena and she gracefully took hold as they walked across the darkened room. Inga held back just a moment and said to Marie, "If men thought with the parts between their ears instead of those between their legs, they would be more dangerous. You watch. Raul will spend the evening stopping by our table to check on me. He is praying that tonight is finally the night of his dreams."

As they all reached the table, Marie noticed that Raul had forgotten her. The men at the table stood and Raul pulled out Inga's chair, "Until later, my lovely señorita." But while Raul was focused on Inga, the woman's attention had already turned to the two men at the table.

***

The men introduced themselves as Helmut Schroeder and Johann Marx. Helena even jokingly asked how a good communist like a Marx could support a strong nationalist Germany. Marie listened intently as the women playfully directed the conversation toward the men's issues of power and wealth. Schroeder and Marx ordered the very best champagne and the women feasted like queens. Dessert was a vanilla cream, mixed with chocolate and topped with cherries. Marie watched Helena drop her spoon. Immediately Helena turned to Helmut and said, "Helmut, I am so clumsy. Would you mind helping me with the last cherry?" Helmut began to hand Helena his spoon when she smiled and said, "Wouldn't you rather use your fingers to feed me?"

Helmut smiled, set his spoon down and picked up the cherry. As he brought it toward Helena, she took his hand in hers. She drew his fingers and the cherry toward her mouth. Helena slowly placed her lips over the cherry and used her tongue to slide it from between Helmut's fingers. Holding his hand, Helena could feel the energy rise up from inside Helmut. Marie was surprised that she even felt an excitement watching the interaction between Helena and Helmut.

Marie's education continued after dinner. The group retired to a table in a quiet side room near the dance floor and the men ordered more champagne. Inga and Helena continued to stroke the men's egos with flattering conversation. Occasionally, one of the couples took time to dance to the soft music being played by the jazz quartet. Marie watched Inga and Johann dancing. The champagne seemed to be getting the best of Johann and he was having trouble moving his feet in unison with Inga's. Marie watched Johann's hand slide down Inga's back and then lower as he tried to reach under her buttocks and between her legs. Inga made no fast movement. In fact, Inga moved slowly along with the rhythm of the music. She lifted her head and kissed Johann's cheek, while at the same time she placed her foot just inside Johann's foot. Johann awkwardly fell to the ground, almost pulling Inga down with him.

Everyone was looking at the couple as Johann rose from the floor and took Inga's hand. They walked back to the table and Marie could hear Inga saying, "Oh Johann, I am so sorry. I am so clumsy. Please forgive me."

Johann replied, "No, no. This was completely my fault. Please forgive me. The meeting today with the Führer has tired me out. I believe that I will retire to my room. I have so enjoyed the evening. Ladies, will you excuse me?" Turning to Helmut, Johann said, "Helmut, I will see you in the morning. Good night all."

Just after Johann left, Inga said to Helena and Helmut, "Could you please excuse us?" Then to Marie, Inga said, "Marie, would you go with me to the ladies room to check the back of my dress? I think there might just be a slight tear." As Marie and Inga walked toward the ladies room, Inga drew Marie close and said, "Marie, did you like the way I finally disposed of our friend Johann? What a clumsy fool."

Marie couldn't contain her laughter and said, "You never once let on that his groping was annoying you and that kiss just before you dropped him was so seductive. He never suspected that you tripped him."

Inga said, "Learn Marie, that like a magician, you too have the power of illusion. This is enough for tonight. We will leave now. I imagine Helena will dispense with Helmut soon. Tomorrow afternoon we have a luncheon scheduled and once again dinner with out of town guests."

CHAPTER SEVEN

Marie found Frau Schafer sitting outside under one of the large firs. As she approached Frau Schafer said, "Well Marie, did you have an educational weekend?"

"Yes, Frau Schafer." Marie could not hide her excitement. "Inga and Helena were so much fun to be with! They are beautiful, charming, and certainly powerful women, Frau Schafer."

Frau Schafer rose and said, "Marie, do not be lost in eager fascination. What they showed you about the power of female sensuality may save your life. Marie, remember that no matter what you might like to think, women are not the physical equals of men. Sometimes just a sweet smile or timely jiggle can be a better weapon than a gun."

Placing her hand on Marie's elbow, Frau Schafer said, "Come with me, dear. It is time to hear of the plans Herr Heydrich has for you and to meet your partner."

Just as Marie and Frau Schafer walked into the great hall, the door at the far end opened. Marie expected to see Reinhard Heydrich appear, but as the man entered, Marie's knees became weak and she felt as though she had just been punched hard. Her breath escaping, Marie whispered, "Hans?"

***

"It is so good to see you again, Marie. I trust you have been enjoying yourself and that Frau Schafer has been a most wonderful host," Hans said.

Confused, Marie asked, "What are you doing here, Hans? I thought that you were on your way to Hannover and then to Hamburg."

"Would you believe my plans changed? Probably not," Hans responded. "To be completely honest with you, I was never going to Hannover. I was always going to Berlin. I needed to take care of some issues before meeting up with you here."

Marie lowered her head and quietly murmured, "Oh, I don't understand."

"I can see that you are hurt by my deception, Marie. I find that somewhat ironic since you tried to deceive me while on the train," Hans continued.

"I know but. . ."

"Stop, Marie," Hans said sternly. "My orders were to meet you. Obergruppenführer Heydrich wanted me to travel with you and see just how much of the secret you could keep. Heydrich has important work for both of us, and he wanted to find out if I thought we could work together."

Marie's tone changed. She was surprised and excited to be with Hans once again. "What do you mean work together?"

"You have been training to be an operative for the Führer himself. We will report to Heydrich, who will then report directly to Führer Hitler," Hans said. He continued, "We will talk more tonight over dinner. I know you have been here for quite a while, but we have two more weeks of training and studying before we are sent out into the dark streets and alleyways of Europe. As I said before, we are being asked to do important work for the good of Germany and its people. We must not fail. I will see you this evening." With that, Hans walked closer to Marie and took her shoulders in his hands. He bent forward and kissed Marie on both cheeks.

***

Marie usually did not take much time in preparation for evening dinners with the other girls. She just filled the water basin and took a quick sponge bath, wiping off the day's perspiration. The bowl of jasmine next to the bath was always left undisturbed, believing the pleasant scent might mark her as weak. Tonight was different. Marie drew a warm bath, crushed some of the dried jasmine and dropped it into the bath water. Marie spent the next half hour soaking in the water and thinking of Hans. She had so many questions. *What did he mean by 'partners'? Where were they going?* This was all happening so fast.

Upon finishing her bath, Marie went to her closet and picked out one of the dresses recently purchased for her by Inga. Marie chose the mauve cotton dress. It was not as elegant or dressy as the others and not as revealing either. However, its design hung attractively on Marie's athletic figure, highlighting her slim waist and long, muscular legs. As Marie walked toward the door, she heard a slight knock. Opening the door, she observed one of the men that worked with the physical training. Marie asked, "Geoffrey, what are you doing here?"

Geoffrey responded, "Hans asked me to show you to the guesthouse. You will be having dinner there. It is on another part of the estate. Not too far, but I will be driving you there."

Marie closed her bedroom door and followed Geoffrey down the hall and outside to a waiting car. Once inside the car, Marie asked Geoffrey, "Do you know Hans very well?"

"I guess I know Hans as well as anybody here. We have been working together for more than two years."

"Working together?" Marie asked.

Geoffrey responded, "Yes, both here at Sanssouci and in Poland. I cannot talk about any of this. If Hans wants to talk about our time, you will need to ask him."

As Geoffrey reached to turn the key, Marie softly placed her hand on his and leaned in close enough for Geoffrey to smell the jasmine. "Can you tell me anything about him? I feel so unprepared to see him tonight. I am still in shock that he is here and not in the navy. Please Geoffrey, anything."

"All I can tell you is that Hans is one of the smartest and bravest men I have known. He follows orders, which is why he had to lie to you. Now that you are his partner, you will never be lied to again. He will trust you with his life, and you must trust him with yours," Geoffrey said. They drove the remainder of the way to the guesthouse in silence. Geoffrey exited and came around to open the door for Marie. As Geoffrey reached in for Marie's hand, he said, "Marie, one more thing. Hans is the best I have ever seen with a gun, knife, or his hands. He will protect you, but he will also expect that you will protect him."

"Thank you, Geoffrey. I will remember that." Marie let go of Geoffrey's hand and moved toward the entrance.

The house was two-story, but small. The plaster, where it could be seen through the massive growth of ivy and ferns, was cracked and badly in need of repairs. It looked as though the forest was slowly devouring the house. This area of the estate was old and beautiful. The forest was thick with both new and old growth spruce and oak. Marie remembered her father taking her on walks in the woods that surrounded their town and explaining that old trees die, drop to the ground and decompose to create the nutrients for the younger trees. Marie could only think that somehow this old house held the nutrients for a new, greater Germany and that she was going to be playing a vital role in this new growth.

Just as she stepped onto the porch, the door swung open. "Good evening, Marie, and welcome." Hans immediately moved forward and embraced her. As they hugged, Hans continued, "Again, Marie, I apologize for the deception and the surprise meeting earlier today. I plan to spend this evening telling you only the truth."

They made their way to a sofa in the small living room. A fire was going, and the embers were glowing with their sooty oranges and reds. Marie absorbed the warmth and thought how good it felt to be here, to be with Hans. As Hans directed Marie to the sofa he said, "Can I get you something, maybe a glass of wine?"

"No, not now, maybe later with dinner. Why the deception and what are we to do? I have spent months training, learning to defend myself and to kill if need be. Frau Schafer tells me that I am good and so do the other girls. All the girls know that we are going to be used in some form of covert operation, but we are never told just what. I hope tonight you will share some answers with me."

Hans picked up his glass of wine and said, "I am going to tell you a great deal this evening. I can't tell you everything because some of the information is still in the planning stages. We are going to be partners. The work is going to be dangerous, but from everything that I hear, you are up to the challenge. First, let me give you some background. Then we will have dinner, and later I will begin to explain our orders. Don't be too anxious; we still have a couple weeks of study and training before we leave."

Hans moved closer. "Germany has not one, but two intelligence and security divisions. The military uses Abwehr, which is run by Admiral Canaris. This organization has been in existence since the last war. It served Germany during that time and it has some long-time agents already entrenched in Europe. These agents were beneficial in giving us needed information for the retaking of the Rhineland. Abwehr also provided key information on troop movements and they are entrenched in high-level government positions both in Holland and Belgium. That is why the military moved west into these countries first. Along with Abwehr's success there has also been failure. Some agents, and even Canaris himself, have let their egos get in the way. They have withheld vital information because they don't want to share the glory with anyone else or any other division. A few years back the Führer created an intelligence agency within the SS called the Sicherheitsdienst. Obergruppenführer Heydrich now heads it. Heydrich reports to Himmler and then directly to the Führer himself. I have been working for more than three years with the Sicherheitsdienst. Most of my work thus far has been uncovering agents trying to sabotage the efforts of the Party and the country. I have infiltrated labor groups and communist cells, and uncovered Jews that have been trying to undermine the efforts of a national Germany. Himmler and Heydrich do not believe Abwehr can effectively handle all the intelligence work in the West. We are being sent as a team to Belgium. I hope that is enough for now. After dinner we will review our orders and our training program."

Hans began to rise, but Marie stopped his movement by placing her hand on his thigh. "Just one question first. Why were you on the train? Were you really there to make sure I came to Berlin, that I followed orders?" The last few words were spoken with just a bit of disappointment and coldness.

"I came, yes, to see if you would follow the letter. If you did not, or if you divulged the information in the letter, Heinrich Froer would have welcomed you to Berlin. He would have shown you around the city and offered you a job working in a laundry room." Hans smiled and laughed, "Well, maybe not a laundry room. Anyway, I was your escort. Other than where I was going, I told you no lies. I enjoyed our time together. To be honest, I could hardly wait these months to see you again, and I even spied on you a couple of times. Remember when you went out with Inga and Helena?"

"You mean the evening we met with the men at the hotel Kempinski?" Marie quickly asked.

"No, the next evening when you went to that awful burlesque underground. What a dreary, foul-smelling place it was. Fortunately for me, there were so many people, and all of your attention and energy was spent on those three young boys."

Marie blushed slightly and said, "I was learning to be playful, Hans. Maybe you should try it some evening. And those weren't boys! They may have looked young, but let me assure you they were certainly manly enough."

"OK! Enough of this! Let's eat, shall we?" Hans offered his hand to Marie and helped her up from the couch. They slowly made their way through the living room and into the dining area.

The dinner was delectable and the conversation entertaining. Both Marie and Hans shared stories of their youth. They both possessed strong athletic prowess, and both had used their competitive skills to achieve status among their peers. Marie felt a closeness to Hans, a bond between athletes. She wondered if they could ever be more than partners in a dangerous life of intelligence. She was still pondering that question when Hans broke her reverie by saying, "Marie, in a few weeks we will be going to Brugge, Belgium. The Reich has learned the early beginnings of an underground cell are working out of Brugge. Agents are using the network of canals and railroads to bring supplies in from England and to smuggle Jews and partisans out from Europe. Our cover will be as brother and sister, newly arriving from the East around Liege. We will find work around the docks and canals. I have some contact names that will be useful in getting lodging."

Marie interrupted, "Will we be speaking Flemish, French or can we use German?"

"I know that you are fluent in Flemish and French. I am fluent in French but somewhat inept in Flemish, so let's try to use French between us. When you speak to others in town, use your best judgment as to the situation. Many people from Liege speak German, so we will not stand out as odd by any means," Hans added.

"What type of preparation will we be doing for the next few weeks?" Marie asked.

"I have information on the underground group including names of leaders and possible meeting locations. Heydrich has also provided us with some photos of possible supporters, although the photos still need to be confirmed by us." Hans continued, "Our time will be spent studying this information and practicing our cover. You will continue with your physical training, and I will join you. We need to know just what our strengths and weaknesses are. Froer and Frau Schaefer tell me you are tough, quick, and decisive; however, they also say you can be too quick and impulsive. You will also need time to learn about my behaviors. Knowing as much as we can about each other will be the key to staying alive."

"I know this will be dangerous, but I am up to this challenge." Marie continued, "I will do everything possible to protect you."

"I know you will, but remember this, Marie. The key to survival has two very important tenets. First, know your enemy and think as they think. Stay ahead of them. Second, and most important, no one is more important than you. Each night you want to return to your bed alive. I will also try to protect you, but I will protect myself first. You must do the same. Staying alive may mean that we leave each other in a difficult situation, but we must make that decision without any feeling or emotion. We will become close, but we must be able to break that bond if need be." Hans raised his wineglass and finished with, "To my sister, Marie. May our work be fruitful and our days be safe."

Marie raised her glass as well and said, "To my brother."

CHAPTER EIGHT

Pennsylvania, 1942

Paul Schaefer pulled his midnight blue, '36 Ford Roadster onto the Emmitsburg Road. The top was down and he had let the Roadster's flathead eight whine out over the long haul from Washington to his family's farm in Gettysburg. He let the wind blow through his golden hair and pound against his aviator's glasses. Paul was twenty-three, a recent college graduate, and creating speed in the classic roadster was one of the true joys in his life right now. The other was working for the government in Washington.

For the past nine months, Paul worked as an army translator. His job was to read new material coming out of Nazi Germany and then translate it for his bosses. Someone above him would decide what to send down the street to the brass at the War Department. Translators had been used since Hitler's rise to power. More translators were hired after Germany's assaults on Austria and Czechoslovakia. After December 7, the United States was all in. Japan brought the war to America; then Germany and Italy, Japan's allies, declared war on the United States on December 11. Now daily briefing materials were being prepared for both the War Department and President Roosevelt.

Getting the job was not easy. Paul was thankful that after two months of interviews and background searches, the government finally offered him a job. The juxtaposition of the interviews and searches were laughable to Paul. On one hand, the government needed people fluent in German and who understood the nuances of German culture, but the government was also suspicious that such people were really German spies. For Paul nothing could be further from that.

Klaus Schaefer, Paul's great-grandfather, had journeyed across Germany to Belgium where he stowed away on a ship sailing to America. He was fleeing the sectional civil strife that continued to pollute the life of decent German people. After arriving in Philadelphia, Klaus was befriended by an old German blacksmith and apprenticed for two years before moving to Gettysburg. Klaus set up a small blacksmith business in town. The area's rich farmland and its location served as the central traffic hub between Harrisburg and farm communities further south. After a short period of prosperity, Klaus once again found himself in the middle of civil strife; on July 1, 1863, the war came to his home.

What the Confederate Army did not steal on July 1st or 2nd, the Army of the Potomac consigned to themselves on July 4th. Having nothing left of his trade, Klaus took the money he had saved and bought a twenty acre wedge of farmland outside the city, up the Harrisburg Road. Paul's grandfather and father had continued to work the farm since 1864. All the Schaefer's, including Paul and his two younger brothers, Anthony and Robert, were born and raised on the Schaefer farm. The Schaefers, all the way back to Klaus, had been religious pacifists, but the family also felt strongly that they were Americans now. Paul's father even served two years in the trenches of France as a military corpsman, carrying medical supplies rather than a gun.

Paul grew up in a family that draped themselves in American traditions and values. Outside the house the children spoke perfect English and thought of themselves only as Americans. They were diligent students in both academics and religious doctrine, because their mother would have it no other way. None of Paul's playmates growing up even knew that he spoke fluent German. It was only inside the house, usually at mealtime, that both their father and mother taught the younger Schaefers about German culture and language, a tradition begun by Klaus.

Paul graduated and was recruited from the Gettysburg Lutheran College. He had majored in military history and theology, certainly an odd coupling, but it was his German background and his history concentration that first attracted the government's interest. Now he was a government employee, and his only digression from the conservative upbringing and job was the Roadster. He found the car just after he was hired. It had been a repo from a Baltimore bank. Now imagining himself as Wilbur Shaw, winner of the Indianapolis 500 in both 1939 and '40, Paul made the final turn onto the gravel and dirt path that led up to the Schaefer farmhouse.

CHAPTER NINE

Promoted to 2nd Lieutenant, Paul now had worked as a translator for nearly two years. He was on a one-week leave from the Pentagon. In 1941, personnel at the War Department were severely cramped. Groundbreaking took place for a new structure, the Pentagon. Sixteen months later, in January 1943, the Pentagon became the new home for the military strategists. Although Paul loved working in the new facility, he had put in for a transfer; his new orders had arrived. Paul was being assigned to a field unit as a translator and interrogator. The Allies had pushed the Nazis out of Africa and now were focusing on Sicily, hoping to end any Italian support for the Axis powers. Soon the Allies were going to invade Western Europe. Everyone knew that Roosevelt and Churchill were making plans that would include an invasion into France, Belgium, or the Netherlands, but no one knew just when it would happen. With these orders in hand, Paul understood he was now going to be more involved. No more sitting behind a desk, reading German documents and communiqués. He was going to be joining the fight and was certain that his mother would be greatly upset.

Against his parents' wishes, Paul's younger brother, Anthony, had told his parents he was going with friends to Philadelphia for the weekend; instead, he signed up for the Marines. Anthony sent a letter to his parents explaining that he admired Paul's work at the Pentagon, but he felt he needed to be directly involved in the fight. Paul still remembered Anthony's final comment.

"*You taught me to love my country and what better way to show my love than to stand up and defend it now. Pray I will return safely, but if I must, I will proudly give my life for the freedoms that I enjoy. Your loving and usually obedient son, Anthony.*"

Paul could not leave without seeing his parents and explaining it was time for him to join the fight as well. He knew his mother would take it hard, now having two sons to worry about; however, at least Robert would be remaining at home. Robert just turned eighteen, but his asthma made him physically unfit for military service.

Just as Paul opened the Roadster's door, his mother came running out of the house, stopping at the top of the porch steps. "Hi Mom. Where are Dad and Robert?" Paul asked as he ran up onto the porch and hugged his mother.

Throwing her arms around Paul and squeezing tightly, she said, "They're out bringing back some of the cows that wandered away when your father forgot to lock the fence gate. He's just not thinking straight worrying so about Anthony. Come inside. I was just finishing making lunch for when they return."

"How is Anthony? Have you heard from him lately? The only letter I received was just after boot camp," Paul asked as he took his mother's hands in his own.

Ignoring Paul's question, his mother lowered her head and said, "Come inside. I need to check the soup. We can talk more while we eat."

"I'll get my bag from the car and be right in," Paul said and he turned to retrieve his bag.

Paul took his bag up to his old room and returned to the kitchen just as his father and Robert were returning. Paul walked up to both men, hugged each and said, "Dad, what's this I hear about you leaving the gate open? I remember a time when there was hell to pay when I left that gate open."

"Times were different then," he said in a tone that emphasized the pain he was feeling over the war and Anthony's participation.

Sensing his father's discomfort, Paul reached again to hug him and said, "I was just kidding, Dad. I know it's tough and everybody in America is feeling the pressure. Don't worry, Dad. Anthony can take care of himself."

Looking back at his mother, Paul said, "So Mom, you were about to tell me what you heard about Anthony."

"We have received a couple of letters. You know about boot camp in California, and then Anthony shipped out to Australia. He will be replacing units that were killed at Guadalcanal. We don't know much more than that. Anthony keeps the letters positive, always saying not to worry and that he will be safe but. . ."

Paul interrupted, "No buts, Mom. All Americans are sacrificing right now. When you write to Anthony you must be positive as well. He needs your support. I need your support." Paul stopped as quickly as he started. He realized this was not the time to bring up his new orders. He was going to be staying for a week. He would help around the farm, bond again with his family, and at the end of the week talk to his parents about his new orders. "I am sure hungry. Why don't we eat something and then I can help Dad and Robert with the rest of the work outside."

***

The week passed quickly, and Paul was happy to have time away from work on the war and the daily stress in Washington. The only stressful times on the farm came during the evening as the family sat around the radio, listening to the daily news about events on both fronts. It was the first time in quite a while that Paul had listened attentively to news reports, and he was amazed at the lack of information being reported to the public. Thankfully, his parents never asked if the information was accurate or if the information was being filtered in any way, but Paul knew it was.

The night before Paul was to leave, the family assembled again around the radio and listened to updates from the front. Robert said,

"I wish I could go. I feel like such a coward staying behind. Every time I go into town people look at me, and I know they're thinking, why isn't he fighting?"

Robert's father immediately spoke up, "You owe no one an explanation. You will be starting college next month. Get an education and, God willing, this war will be over before you finish."

"I agree with Dad," Paul said, adding, "in fact, while Anthony and I are away, we are going to depend on you to watch out for Mom and Dad and to be here to give them a hand."

Paul's mother quickly caught the meaning of Paul's statement and asked, "Where are you going Paul? Your work for the military is in Washington, D.C."

Paul stood up and faced his parents who were sitting in chairs on both sides of the radio. "I came home this week because I was on leave prior to a change in orders. I leave Monday for Fort Jackson, South Carolina. I requested to be transferred to a unit going to Europe." Paul immediately turned to face his father. "Dad, you fought in the last war and. . ."

Correcting Paul his father said, "I never fought. I never carried a gun. I helped save lives, not take lives."

"You're right Dad. You helped save lives, but times are different. Anthony and I and everyone else in the service are trying to save lives as well. If America doesn't help to stop the Nazi and Japanese aggression, none of us will be safe. The army needs me to help. An invasion of Europe is coming, Dad. You don't get that news on the radio. After listening for a week, I realized you don't get much of the news, the real news, on the radio. I will be training at Fort Jackson and then ship out for England. America and Great Britain are committed to taking back France and driving Hitler back to Berlin. I don't know how long we will train in England, and I might not even be able to write. This is not easy for me, but it is something that I must do."

Paul walked over to his mother and knelt in front of her, taking her hands in his, "Mom, you sent me off to school saying take care of your brothers. Can you see that by going to war that's what I am doing? I am taking care of them, you, and all Americans. I love you, Mom. I'll do as much as humanly possible to be safe." Paul raised her hands to his lips and kissed them. "I need to go and pack. I will see you all in the morning before I leave." He turned and made his way up to his room, while his mother silently wiped tears from her cheeks.

***

The morning sun was just peeking up over the hills. Eventually, the heat would melt away the early fog. For now, the fog draped itself across the Schaefer farm like a wool blanket over a newborn baby. "Good morning, Mom," Paul said as he walked into the kitchen and kissed his mother's cheek.

"There's juice on the table. Bacon and pancakes will be ready in just a few minutes," his mother replied.

Paul's father and Robert joined him at the table. "What time are you leaving today?" Paul's father asked.

"Right after breakfast. I just need to go to the train station. I am catching the train back to Washington, and from there I will catch a transport to Fort Jackson," Paul said. Looking at Robert, Paul asked, "Robert, could you give me a ride to the station?"

"Sure, but what about your car?" Robert asked.

"Well, I was hoping you might take care of it for me while I am away. Girls love it! You know, I've been fairly lucky with it."

"Stop. Maybe that's a conversation you two should have on the way to the station. Mothers don't need to know everything," Paul's mother chided as she handed Paul the plate of pancakes.

Taking the plate, Paul gave Robert a wink and said, "Okay, Mom."

"Great!" Robert said. "I probably should drive it to the station, so you can make certain I know how to work everything. I'm ready to go whenever you are."

"Well, let me savor this breakfast just a bit longer. I'm not so certain I'll get this type of food or service for a while."

An hour later, Paul and Robert were waving to their parents as they made their way down the gravel roadway toward the Emmitsburg Road. "I can't wait for school to start now. This is going to be a great year," Robert said as he shifted into third gear and the Roadster fish-tailed slightly in the gravel.

"Make sure I get the car back in one piece," Paul smiled and said. Then he closed his eyes and relaxed, for he knew relaxation would be a rare commodity where he was headed.

CHAPTER TEN

Hans and Marie were stunned to learn that Czech and Slovak soldiers had assassinated their commander, Reinhard Heydrich, in Prague. The state funeral brought out thousands of mourners, and the Führer himself laid numerous military medals on the casket. Hitler called Heyrdrich a 'great German hero'. Hans and Marie attended the funeral to pay their respects, but they also came to meet with Heinrich Froer, their handler in the Sicherheitsdienst.

"Will this unfortunate event alter our assignment?" Hans asked Froer as they walked out of the Chancellery.

"I do not believe so. For a short time, Himmler will take back control, but will eventually replace Obergruppenführer Heydrich with someone as capable. This unfortunate event may only delay your assignment."

"Good. Marie and I should soon be finished with our infiltration into that communist group working in Potsdam. Next week we will hand over our information to the Gestapo. They will have everything they need to make the appropriate arrests."

"Fine." Froer's car pulled up and the SS driver came around to open the door. "I will be in touch as soon as your new orders come through."

Marie and Hans turned together to walk back toward the S-Bahn station, while Heinrich Froer slid into the backseat of his car.

***

Hans and Marie waited two months before Heydrich's replacement, Ernst Kaltenbrunner, summoned Froer to his office and informed him of their assignment. Froer met Hans at Gestapo headquarters. Upon seeing Froer, Hans stood at attention, "Heil Hitler."

Froer returned the salute. "Please, Hans, have a seat. Obergruppenführer Kaltenbrunner has passed your assignment on to me."

Hans said, "Very good. Marie and I were tired of rounding up local communist radicals. I know the danger they pose to our leadership and to our country, but. . ."

Froer interrupted, "Hans, all enemies of the Führer are enemies of our country. Each assignment is equally important."

"I'm sorry. You, of course, are correct. Marie and I were just hoping that the assignment in France, as you had mentioned, would come through."

"That is why you are here. I have received orders to send both of you to Brugge. We have found a link between French Resistance and the escape of important Germans, French, and Belgians through Brugge. We also have limited information that British agents may be arriving through the same source."

"Did you receive this information from Admiral Canaris?"

"No. Abwehr is unaware of this possible connection. For now Obergruppenführer Kaltenbrunner wants to keep it that way."

"When do we leave for Brugge?"

"I am sending Marie there next week. She will find a suitable location for you both to live. It might be easier and less suspicious for a woman to obtain lodging. The other reason that I am sending Marie first must remain between only the two of us."

Hans looked bewildered by Froer's remark. "Marie is a very good agent. Do you have reservations?"

"I do not. Remember, I was the one that recruited her. You, on the other hand, are the leader and too important to lose. This is Marie's first assignment outside of Germany. If she makes a mistake and is compromised, we will only be losing one agent."

Hans stood. "I understand, but she will not fail. She is every bit as capable as I am to carry out your orders. I will relay your orders to her and let her know that I will follow once she obtains an apartment."

Froer now stood and stuck out his hand. "Very good, Hans. Find this leak and then turn it over to the local Gestapo."

Hans shook Froer's hand and returned to give Marie the news.

***

Marie had little difficulty finding an apartment close to the restaurant the SS surmised as the meeting location for transfers in and out of the country. Finding a job was not difficult. Marie was young, pretty, and she easily unveiled the charm taught by Inga and Helena. Marie notified Hans that she was working in a small grocery and flower shop that abutted the restaurant identified by the SS.

Hans arrived the following week and found work on the docks as a loader. Froer's plan centered on Hans and Marie finding the link between partisans, the Resistance and to the escape of high-level Jews. Froer expressed Kaltenbrunner's desire to strike a severe blow to the Resistance movement and to do it quickly.

Now winter was taking a strangle hold over Brugge. Marie grew up in the cold of the mountains, but this was a deep and bitter, wet cold. She continued to fight off a terrible cough and fever. One night at dinner Hans said, "Maybe this assignment is not for us. I will call Himmler about replacing you. You are too sick to do any work and too weak to be of any help in an emergency."

Marie stood, pushing the table toward Hans, and said, "Don't you dare! I have never quit! I will never quit! Give me a couple more days to regain my color. Mr. Sholl at the store loves me. I have made many friends in the area, and I make the regular deliveries now to the restaurant. I come and go and no one pays attention. I know that I have seen some of the people that we are looking for. Everyone trusts me. Don't throw all of my work away. I can do this, Hans. Just wait a few more days."

"All right, a few more days. Now drink your soup and get to bed," Hans said.

***

The threat by Hans and a few more days were all Marie needed. She regained her strength and color and was back to her old self, bantering with Hans at every chance. Hans came home early and found Marie cooking stew. "Marie, we may have a problem," Hans said as he entered the front room.

Marie looked up from the boiling pot, "What do you mean, a problem?"

"A man, Richard Koch, came by the docks today looking for Mr. Korr, my foreman. Fortunately, my partner, Robert, talked to him. I had gone to get some harness hooks for the boxes we were loading. As I came around the cargo crates, I saw the two of them talking. Marie, I knew the other man from my assignment in Poland. He was the leader of the communist rebellion in Warsaw. We thought we had him captured, but he escaped. Canaris and Himmler have been working together to capture him. He is either here to bring in some of the Belgians and French, or he is trying to get out of Europe. We have to stop him."

Marie asked, "What do you suggest? He might not even return."

"Robert said that Korr was gone for the day and would not be back until tomorrow. Robert said to come back just before the end of the day, around 4:00 p.m. I will make up an excuse to leave early. I will watch for their meeting and then follow Koch. Hopefully, he will lead me to where he is staying. Then I will make a decision as to steps we will take."

Marie responded, "I will listen carefully tomorrow for his name when I make my deliveries. Maybe I can find someone that knows him."

Hans warned Marie not to press too hard. "Koch escaped my grasp once. I don't want to lose him again."

"Sit down and eat. This stew won't stay hot for long," said Marie as she brought Hans a bowl.

***

In 1938, Richard Koch traveled to Moscow to meet with members of the Soviet Union's military intelligence. He had been a communist leader in France for more than ten years. Influenced by Marx's writings and the success of the Russian revolution, Koch attempted to set up communist labor movements in France and later at the University in Poland. He despised Hitler and Nazis. He saw the Nazi party as a vicious antagonist to the citizens of Europe. Koch was eager to work for the Resistance, traveling to many parts of Europe, currently working in Brugge.

Koch returned the next afternoon at half-past four. As he had told Marie, Hans excused himself from work early and found an excellent observation window in an old abandoned building just across the dock from Korr's office. Hans knew that after the meeting Koch's exit would take him down the walkway and alongside the building Hans now huddled in.

Hans followed Koch that first night and again the next. Robert told Hans he had found out that Koch had set up a special shipment with Korr. Two cargo containers were being delivered sometime within the next four days. The containers were going to Ireland–something about farm equipment for a dairy–just outside of Dublin. Hans knew the farm equipment was just a cover and figured Koch was setting up a plan to flee the continent for Ireland. The SS knew someone, or a group of partisans, was using the Brugge docks as a shuttle point from the continent over to Britain and Ireland. Hans now believed Korr was also working with the conspirators.

As Hans pushed open the door to the apartment, he excitedly asked, "Marie, where are you?"

Marie's voice came from her bedroom. "I am changing and washing up. I worked all day today loading deliveries and one of the flour canvasses split. I was covered in flour and needed to get out of these clothes."

Hans was so excited about the information he had uncovered that he did not even listen to Marie's comments. When he heard her voice come from the bedroom, he immediately rushed in. Marie was standing in front of her nightstand, a pitcher and basin resting on top and a mirror hung on the wall in front of her. She had a wet cloth in her right hand and her left arm was raised above her head. Just as Hans entered, he caught a glimpse of her hand slowly wiping over her left breast and moving toward her armpit. In all the weeks together, this was the first time he had seen Marie undressed. He knew that she was athletic, trim and muscular, but he had no idea just how beautiful her body was. He stopped short as Marie looked at him through the mirror's reflection. "A gentleman usually knocks!" she said. "Or, maybe you burst in here to have your way with me. If so, I think you will find that, although as you can see I must be unarmed, I will be a formidable opponent." Other than her comments, Marie never made a move to cover-up. Marie was not embarrassed about being naked in front of Hans.

"I am so sorry, Marie. I have some important news, and I guess I didn't even listen to what you were saying."

His apology was answered when she winked slowly and said with a seductive whisper, "Well, Hans dear, if you wouldn't mind handing me that towel on the closet doorknob. Then you may take your eyes back out of the room, and I will finish here and come to listen to your great news." For the first time since entering the room, Hans took his eyes off Marie, picked up the towel and handed it to her. He turned and exited, closing the bedroom door behind him.

A short time later, Marie opened the door and came out into the small combination living room and kitchen. Since their time in Brugge, Marie had occupied the bedroom alone, and Hans slept on the sofa in the living room. "What news would make you lose all composure and turn you into a gawking teen?" Hans did not respond right away and Marie continued, "Oh, come on, Hans. I'm just kidding with you. We both knew that we could not continue to live in these small quarters and work together without, at some time, realizing we have bodies under these clothes. I am going to take your boyish embarrassment as a compliment that you liked what you saw. If it makes you feel any better, I have used the small mirror on the kitchen shelf to watch you change over in the corner after breakfast. I know you thought I was doing the dishes like the obedient female that I am," she smiled and continued, "but I figured I might as well enjoy some of the scenery while I worked."

"Marie! I never thought you would."

Marie quickly interrupted, "Let's not say any more about this. Let it go. We are both adults and we have a job to do. It seems like so long ago now, but what news do you have?"

Hans began to unravel the story of Richard Koch, including his early communist propaganda work at the University in Warsaw and then his saboteur work after the Germans controlled Poland. He explained that one of Koch's bombs had killed three high ranking Nazi officials and the regional administrator for Hitler in Poland. The SS wanted Koch badly. Hans said that he had almost infiltrated Koch's group when Koch simply disappeared.

Hans also relayed that he followed Koch for the past two nights and had information that indicated Koch was attempting to sneak out of Belgium within the next few days. "Koch met a man on a small fishing boat and was on board for more than two hours. When the two emerged from the boat's cabin, I heard the other man say the boat was seaworthy even if it did not look to be. Koch then mumbled something about it only needing to cross the channel."

Marie listened intently and finally said, "Hans, I need to see this Koch. How can I do this tonight?"

"Why do you need to see Koch?" Hans inquired.

"Today, while I was sweeping up my mess back behind the store, I heard some loud voices at the back of the restaurant. I could tell someone was just inside the door and then the backdoor slowly opened. I quickly crouched down behind the cart I had been unloading and saw a man walk out the restaurant door. I heard him say to someone inside that he did not care what it took to get it ready, but he was leaving the day after tomorrow with or without the others. I had never seen this man; it may be nothing, but it may also have been your Richard Koch."

"Okay. Go change into something warmer and darker. I will take you to where Koch is staying, and we will see if we can get a glimpse of him."

***

Koch's room was in the back of a laundry a mile from the flat rented by Hans and Marie. Earlier, Hans had watched as Koch entered the room from the alley behind the laundry. There were no lights in the alley. Both Hans and Marie walked down the alley, hugging the darkened walls of the buildings across from the laundry. Hans and Marie were two buildings north when they saw a light come on near the vicinity of Koch's room. "Quick, up against here!" Hans whispered to Marie, as he pushed her shoulder toward the alcove of an entry door. "I can't tell if that is Koch's room or the one next to his. Let's wait a moment and see what happens."

Just as Hans finished his statement, the light went out and the door opened. A man walked out and shut the door. The figure walked toward Hans and Marie, while Hans quietly slipped his Walther PPK from his coat pocket. Stopping beside a car parked just in front of the crouching pair, they heard a scratch and then saw as the soft flame of a match moved from the car's bumper up toward the man's face. As he worked to light his cigarette, Marie strained to see his face. The match went out, but the red ember glowed as the man took a deep drag from the cigarette. Hans was still pointing the Walther directly at the figure as the man turned and began to walk north, out of the alley. "I can't be certain, but I think that was the man I saw earlier today at the restaurant," Marie said.

"I am certain," Hans said, "that we both just looked at Richard Koch. If what you said was true he might be going to the restaurant now to meet someone. I know another way back that should get us to the restaurant before Koch makes it there." After Koch turned the corner, Hans and Marie rose from the alcove and proceeded south out of the alley. When they arrived back at the restaurant, Hans told Marie to find a secure spot to watch from the front; he would go back into the alley and watch the backside. "Don't do anything, just watch. Make note of anyone that goes in and try to get a look at his face. If Koch is coming, he should be here soon. In twenty minutes, make your way over to the corner greens. We will pretend to be having a romantic tryst near the fountain's bench. Now go and find a good location."

Just as Hans turned to leave, Marie grabbed his arm and turned him toward her. She hugged him and kissed his cheek. "You be careful too."

"In twenty minutes." They both turned to find secure shelter.

***

Marie was at the bench when Hans arrived. There were soft lights at the corner. She was certain by the gait that it was Hans, but she held the knife in her right hand just in case. There was no one else in the park, but to be certain that they looked the part of lovers meeting, Hans hugged Marie tightly. Marie felt his warmth and liked the feeling; she hugged back just as strongly. "Let's sit over here," Hans said. They sat closely on the bench as his arm draped over her shoulder and pulled her head to his. "Nothing moved in the alley. Anything on your side?"

She was enjoying this more than she thought. Marie snuggled closer to Hans and said, "I saw the man from earlier. Whoever he is, he went inside the restaurant."

"Good, let's see what we can do about getting into the restaurant," Hans replied.

"Wait, I'm not done. There's more. Another man went in just a few minutes after Koch."

"Did you get a good look at him? Do you know who he was?" Hans was anxious now.

"Hans, the other man was Mr. Korr! You introduced me to him just after you started work on the docks. Remember the night you worked late, and I brought you over some supper?"

"Ah! I thought as much. Koch and Korr had a meeting about these boxes being shipped to Ireland. They are working together. We may not have another chance. Somehow we must get inside and stop them."

Marie continued, "One more thing you should know. They posted a guard or someone outside. He is sitting on a stool near the front door. The good news is that I know him. His name is Jacque. He usually cleans the restaurant at night or early in the morning. I have chatted with him often, as he is usually leaving when I am coming to work. There is no way we can get to the restaurant without Jacque seeing us, and I am sure that someone is also watching the back door."

"Maybe not us, but what about you, Marie? Do you think you could use your charm to get close enough without this Jacques setting off an alarm to those inside?"

They were still close and Marie took her right hand and cupped the side of Hans' face. Their lips were almost touching and Marie said, "Certainly love. I am glad that you have finally noticed that I have assets." Marie was up off the bench and already moving across the green, toward the restaurant.

Hans caught up and took Marie's hand. "Be serious, Marie. Take him down quickly and quietly. When he is secured, I will move in with you. We know there are at least two others inside, so we need to get in quickly. You always carry a knife and that stiletto. Did you bring your gun as well?"

"Certainly, she said. "A woman can never be too careful at night during these dreadful times."

"Marie! This is not your schoolyard game. This is about who lives and who dies." Hans' voice was different. Marie had never heard him like this.

Marie said with conviction, "I know my job. Let's go find Koch and Korr."

CHAPTER ELEVEN

Marie started for the restaurant, but stopped and made a final check of the weapons she was carrying. She had the stiletto that held the bun in her hair and a knife strapped to her ankle; tonight she also carried a French 7.65 mm B.N.C.I. revolver. The revolver was small enough to hide and did not carry the kick of Hans' Walther. Marie made one more stop by a house bordering the greens and found a small basket. Marie loaded the basket with some of the flowers from around the house. She hoped with this she could create enough of a distraction to take Jacque down before he could warn those inside. Finally, Marie unstrapped the knife from her ankle and placed it in her right hand.

She started down the sidewalk and only looked back once to make sure that Hans was ready. He gave her a nod and then slipped back behind a wooden crate. There was a light on just above Jacque and the door he was guarding that created an ample view, but she was uncertain exactly when Jacque would notice her approach. About twenty yards into the walk, Marie noticed Jacque stood and looked in her direction, bringing the rifle he had slung over his shoulder into view. Marie, afraid that Jacque would sound the alarm, immediately called to him.

"Jacque, how are you this evening? It is Marie. Mr. Martine asked me to come back and make an arrangement of flowers for a special customer. I had to find the flowers and bring them back to the store." Jacque tipped his hat, and Marie could see by his wide grin that he was relieved it was only Marie. She also knew that his lapse would cost him his life tonight. She picked up her pace, so as to not give Jacque time to change his mind or reconsider his options.

Only a few feet from him now, Marie said again, "Hello, Jacque. It's me, Marie. I certainly wish I was not back working again tonight. Why are you outside with a rifle?"

Jacque hesitated, as if searching for a response that would fit sitting outside with a rifle in hand. "Mr. Donue, the owner of the restaurant, said there were some kids vandalizing buildings. He asked if I would sit outside to protect his building and maybe chase off a couple hooligans," Jacque finally responded.

Just as Marie was close enough to touch Jacque, she dropped her basket of flowers. "Oh, clumsy me. Sorry, Jacque," she said as she bent down to pick up the basket.

"Let me help," Jacque said as he bent down toward Marie.

Marie still had the knife in her hand and as Jacque moved down, Marie thrust up and caught Jacque in the throat. His eyes bulged, and he grasped Marie's right hand. As he clutched her hand, Marie quickly used her left hand and pulled the stiletto out of her bun. The stiletto's thrust went deeply into Jacque's back, piercing his heart. Jacque released his hands, closed his eyes, sighed and crumbled to the ground. Marie pulled both weapons out as Hans ran toward her. Before having time to reflect on what had just happened, Hans arrived and knelt beside her saying, "Good work."

Marie wanted to say something, but instead just wiped the blood from both knives on Jacque's jacket; she placed the ankle knife back in its sheath and the stiletto in a vacant sheath carried behind her belt. She also rolled her hair up, stuffed it under a wool cap that she retrieved from her coat pocket and rubbed some street grease on her face. "I don't want anyone to recognize me if I can help it." Finally, she took the revolver out and chambered one round. Hans chambered a round as well.

They moved up to the door and Hans said, "I will move in first to the right. Be prepared to quickly come in behind me. Let's presume they are armed and be ready to fire. It will be beneficial to keep either

Koch or Korr alive but not if it endangers either of us. Hans looked straight into Marie's eyes and could sense that she was still thinking about the life she had taken at the front door. "Are you ready?"

Marie could only nod. Hans twisted the doorknob, pushed the door open, and moved inside. Koch had rigged a tripwire just inside the door, tripping Hans as he entered. Hans' sudden crash to the floor alarmed everyone inside. Two men seated by the fireplace to the right grabbed their guns off the table and fired at the door. Marie stayed crouched behind Hans and could see the two men at the table. Five bullets struck the door and the jamb just above her head. Clutching the revolver in both hands, Marie fired her first round, striking one of the men in the chest. As he crumbled to the floor, she sighted the second man and fired. The second bullet hit the second shooter just below the right eye, driving him back into the fire. Only after the two men at the table were down did Marie turn her attention toward Hans. "Hans?"

"I'm fine," Hans said as he scrambled across the floor. "Move in!" Four men were near the back of the restaurant. Two of the men returned fire toward the door, while Koch and Korr moved further back into the kitchen area. Hans, still laying low on the floor, stretched around a downed table and fired. Hans' shot struck one of the men, sending him back over a table. The other shooter surprised Marie and Hans by running toward them. Marie fired as the man launched himself toward her. Hans did not wait to see the outcome of Marie's shot as he quickly rose and ran toward the kitchen. As Hans entered the kitchen, he could see that Koch and Korr were opening a trapdoor in the kitchen floor. "Stop!" Hans shouted. Ignoring the order, Koch jumped down the opening in the floor. Korr reached inside his jacket and pulled out a small caliber pistol and fired at Hans. Hans, ducking low again, returned fire, hitting Korr in the arm and knocking the pistol to the ground. As Hans moved toward Korr and the trapdoor, Korr tried to lower himself down the hole. Two shots rang out from down in the hole, and the concussion of the shots propelled Korr back onto the kitchen floor. Koch or someone else from down under the floor had shot Korr, once in the head and once in the chest. Figuring it unsafe to attempt lowering himself into the hole, Hans quickly moved back to check on Marie.

Back in the dining area, Hans saw Marie rising from the floor. Her assailant was down, and her knife was sticking out of the man's chest. Marie's cap was off, and her hair was hanging down around her face. Hans now saw blood running down around her left eye and spotting on her jacket. "Marie, you're bleeding! Are you okay?" Hans asked as he bent down toward her. Closer now, Hans saw tears mixed in with the blood.

It was no longer a competitive game; winning meant living while losing meant death. Marie thought Oberleutnant Hoster would have been proud at the instinctive way in which she had defended herself and killed these men tonight, but she was not quite as sure now. She just looked up, tears still forming in her eyes, and placed her arms around Hans and squeezed. Hans squeezed back as they sat huddled together on the floor.

CHAPTER TWELVE

Paul arrived at Fort Jackson just as fall was setting in on South Carolina. It was the first time Paul had been this far south, and he was surprised by the warm climate still lingering in the air. Unlike back home in Pennsylvania, the trees in South Carolina had yet to turn into the fire burst of oranges, reds and yellows. Paul noticed that much of the area even seemed tropical, with Palmetto trees most prolific. He read that the Palmetto had just recently been officially named the South Carolina state tree. Fort Jackson sat outside Columbia, the capital of South Carolina. By 1942, Fort Jackson was the third largest city in the state. The Fort was first commissioned in 1917 to help prepare troops for WWI and then abandoned by the War Department in 1922. However, in 1939, Secretary of War Woodring reassigned Camp Jackson to active status, officially for training new recruits. Paul, however, was not arriving today with a group of new recruits. His transfer papers were handled by the War Department and signed by Chief of Staff, George C. Marshall. Paul's orders were to report to Major Dwayne Poder, Army Intelligence.

Major Poder, a career military man and veteran of WWI, was assembling a group of officers fluent in German. These officers, assigned to army ground troops, were to be used as translators and interrogators once Allied forces assaulted Hitler's Atlantic front. Paul's meeting with Major Poder was scheduled for 1500 hours; with the earlier train delay, it was already 1430 hours as the taxi pulled up to the guard station.

Paul extended his papers out to the guard and asked, "Corporal, could you direct me to Major Poder's office? I am almost late for our appointment."

The corporal looked at the papers and at Paul, then saluted saying, "Yes sir, I can give you that information. Take this road up to the first stop sign and turn left. Take that road through two more stops and the building on your right houses Major Poder's office." The corporal then stepped back and gave Paul another salute as the taxi pulled forward.

Arriving at the building identified by the corporal as Major Poder's, Paul gathered his coat while the driver opened the trunk and set Paul's suitcase on the ground. Paul asked, "What do I owe you?"

"Two dollars and ten cents," the cabbie said.

Paul pulled out three dollars and gave it to the taxi driver and said, "Thanks for the ride."

"No problem. You take care of yourself now," the cabbie said as he shut the trunk and pocketed the three dollars.

Paul laid his coat over the bag, picked up both and moved quickly toward the door. Entering the outer office, Paul saw a young clerk working at a reception desk. "Excuse me," Paul said. Before he could finish, the clerk rose, sliding the chair backwards and saluting.

"Good afternoon, sir. How may I direct you?" the clerk asked.

Paul returned the salute and said, "I am looking for Major Poder. I am sorry that I am running late, but my train was delayed."

"You must be Lieutenant Schaefer. The Major is expecting you, sir. Just leave your bag with me and have a seat. I will let Major Poder know that you are here."

The clerk returned a short time later and said, "Lieutenant, please come this way." The clerk held the door open for Paul; as they walked in, the clerk addressed Major Poder saying, "Major Poder, this is Lieutenant Paul Schaefer." Paul walked to the front of Major Poder's desk, saluted the Major and stood at attention.

"At ease, Lieutenant. Please have a seat." Then addressing the clerk, Major Poder said, "Please bring us some coffee, Corporal."

"Lieutenant, do you like coffee or would you prefer something else?"

"No, coffee is fine, sir," Paul said.

Paul sat studying Major Poder. The Major was tall and thin, looking to not weigh more than one hundred and fifty pounds. His hair was the color of rust, and Paul thought it was longer than the military usually likes. He spoke with a soft, academic voice, sounding more like one of Paul's theology professors than a military officer. Major Poder spoke up. "Lieutenant Schaefer, I understand you asked for reassignment from the War Department to a combat unit. Is that correct? I also see in your file you have received commendations for some of your previous work there."

"Yes sir, I asked for this transfer. I believe it is time for me to do more than read letters, documents and communiqués. I have college friends that have already sacrificed a great deal, some even their lives, and I just figured it was my turn to do more."

"Son, everyone in this country has made sacrifices. What you were doing was just as important as your friends, albeit safer. I have no problem with the men who stay here and work for the government instead of living in the trenches, but that is not my call, Lieutenant. As for this transfer, I am happy to have you aboard."

Paul was just about to speak up again when the door opened; the clerk returned with a tray, complete with a coffee pot, sugar, cream and two cups. He laid the tray on the desk in front of both men and asked, "Anything further, sir?"

Major Poder said, "No, that will be all. Thank you and close the door on the way out." Now addressing Paul, the Major said, "Please help yourself, Lieutenant." Paul took the pot and poured some coffee into his cup. As the Major opened his desk drawer and produced a bottle of Jack Daniels, he asked, "Cream, sugar, or something a bit stronger, Lieutenant?"

Paul said, "No thank you, sir. I believe I will just have it black right now."

"Suit yourself, Lieutenant," the Major said as he filled his cup with Jack Daniels, topping the cup off with just a dash of coffee. "Now Lieutenant, if anyone asks, you can say that you shared a cup of coffee with your new commanding officer and it will not be a lie." Major Poder gave Paul a wink and then relaxed back in his chair. "Lieutenant, I sensed you were just about to say something when the coffee arrived. Go ahead."

"Major, General Marshall said he was transferring me here to become part of an intelligence group, but he did not elaborate." Paul then asked, "Could you elaborate, sir?"

"Yes, Lieutenant. You certainly know that we have been extremely successful this past summer, pushing Rommel out of Northern Africa and advancing into Sicily. It's been one hell of a fight, Lieutenant. We've lost too many good soldiers. General Eisenhower has had a time of it, keeping the English and American troops moving forward. Although difficult, Patton has taken Sicily and made a base there, while Clark just launched Operation Avalanche, assaulting the Italian coast near Salerno. Soon we will be advancing up through the heart of Italy and, with any luck, ending Italian support for the Nazis."

"Sir, my Italian is not very good."

Before Paul could finish, Major Poder said, "No, no. I am not sending you to Italy. Lieutenant, plans are underway for an even larger invasion against Hitler's Western Atlantic front. I can't go into any details about it, but I can tell you that you and twelve other German-speaking officers are being assigned to platoons here at Fort Jackson. You will be training with and leading your platoon against the best German panzer platoons in Europe. When we land in Europe, we are going to need men that can interrogate prisoners and read any materials we confiscate. Time will be critical. Washington cannot wait for someone here to translate materials and then send it back to the field. That's why you are here, Lieutenant. You are going to give us the quick turnaround that General Eisenhower believes will be critical to our success. Your platoon will be one of the first landing groups on the beaches of Europe. Training will begin here and continue in England. Once in

England, training will become intense and will continue until General Eisenhower is ready to launch an attack on Hitler's defenses."

Paul finished his coffee and said, "Thank you, sir. I was hoping my assignment would be something like this. I am ready to do my part, sir."

Major Poder said, "Son, I hope that by the time you are needed, you will be ready. You worked in Washington, and you know those Generals are always doing casualty predictions. On this invasion, even those Generals just somberly shake their heads. This invasion is going to be the worst of the worst. There will be no room for failure and nowhere to retreat. You understand what I am saying, Lieutenant?"

Paul stood up and said, "Yes sir, I do. I'll do my best, sir." Then Paul asked, "When will I be meeting my platoon, sir?"

"I have scheduled a meeting for tomorrow morning with Sergeant Coffey, your platoon leader. Sergeant Coffey and your platoon have been here training for eight weeks. You will meet Sergeant Coffey and then your platoon. Now, ask the corporal to show you to your quarters. That is all, Lieutenant." From his chair, Major Poder returned Lieutenant Schaefer's salute. Paul turned and walked out to find the corporal.

***

Paul rose just after 0500 and prepared for his meeting with Major Poder and Sergeant Coffey. John Coffey, also addressed as Sarge by his platoon, was a southerner from Virginia, just outside of Manassas Junction. He was gangly, but with tremendous strength for his body size. What Coffey lacked in size he made up for in tenacity. On more than one occasion, Coffey had become involved in misunderstandings that led to physical confrontations. He'd seen enough dog fights in his day to know victory went not to the biggest dog, rather to the dog that never stopped coming at its opponent. Sergeant Coffey had never heard the phrase 'fight or flight'. He only knew fight and his fighting had cost him promotions, but this might now change. Uncle Sam wanted fighters. From what Coffey knew, he was off to England to train and to take his fighting spirit to the Nazis. No one was going to pull this American hound dog off a German shepherd.

Sergeant Coffey was sitting just outside his barracks when Paul and Major Poder drove up. Snapping to attention as the two men walked up, Sergeant Coffey saluted saying, "Morning Major, Lieutenant. The men are just finishing breakfast and should be assembled back here in fifteen."

Major Poder said, "At ease, Sergeant. I would like you to meet Lieutenant Paul Schaefer. He has been assigned to your company. I have already briefed him on your training. He will be involved from here on with the remainder of your training, getting everything ready for transfer to England."

Sergeant Coffey raised his hand, "Good to meet you, Lieutenant Schaefer. I believe ya'll will find this to be a fine group of men, sir."

Paul returned the handshake, noticing the strength of Coffey's grip, "I am pleased to meet you as well, Sergeant Coffey. Major Poder has briefed me as to your previous training, and I am anxious to meet the rest of the company. I understand you are conducting a field exercise this morning, Sergeant."

"That is correct, sir. We have a five-mile march to the field point and then will commence with a navigation and compass course. Were ya'll planning to drive out and observe the exercise, sir?"

"No, sergeant. I was planning to march out with you if you and the men have no objections," said Paul.

"No objections at all, sir. It's just that in my time with the army, sir, the officers don't always like to go through all the training, if I may speak honestly," Coffey replied.

At that moment Major Poder interjected, "I see that you two are going to work out just fine. Lieutenant, Sergeant, I believe I will leave you two to prepare for your morning training. Stay at ease. Lieutenant Schaefer, remember that I will see you this evening at 1900 hours."

"Yes sir," Paul said, adding, "let me get my gear from the jeep, sir."

When the two men arrived at the jeep, Major Poder said, "Good move, Lieutenant. The quicker you become part of the platoon the better. Just be sure not to push too hard too soon. Get to know Coffey. The men like and respect him. For you to be effective, the platoon will need to see that Coffey respects you as well."

"I will keep that in mind, Major. I'll be at the Officer's Club tonight at 1900 hours, sir," Paul said as he grabbed his gear from the jeep. As he turned and walked back toward the barracks, his stomach turned in anticipation, or maybe fear, as to just what lay ahead.

CHAPTER THIRTEEN

After checking Marie's head wound and each of the bodies, Hans and Marie returned to the flat. Disappointedly, they had found no papers on any of the men and they had no prisoners to interrogate. However, Hans did recognize one of the first two shooters as a dockworker and was certain the Brugge docks were somehow connected to the underground movement. He would report this information back to Froer.

Upon arriving at the flat, Marie went to the bathroom and washed the grease, blood and dirt off her face. She looked into the mirror, saw Hans walk into the bathroom and felt him gently touch her shoulders. Turning Marie around, Hans said, "Let me take a closer look at the cut now." Reaching into the medicine cabinet, Hans retrieved some tape and made small butterfly bandages to close the wound. "You might also have a concussion, so let me know if you are experiencing any headaches or blurred vision."

"I'll be fine. It's nothing really. I'm sorry we did not get any information. I guess we failed," Marie finally said.

"Marie, we never fail as long as we come back alive. We probably stopped the shipment Koch and Korr were talking about and that's good. True, more information would have been helpful, and they will now move their operation to a different location. We will send a report to Hauptmann Froer, and the SS will increase patrols at the docks. I am going back to the docks tomorrow and see what else I may find. I need to go through Korr's files before anyone knows he is dead."

"I'll go with you," Marie replied.

"No! No one knows that we are connected. You need to return to the flower shop and restaurant. Listen to everyone and see if anyone is talking about the shootings from last night," Hans sternly said. Then in a calmer, more relaxed tone, Hans said, "But for tonight it's over. You take a bath, and I will fix us something to eat. I am going to put on some Brahms. That might help to relax us."

The small flat was soon filled with Brahms' Symphony No.1. As Marie finished the dinner dishes, Hans took a bath. With little warm water available, Hans returned quickly wearing pants, but without a shirt. Marie gazed at Hans' lithe, muscular shape. Marie walked over to Hans who was sitting on the sofa. He looked up as she slowly lowered herself onto his lap. "What's wrong?" he asked. "Are you still upset about this evening?"

"It's more than that," she replied. "Hans, we could have been killed just as easily as those men."

Hans silenced her by placing a finger over her lips. "Stop, you cannot get this emotional about it. We did our job. People died. In war men and women die. It's sad. Even barbaric. One day it will stop, but for now we must continue the work we were sent here to perform."

Marie took Hans' fingers and gently kissed them. Holding tightly to his hand, Marie said, "I know about that and I will do my job, but I also now realize that I might be the one to die. She then placed Hans' hand on her breast. "Hans, I don't want to die without ever loving a man. I want to feel the warmth and pleasures between a man a woman."

Marie then let go of Hans' hand and brought her own hands up his chest and settled them on his face. Lightly holding his cheeks, Marie bent forward and kissed him. He returned the kiss deeply, while slowly unbuttoning Marie's blouse. Hans slid the blouse over her shoulders and let it fall to the floor. She stood, unsnapped her bra and slid her skirt and underwear off. Hans began to rise and undo the belt holding up his trousers, but Marie moved forward and pushed him back onto the sofa. She leaned forward and unzipped his pants. In the background, Brahms' Symphony continued to play, but now Hans' soft sighs and the sound of Marie's pounding heart filled her head.

CHAPTER FOURTEEN

For three months, Paul's platoon trained at Fort Jackson under the watchful eyes of both Lieutenant Schaefer and Sergeant Coffey. The men, most only eighteen to twenty years old, were from various parts of the Eastern United States. Like Paul, many of the men had brothers already fighting against the Germans, Italians or Japanese. During this time, two of Paul's men received the sad news that their brothers had been killed in battle. Paul took the news as hard as his men, constantly thinking about Anthony and the tough time the Marines were having advancing against entrenched Japanese forces on those little volcanic drops of land out in the Pacific.

The other source of negative news for some of Paul's men was the occasional letter from a girlfriend telling them that maybe it was time to break things off. The letters seemed sincere, but the outcome was the same in the eyes of Paul's men; their girlfriends had found someone still back home that they were now snuggling up to for warmth and compassion. So goodbye and take care of yourself. When received, one of these letters sent the platoon into a state of agitation that, to an outside observer, made the platoon look like a pack of rabid dogs. An innocent, joking comment about another's body odor could be enough to set off a melee that, by the time it was over, had engulfed seven or eight men. After things settled, hard looks and stone silence embraced the platoon for days. Sergeant Coffey believed the best way to overcome these episodes was to take the men on what he liked to call 'family time'. Really, it was a full gear run through the backwoods of Fort Jackson, sometimes up to fifteen miles. By the end of the maneuver, the men had struggled, suffered, worked together and, most importantly, refocused any lingering animosity toward Sarge.

***

Late in November, the platoon received orders to ship out for England, effective December 7. No one missed the irony that they were leaving exactly two years after the attack at Pearl. Each man was also given a five-day pass. Some members returned home to see family, to check on their sweethearts, or to have a last Thanksgiving home-cooked dinner. Others, like Paul, decided that going home for such a quick visit might do more harm than good. These men ventured off to more local areas, like Columbia and Charleston, in the hope of finding some southern comfort.

The evening before leave was to commence, Coffey approached Paul and said, "Lieutenant, I'm going home for just a couple days and thought I would see if you might like to ride along. My cousin is driving down to pick me up tomorrow."

"Thanks for the offer, Sergeant, but I think maybe I'll just get some things done around here," Paul replied.

"Lieutenant, if I might," Coffey said as he pulled up a chair next to Paul. "Ya'll been working just as hard as any man in this group. Fact is, you might be the only Lieutenant that continues to go out and sweat right alongside the men. You need a break, Lieutenant, if for no other reason than to get away from this cooking. It's god awful, and that's on the good days."

Paul sat quietly, not responding, replaying in his head the sounds of extended family sitting around the dinner table, chattering about events that now seemed less important. Finally responding, Paul said, "Okay. A bit of home cooking would be an enjoyable change. Thanks, Sarge."

"Great! My cousin will be here tomorrow around 1100," Coffey said as he rose and left Paul's room. Just as Coffey was exiting, Paul pulled out Anthony's last letter while looking at the headlines of the paper on his desk.

CHAPTER FIFTEEN

Hans stretched his arm around Marie's snuggling body and kissed the back of her neck. They were in Marie's bed, having moved there during their second passionate liaison of the evening. "Last night was wonderful, but we must forget that it happened, live as we have, and complete the work that Hauptmann Froer has assigned us," Hans said without much emotion attached to it.

Saddened by Hans' cold tone, Marie said, "Yes, I know. I can go back and live as we did in separate rooms and we can do our work, but I will not forget anything about last night. The sensations I experienced were more intense than anything I ever knew possible. Do you think that Inga and Helga experience those feelings every time they are with a man, or after time does it become uninteresting?"

Hans gave Marie a quizzical look, "Am I to believe now that I was just an experiment in your seduction training seminar?"

Marie placed her arms around his neck and said, "Not at all." When she finished, she lightly gave Hans a peck on the cheek and said, "No more talk of last evening. Go to the dock and see what information awaits in Korr's office."

"You should go back over to the flower shop this morning. Don't bring up anything about last night, but listen to see if anyone else is talking. Most of all, be careful. If you think someone recognizes you from last night, don't wait around. Get back here as quickly as you can and make certain no one follows you. I will see what I can find out at Korr's office and will meet you back here later this evening." Hans got out of bed and began to dress. After quickly eating some bread, he grabbed his hat and coat and hurried out the door.

***

The streets were busy for a Saturday morning, with men and women on bikes riding toward the square where the farmers' market was held. The market was a bustling affair, with families buying fruits, vegetables and dairy products from local farmers. Unfortunately, with the war going on, the German military was commandeering the majority of the crops. Marie and Hans suffered like the rest of the civilian population. Most families rushed to the market early in the morning to scavenge the best products available. Hans and Marie shopped there early most Saturdays as well, but not today.

Hans did not return to the flat last night, and Marie was worried. This was the first time Hans had not returned in the evening to relay news of his observations. Marie could only believe that whatever Hans found was so important that he needed to keep up a continuous vigil. She made her way along the street now, thinking the encounter with Koch and Korr most likely did jeopardize their latest shipment; but they still didn't know what the shipment was. Maybe Hans was lucky enough not only to find information on the shipment, but to also find a transmitter with a security check. With the transmitter and security check, Hans or Marie could impersonate a field agent and send false information back to London. Through false communications with London, they might also learn the names and residences of key underground agents in the region. While working alone on an assignment in Lyon, Hans had used a transmitter and security check to gather information on a drop being made by the SOE, the British spy organization. The Gestapo was waiting at the drop area for the team, hoping to turn the agents and use them for further intelligence gathering. Unfortunately, the agents proved to be unwilling, and all three gave up their lives with simple cyanide pills.

Arriving at the docks, Marie found them deserted as expected for a Saturday. Most of the loading and unloading took place midweek, and now she saw only a handful of workers at the far end of an adjacent dock. They were immersed in loading crates on a flatbed truck and paid little attention to Marie as she walked toward Korr's office.

It made no sense that Hans did not come home last night and now was nowhere to be found. Marie eased herself between two trucks parked next to Korr's office and listened carefully for any sound of others. It's too quiet, ghostly quiet, she thought as she unstrapped the ankle knife and felt for the pistol in her coat. Staying low, she scurried to a spot just under one of the side windows and peered inside. No one! The office was empty, but she did see papers scattered about the floor and two chairs overturned–a sign of a struggle for sure. Maybe Hans had found a lead and was following up because time was of the essence, she considered. Marie hesitated for a moment thinking, if Hans found something so important, he surely would have stopped by the flat to tell her. She knew she had to follow Hans, whatever that meant. To do that, she needed to get inside the office. The front door was partially concealed by a stack of boxes, so Marie moved to the door and took hold of the doorknob. The knob easily turned in her hand. Cautiously she opened the door and entered.

Marie slowly drew her pistol, but within the first few steps, she knew the eerie silence and the smell of death was all that consumed the office. Quickly, she made her way over to the desk and stopped. A trained soldier, she screamed, but a silent scream at that. Marie dropped to her knees sobbing. Hans was hardly recognizable as he lay in a pool of blood, mixed with blood from another man lying dead next to him. It was apparent that Hans probably killed the other man, but was overtaken by others. From the bruises and the cuts on his body, it was also apparent that Hans had suffered greatly before he died. "Hans, why did it have to be you? Why didn't you let me come with you yesterday?" she mumbled out loud as she cradled Hans' head in her lap. Marie sat there just holding Hans, trying to squeeze life back into his bruised and beaten body.

Shaken from her thoughts, Marie heard voices originating from the dock outside. Immediately, she looked up and listened for the sound of the front door. It remained closed, but she knew she could not stay there. She also realized she could do nothing with Hans' body. Whoever killed Hans, probably Koch, might be waiting to see if anyone came to look for him. Somehow she must now find a way out and leave with no signs of her presence. Marie kissed the top of Hans' head and slowly slid it off her lap. "Hans, you told me we might need to leave each other for our own protection, but I never thought I would leave you like this." A tear rolled down Marie's cheek and fell onto Hans' head. "Hans, I will find who did this, and they will pay with blood," she whispered.

Rising from the floor, Marie moved over to the window nearest the front door. The voices she heard came from two men standing next to the crates she had herself just hidden behind. The men were smoking and chatting with each other. They did not seem to be stationed there as lookouts, but she could not be certain. The best plan would be to find another way out. She moved back to the rear of the office where she recalled seeing another door. Slowly opening the door, Marie saw that the other room was a lavatory. The building must be old she thought because the toilet was nothing more than a wooden bench with a seat attached to the top. She looked down the toilet hole and could see the water below.

"I doubt they would consider my exit by this means," she said to herself as she slithered down the toilet hole. Large beams supported the office and dock. Marie was able to find footholds to use as she squeezed through the hole and crouched under the lavatory flooring. The wood was slimy, with the potent smell of urine and excrement. Holding her breath as much as possible, she continued to climb down the supports until just above the water. Tied up to the side of the dock was a small wooden dingy, with oars and some tarps folded in the front end. Marie climbed into the dingy, opened one of the tarps and slid underneath.

She lay there for hours, occasionally peering out to see how dark it was getting. When nightfall finally descended on the wharf, Marie climbed back up to the dock area and looked for signs of a surveillance. There seemed to be no signs of men waiting or watching the office, but she could not be certain and felt the best option for escape was the dingy. Climbing back down, Marie slowly untied the dingy and quietly took up the oars.

It took close to an hour to make her way out and around two of the adjacent docks. She tied the dingy off and climbed a ladder to the platform above. Marie knew nightfall would bring German patrols down to the dock and figured Koch and his men would make certain to be gone from the area by this time. Marie made her way down the streets toward her flat, also making certain she avoided German patrols. She was not afraid of contacting the patrols, but she did not want to be picked up and be brought back to an SS station only to prove she was working for the Sicherheitsdienst. That was wasted time she did not have.

Marie walked back through the square where, earlier today, families had relaxed and spent a sunny winter day just trying to forget that this war had changed their lives. Back at the flat, Marie quickly showered and changed from her soiled, smelly clothes. Some of the local cafes were now in the process of serving supper, and Marie walked into one that looked crowded, remembering Hans' advice. "When you are trying to hide, it is best to hide in a crowd," he had said. Marie's eyes gazed around the cafe, identifying exits just in case a quick departure was needed, and took a seat at a table close to a side door. She was famished, as she had left the flat without eating this morning, figuring she would meet Hans and dine with him. Now, almost twelve hours later, her body was weary and crying for food.

The waiter, a young boy maybe ten and probably the son of the owner, came over and offered Marie a menu. He smiled and asked if she wanted him to take her jacket. "No thank you," Marie replied. "I am a bit chilled and would like to keep it on." More accurately, Marie knew that her pistol was in the jacket pocket and sewn inside the seam was money just for situations like this.

The boy said, "I will give you a moment and return for your order then."

"Thank you," Marie replied. The boy turned and walked over to another table as Marie held the coat with both hands and gently tore the seam. She reached inside and produced twenty Belgian francs. Her thoughts returned to Hans. He was a strong-willed man, a soldier, and would do anything to protect her, but she also knew that everyone had limits as to the pain they could endure. Quick visual images of a beaten Hans raced through her brain, like a runaway train racing through a depot. She could not be certain that he did not give her up or give up the location of the flat. Maybe that was why no one was at the dock. After eating, she knew what she had to do.

Working her way back to the flat took most of the night. Carefully, she surveyed each street, looking for anyone that was unfamiliar or out of place. She scrutinized windows, looking for movement. Believing no one was watching from outside her apartment, she still could not be certain Koch and others were not waiting for her inside. Marie walked to the back of the building and down the steps to the basement door. The door was locked. Shielding her hand in her coat pocket, she struck the glass window. Pushing the broken pane inside, it cracked and clanked as it hit the floor. Marie hoped the noise would not be heard by anyone. At this time of night, no one would be in the store, which occupied the ground floor, and Hans and Marie were the only resident occupants. The owner of the store and building lived in one of his other properties on the next street over.

Once inside, Marie worked from her memory of the basement lay-out. The only light came from the glow of the building's boiler firebox. Tucked away in the corner of the basement and behind a pile of boxes was a small door clasp. Just after moving in, Hans and Marie made a small alcove in the plastered wall with a trapdoor to cover the opening. Inside the alcove safe, Marie found both of their SS credentials, the information for contacting Froer, five hundred francs and a small explosive device that now would come in handy.

Taking the can she brought with her, Marie poured the gasoline on the floor just under the boiler. Next, she placed some boxes of materials and a mattress on top of the liquid and placed the explosive device just under the boiler. The detonator had a small time fuse attached, which Marie set. Once set, Marie only had five minutes to get out, but she took a moment and closed her eyes. It was only one night, last night, but she could feel Hans' hands slowly, gently gliding over every part of her body. She felt his weight as he pressed on top of her, and she began to move as she had moved under him last night. As quickly as those visions came, they vanished into the dark catacombs of her memory. She was out the door and into the darkness of her new life, alone.

CHAPTER SIXTEEN

Paul reread Anthony's latest letter.

Dear Paul,

I am sending this letter to you from my transport ship. We are on the move but we have not been told where we are going. We have been told we need to take out some Jap landing strips. This will be my first taste of fighting the Japs and I am scared, Paul. They say the navy will pound the hell out of the Jap positions, so we should not encounter much in the way of resistance once we move ashore. But you never can be sure. Paul, I am ready to do this. I'm ready to fight alongside my brother Marines, to take this little piece of volcanic rock in the middle of the ocean and to move, hopefully, one step closer to ending the Jap aggression.

I understand from your last letter you are about to ship out to England and eventually take the fight against Hitler all the way to Berlin. Good luck and let God be with us both.

Semper Fi.

Your brother,

Anthony

P.S. Don't say anything to Mom or Dad. They still think I am training down off Australia. I will write them when I am safe.

Paul laid the letter down and picked up the paper again looking at the headlines: MARINES VICTORIOUS AT TARAWA. JAP LANDING STRIP DESTROYED. Reading further, however, the article stated that victory came only after heavy Marine casualties of more than 3,000. Marines were cut down by enemy machine guns as they slowly inched their way across the coral waterline to the beach. Fighting took days before a beachhead could be firmly established and the Japanese landing strip secured. *Was this the island that Anthony referred to in his letter?* Paul prayed that, if it was, Anthony was not a casualty. He thought about calling his folks to let them know but decided to honor Anthony's wishes.

***

Coffey knocked on Paul's door, sticking his head in saying, "Lieutenant, my cousin is here."

"I'll be right with you," Paul said as he finished zipping up the black day bag.

Out at the car, Coffey said, "Lieutenant, this is my cousin, Jack. Jack, my Lieutenant, Paul Schaefer."

The men shook hands and Paul said, "Jack is it? Just call me Paul. Thanks for the invite and for picking us up." Paul noticed that Jack was about Robert's age and that he walked with a limp, as though his right foot was injured.

"Nice to meet you too, Paul. Just throw your things in the trunk and we'll be gettin out of here. Where ya'll from?" Jack inquired.

"Pennsylvania," Paul said. "Gettysburg."

"Isn't that where Lee was just about one day short of kicking some Yankee butts and ending another war?" Jack asked somewhat rhetorically. He continued, "How do ya'll think we would be handling this war today if we were two countries instead of one?"

Closing the car door, Paul said, "Thank goodness Lee didn't listen to General Longstreet, Gettysburg wasn't lost and those Yankees kept this country as one. Right now we need everyone united in this fight."

"Ya, I guess that's probably right." Then Jack turned to Coffey, "John, I talked to your Momma last night, and she was so excited she was squealing like a pig in heat. When I get you home, she's likely to chain you up in the basement till this thing's over."

"Let's just get going, Jack," Coffey said as they pulled out of the gates at Fort Jackson and headed for home.

***

"Well, this is it," Coffey said to Paul as they pulled up to the single story combination stone and wood-sided home. The original structure was made of mortared stone, but additions must have been made that were plank wood siding. The siding was peeling and the roof, covered with moss, looked to be in a similar state of disrepair. Coffey said, "She ain't much to look at since my Pa died six years ago. We've been trying to do some small improvements, but money has been tough. That's one of the reasons I joined the army, so I could send money back home to Momma, but now that she's got some money, there's no one around to fix up the place."

"Hey, don't worry. It looks great. Maybe we could spend a couple days around here doing some things for your mother," Paul said.

"You think so? You wouldn't mind, I mean. That would be great," Coffey said exuberantly. He added, "Momma would love it if we could just fix a couple spots on the roof that have been leaking for some time and maybe slap a little paint on some of the siding. Thanks Lieutenant, but I don't want you to think that I invited you here to join a work party."

"Not at all, Sarge. I'd like to stay busy—keep my mind off the war for a few days. Besides, I don't expect your mom to feed me for nothing. A man has to earn his keep."

"Whatever you say, Lieutenant," Coffey chuckled in agreement.

"Paul, the officer corrected. "Please, call me Paul while we are here."

"Well, I don't think I could do that, Lieutenant."

"What if I told you it was an order, Sergeant?"

An order, huh?" Coffey said with a grin. "Come on, it's time you met Momma."

***

Just as both men reached the porch, the front door opened and Coffey's mother, Ruth, appeared. Physically, Ruth looked younger than Paul had expected, but she was stooped over, propped up with a cane. As Coffey reached his arms around her, she raised up and squeezed tightly, tearfully sobbing, "My boy is home. My boy is home."

Coffey kissed his mother on the cheek and then gently released her saying, "Momma, this is my Lieutenant, Paul Schaefer." Ruth reached and took Paul's hand in hers.

"I am pleased to finally meet you, Mrs. Coffey. John has talked often of you," Paul said.

"Please, Lieutenant Schaefer, call me Ruth."

"Yes ma'am, but only if you call me Paul," Paul said as he picked up his bag.

"John, show Paul to one of the extra rooms and then come back. I have some lunch made for us. Smoked catfish and blackberry jam sandwiches with lemonade." Ruth called from the porch, "Jack, come in and have some lunch as well before you head back home."

"Yes ma'am," Jack said adding, "thought maybe you forgot about me, with all the hugging and kissing up there."

"Just git yourself in here and help me with the lemonade and lunch tray," Ruth concluded as she walked inside trailing behind her son.

Paul returned to the front room and began to inspect the surroundings. A relic of the 19th century, the front parlor was anchored to the earth by a large stone fireplace, complete with a swing rod that held a large cast iron pot. The interior walls were rough plaster with numerous cracks, no doubt from the constant change in temperature. The split plank floor was uneven, accented by large gouges, worn smooth over time.

Coffey entered and watched quietly as Paul walked around inspecting the room. "It's a museum piece alright, but it's the only home I've ever known," Coffey said startling Paul.

"It's a great home, John. I love the history. My parents had an historic home like this up in Gettysburg, but they tore it down to rebuild about fifteen years ago. It always saddened me." Paul then asked, "Has this home been in your family for a time?"

Coffey said, "Take a seat here, and I'll give you the quick history. It was built on the Rawling plantation sometime in the late 1700's. The Rawling's house was located on the other side of the hills, just northwest of here. The stone portion of the house was originally built as one of three slave quarters. There was an overseer's house nearby, but it burned down just after the war. This was a tobacco plantation, and the field slaves were divided between the three areas, working their section of land for the Rawling family. My great-great-grandmother was a slave bought in Richmond around 1855. She was only thirteen at the time and everyone just called her Coffee because of her light creamy color. Mr. Rawling had taken a liken to Coffee, but Mrs. Rawling didn't quite take a liken to Mr. Rawling taken a liken, if you know what I mean. So Coffee lived here maintaining this house while the others worked the fields."

Paul gave Coffey a stare and started to say, "But. . ."

Coffey knew that look, had even seen it before. "Yah, gee Sarge, you don't look black."

"I'm sorry, John. That's not what I meant by. . ."

Coffey stopped Paul again saying, "It's fine. Let me finish. This story does have a happy ending. Anyway, Mr. Rawling's son, Thaddeus, was about sixteen and took a liken to Coffee as well. Whenever possible, he would come out here and sneak visits. Thaddeus wasn't the only white man to leave a half-breed bastard child on the plantation. Unlike others, however, Thaddeus did care for Coffee, but with secession Thaddeus left to join Lee's army. The Rawling plantation survived the first battle of Manassas but not the second in 1862. The plantation house was burned to the ground and the land razed as the North moved back toward Washington. Thaddeus returned after the war to find his plantation home destroyed, his father dead, and his mother gone. She left to live with relatives in Mobile. The stone slave quarters were still erect. Thaddeus' son and Coffee were still here with maybe five others. 'Carpetbaggers' came and divided up the property, leaving Thaddeus with some 10 acres. Thaddeus worked the land and lived here with Coffee. It was a difficult relationship, but from Coffee's diary it seemed they cared for each other. They had two more children, both daughters, and all three children looked more white than black. When their son, Joshua, was sixteen, he left home and went to Baltimore to work on ships. Six years later, Joshua heard that Thaddeus died and decided to return home with his new white wife. Lieutenant, I am sure you can figure the rest of the story. Joshua used the name Coffey instead of Rawling and as time went on, well here I am."

"What about the daughters?"

"One of them died as a child, and the other also left and went to New York. She married a white man and never returned. I imagine no one ever knew that her mother was a slave girl. Thaddeus and Coffee stayed out of the way of society. If anyone came around, Thaddeus became the benevolent master again to his former slave."

"If the army even knew that I had Negro blood, they would make me a cook or custodian in one of those black regiments. It's wrong, Lieutenant. You people in the north said you went to war to free slaves, but none of you really wanted anything to do with them when it was over."

"Sadly, you're right. Maybe someday we will see a change. Say, let's leave this at the happy ending and have some lunch."

CHAPTER SEVENTEEN

Marie made her way to the train station. The transmitter, used by Hans and Marie to contact Froer, was now part of the rubble in her burned-out flat. However, papers recovered from the basement gave her the name of an SS contact in Brussels, Dr. Manfred Schneider.

Arriving at Dr. Schneider's office six hours later, Marie found the office locked. She rang the doorbell and waited a few moments before a man appeared. He looked to be in his early sixties, with silver hair and a small goatee. He was large, maybe six foot four and close to three hundred pounds. "May I help you?"

"I am looking for Dr. Schneider," Marie said. "My name is Marie Monin from Brugge. I understand that Dr. Schneider helps young women in distress." Her papers identified this as the code she would use with Dr. Schneider.

"I am Dr. Schneider. Please come in, Fräulein Monin," he said as he waved her inside and closed the door. Dr. Schneider walked Marie to a sitting room just inside the front door. "I was just in the kitchen making some tea. Would you care for some?"

"Yes, that would be very nice. Thank you," Marie said as she took a seat in one of the large leather chairs.

Dr. Schneider returned a short time later and gave Marie a tray with a cup of hot tea and some cream and sugar. Concern showed on Dr. Schneider's face and his tone changed. "If you are here Fräulein Monin, there must have been some problem in Brugge."

"Please call me Marie and, yes, there was a terrible incident," she said, adding, "Hans was killed by a group that we were tracking at the docks." Marie then went on to detail the altercation and killings at the restaurant, finding Hans' tortured body, the connection between Koch and Korr, and Koch's escape. She also explained the destruction of her flat and any evidence of their activities there. Marie concluded that she needed to get in contact with Froer.

"I agree," Dr. Schneider said. "I will contact the Sicherheitsdienst immediately. Hauptmann Froer will certainly be saddened by the loss of Herr von Schroedder."

Marie was surprised by Dr. Schneider's use of Hans' last name, as she had not mentioned it during their meeting. "Did you know Hans, Dr. Schneider?"

"I met him only once back in Berlin, during the time the two of you were training. Froer sent me updates as to your work in Brugge." Dr. Schneider rose from his chair and walked over to Marie. "I have a spare bedroom just down the hall. Please come with me, I'll show you."

Marie followed Dr. Schneider. "Thank you. Will you be contacting Hauptmann Froer this evening?" Marie asked.

"Make yourself comfortable. I will contact the Hauptmann's office immediately, although he may not get back to me until morning. Once again my dear Fräulein, make yourself comfortable. I will let you know as soon as I hear from Hauptmann Froer." With that Dr. Schneider closed the door, leaving Marie to her private thoughts of finding Mr. Koch.

***

"Hauptmann Froer will be here by tomorrow evening," Dr. Schneider informed Marie over breakfast the next morning. "He was quite shaken by the death of Herr von Schroedder and wants to speak with you in person."

"That's fine. The sooner he arrives, the sooner I can return to Brugge and find Koch."

"Patience my dear."

"I apologize for my ardent behavior, Dr. Schneider, but Hans believed Koch was attempting to flee to the safety of England. We may have stopped those plans for now, but I am certain he is continuing to make plans to flee this area. I need to find him before he can do more harm."

"I understand your concerns, but one good agent is already dead and the Reich does not need to lose another hastily. I am sure you and Hans were close and his death is unfortunate, but there is a larger cause. Germany is at war, or have you forgotten? This is not just your war but a war that the German people cannot lose again. If Hauptmann Froer believes it is in the best interest of the Reich for you to find Koch, he will send you back. If not, you shall abide by his decision and return to your work in the field, wherever that may lead you."

"Hans lost Koch after Warsaw, but now he is back. Hans paid for that with his life. What could be more important to our cause than to find Koch and stop the underground movement within Belgium and France? The partisans in both countries have plagued our military movements for months, and now I might be able to destroy them for good. I know what Koch looks like, but he does not know of me. I only need a few months to locate and end Koch's network. Please help me, Dr. Schneider. I need to convince Hauptmann Froer that my work is for the good of our entire cause."

"I will relay your concerns, and we shall see if we can convince him of your continued desire to help the Reich."

***

It was late in the evening when Froer arrived at Dr. Schneider's. The three immediately went into the same sitting room Marie and Dr. Schneider had used the prior day. Froer began, "Marie, I was saddened by Dr. Schneider's communication. Hans was a good friend to both of us, and his death is a great loss to our cause."

"Yes, that is why I need to return to Brugge. I must find those responsible. . ." Marie began to say but was interrupted by Froer.

"I share your malignity for these partisans and Koch in particular. If I send you back, I must be certain that there is a greater outcome than a young girl's singular revenge."

"Hauptmann, this is not about one woman's revenge," Marie said while staring straight into Froer's darkened eyes. Marie drummed up all of her courage and continued. "Just last June you were able to capture Jean Moulin in Caluire and severely hinder the Resistance movement in France. Hans and I had information regarding Koch's involvement with Moulin, also information regarding Moulin's replacement. I need to return to Brugge, retrieve the information and follow those leads. I have seen Koch. I know him, and I am the best you have at gathering information on the new heads of the Resistance." Marie hoped Froer did not ask further questions regarding the information, for most of it was a lie.

"I will allow you to return but only for a short time. By the end of the year, you will be departing this region for another assignment. I cannot go into details now, but you can be assured it is of the greatest importance to the Führer."

"Thank you, Hauptmann Froer. I will complete this assignment and be ready when the Führer needs me."

Froer rose from his chair, as did Dr. Schneider and Marie. Turning to Dr. Schneider, Froer said, "Doctor, it is late, but I have some friends here in Brussels that I am meeting. They will give me lodging this evening, and I will return to Berlin in the morning. Then to Marie, Froer said, "Marie, return quickly to Brugge and find Koch. End his involvement and get me names of those taking Moulin's place in the Resistance." Froer picked up his hat, moved to the front door and was gone.

"Well, Fräulein Monin, it looks like you are returning to Brugge. You need some sleep. I will make train arrangements for you," Dr. Schneider said.

"Thank you Doctor, I will be ready early." Marie turned and retired to her room, alone with only thoughts of revenge.

CHAPTER EIGHTEEN

The time passed quickly for Paul and John. Days were spent making the roof repairs and replacing and painting the wood siding. Evenings were something special. Ruth's mouth ran nonstop, and Paul loved it. It was as though Ruth had waited her entire life to tell family secrets to a stranger. Photos of family members accompanied most of Ruth's stories. Between photos Paul tried to catch a glimpse of Coffey's reaction to the stories only to see Coffey shaking is head and smirking.

The morning of their departure, Paul walked along the side of the house, his duffle bag in hand. Ruth was sitting in the old rocker on the front porch. "Good morning, Mrs. Coffey."

Ruth said nothing in return, her face frozen in terror. Paul slowed and said, "Are you okay, Mrs. Coffey?"

Still no reply, but Ruth slowly lowered her head, looking down to the right of the rocker. Paul looked in the direction of Ruth's stare and saw a copperhead snake lying just to the right and behind the rocker. "Don't move, ma'am."

Paul moved slowly around the porch to the steps, coming up behind the snake and making enough noise to draw the snake's attention. The snake responded, moving from beside the rocker toward the porch entrance. Paul continued to move carefully, making certain that the snake focused its attention on him and not Mrs. Coffey. As the snake slithered away from the rocker, Paul moved back off the first porch step. As he moved off the step, he caught sight of a spade leaning against the porch rail. Holding the duffel bag in his right hand, Paul took the spade in his left.

The snake had moved far enough from Mrs. Coffey that she was out of danger; Paul was still in the snake's path, although it seemed to him that the snake was attempting to leave and not attack. Suddenly, sounds of footsteps striking the wood entry floor were heard just inside the screen door. The foot sounds coupled with Paul's presence forced the snake to move into a coil position with its mouth opened wide and making a terrible hissing noise. Paul screamed, "John, stop!"

Paul knew he had to act quickly. He pushed the duffle forward, prompting the snake to strike at the bag. The strike hit the top of the bag, just missing Paul's hand. Paul swung the spade, pushing the snake back down to the porch. Immediately, Paul dropped his bag onto the snake's head and stabbed down with the spade, cutting into the snake's body. Paul continued to thrust the spade until the body was severed into three pieces.

John opened the screen door. "Paul!"

Paul said, "I'm fine. Go check your mother."

John moved around Paul and the snake. "Mom, are you all right?"

Ruth rose from the chair. "I'm fine now, but if Paul had not walked by when he did. . .well, I don't know."

Paul walked over to Mrs. Coffey, and she put her arms around his neck. "Thank you, son. You saved an old woman's life."

Paul said nothing as he returned the hug.

***

The three were standing on the porch as Jack's car turned up the dirt road to the house. John said, "Jack looks like he is in a hurry. I best get my things."

Paul let go of Mrs. Coffey and grabbed the spade. "I should probably get rid of this guy as well."

"Hurry up there, boys. I got me a date for this evening, and I don't like to keep my sweetie waiting," Jack said as he jumped out of the car and popped the trunk open.

John yelled out the screen door, "Be right there, Jack."

Jack hustled up to the porch and saw Paul throwing pieces of the copperhead over the porch railing. "Had a visitor this morning, it seems."

Ruth appeared, wiping tears with her apron. "That we did. Paul saved me from it."

Paul said, "It wasn't that much."

"It was to me!"

John walked back through the screen door. "Momma, are you going to be okay?"

Still crying, Ruth said, "I will, but what about you? I know I can't stop you. Lord knows I tried that before. You take care of yourself, and you watch out for this fine fella as well," Ruth said as she took hold of Paul's arm. Ruth gave John a big squeeze and kiss. She then turned and hugged Paul whispering, "Thank you, son, for all you've done for an old lady. Your momma raised you well and should be proud. You take care of my little boy and make sure you write to your family."

Paul hugged Ruth back, "Yes Ma'am, John will be just fine. I'll make certain he sends you a letter weekly, and when this war is over we'll both be back to finish up the repairs. That's a promise."

"I'll hold you to it."

Jack hollered again, "Let's go, boys. The meter's ticking!"

CHAPTER NINETEEN

Sales were average for the day. Most of the customers were local housewives shopping for bread. Sebastian and another cook worked the ovens in the back while Marie worked the front counter. She enjoyed the socializing with customers, and each day she seemed to feel more accepted as one of the locals. However, as friendly as the citizens of Lille were, they could not match the warmth of Germans. Marie felt Germans were open and honest, loving to sit and pass the time with each other. She could remember the days in the park, watching her father talk to so many people. Some would even come over to her and offer to push her on the swing for short periods. But she found the French guarded, as though they had a huge secret to hide. Maybe, she thought, this was why it was so easy to carry out her assignment in France.

After two months of work at Sebastian's bakery, Marie knew the routine–not the cover routine of selling pastries to these lonely and weary housewives, women struggling to look after a family torn apart by the war–Marie knew the routine used by Sebastian to pass information along to the French Resistance. The head of the Resistance, Charles de Gaulle, was from Lille, and the movement was strong in the area. Although de Gaulle had fled France three years prior, he still commanded the Resistance movement from England. Jean Moulin, the resident leader, had been captured in June of 1943. Marie now had information that one of three men had taken over as the resident leader.

Once a week Sebastian baked extra bread. The drivers, Peter and Harold, would stop by, pick up the bread and deliver it to three churches in Lille. The bread was to help feed some of the orphaned children or families that were destitute. Marie learned Sebastian placed strategic information into the loaves before delivery. He then somehow tagged the bread; when delivered, the information was extricated and sent to De Gaulle or other partisans.

This evening Peter and Harold did not show up, and Marie could tell Sebastian was agitated. As the time to close came near, Sebastian finally said, "Marie, I am not sure what happened to Peter and Harold today. We may have to deliver these boxes to each parish. Would you mind working a bit extra this evening?"

"Not at all," answered Marie, while she continued to wipe down the counters. "Do you think they are all right?"

"Oh, I'm sure they probably just had some car trouble and no way of getting a message to me. I will check in with them later this evening. You finish with the cleanup here, and I'll load the truck with the boxes of bread."

"Fine, Sebastian. I will be done in just a few minutes. I will lock up and meet you out back."

Marie locked the back door and jumped up into the truck's cab, immediately smelling a pleasant aroma inside. Marie realized Sebastian had just put on some cologne, and the smell was inviting. She slid over on the seat, just close enough so her dress would brush up against Sebastian's hand as he used the gearshift. "Where are we off to first?" she asked excitedly.

"We will start with St. Michel, then circle back to Sacre Ceur over on Rue Nationale and finish up with the largest delivery to Notre Dame de la Treille. The boxes are marked for each church and they will be expecting us. We deliver the boxes to the Monsignor's residence, and then they ready the bread for distribution to needy parishioners."

Marie smiled saying, "You are very kind, Sebastian."

"It's nothing really. I can afford it and, who knows, maybe it will buy me some extra points later if I need them."

The pastor was waiting at St. Michel. Marie and Sebastian unloaded three boxes. As they were readying to leave, they heard from the doorway, "God bless you, my children."

The second stop was the Sacre Ceur. There were three more boxes to unload, and they had to be carried around to the far side of the church. Sebastian told Marie to take the smaller box. He would take one of the larger boxes and come back in a moment for the second box. Marie cocked her head to the side, gave Sebastian a disgruntled stare, but grabbed the smaller box anyway.

Back in the truck, Marie immediately said, "Did you think because I'm a female that I couldn't handle the larger boxes?"

"Of course not, it's just. . ."

Marie cut Sebastian off. "It's just what? Are you going to try and tell me you didn't want me to hurt myself? I'll have you know I can perform any work that a man does, probably better."

"Okay, okay! There are six boxes for the next stop at Notre Dame. Each box is to be taken across the yard and up two flights of stairs. Let's see if you can back up all this jabbering."

Marie's competitive hormones were flowing like a rushing stream, melting after a heavy snow season. "Not only can I match you, mister, but why not wager a bet on who can get their three boxes delivered and be back to the truck sitting here first. Maybe say, loser buys dinner?"

Sebastian smiled warmly and placed his hand on Marie's leg. "Okay, but please don't ruffle your dress or muss your hair. Remember, women are to admired by the beholding eye."

Marie removed Sebastian's hand from her leg and ended the conversation abruptly with, "How soon do we get there?"

Ten minutes later, Sebastian pulled the truck up along Rue Basse, just beside Notre Dame de la Treille. As they arrived at the back of the truck, Sebastian pointed toward the large building across the courtyard. "We cross around the large fountain, enter the double doors at the top of the stairs and place the boxes just inside the second room to the right. Any questions, madam, before the starter fires his gun?"

"Only one. Do I get to choose where you take me for dinner?" As soon as she completed the statement, Marie reached in and grabbed two boxes. She pulled the boxes tight to her stomach and started to move quickly across the yard. Sebastian stood for a moment just watching Marie. He admired her competitive determination, but more than that he admired the outline of her athletic body. Watching her long legs striding forward and the dress pulling tighter across her backside was stimulating. As Marie began to ascend the stairs, Sebastian thought to himself, *I had better get moving.*

They passed on the stairs. Sebastian was going up while Marie, having already delivered two boxes, was heading down. Quickly he moved into the room, dropped off his boxes and started back down the stairs. He saw Marie was back at the truck, gathering her last box. Sebastian only touched three steps on the way down and swiftly raced across the courtyard. He grabbed his last box from the truck and turned to see Marie trip on the bottom stair. Her box fell forward onto the next step, and she looked back over her shoulder. Sebastian couldn't help but wonder if she was tired or if she was playing a game with him, waiting for him to catch up. Whatever the reason, Sebastian was not going to be beaten by a girl. He managed to get to the bottom of the stairs just as Marie went inside. Sebastian caught the stairs two at a time and was now only a few meters behind Marie. He was gaining on her and she knew it, but it was going to be close. She was a few meters from the fountain as Sebastian flew off the last step. As he sprinted toward her, Sebastian realized if he ran through the fountain instead of going around, he would be able to pass her. Sebastian leaped the short fountain wall and started through. Marie turned back just in time to see Sebastian catch his foot on something underwater and sprawl forward into the muddy water and algae. Sebastian quickly looked up and saw Marie standing at the truck laughing. He slowly lowered his head, slapped at the water, and proceeded to raise himself and walk toward the truck.

"I didn't realize it was also a swimming race," Marie said as Sebastian looked for a blanket to dry himself off.

"No smart remarks! Let's just say the best *man* won today. Before I have the pleasure of buying you dinner, would you mind if I stop by my flat to clean up? It's only a couple blocks over."

"Not at all." Sincerely, Marie added, "I hope this will not ruin our friendship or end my employment. Are you hurt?"

"Only my pride and no, this helps your chances for advancement." Laughing, Sebastian continued, "I am going to place you in charge of store security. You get to chase anyone suspected of stealing pastries from the table trays."

"Thanks, will the promotion get me a pay raise as well?"

"We can talk about that over dinner. Here we are."

Sebastian opened the door to his flat. As they entered, each was struck by the stale air and heat. "It was cooler at the bakery today working the ovens don't you think?" Marie started.

"I think you're right. I am sorry, but I must leave all of the windows closed; too many young thieves in the neighborhood. I also forgot to turn the heater down when I left this morning." Marie smiled and nodded her forgiveness. Sebastian walked over to the balcony, swung open both doors and then crossed the room to open a window. "This might help to get some fresh air to move through. Let me pour both of us a glass of wine. You can sit near the balcony and catch maybe a wisp of air. I need to wash this mud and dirt off before we go to supper. I will not be long."

"Oh, don't worry about me. Take as much time as you need. I will just sit here and think about everything I want to devour later this evening." As Marie was finishing, she rested back on the sofa and lifted her legs onto the coffee table. Her dress fell back just enough for Sebastian to see her legs from the knees down. The sight of her muscular calves and her painted toenails sent a sparkle from his eyes and created a spark further down through his body. Marie smiled, raised her glass, and said, "If you just stand there and stare, we will never get to the eating." Eating was the last thing Sebastian had on his mind right now.

During these months of working together, she had teased Sebastian constantly. In such a small working kitchen, Marie continuously brushed up against him as she passed by. He knew there was enough room to pass, but she enjoyed the physical contact as much as he did. She would send out small hints that maybe there could be more than a working relationship, but each time the message would end abruptly. Just last week, Marie naively asked Sebastian if he ever thought what it would be like to make love after rolling in the flour bin. After her question, Sebastian walked up to her and touched her waist. Marie laughed and reached up brushing some flour off his cheek and said, "Silly Sebastian, we have work to do feeding the starving people of France."

Sebastian, the gentleman, smiled kissed her forehead, "When this war is over, we will make more than pastries together." His thoughts were constantly of Marie. *If this war were not so crazy maybe there could be more between us.* Over the past few days, Sebastian had thought of telling Marie about his other work, about what was really in some of the bread delivered to the churches. He wanted her to know, but he didn't dare risk her involvement and possibly her life. She was too young and optimistic to be dragged into this ugly aspect of his life. Maybe after France was free, he would act on his impulses.

Sebastian raised his glass to Marie and said, "I will be a good boy now and take my leave to freshen up. Please, continue to relax and make yourself at ease. There is more wine on the table, and I will lay out some grapes and fresh oranges. Here, let me also turn on some music for you."

Marie could hear the bath running. When the water stopped, Marie walked over to the door and said, "Sebastian, I am going to turn up the radio so you too can listen while you bathe. Marie walked back over to the radio and turned up the music. She recognized that it was Bach but a very poor arrangement and delivery. Marie began to carefully walk around the kitchen and living room. Like a cat, her eyes darted from object to object. Where would Sebastian hide the maps, papers and names of those he considered leaders? Time was running out. Froer needed to know what information she had, and soon.

Like the cat she always had been called, Marie sprang quietly from place to place. She lifted chairs, opened drawers, looked under the sofa and tables, and even climbed a chair to look up in the ceiling fan. Nothing looked as though it might hold information on the Resistance movement or transmittal devices used to send and receive information from the Allies.

Maybe in the icebox she thought. Opening the door, the cold air felt perfect. She didn't have time, however, to enjoy the moment. Quickly, Marie looked in the canisters, down in the bottom of the fruit bowls and in between some wrapped cuts of meat. As she was beginning to close the door, she heard Sebastian behind her say, "Can I help you find something?" He was standing in the kitchen doorway, wrapped only in a towel.

Out of Sebastian's sight, Marie reached in the icebox and picked up an apple. Taking a bite as she turned, Marie smiled and said, "I hope you don't mind, but after the grapes and the oranges I was still hungry." After taking a bite, she raised the apple saying, "A bit of the poison fruit."

The sun was setting, but there was still light coming in from the balcony. The light struck Marie much like a spotlight strikes the star on a theatre stage. Sebastian froze as he stared at Marie's dress. It was not the one she wore earlier in the day, and Sebastian guessed Marie had this one folded in her bag. Marie was now wearing a thin dress, with buttons that went from top to bottom. The buttons, however, were undone and Marie had taken off her undergarments. She stood in front of Sebastian as his eyes worked their way up her body. He could just see the top of her pubic hair, then her belly button, her flat, muscular stomach, and finally her small round breasts. Marie took another bite of apple and looked over to the sofa and the bra and panties saying, "I thought with less on I could take more advantage of the cool breeze. Please don't get the wrong idea."

There was only one idea on his mind now. He continued to stare at her breasts as they rose and fell with each breath. Marie's nipples were overly large for such small breasts, and each nipple was hard and erect. Between her breasts he could also see small drops of perspiration beginning to move down toward her stomach. She looked down; with her index finger, she wiped the sweat and then slowly sucked on her finger. She moved her finger in and out over her luscious red lips. Marie whispered, "My father said the same genes that made me athletic also made me sweat more than other girls. I hope you don't mind? I mean that I am athletic and competitive. Some men don't like women to be too masculine. It frightens them, I guess. I have found that men always like to be in control." Marie reached back down, cupped her left breast and continued, "Sometimes strong, controlling women can actually be quite relaxing for men."

Sebastian tried to respond; however, standing there with just the towel wrapped around himself, all he could do was smile and stare. Marie knew she was in control of the situation and said to Sebastian, "You look so excited and tense. Come over here and sit in this chair. Let me massage your neck and shoulders. I might be able to relieve some of that tension."

Sebastian walked over and sat while Marie moved forward. She straddled his legs and began massaging his shoulders. As she did, Sebastian raised his hands and placed them inside the open dress. Marie didn't acknowledge his movement. She just continued massaging the muscles along his shoulders and neck. Sebastian reached higher and with his right hand he slowly cupped her breast. Her nipple was rock hard. Sebastian pulled her closer and stretched his tongue to lick the end of the nipple. He could taste the sweat, but he also could taste the wine. She had planned this seduction he thought, but he was intoxicated with her passion and he didn't care anymore about his work, the war, or the silly idea of who was in control. He only knew he wanted her.

Marie moved her hands up his neck and began to slowly move her fingers over his spine. As she palpated the landmarks of the cervical vertebrae, she felt for the intervertebral disc space between each disc until her left hand stopped between C2 and C3. Sebastian was still slowly guiding her breast into his mouth. He gently moved his other hand down over her stomach and between her legs. She was warm and responsive. Marie never took her left hand off Sebastian's neck, but as she moved in closer she whispered, "Good thing I ate the fruit because I don't think we will be having dinner." Sebastian smiled because he was thinking the same thing.

Marie reached up to the long, red hairpin that still held the auburn bun behind her head. When the stiletto came out, her hair fell down to just past her shoulders. Sebastian's mouth released her nipple and he tried to look up. She kept his head between her breasts and plunged the stiletto into the space below C2. Immediately, blood and spinal fluid began to seep from the wound and run down the back of Sebastian's neck. Paralysis was instant. He convulsed some, but otherwise could not move. Death would be enveloping him soon. The last words Sebastian heard were Marie's, "There are more than thieves to worry about during time of war my dear, Richard Koch." Marie held him close to her for just a few more minutes and then let Koch sink to the floor.

CHAPTER TWENTY

General Morgan's staff assembled early and walked together down King Charles Street toward the War Room bunkers. The underground rooms were in the Whitehall area and were the center of military planning. The significance of today's meeting was not lost on anyone. Prime Minister Churchill had summoned Morgan and his staff to the meeting and called it the highest priority. Once inside, each man made his way along the tight corridors to the cabinet room.

The room felt small, with low steel beam supports crossing overhead. Wall fans circulated the stale air, piped in from vents at street level. On the wall was a large map showing Great Britain and the European continent. Pins placed on the map outlined Allied advances up the Italian coast.

Operation Husky, the Allied invasion into Sicily, began in July. By September, Operation Avalanche saw Allied forces land on the Italian shoreline. Both operations were considered a success, but there was no denying the statistics of heavy casualties on all sides. Churchill summoned Morgan and his staff today to discuss plans for a new and even larger invasion of the continent, which would take place in the coming year. Lieutenant General Frederick E. Morgan was a WWI veteran and a British career soldier. He had recently been appointed as Chief of Staff to the Supreme Allied Commander. In a memo, Churchill informed Morgan that it would be his job to begin making preparations for Operation Overlord, the next invasion of Europe.

Morgan and his staff took their seats at the table. The black leather seats, small and hard, were not made for comfort. No one wanted to be sitting long. As each man sat, he withdrew a cigarette from his pack or pulled out a pipe and tobacco bag. Grey smoke filtered up, filling the room. After a ten-minute wait, Prime Minister Churchill entered, adding to the smoke by taking three large puffs of his usual cigar. Behind Churchill, Home Secretary Herbert Morrison entered, taking a seat to Churchill's left.

Secretary Morrison was a member of the Labour Party, part of the coalition government formed by Churchill in 1940. Morrison's office oversaw issues originating within Great Britain. Watching the two men was like watching a Laurel and Hardy movie, without the antics. Churchill's rotund body and ill-fitting jacket played against Morrison's tall, lean, well-groomed figure. Morrison's round spectacles and quiet demeanor also gave him the appearance of an academic rather than a politician.

The men at the table stood and waited for the Prime Minister to take his seat at the head of the table. General Morgan sat to Churchill's right. "General Morgan," Churchill began, "sorry to keep you waiting."

"Not a problem, sir. We only arrived a short time ago and used the time to review our advances up the Italian coast."

All the men turned to look, once again, at the European map. "Yes, General. We have only been there a month and already have found success in splitting the German and Italian lines of defense." Churchill continued. "Hope now centers on Germany bringing additional troops to Italy and transferring divisions out of France and Belgium."

General Morgan said, "That would be a significant advantage for us, but our intelligence continues to report heavy panzer movement within France."

"I am afraid that is true at this time. An invasion from the west is still a ways off. Maybe at a later date a few panzer divisions will be gone." Churchill took a long drag on his cigar. "But we are here this morning to indeed look at a western invasion, the largest and most important invasion of the war."

Each man raised his pen, ready, if needed, to take copious notes on the plan at hand. Churchill began, "In three weeks time, the British government and the War Department will be sending notice to the Devon County Council, informing the council of a pending removal of citizens living within some thirty thousand acres. The beaches of Lyme Bay will become the center for Allied maneuvers." As Churchill spoke, a soldier placed a new map on the wall, showing an enlargement of Devon County. A triangle outline showed Torcross and Blackpool Sands along the bay moving uphill to Blackawton. Within the triangle could be seen dots representing seven other villages as well.

General Morgan asked, "Just how many citizens will be leaving?"

Churchill responded, "Our estimates are nearly three thousand people. Each will need to be assisted in relocating."

Some staff began to shift in their chairs, tension visible on their faces. Recognizing their posture, Churchill addressed the staff. "I know some of you may have difficulty accepting the removal of British citizens from their homes. But these are extreme times, and they call for utmost sacrifice from all of us."

One soldier at the end of the table, Colonel Allison, said, "Mr. Prime Minister, if I may speak, sir."

Churchill stared, biting down hard on the end of his cigar. "Certainly, Colonel. Say what you will."

"I myself live within this area, just outside of Strete. Due to my position, my wife and family will easily be able to move from the area to London."

"Good. See it is not that difficult."

"Mr. Prime Minister, if I may continue. There are many around us that are not in a position to move easily. Some are quite old and movement will be almost impossible. Some have little in the way of finances to make a move. Others are young wives and mothers, alone while their husbands are serving our country."

"I understand this will be difficult, Colonel. That is why Mr. Morrison and all of you are here. You will need to begin the logistical plans for relocating and compensating these families. The British government will do as much as possible to assist families in relocating or with finances to ease their burdens."

General Morgan spoke up. "Mr. Prime Minister, how long will these families be away from their homes?"

"General, we don't have an answer for that as yet. Six months would be a minimum, but it is reasonable to consider a time greater than a year."

"When with the removal begin, sir?"

Churchill turned to Secretary Morrison. "Why don't you address that, Mr. Morrison?"

Herbert Morrison removed his pipe, placing it on the table. "Yes, Mr. Prime Minister, I would be most happy to respond. Our office, in conjunction with the War Department, will be sending notice by the first week in November. Meetings will then be set up within each village."

Once again, Colonel Allison broke in. "How will people be notified? How will some of the more elderly. . ."

Churchill interrupted. "Colonel Allison, please remain silent! Your questions will be addressed, and if not, you may send a communiqué up the chain of command."

Rebuffed, Colonel Allison said, "My apologies, Mr. Prime Minister."

Churchill finished by saying, "Removal was not an easy decision to make, but one that must be made in order to successfully accomplish our goals and to end this war sooner rather than later." Turning back to Morrison, "Please continue, Mr. Secretary."

"The meetings will be held with the support of each village council and pastors of local churches. Questions from locals will be addressed, and the timeline of removal will be discussed."

General Morgan asked, "Mr. Secretary, how long do you expect the removal to take?"

"Everyone needs to be removed by the 20th of December, so six weeks. U. S. and British engineers along with building crews will be there on the 20th to begin the process of erecting new barracks. Training troops start to arrive just after the new year."

Prime Minister Churchill concluded the meeting, "General Morgan, your staff, working with the Home Secretary, has three weeks to get whatever you decide is needed to assist the citizens of Devon in moving their belongings out of the training area. Good luck, General."

Each man stood as Prime Minister Churchill and Secretary Morrison rose to leave the room. Now the only sound was a humming of the fans as they worked to circulate the stale, smoky air. Staff members placed their pens, notebooks, and unused smoking materials into satchels, pushed in their chairs and headed back out to King Charles Street.

CHAPTER TWENTY-ONE

With his dizziness and dry heaves back again, Paul had been sitting up on deck for most of the past two days. They were just days out of England. His transport ship, the *S.S. George Washington Carver,* was running a zigzag pattern. It was not helping Paul feel any better. The pattern was mandated by the navy to lessen the chance of German U-boat attack. Everything about life below deck made Paul sick, from the stench of body odor and urine to the cigarette smoke that lingered in the air like hazy fog. Fortunately for Paul, being a lieutenant had its privileges, one of which was the ability to sleep up on deck. While Paul was on deck, Sarge took care of watching the company down in the ship's lower levels and came up daily to brief Paul on the company's activities.

Today, Sarge found Paul leaning against a pile of rolled fire hose and said, "Lieutenant, how's it going this wonderful afternoon? Keeping some food and water down, are ya?"

Paul looked up, with a face that reminded Sarge of an old hound dog, and just nodded. As he looked at Sarge, however, Paul sensed there was something else. "Honestly, Sarge, how are the men holding up?"

Sarge replied, "They look a whole lot better than you that's for sure. But I'm afraid if we don't get to shore soon, we might just have ourselves a little war down below. Those New York wops are giving some of my Southern boys a bit of a time of it. A Southern gentleman can only be gentle for so long, if you know what I mean." Paul certainly knew what Sarge meant as he had witnessed Coffey taking apart a guy in a pool hall a couple of days before they shipped out. The local, twice the size of Coffey, disliked being hustled in a game of pool by a soldier, and he was going to give Coffey an education. Unfortunately, the local was on the receiving end of an education in size and strength versus cunning power and determination. The fight ended only after Paul and a couple others from their company pulled Coffey off the big man and hurried him back to the base. The local sheriff came to the base and met with Major Poder. After the meeting, Major Poder called Paul into his office.

Paul knocked and opened the door. "You wanted to see me, Major?" asked Paul.

"Come in, Lieutenant, and have a seat," Major Poder said from behind an old oak desk, cluttered with papers. I just came from a meeting with the town sheriff regarding Sergeant Coffey's activities from last night. That fellow at the pool hall is going to make it, but the sheriff said he'd be in the hospital for a time. The only reason the sheriff is not arresting Sergeant Coffey is because enough witnesses came forward to say Coffey was only defending himself when the fight started."

"Yes sir, that's true. Coffey attempted to stay clear of the guy, but he wouldn't let up," Paul said.

"Lieutenant, there's a point at which defending yourself goes beyond acceptability and moves over to that darker side of being the aggressor. I know you've just recently been assigned here, but this is not the first confrontation that led to hospitalization for one of Coffey's victims. Coffey would most likely be a lieutenant by now and leading a company, if not for his violent side." Major Poder stood and said, "Lieutenant, Sergeant Coffey is just what this army needs right now. He is a damn good soldier and probably going to kill a bunch of Nazis before this thing is over, but you need to keep him under control. Coffey stays on the base until you ship out day after tomorrow. When you get to England, Lieutenant, keep Coffey close by. We don't need to make enemies of the English. Any more trouble out of Coffey and I'll court marshal you both. Am I clear?

Paul stood and saluted saying, "Yes, sir. I understand and thank you, sir."

Major Poder half-heartedly returned the salute and said, "That is all, Lieutenant. You are dismissed."

Paul got up from his makeshift quarters, vividly recalling Major Poder's words. He said, "Jesus Christ! The Major's already warned me about your behavior—and now they start up. Christ, I'm going to be court-martialed before I even get to Europe! Lead the way, Sergeant. I am responsible for you and these men, and I will not tolerate any fighting between them. We are going to save that hostility for the Germans. You understand me, Sergeant?"

Sergeant Coffey turned toward the ship's hatch, "Yes, sir." Coffey then added, "Sir, may I say you're looking mighty fine and fit today. I'm sure these boys will get over their sectional squabbles once we're facing the enemy." As they headed down below, Coffey leaned in closer to Paul and said, "Lieutenant, you might want to change that shirt and splash a little water on yourself before you meet with the men." Paul looked down to see the dried vomit on the front of his shirt and nodded.

***

Sergeant Coffey assembled the men together, and they were standing at attention when Lieutenant Schaefer walked in. "At ease, men. Sergeant Coffey informs me that some of you have been discussing family lineage and American history."

Some of the men began to nervously shuffle and whisper. Finally, Corporal Johnson from Georgia who was standing just in front of Paul said, "Lieutenant, how do we know that once we get into a fight that these wops won't turn on us and fight with the Italians or even the Germans?"

Paul's hand moved like a striking rattler and grasped hold of the corporal's shirt. Stunned, Corporal Johnson tried to move back, but Paul moved in even closer. Only inches separated their faces. No one in the room moved or made a sound. To the members of the company, Lieutenant Schaefer had always been a hard worker, but quiet and reserved. Some of the men even questioned whether the Lieutenant could lead them in a fight. Tightening his grip on the shirt, Paul forcefully said, "*Sprechen Sie Deutsch, korporal? Ich bin Deutscher. Wollen Sie mich toten?*" Letting go of the corporal's shirt, and not waiting for a reply from his shaken corporal, Paul looked at everyone and said, "All of you listen to me. We land tomorrow in Bristol and will be training for something big. We're going to be very close to each other for a long time. We're going to need to depend on each other and to trust each other. We aren't Germans, Italians, Irish, Swedes, or English. We are Americans, and you damn well better understand this! Paul then turned to Coffey and said, "Sergeant, I will hear no more about these problems. You have my permission to take whatever steps deemed necessary to keep these men in line. Are we clear, Sergeant?"

Sergeant Coffey crisply stood to attention, as did the entire company, and saluted, "Yes, sir! There will be no further problems, sir! You have my word on that, sir!"

Lieutenant Schaefer returned the salute and said, "Sergeant, come with me. I would like to speak with you further."

As soon as Paul and Coffey were beyond the door, Paul said, "I think I'm going to be sick again. There's no air down here. I need to get back up on top deck."

"You bet, Lieutenant. Let me help," Coffey said as he placed his arm around Paul's back. "Lieutenant, you were good in there. A nice German language lesson for everyone, yes indeed, sir. Oh, and don't you worry about us, Lieutenant," Coffey said, now back in his down-home Southern drawl, "by the time we pull into Bristol, I'll have those Southern boys singing Dixie in Italian." The two men laughed and walked in silence up to Lieutenant Schaefer's top deck penthouse.

***

Paul pulled the jacket up around his neck as the *George Washington Carver* tied itself to Avonmouth Dock on the Bristol Channel. As his transport was entering the harbor, Paul could make out at least six other U.S. transports already tied up or anchored just inside the harbor entrance. Numerous other cargo ships were in the process of unloading containers, tanks and other military equipment. There were men and equipment assembled on the docks as well, and Paul saw a mix of American and British soldiers scurrying about. Since entering the Bristol Channel, small-armed patrol boats continuously were cutting paths across the line of Paul's transport. Large gun casements were also visible on the surrounding hills.

Winter had uncomfortably engulfed England with a frigid, damp drizzle that cut to the bone. Paul thought Gettysburg was cold; this was biting cold! He wondered how his men would adapt to English weather, especially those from the warmer areas of the deep South and Southwest.

Officers were briefed the night before about disembarkation procedures, and Paul waited for Coffey to assemble the platoon at the starboard end of the ship. As the men began to appear, Paul observed their body language. Some men began to shake uncontrollably as they exited from the doorway, while others set down their duffle bags and pulled their jackets up tighter around their necks. Paul had snugged his jacket up just minutes earlier. He also could hear grumblings but could not make out exactly what was being said, although he knew it probably was not positive.

Paul joined the assembly. The men stopped, dropped their bags and stood at attention. "At ease, gentlemen. Welcome to England." The drizzle was turning to rain, and the men lowered their heads in the hopes of letting the rain run off their helmets and away from their faces. Paul continued, "We will get you out of this rain as soon as possible."

Then Paul addressed Coffey, "Sergeant, we are to assemble at station 121. It should be down at the west end of the dock. From there, we will be boarding a truck that will take us to temporary barracks at Taunton, a town just south of here. We will set up there, awaiting further orders to move to our permanent quarters in what the English refer to as the South Hams.

CHAPTER TWENTY-TWO

Focused on finding information that might tie Koch to de Gaulle's Resistance movement in the region, Marie stepped over the recently departed Sebastian, AKA Richard Koch. She knew she had time to search, as no one was expecting Koch this evening. He had made it clear only minutes before that he was interested in spending the evening with Marie–alone. It would be dark soon, and Marie weighed the issue of lights. The lights would not attract suspicion; however, they just might attract company. Deciding she did not need any further disturbances, the lights remained off.

Koch's bedroom was small, with only a bed, nightstand and armoire. There were no pictures on the wall, but there was a photo on the nightstand. Marie lifted the picture and looked at a slightly younger Koch, smiling at the camera. There was also a woman in the picture, holding Koch's head and kissing his cheek. A quick flash of Hans registered in her mind, and she thought, "*It looks as though we both lost someone we loved.*" She set the picture down and began rummaging through the room. Finding nothing, Marie moved to Koch's bathroom.

The bathroom was spartan. Quickly Marie realized little could be hidden in there. She believed Koch would have kept important material nearby; therefore, a new search of the bedroom was required. Marie dismantled as much of the bed and nightstand as she could, finding nothing. She returned to the picture and tore the backing and picture out of the frame. Nothing was hidden behind the picture. As she went to place the frame back on the table, she knocked the picture to the floor and it slipped under the armoire. Marie knelt down to retrieve the picture. As she did, she noticed the picture had snagged in a crack in the floor. She examined the crack for a time. It was not jagged, as might be expected with normal expansion and contraction of a wood floor. The line was straight and felt as though it may have been cut into the wood.

The armoire was heavy, but Marie was able to slide it far enough down the wall to expose the floor beneath. Back down on her knees, Marie felt for the cuts made in the floor, but she was unable to find a way to lift the boards. She rose and went into the kitchen, where she found a large broad knife. Returning to the bedroom floor, Marie used the knife to pry up the wood. Excited, Marie felt her heart beating within her chest. She reached into the chamber and found a leather satchel.

Marie extricated a number of papers from the satchel. By now, it was too dark to read the material. Realizing the importance of her discovery, Marie decided to take the risk of turning on the bedroom light. With the light on, Marie sat back on the bed and looked through the material. There were names and dates, most of which made little sense to her, but there was a reference to Brugge and another to Jean Moulin.

On another sheet, Marie found three other names: Emile Bollaert, Pierre Brossolette, and Claude Bouchinet Serreulles. These names meant nothing to her, but if they were tied to Moulin and Koch, she knew they would be helpful to Hauptman Froer. These men might be taking over the movement for Moulin. Marie turned the light off, replaced the floorboard and returned the armoire to its proper place. She decided to get this information to Froer and let him decide the next best move. By tomorrow evening, Koch–or Sebastian–would be missed, and someone would come looking. Froer needed to have the Gestapo watch the apartment and be ready to move in.

Marie returned to the outer room and gathered her undergarments from the chair. Fully dressed now, with satchel in hand, Marie made her way out and back to her apartment.

***

Inside the apartment, Marie retrieved her transmitter and made contact with Froer's office. She informed Hauptmann Froer that she had terminated Koch and retrieved information on the Resistance movement. She was told by Froer to go immediately to Gestapo headquarters and find Hauptmann von Hagel. He would review the information and send SS men to watch the apartment. He then told Marie to make arrangements for a train to Berlin. He wanted a meeting with her there. When Marie inquired as to the purpose of the meeting, Froer told her it was of the utmost importance and to be in Berlin by the end of the week. He stated her work in France was finished and that she would not be returning. Her new assignment would take her to another country. When Marie began to ask questions, Froer said, "It will all wait until I see you."

Upon returning from her meeting with von Hagel, Marie began the process of packing. She still had a number of items that belonged to Hans: pictures, a revolver, and personal letters. She thought for a moment, *"You told me we needed to have a will to live, but without you it is difficult."* As tears dropped from her cheeks, Marie threw the pictures and letters into the stove's fire. She wrapped the revolver in cloth and placed it in her suitcase along with her possessions. Marie finished packing her things and made arrangements for her trip back to Berlin.

***

Berlin was cold, even for December. Tiergarten Park was frozen, with snow still covering the ground and the barren trees giving it a desolate, haunting look. Marie crossed the park and walked on toward the Sicherheitsdienst headquarters. Since the assassination of Obergruppenführer Heydrich the prior year, the Sichercheitsdienst was briefly under the direct control of Himmler; now Ernst Kaltenbrunner was director. Marie still reported to Hauptmann Froer, however. Froer was expecting Marie this morning, and she was anxious to find out what Froer's plans were for her.

Marie walked in and showed the soldier at the door her papers signed by Froer. The soldier led Marie to an office, which resembled Froer's office in the old Sichercheitsdienst building near Alexanderplatz. The walls were covered with pictures taken by Leni Riefenstahl of the 1936 Nuremberg Rally and the Berlin Olympics. Behind the large oak desk, a large photo of Froer with the Führer hung next to a German flag—the flag of the German Reich. Marie was sitting in a chair when Hauptmann Froer entered. Before she could move, Froer said, "Please, Marie, remain seated." He walked over, took her hand and gently kissed it. "It is so good to see you this morning."

"Thank you, Hauptmann Froer."

"Please, Marie, after all this time, just Heinrich."

Marie smiled, "Yes, Heinrich. You know of my work in Lille. Did my information prove useful?"

"We believe so. After you left Lille, von Hagel's men were able to capture someone going into Koch's apartment. With a little prodding, he provided information on the Resistance. Some of the information we shared with Admiral Canaris at Abwehr. We are linking the names you provided with information that Admiral Canaris had and are now hunting down some of the new leadership. Your information was very valuable. I am only sorry we were not able to interrogate Koch before his death, but I am certain if you could have taken him alive you would have." A smile began to emerge on Froer's face as he finished speaking.

Marie could not help but see Froer's change of expression. "Oh, most certainly. There was very little I could do to control the situation enough to take him alive," Marie lied.

Heinrich Froer's eyes locked with Marie's gaze for a brief moment. "Indeed," he said before continuing, "Marie, you are aware that since the Americans joined up with the British, things have been more difficult for Germany. The Allies have advanced into Italy, and the Führer is concerned with an invasion into either France or Belgium. Admiral Canaris' people have been unable to turn out any intelligence on this subject. The Führer wants this office, and you specifically, to go to England. Plans are underway for you to travel back to Brugge and to be taken into England by boat. Since you are fluent in French, your identity will be that of a French refugee. Make your way to London. Find places that you might mingle with high-ranking British or American officers. We are looking for communiqués that might give a date or location of the Allies' next attempt to invade Europe. The last bit of information obtained by Canaris' people only identified a large buildup of Americans in England." Froer's eyes narrowed and his face stiffened. "Marie, I need information and I need it soon."

Marie asked, "Does Admiral Canaris know of my assignment?"

"No. We believe some of his people have been turned and are now working for the British. That is why only my office knows your assignment. Find out what you can and report back to me as soon as possible."

"When do I leave?"

"I wish you could spend some time and relax, but I need you to leave this evening." With that, Froer stood and walked around the desk. Marie also stood as Froer approached. Taking her shoulders in his hands, he said, "All of Germany depends on you."

Determination set upon her face. "I will not fail you."

PART II

SOUTH HAMS

CHAPTER TWENTY-THREE

France, 1943

The frigid morning drizzle penetrated Marie's body while she stood waiting with sixty other women and children for a transport to Dover. The group of French and Belgians was part of Hitler's Christmas goodwill program. He was allowing a group of women and children to leave occupied Europe for Great Britain. The reality, however, was Froer's plan to get Marie into Great Britain. Marie slid the documents from her coat pocket and looked at them. The excellent forgery, even down to the coffee-stained corner, impressed her. Marie still worried about passing the entrance inspection. Once in England, she would unlikely raise any further suspicion; however, if she were caught, Froer would know soon and not be wasting valuable time retrieving compromised information. It was the perfect plan.

Marie spoke to no one while waiting to board and only smiled at the young mother and baby sitting next to her on the bench. Three German soldiers patrolled the Brugge dock while two more stood guard at the boat's ramp. The boat Marie believed to be the one taking her to Dover rose and dropped in the choppy waters. Finally, an order was given for all the refugees to line up for document inspection. Each refugee was allowed one suitcase or bag, and each was required to take care of transporting it onto the boat. Marie watched mothers struggle helplessly, trying to figure how to carry their babies and their luggage as the soldiers stood by laughing and smirking. Marie was disgusted to hear one soldier say that any suitcase left on the dock was free booty

for them to pilfer through, although he doubted there would be anything worthwhile in the suitcase of a refugee. The woman occupying
the seat next to Marie was having trouble moving her suitcase while
holding tightly to her crying baby. In frustration, she dropped the suitcase and continued forward. Just as one of the soldiers went to pull
the suitcase away, Marie bent down and took the handle, glaring at the
soldier. Then in perfect French she said to the woman, "Let me help
you. I have a free hand."

"Merci," the woman said to Marie as she pulled out her papers and
handed them to the soldier at the boat ramp.

After they boarded, Marie followed the woman into the central
cabin and placed the suitcase down at the end of the bench seat. It had
not been her plan to converse with anyone, trying to be as forgettable
as possible, but the cruel actions of the soldiers had changed that.
Marie introduced herself to the woman and found out that a German
soldier had raped the mother. Her family believed she willingly had
a romantic tryst with the soldier and now rejected both mother and
child. Saddened and embarrassed, she decided to leave and start
over in England. Marie felt somewhat uncomfortable listening to the
woman's story and seriously wondered why a stranger would tell her
such private details. Marie was relieved when the woman excused herself, placed a blanket over her shoulder and unbuttoned her blouse to
breast-feed her daughter. Marie laid her head back in cynical reverie,
wondering if the woman's story was a lie. Why not, Marie thought, her
own story was nothing but a lie.

***

The crossing was exceptionally rough, even for this time of year, with
the boat fighting to lumber over eight-foot swells. The cold, damp wintry weather kept everyone inside the cabin. Only two small windows
were open, letting in some frigid but welcomed fresh air. Marie struggled to stay upright as she walked around, venturing over to one of the
open windows a few times to escape the stale stench of body odor and

seasickness. The putrid aroma triggered memories of the escape she had made through the toilet hole in the office where she had found Hans' body. Gazing out at the gray, cold English Channel, she wondered, *will I always be a prisoner to thoughts and memories of you, Hans?*

British soldiers awaited the arrival of the refugees. In contrast to the embarkment, soldiers helped load luggage onto transport trucks. Each refugee was ushered into a warehouse that had been converted into a temporary immigration office. Documents were inspected and French translators were helping British officials ascertain if the refugees were legitimate casualties of war or if they, in fact, were agents dangerous to British security. Marie knew some of the interviewers were most likely working for the British Special Operations Executive, or SOE. German military intelligence units passed on information to Froer regarding both the existence and work of the British SOE and its American counterpart, the Office of Strategic Services, or OSS. Both the SOE and OSS were sending agents onto European soil as well, assisting underground movements in German-held territories. The SOE was also running agents within Great Britain, attempting to track down German spies that did infiltrate their shores. Marie recalled Froer saying SOE agents were very good, and *Abwehr* already had lost a number of agents within England.

When it was her turn, Marie took her seat on the hard, uncomfortable wooden chair, sitting directly across from a British official. The official did not need a translator as he spoke French, although it was French with a terrible English accent. Marie wanted to laugh at some of his pronunciations. He quizzed her for more than twenty minutes about the loss of her parents, her life as a baker and other facts regarding life in France. He also wanted to know where she would be staying in England and possible work she might secure. Marie said she was on her way to London where she hoped to find work in a bakery. He stamped London on the top of a document. She was told she would need to notify London officials of her residence when established and keep in touch with British officials for the first six months. A review of her documents and another meeting would take place after that six-month period. When he was finished with the questions, he said to Marie, "Miss, you will now take your bag and proceed to the transport truck that will take you to the train station. From there, you will catch a train to London. There will be an agent meeting you in London. Give him this paper, and he will help with temporary shelter."

In perfect French, Marie said, "Thank you for your assistance."

Then, as she rose from the chair, the official said in German, "Guter Tag."

During Marie's training, it was stressed that one of the simplest tricks was for an agent to drop a German phrase into casual conversation. If a spy was not on guard, the instinctive response would be to reply in his native language. Marie responded, "Je ne comprends pas."

Returning to French, the officials said, "Desole. Ayez un jour agreable."

"Merci," Marie said as she turned and walked toward the train transport.

***

Marie closed and locked the door of her temporary shelter room. She secured the room from the London agent upon her arrival after he, once again, reviewed her papers and asked questions regarding her past. Marie was prepared and confident the official suspected nothing was out of the ordinary for a French refugee seeking shelter and protection in England. It was now late, and Marie decided to just unpack her things and get a good night's sleep. After taking her belongings out of the suitcase, she checked the two secret compartments hidden within the sides. Marie had been quite surprised that no official and only one soldier had opened her suitcase, making a quick obligatory shuffle through her clothing. She thought to herself, *what fools. If this is my foe, my task should be quite easy.* Then, from the hidden compartments, Marie took out another set of false identification, her transmitter for communications with Froer, a Beretta and five hundred pounds. The money was certainly enough to live on for quite some time and could be used to be friendly toward people that might become generous with information regarding British or American military movements in England. She kept out fifty pounds and placed the remaining money, identification documents, the Beretta and the transmitter back in the secured compartment. As she dozed off to sleep, she was actually excited about the opportunity to see London for the first time.

As Marie ventured out the following morning, she was overwhelmed by the destruction of London. She had read news reports regarding the German air wars over Britain, recalling headlines of the June, 1940 address by Churchill to the House of Commons. The article reported Churchill making a statement that France had fallen and he expected soon the Battle of Britain would begin. Now more than three years later, she was not prepared for the destruction she witnessed. Marie walked along entire streets of burned-out buildings, skeletal structures of their once massive brick facades. She recalled reading of German Luftwaffe and the British RAF engaged in air battles lasting from sometime in the summer of 1940 until May of 1941. The Führer believed the British Royal Air Force needed to be destroyed prior to any successful German amphibious assault. After more than four months of constant air assaults, Hitler was no closer to a victory. Frustrated, the Führer moved his Luftwaffe to the Eastern front and began a major air assault against Russia. Marie read that German rockets continued to land on English soil well into May.

One crumbling edifice, in particular, caught her attention. Marie stopped, looking at a simple memorial. Laid within the pile of crumbled bricks were flowers and two crosses, with a sign reading, "May our children find peace with God." Below the words were printed the names, birth dates and the day of their deaths. Both were girls, one ten and the other six. Somberly, Marie continued her journey through the streets of London.

It was two days before Christmas, and English citizens were trying to be as joyous as possible. Buildings, once offices and stores, now had signs hung advertising free soup and bread, free coats and shoes, rooms to rent, and offers for limited work opportunities. People on the street were friendly and merrily wishing each other a Merry Christmas. Marie realized the British citizens were showing the same resilience that Germans showed after World War I. There was a feeling of pride in having weathered the worst of the storm and the feeling that tomorrow would be a brighter day. Marie felt compassion for the British, but she had not lost sight of her duty and reasons for the assignment in London. On the walk back to her lodging, Marie spotted three American military men entering a pub and decided to follow them inside.

CHAPTER TWENTY-FOUR

After sending Sergeant Coffey and his men to find the assembly location, Paul made his way to the briefing meeting being conducted by Major Poder. The army was using one of the warehouses as a meeting facility. Walking inside, Paul was overwhelmed by the musty stench of damp timbers. The roof was leaking in many places, and buckets and blankets were being used to catch the steady drips. There were only a few chairs available and those, most assuredly, were for higher ranks. Paul stood in the back with the other lieutenants.

"Sorry about the accommodations," Major Poder began. "I will make this quick, so you can get back to your men."

Paul listened carefully as Major Poder spent the next twenty minutes briefing them on South Hams, the training area secured by the British government. Major Poder explained that the area was in Southwest England and comprised approximately thirty thousand acres, including seven villages and even more rural farms. In November, the English War Office had sent notices out to local officials and clergy explaining that the government needed the land for training exercises. Everyone living in the area had been given six weeks to move all of their possessions to somewhere outside the secured areas. Evacuees were told they should expect to be out of their homes anywhere from six months to a year. Major Poder continued by telling the officers that by now, the end of December, the area was vacant. The 531st Engineering Regiment was already on-site building new barracks for some fifteen thousand U.S. troops.

Major Poder concluded with, "Gentlemen, although we have come to help the British, we are still guests in their country. You and your men will run into people that have been displaced by these actions, and they may not be quite as appreciative as you might hope. As you leave, go to the back tables and pick up a pamphlet for each of your men. Read it and go over it with your men. It will explain English customs and will help you better understand the English people. Get to your men and get settled in. That is all."

With the Major's conclusion, all of the seated rose and waited for Major Poder to exit the front of the room before they moved toward the back tables. Paul picked up a handful of pamphlets and began flipping through the pages. The first item to catch his attention was a line in large bold print, "THE BRITISH ARE RESERVED, NOT UNFRIENDLY." Paul laughed to himself as he recalled one of his professors who was English. Paul remembered him as a stuffy, arrogant son-of-a-bitch. Now come to find out, Paul laughed, the professor was just reserved.

***

Paul found Coffey and the others sitting under a tarp, awaiting transport. The rain had not let up, and the men were cramped together with their bodies uncomfortably entangled. As Paul approached, he immediately said, "At ease, men. Stay dry, but while we wait for our truck, I brought you some reading material." Paul handed the pamphlets to Coffey to distribute and continued, "Major Poder asked that we go through this together so we might better understand our British hosts."

Private Thomas asked, "Lieutenant, is this going to tell me how to get laid by a proper English lady?"

Everyone laughed. From somewhere within the mass of bodies came a reply, "For you to get laid by any lady, she would need to be both blind and near death." Once again, laughter erupted.

"Okay. Good to see that you want to make as many British friends as possible," Paul said.

Private Dicatto asked, "Hey Lieutenant, it says that a great place for recreation is the pub. When do we get some R & R?" Then Dicatto addressed Private Thomas, "Johnny, I'm sure that we will find some of those English ladies there."

Before anyone could respond, Corporal O'Shea asked in a serious tone, "Lieutenant, what do they mean here that 'if you are Irish the wars are over. Let it go, because we are here to help the British'." O'Shea continued, "I came here to help the USA, not to help out these British bastards. They never did anything for my ancestors 'cept lock them up or slaughter them like sheep." All of a sudden the jovial atmosphere became tense. Paul saw the men uncomfortably attempting to move away from O'Shea.

Just as Paul was about to comment, Sergeant Coffey said, "O'Shea, when we take that R & R at one of these pubs, we're going to sit you down in a corner with a pint of their finest stout and a shooter of good old Irish whiskey. We may even find some redheaded Irish lass to bring it over to you and sit on your lap while you commiserate about the hardships of British rule." Coffey's comment broke the tension, and those around O'Shea began to nudge at him. Paul saw O'Shea smiling, maybe even turning slightly red-faced.

"Okay, men. I believe our British lessons are over for today." Pointing to three trucks pulling up, Paul said, "One of these might be ours."

Sergeant Coffey then addressed the men, "Make certain you have all your gear. Dicatto, you grab the Lieutenant's gear. Let's move out." The platoon slowly began to rise, stretching their cramped, cold bodies. Now able to get into their pockets, some lit up cigarettes. Each picked up his rifle and duffle bag, moving back out into the rain and to the back of a transport.

***

Taunton was approximately fifty miles south of Bristol. Paul asked Sergeant Coffey to sit up front with him on the ride down. "How do you think the men are going to adapt to these new surroundings, Sergeant?" Paul asked.

"You mean Corporal O'Shea?" Coffey asked in reply.

"Not just O'Shea, but he is certainly a concern. I mean the rain, the British people, the stress of training. All of it, I guess."

"You know, Lieutenant. These men have trained hard. They have come to believe in each other. I'm not saying everything will be easy, but they know why they are here and that this war depends on their success. They won't let you down. I'll keep them in line. Just let them have their jokes and ease into this gently."

"I hear you, Sergeant. You know I trust you, John. Don't take this wrong, but what I said about them goes for us as well. This is only going to get tougher. I've seen your temper when you are backed against a hard rock and . . ."

Before Paul could finish, Coffey interrupted, "Don't worry, Lieutenant. My fight's with the Nazis, not the British." Coffey then smiled and turned to gaze out the window toward the English countryside.

The road to Taunton was narrow, with most bridges closing to just one lane. Thankfully, there were few cars on the road. Both Paul and John remarked at the oddity of driving on the left side of the road, and twice they tensed up as their driver pulled out into traffic. Paul said, "I'm certainly glad you're at the wheel, Corporal. I would have killed us by now."

The corporal responded, "That's for sure, Lieutenant. They had us driving alone for a couple weeks, just preparing for troop arrivals. A couple guys in the motor pool crashed big time. They went to make right hand turns and forgot to get over a lane, and sure enough, had head-on crashes. The local constable demanded that we practice somewhere off the main roads, so we were not placing English citizens at risk. Since some of the South Hams were already vacated, we practiced there each day and had to pass a test before they let us drive troops. I guess Uncle Sam didn't want us to kill any of you before your big day."

Finally, the rain stopped. Sunlight began to peek through just enough to make the foliage of the countryside glisten, reminding Paul of the rolling hills of Pennsylvania back home. Sheep, goats and cows contentedly grazed in grassy pastures. Small sections were tilled, but the majority of the land seemed to be grazing land. The one noticeable difference between Pennsylvania and England was the fences. Paul grew up building and mending split rail fences made from trees felled to clear the land. Thickly entangled vines and shrubs called hedgerows separated the English pastures. It was a natural fencing, difficult to see through and high enough to make windbreaks. This was one of the reasons for the military's decision to practice in England. American ground troops would encounter hedgerows in France; from the looks of them, Paul thought the hedgerows were going to cause a great deal of difficulty for ground movement. *Too many good men are going to die in these hedgerows*, Paul thought as he closed his eyes, seeking a couple minutes of rest.

***

The barracks at Taunton were nothing more than a tent city, located five miles south of town. The area was fenced with barbed wire, but the only visible guards were located at the gates. As the truck slowed, the driver stuck his head out and said, "Another load of Uncle Sam's finest."

The guard looked at his sheet and the number on the side of the truck and said, "Turn right just inside the gate. Make your way along the west end road to section Bravo. There will be a sign overhead. Use the row of tents to your right."

The gate swung open, and the driver proceeded forward. Coffey said, "Wow, Lieutenant, I sure hope we don't stay here for too long. With all the rain, this is nothing but a mud hole."

"As soon as we are settled in, I'll go and see what I can find out about our length of stay and our duties while we are here. Sergeant, remember you are in charge. I don't want to hear any moaning when I return."

"Yes, sir," Sergeant Coffey responded as they disembarked from the truck. Immediately, Coffey walked to the back of the truck and began spouting orders. "Grab your gear and form up here. Dicatto, Severs, Thomas, you take tent one." Paul could hear Coffey continuing with the tent assignments as he walked down the muddy road toward a sign that said HQ.

An hour passed before Paul returned with information. Finding Coffey, he said, "Sergeant, have the men form up here. I will go over the details with everyone."

Paul relayed information regarding their scheduled stay up to the third of January, which would be ten days. "During that time, we will be attending briefings on land topography, amphibious assault techniques and weapons usage. We will also be going on maneuvers to get accustomed to moving through those hedgerows you might have seen as we drove in."

Sergeant Coffey spoke up, "Lieutenant, what about Christmas tomorrow and New Years?"

Paul answered, "Thank you, Sergeant. There will be a Christmas dinner served in the mess. Sorry, but there will be no entertainment." The men began to groan, and Paul could tell that they were upset. For many of his men, this was probably the first time they had spent Christmas away from their families. In fact, as he thought about it, this was his first time as well. "I do have some good news for you. Everyone has an eight-hour pass for New Years. There will be vehicles leaving in the evening for Taunton."

Someone hollered out, "Johnny, we're going to find you that English lady."

Then another said, "And O'Shea, Sergeant Coffey's going to find you that pretty Irish lass."

Paul interrupted the laughter by concluding, "We have some training to do before New Years. And as for New Years, let me make it clear that I want no one returned by the MP's or the local constable. Are we clear on that point?"

Then men quietly groaned, "Yes, sir. We're clear."

136

Turning to Coffey, Paul said, "Sergeant, prepare the men for an 0600 Christmas morning march. No packs or weapons. This will be our first visit to the English countryside and a close-up look at those hedgerows."

***

The men were formed and ready at 0600. Paul addressed Sergeant Coffey, showing him a topography map, "Sergeant, we will move out through the back gate and along this ridge for two miles. There is a road back there that will take us down into some farmland. The owner of the land gave the military approval to walk around but strict orders not to endanger any of his sheep."

"Yes, sir. Will we find some hedgerows down there?"

"That's what I have been told. Let's move out and take a look."

Sergeant Coffey moved to the front of the platoon and directed the men to move out. Paul stayed toward the rear. He was happy to see the men were actually upbeat, and some even were eager to see the English countryside.

By 0800, they were in front of a large section of hedgerows. Everyone walked along the edge of the shrubbery until reaching a point where they found a small break in the wall's vegetation. This opening worked as a connecting gate to the divided pastures. Paul turned to his men, "Once we make it up the beach and into the French countryside, this is what we are going to encounter. Any thoughts?"

"This is a bit dicey, Lieutenant. This vegetation may make good cover for hiding, but it sure ain't going to stop any bullets."

Someone else asked, "Will we all be going through this little opening?"

Sergeant Coffey responded, "If I were the Germans, I would set up my machine guns to center on these openings, wait until a large group converges, and then open fire. It will be a slaughterhouse."

Thompson said, "Maybe we should be carrying machetes to make our own openings."

Johnson added, "Or maybe get some of the tanks to blast the hedgerows and the Krauts behind them to shits."

The last response seemed to get a rise out of everyone. Paul said, "I brought you out here to see some of what we will be up against. Tomorrow we begin the briefings. Pay attention, listen carefully and ask questions. Your life and the lives of everyone in this platoon depend on it. Now let's get back to camp. There will be a mail run going out tomorrow and only one more before we begin training down in the South Hams. Get your letters written. Your family will want to hear from you, because it may be a while before they get another letter from you. Remember, nothing in the letter about where we are or about the training. Christmas dinner is at 1600 hours."

***

Back in his tent, Paul thought about the comment he made to his men regarding writing letters and felt badly that he had not written home in weeks. He rationalized his behavior with the idea that nothing much was happening.

Paul was also bothered by the thought that he had not heard from Anthony in more than a month. He hoped his brother was still safe and expected that was the case since he had not received any note that said otherwise. Although, if Anthony had just been wounded, the war department would not necessarily notify the family quickly. Tonight, after returning from dinner, he would write to his parents, Anthony, and even to Robert. Paul was curious to find out about his car and if it had helped Robert break the ice with some of the girls at school.

CHAPTER TWENTY-FIVE

After an hour in the pub, Marie walked away with mixed feelings on the success of her mission. The three military men were friendly enough, but they provided no information on a buildup or planned invasion of Europe. The men were officers spending the holiday on leave in London. Each man served in Patton's 3rd Army, seeing action in North Africa and most recently Sicily. Their explanations on driving Field Marshall Rommel from Africa were quite animated; however, they were quite restrained every time Marie approached the subject of future confrontations with the Germans. She decided to continue hitting the pubs around London, searching for other American officers. Eventually, she told herself, one of them would make a mistake and say something that would put her on the track of future Allied plans.

Upon leaving, Marie decided to practice using the subway, or the Underground as the British called it. Knowing just how the system worked, how the lines connected, and how to navigate its many stations and substations might be critical in the event of a needed escape out of London. Earlier in the day, she had walked by an Underground sign near Piccadilly Circus, so she backtracked in that direction. It was starting to rain lightly, and Marie pulled her coat higher around her neck. She recalled Hans once saying that *the sour disposition of the Brits was due to the constant gloomy weather.*

Within minutes, she was at the station and proceeded down the steps. Once inside, Marie welcomed the relief from the rain, but the relief soon gave way to the foul, stale air found in the Underground. There were a few bedrolls and at least two cots visible, signs that some people continued to make the Underground their home. Marie knew, during the air bombardment of London, thousands of Londoners had sought refuge in the Underground. She learned the government initially tried to stop citizens from taking refuge there, but in the end they set up shelters with cots, latrines, and food supplies for those seeking safety.

Finding the pay station, Marie bought tokens and picked up a map of the entire system. Inside a car, Marie sat down and opened the map. She was on the Piccadilly Line. The map showed the route cutting through London on more or less a north and south direction. She chose to take the train to South Kensington Station, switch to the Central London Railway Line and get off at Westminster. The Central London Rail Line ran east and west along what was called the Victoria Embankment. Marie refolded the map and placed it in her coat pocket, knowing she needed to commit the Underground layout to memory. The best way to do that was to spend the next few days riding trains for a good part of each day. She planned to take a new line each day, get out at every stop and go above ground to survey the surroundings. When she mastered each line individually, she would combine lines until she could navigate the entire system and know which stations gave her the best opportunity to fade into the background of London life.

Marie made her line change, and after fifteen minutes, was exiting the Central Line at Westminster. The rain was still falling, so she found a small store that carried umbrellas and purchased one. Standing across the street from the Abbey at Westminster, Marie recalled her history lessons. Westminster Abbey was the site of English coronations from as far back as William the Conqueror, in the 11th Century. The cathedral looked as though it was only slightly damaged by the bombings.

Along with the Abbey, this area was also the center of the government but not necessarily the monarchy. In her briefings, Marie had learned that Winston Churchill was asked to become Prime Minister and to form a coalition government. Churchill was the power behind the British government, at least on the issue of war. The House of

Commons, 10 Downing Street, and Whitehall were all located in this area, evident by the number of soldiers roving through the streets. Most of the soldiers Marie saw today were officers, briskly walking about with satchels in hand. She was told Churchill's War Board was set up somewhere in the area, but no agent had yet found the exact location. It was not her priority to find Churchill or the location of secret meetings, but if she happened upon any information it would be good news to Heinrich.

Marie spent another couple hours wandering the streets before deciding to take supper at one of the pubs. She found a pub, Hotspur's, located just a few blocks from the Abbey on Queen Anne's Street. The pub was lively, smoky and loud. Most tables were jammed with men, and the few women she saw were surrounded by an active pack of men in heat. "Not tonight. I'm just too tired," she thought. Just as Marie turned back toward the door, a gentle hand touched her elbow.

"Pardon my intrusion, Miss, but I become depressed when a beautiful young woman steps into my tavern, only to quickly turn back toward the exit." Reaching for Marie's hand and taking it softly in his, he continued, "My name is Harry, and I am the owner of this humble tavern. I would like nothing more than a chance to show you that my little establishment, if given a chance, may grow on you. Please." With a cheerful smile and a wave of his hand, Harry pointed toward the inside of the pub.

Harry looked to be in his fifties. He was not too tall, but his wide shoulders enlarged his presence. His closely shaved head and a salt and pepper goatee made him look a bit mysterious. His skin was rough and tight, with wrinkles expanding across his forehead. Harry looked like a man that had seen much in his life, gotten out of a few jams, and had control over many situations, or at least he believed he did. Quickly, she sized up Harry as a man that handled situations by using his mouth or possibly his fists. "Oh, thank you, Harry, but it has been a long day. I was looking for just a quiet place to take supper."

Harry looked quickly at the crowd and then back to Marie. "Yes, the wolves here can be treacherous and overbearing at times, but such things are common during times of conflict. I understand what you are saying; however, please join me at my table. Everyone will assume you are my guest, and no one will bother you."

Once again, Harry gently touched Marie's arm and moved toward his table. Marie was hungry and decided Harry might prove to be a worthy asset of information. Without further hesitation, Marie followed Harry's lead. Harry continued to speak softly to Marie, "Thank you for staying. My reputation would have been ruined if someone with your charm had left without having even one drink. As I said, my name Harry. What may I call you, my dear?"

Now intrigued by his charm and not concerned about her safety in such a public setting, she answered, "Marie." As they walked toward the table, Marie reappraised her earlier conjecture; *he uses his mouth much more than his fists.*

Harry escorted Marie to the far end of the bar, where a small table was set for dining. A partially consumed pint already sat at the table. "Please sit here, Marie." Harry said as he pulled out a chair. "The first pint is on the house, but I don't want you to get the idea I am just using my position to gain any unconscionable advantage. So dinner and your other drinks are yours to clear with the house. Now, what may I get you?"

Marie looked at his glass. "I'll have what you are drinking, since it must be safe. I would also like some jacket potatoes, with ham and cheese," she said with a smile.

"An observant choice in liquids, my dear girl. As for dinner, why don't I throw in some sautéed mushrooms to make it just a bit healthier for you?" Harry turned and walked back behind the bar, spoke to the bartender and then retreated into the kitchen.

Quickly, the bartender came over with two fresh pints, taking the other glass from the table. "Your supper will be right up, and Harry will return momentarily," the bartender said before turning to leave.

Marie used the time to survey the crowd. Most of the male patrons looked to be much older than Marie, who would turn twenty-three in another month. Many men were also in uniform, but she could see they were all British soldiers, not Americans. She noticed an equal number of men in civilian clothing, primarily gray or brown suits. Mixed in with the men were women, girls really, that seemed engrossed and enchanted at the opportunity to find male companionship, if even for just one night. Marie watched the girls. Each girl caressed a cigarette between her fingers, with the end imprinted with her favorite shade of red lipstick. The lipstick and perfume were most likely reapplied each time they took leave to the ladies' room. Marie laughed to herself as she watched the girls stroke the hands and cheeks of the men with them. Marie was caught in her preoccupation when Harry returned.

"Quite the mating season, would you agree? War does bring out the romantic in us all," Harry said as he took his seat.

Embarrassed by Harry's perfect observation, Marie said, "Oh, I'm sorry. I shouldn't be staring."

"No need to be sorry, and don't think for a minute that you've invaded their privacy. They are so engrossed in the moment and the opportunity that might soon present itself that you could sell tickets and they wouldn't care." Harry carefully set down two plates, one with the potatoes and the other the mushrooms. Marie's stomach turned as the aroma of the mushrooms found its way to her nose. Harry took up the seat across from her. "So tell me, Marie, what brings you to London? Your accent sounds French but with just a bit of German at times."

Marie didn't show any shock but was taken back by just how astute Harry's observations were regarding her accent. Feeling it best to give a believable answer, Marie said, "Harry, you are quite observant. I am a French refugee, arriving as a part of Hitler's Christmas generosity. I have only been in England for a short time. As for the German accent, I am from Strasbourg. Some of my ancestors came from Switzerland to France, by way of Germany."

Harry seemed to accept Marie's answer without any questioning look or expression. He continued, "So what are you going to do here in London? There are factory jobs and some secretarial jobs around,

143

but finding work has been difficult with so many new refugees similar to yourself showing up."

Lying with a smile, "I have already found work at a small bakery near my flat. My parents owned a bakery in Strasbourg. I have worked making breads and cakes since I was old enough to reach the table and mix the dough. To get the job, I had to make a cake for the owner's mother-in-law's birthday. I guess he figured if she liked it, I was good and if she didn't, I wouldn't get the job, but . . ."

Harry finished the statement. "But it was only his mother-in-law anyway." They both laughed, and Marie focused once again on the meal.

"So tell me, Harry, how did you come to use the name Hotspur's for the tavern?"

"I forgive you my dear sweet girl, as you do not hail from here." Harry continued, "Sir Henry Percy, lovingly known as Harry Hotspur, lived in England in the late 1300's. He was a gallant and, at times, impulsive warrior who was made immortal in Shakespeare." Reaching across the table and touching Marie's hand, Harry began to quote from *Henry IV*:

"And now am I,

if a man should speak truly,

little better than one of the wicked."

"Quite the contrary, Harry. I find you to be quite the charmer. If I stay here long enough, I am confident you will become a fine tutor of English history."

For the remainder of the meal Marie and Harry each bobbed and weaved through their conversation, Harry working at being the charming, polite host and Marie showing just enough interest to keep Harry thinking that with time this might work into something more than a quiet dinner. Finishing her second pint, Marie said, "Harry, you have been the perfect host. It would have been a tragedy had I walked out the door earlier." Reaching into her bag, she continued, "Now, you said there were no free meals, so what do I owe for this splendid meal and conversation?"

"It is two pounds twenty, but if you would like, I could keep a running tab for you. I do that for many of my regulars."

"Aren't we getting ahead of ourselves? I have only been here once. I wouldn't call me a regular. . . yet," Marie said as she brushed Harry's hand and handed him two pounds twenty.

"Okay. I will take your money this time, but I do hope you will become a regular."

Harry pulled the chair out for Marie and helped her with her coat. At the door Harry said, "Marie, thank you for staying and making my evening all the brighter. When might I expect a return visit?"

Marie rose up and gently kissed Harry's cheek. "I will be back soon. You might even help me to meet new friends." Marie exited to the sidewalk and once more faced the rain, leaving Harry smiling at the door.

CHAPTER TWENTY-SIX

*N**ew Year's Eve. Tomorrow begins 1944, and we will have been at war for just over two years. My first New Year's away from home but probably not my last. Just how soon will we be ready to take this fight onto European soil?* Paul thought for a moment as he exited his quarters and sauntered toward the makeshift officers' lounge. In fact, the officers' lounge was nothing more than one large, wood-sided building, divided into two sections. One section held the mess, with two sets of long tables, chairs and a buffet line down one wall. The other side of the building was a small lounge area, complete with a bar and some small tables and chairs.

Earlier, Paul had left the squad under the supervision of Sergeant Coffey and watched as the trucks rolled out of camp toward Taunton. Command had given the men an eight-hour pass to celebrate New Year's in town, instead of keeping them on base. Each Lieutenant was warned that any man missing curfew or being hauled in by the MP's would be under house arrest until the war was over. No one was certain what "house arrest" meant, but Paul let Coffey know that it was his responsibility to ensure they would not need to find out.

Entering the lounge, Paul noticed three lieutenants sitting amicably at one table. He picked up a plate and some utensils and walked over to the food. New Year's dinner consisted of warm lamb, sweet potatoes and green beans. Paul scooped some of each onto his plate then walked over and picked up a mug of beer. With plate and mug in hand, Paul took a seat at the end of the table. He sat next to Lieutenant Richard Hooker, who was also from Pennsylvania and spoke German.

"Hey, Paul," Hooker began, "your men finally get off?" Lieutenant Hooker was referring to the transport of the squads to Taunton. Paul's men were one of the last groups to be driven to town.

"They did, although none too happy about being last. They figure by the time they get to town, all the women will be in the clutches of their competition," Paul said as he slid his chair in.

"My guys were elated to be the first ones out. I just hope everyone makes it back without any problems. We certainly don't need Major Poder on our ass."

"I second that," Paul said. A radio played softly in the background. Paul asked, "Has there been any current news on?"

Hooker said, "The BBC gave a report about fifteen minutes ago. The President is expected to give a New Year's Eve address, but that won't happen until 1800 hours Washington time."

Paul asked, "What was in the BBC report?"

"Nothing really about Hitler or Europe. They did report some old news about Tarawa, out in the Pacific. Sounds like the Marines took a beating with their amphibious assault but finally drove the Japs off the island. They're saying the next fight will be the Solomon Islands."

"I understand we are going to be using similar landing craft when we get the chance to hit European shores. I hope command is learning something from each of these assaults and shares it with us soon."

"Let's hope. Now eat that dinner before it gets colder and the beer gets warmer," Hooker said.

***

It took Coffey and his men four stops to find a tavern not already bulging at the seams with soldiers. The tavern was called The Hare and The Hound. It was good-sized, with a long wooden bar and close to twenty tables on the floor. The air was stale and smoky, but that didn't bother any of the men as long as the beer was "British" cold and the women were not. Coffey saw three tables near the back and motioned for Private Dicatto to head in that direction. The men began to take seats while Coffey said, "Benson, Thomas come with me. Let's head up to the bar and grab the first round for everyone."

"We need eight Old Toms and one shot of Jameson," said Coffey as the bartender leaned in toward Coffey to better hear the order. Coffey pointed toward the three tables and laid ten pounds on the bar. "This will start as a down payment on our tab." He continued by asking the bartender, "The young lady with the red hair washing glasses down at the front of the bar, would you know her name?"

"Sure, name's Charly Rice," the bartender said. "She works waiting tables a couple nights a week and sings here on weekends and special holidays. In fact, she's going to be singing later tonight, but she came in early to help out because we had heard you Yanks would be coming into town."

Coffey grabbed a beer and the whiskey and said to Benson and Thomas, "You guys take these back to the table. Give everyone a beer except O'Shea. Tell him that his is on the way." Coffey then headed toward Charly Rice.

Charly was an attractive young woman in her mid-twenties maybe. It was hard to tell because the bar was dimly lit due to a burnt out bulb. To Coffey, she looked to be well proportioned with long wavy red hair falling gracefully upon her shoulders. Her face was thin and milky white, and she was wearing bright red lipstick. She was setting a couple mugs on the bar as Coffey approached. "Good evening, Miss Rice." Charly looked at Coffey, trying to place his face. "Excuse me. I'm sorry. The bartender told me your name."

Charly set the mug down that she was drying and reached out her hand, "Good evening, Sergeant, and welcome to The Hare and The Hound."

"The name is John Coffey," he said as he took her hand. Her hand felt strong, more like she had done outdoor manual labor.

Charly was taken by just how handsome the sergeant was and asked, "What can I do for you, Sergeant?"

"Please, Miss Rice, call me John. My men just call me Sarge."

"I'll go with John. So what can I do for you, John?"

Well, Miss Rice, it's not so much for me. Rather, it's for one of my men. You see, he's Irish. I promised him that I would find an Irish lass to serve him his beer. He's kind of homesick, you know. Anyway, I was hoping you might help me out. I'm not even certain you are Irish, but the red hair . . ."

"John, why don't you just call me Charly? These times require a less formal sense of social identification."

"Yes, Ma'am. Sorry, Charly." John asked, "If you don't mind the question, how did you acquire the name?"

"Nothing special. My father was hoping for a boy, and the name Charles has run through our family since the time of King Charles I." Charly frowned and said, "I'm sorry, John, but I'm Welsh not Irish." Coffey looked dejected. Before he could say any more, Charly continued, "but I do understand how your Irish soldier must feel here in England, being Irish and all."

Coffey replied, "Well, Miss Rice,–I'm sorry–er, Charly, I don't think he would mind if you're Welsh as long as you aren't English. I mean if there is a difference and all."

"Believe me, John, there's centuries of differences. The bloody English were none too kind to my ancestors either. Leave the beer and whiskey here and go back and tell your soldier that his drink is about to be served."

Coffey smiled at Charly. "Thank you so much," he said and then turned to walk back to give O'Shea the good news.

Not more than a couple minutes passed before Charly picked up the beer and whiskey and moved toward Coffey's table. Coffey saw Charly make her way through the crowd and could see she had taken her sweater off. Charly wore a white blouse. As she moved closer, he could see the top two buttons were undone. Coffey shifted a bit in his chair, thinking just how grateful he was to be sitting beside O'Shea.

Charly approached and noticed O'Shea was the only soldier at the table without a beer. "This must be my Irish savior," she said in her best Irish brogue, leaning forward with the beer and placing the whiskey on the table.

O'Shea's eyes bulged, and he sat up higher in the chair. "The name's William O'Shea, Corporal, United States Army."

"Thank you, William, but I am not here to arrest you. I just thought two Irish souls should share a drink before the night gets too far along and I have to go to work." Charly smiled and continued, "Now, William, why don't you pick up that whiskey and give it a strong pull?" Charly was still leaning forward, and both William and Coffey stared at the blouse as it fell open further. Each man at the table was now jostling in an attempt to move in behind O'Shea. Coffey also noticed perfume smelling like sweet lilacs that Charly obviously applied prior to delivering the drinks.

O'Shea finished the whiskey and placed the shot glass on the table. As he did, Charly took the pint of beer and brought it to her lips, taking a healthy mouthful. Everyone could see where the red lipstick made its mark on the glass. Turning the glass, she gave it to O'Shea. He took the pint and finished it. "My you were thirsty, William," Charly said as she picked up both glasses. Let me go and fetch another pint for you. Now don't go away." Charly leaned in and gave O'Shea a slight kiss on his cheek.

She was halfway across the room when the table broke out in raucous chatter. O'Shea turned to Coffey. "Thanks, Sarge. She's the most beautiful woman I've ever seen." Smiling, Coffey took another strong whiff of the lingering perfume and said, "You are so right, Corporal."

***

As evening progressed, some of the men wandered off in search of female companionship with the strict orders to meet back at The Hare and The Hound by 0030. O'Shea, Coffey and two of the married men stayed back, hoping to see more of Charly Rice. The drinks kept coming, but only once did Charly deliver them saying, "I see my Irish brigade has diminished, but, alas, my savior and his gallant leader remain." She placed the pints on the table, smiled and gave Coffey a wink. "Don't be leaving, because I just need to change before I take the stage."

Coffey was quite happy Dicatto had found this table as it sat at the front and just left of the small stage. The bartender came over and pulled the microphone from the corner. An old upright piano sat against the back wall. A male patron sitting at the end of the bar left his stool, pint in hand, and proceeded to take a seat at the piano. Placing the beer on the top of the piano, the man lightly brushed the keys, making a few melodic runs. As he did, Charly walked onto the stage. The pub erupted in boisterous applause, whistles and cheers. Her hair was curled just a bit more, and she had applied some rouge to her cheeks, giving them a rosy glow. Charly also had changed out of her slacks and blouse and was now wearing a dark green dress. It was pulled tightly around her narrow waist, accentuating both her breasts and hips. O'Shea leaned back toward Coffey and said, "Sarge, look at her. She's beautiful." Coffey did not respond. He just stared, wide-eyed with anticipation.

Charly welcomed the crowd, thanking the citizens for their patriotic sacrifices and the soldiers for their heroic endeavors. The notes from the piano began to fill the room, as Charly's voice rose with *I'll Be Seeing You.* Her voice was deep and rich. Coffey closed his eyes. Her voice flowed over him like a meandering creek flows over mossy rocks, leaving a part of itself behind to linger and soak in.

Coffey did not want Charly's singing to end, but she finished the evening by saying, "My last song tonight, *We'll Meet Again,* is for my new American friends. The song was made popular by British recording and film star, Vera Lynn. These Yanks may not be familiar with it." Looking at Coffey's table, Charly sang, *"We'll meet again. Don't know where, don't know when, but I know we'll meet again some sunny day."* At the end of the song, Charly placed her hand to her mouth and gave a big farewell kiss to the audience. The men went wild with applause, giving her a standing ovation. Charly bowed, threw another kiss and exited through the door near the piano.

Coffey waited for Charly's return. Finally at 0020, dispirited by Charly's sudden disappearance, Coffey gathered up the squad and left for the rendezvous point.

CHAPTER TWENTY-SEVEN

Marie's subway education continued as did her trips to Hotspur's. Harry used all of his charm, but it still was not enough to entice Marie back for a New Year's Eve party. She did, however, find a New Year's party thrown for soldiers at The Queen's Hall, near Regents Park. Changing her focus to soldiers of lower rank, with possibly less awareness of a need for secrecy, Marie hoped to hear of training exercises or landing dates. Although residing in London for less than two weeks, Marie was feeling pressure to find where the Americans were settling.

Yesterday, Marie received a communiqué from Heinrich stating American transport ships were spotted at the docks in Southampton, Bristol and Liverpool. Heinrich also informed Marie that intelligence information showed a buildup of troops in Scotland. Marie thought, *why would American troops land in the south of England and then move north to Scotland?* She told Heinrich that she still believed the Americans were assembling in the southern region of England, and she would have information within the week.

Unfortunately, the New Year's party was another failure. Sure, there were plenty of soldiers and she cozied up to many, but she found out most of the men were just new British recruits, not yet deployed. The only information they provided was related to their enlistment training. They were eager to talk about getting into the fight, but they had no information about where they were going or when they would leave. The only consistent piece of information she gathered was that each soldier wanted desperately to spend New Year's in bed with a woman, any woman.

***

Three days into the new year Marie found herself, once again, traveling the Central Rail Line to Westminster and taking the walk up Queen Anne's street to Hotspur's. Today's foray, however, was different. Today, Marie brought a double-edged, five-inch knife as part of her accessories. It was small enough to conceal but would be enough to slit someone's throat or pierce the human heart. Heinrich made it clear that she needed to produce some information. She could sense his urgency in his brief communiqués of late. This morning Marie felt his piercing eyes judging her from the great distance that separated them. She needed time to develop a contact, but Heinrich made it clear that time was not on Germany's side.

Marie opened the door and saw the pub was less crowded than usual for midday. Harry saw her and walked over. "Marie, we missed you the other night. I hope you were able to bring in the new year with someone special." Harry gave Marie a hug and continued, "Please, let me take your coat."

Marie pulled slightly away and said, "Harry, thank you, but I think I will leave my coat on. I'm still cold from the walk over and cannot stay for long. I am on my way to look at a new boarding room. My landlord asked me to move because his cousins are moving to London and need a place to stay. I just stopped in for a quick bite."

"I am glad you stopped by, even if it is for just a short time. Too bad about your rooming situation, but I understand many people are making adjustments during these times. In fact, I would like you to meet my niece. Her family just moved to London as well. They were displaced a short time ago."

Just as Marie was about to ask for more details, Harry waved to a woman coming through the kitchen door. "Oh, Catherine, could you come over here a minute? I would like you to meet someone." Catherine looked to be slightly older than Marie with her hair in a short bob cut. She was large, not heavy, but rather big-boned. She was wearing a dress that went to her ankles, a long-sleeved top and a cook's apron. Harry turned back to Marie, "She is working for me, at least for a short time."

Catherine walked up, wiping her hands on her apron. Harry made the introductions. "Catherine, I would like you to meet Marie. She is a newcomer to London as well but by way of France. Unfortunately, Marie was forced to flee those iniquitous Nazi predators."

Marie smiled and reached for Catherine's hand. "Nice to meet you, Catherine. Your Uncle Harry has been very kind to me, making me feel quite at home." Marie then asked, "Harry says you are also new to London. Where was it you moved from?"

Before Catherine could answer, Harry said, "To quote Shakespeare, 'The past is prologue'. Why don't the two of you sit and get to know each other better while I get Marie a bowl of hot stew?"

Marie quickly scanned the pub for someone that looked as though they might have some information but saw no one as of yet. She decided to have the stew while she watched and waited. "Thank you, Harry. Stew would be very nice and maybe a cup of tea."

"I'll be right back. Please Catherine, have a seat and keep Marie company. I can handle the kitchen for now." Harry then turned and made his way through the kitchen door.

Catherine immediately began, "So you are a refugee from France, Marie? When did you arrive?"

Marie said, "The middle of last month. The Nazi's took everything. My family is gone. So when Hitler allowed for refugees to leave, I came here." Marie then asked again, "And how did you find your way here, Catherine?"

"Similar to you," Catherine began, "but my family lost everything to our own government."

Catherine looked angry, and Marie saw her face tighten. "How so? I don't understand. The English government took your property?"

"Yes. Churchill and Parliament passed a law stating families in the South Hams must relinquish their land and homes for military use by

American and British troops. There will be some large-scale maneuvers in the area of Lyme Bay. We had less than six weeks to pack up and leave."

Adrenaline shot through Marie like a lightning strike. Taking just a moment to breathe, Marie replied, "I'm so sorry for you and your family. It must be a very important endeavor for the government to take such a drastic measure."

"Our minister at church told us that the government needed the land for the Allied Forces to carry out their landing practice." Catherine's expression turned from anger to sorrow and she looked as though she might cry. "I already gave the government my husband. He has been gone now for more than a year. The farm was all we had. I was trying to keep it going and now this." Catherine continued, "A British officer at the church meeting proclaimed the sacrifice was the patriotic thing to do. As good English citizens, we needed to keep our chins up."

Marie had many more questions but didn't want to sound too eager or uncaring. Fortunately, she was able to pause for a moment as Harry returned with the stew. As Harry placed the stew down on the table, Marie looked up, making eye contact with him. Smiling, she asked, "Harry, would you mind it terribly if Catherine stays a bit longer to chat while I eat? We are consoling each other over our recent relocations."

"I can cover for ten to fifteen minutes more," Harry said. "Catherine, by then I will need you to work the bar, as the lunch crowd should be arriving."

"Will do, Harry. I will just be a moment more."

Realizing time was of the essence, Marie began, "So Catherine, you were saying that you moved your things. How long did the government say they would need your farm?"

"Anywhere from six months to a year."

"That's terrible. How many families were forced to move?"

"I don't know for certain. We heard that seven or eight villages were completely vacated, and I am sure all the farms in the area were vacated as well. The government probably displaced more than 4,000 people."

Marie could not believe this revelation. She finally had valuable information to send to Heinrich. Catherine rose to leave. Marie quickly asked, "How could all these people just up and leave? Where did you say this area was located?"

"In Devon County. We had a farm just north of Slapton village. Since my husband is away, my baby and I were looking to stay with friends in Dartmouth. Then my Uncle Harry called and said we could come stay here for a while and that I could work at the pub. It was nice to meet you, Marie, but I better get going. Come by again."

"I'll try. Catherine, I am so very sorry for your loss."

Marie didn't see Harry as she prepared to leave, so she walked over to the bar and said to Catherine, "This is for my stew and tea. Tell Harry that I will stop back by when I get moved into my new flat."

"Will do," Catherine said as Marie turned and headed out the door. The outside air was, once again, cold and damp. She placed her hands in her coat pockets, felt the knife and thought, *no need for this today.* Marie rushed back to the Underground, rehearsing just what information to communicate to Heinrich.

CHAPTER TWENTY-EIGHT

Marie threw open the door to her flat and raced toward the hidden transmitter and the map of Great Britain. Searching the map, she located the area Catherine described as Devon County, which included Slapton and Dartmouth. Devon was southwest of London, approximately 320 kilometers. Marie did not have a map of the rail system but believed she could use the train to get near the area. Heinrich would certainly want her to leave quickly and to relay information on troops, training, and any news of an European invasion. Cranking the transmitter up, she waited only a few moments to find a connection.

Marie quickly relayed information stating British citizens in Devon County had moved out of the area, allowing Allied troops to begin training. She stated that she would be leaving the following day for Devon but would not risk taking her transmitter with her. It would be at least two weeks before she sent any further messages. She also aggressively restated her doubt of any large-scale training being conducted Scotland. Her training had taught her not to stay on the line for long. British SOE was known to set up retrieving centers within London neighborhoods. The centers were equipped with devices used to pick up radio transmitter signals. Marie placed the transmitter back in its hiding place and took out one hundred pounds. She placed the money on the bed next to the suitcase she had just pulled out from under the bed. Looking at the bed, a thought came to her. *If Catherine's information is correct, people are leaving Devon not traveling to the area. If I pack a suitcase, I will certainly draw more attention to myself.* Marie slid the suitcase back under the bed, grabbed a purse, and went to find a bag that might not look out of place but also would hold some clothing and personal items.

***

The next morning, Marie found herself at Paddington Station's ticket counter.

"May I help you, miss?" the counterman asked as Marie approached.

"Yes sir, thank you. I would like a ticket to Dartmouth." Marie used the name of the largest city Catherine had mentioned yesterday.

"I'm sorry, miss, but the train only goes as close as Totnes. You will need to then catch a bus to Dartmouth. I hear most people are leaving the area. If I may ask, what business do you have in Dartmouth?"

Marie anticipated the question and quickly responded, "My sister lives just up the Dart River, and she is coming to live with me for a while. I am going down to help her bring her two small children back. Her husband, Robert, is in the RAF and has been away for more than a year."

The ticket agent smiled, "Wonderful for her she has such a thoughtful sister." The counterman slid a ticket to Marie as she passed a five-pound note to him. "Track 4, miss."

Marie smiled, "Thank you, sir." As she turned to walk toward Track 4, she eyed two Bobbies and thought about the decision not to take her suitcase. She was still carrying a switchblade for protection. She doubted that anyone would take much notice of a young woman traveling during daylight hours. If they did, she was ready to silence them and ditch the body.

She found a seat in one of the general seating cars. There were only six seats taken. The counter agent was right; not many people were traveling out of London toward Devon County. As the train lumbered out of Paddington Station, Marie stared out the window at the billowing smoke of the factory stacks surrounding the tracks. Tired from the events of the last twenty-four hours, Marie placed her ticket on the seat back holder and closed her eyes to sleep.

When she awoke, a bit stiff, Marie stood and stretched. Looking around, she saw the car was still nearly empty. Furthermore, she had no idea just how long she had slept or where the train was, but the landscape had changed dramatically. The urban soot, greyness of factories and the long rows of apartment buildings had given way to a lush green landscape of rolling hills and pasturelands. Sheep were grazing in the fields that were partitioned off by hedgerows of thickly tangled shrub branches, barren in the winter cold. The peacefulness of the pasture made her think of home, although the Rhine Valley was much steeper than the rolling hills of rural England.

She wanted to find out just where the train was and began to move toward a gentleman sitting four rows ahead of her. However, just as Marie began to walk forward, the conductor entered the car and announced, "We will be arriving in Totnes in ten minutes. End of the line in ten minutes." Marie sat back down and began to plot her next move.

Leaving the station, Marie could see Totnes Castle, a Norman structure built around the time of William I. She had read that Totnes was a market center and someone on the train had mentioned a farmers' market near the center of town. She was hungry and decided to search out some food before traveling to Dartmouth. It did not take long to find the market, and Marie took a chair in one of the small cafes lining the street. A young waitress, still in her teens, with dark, stringy, unkempt hair came over to the table. Marie asked for the fish and chips with a cup of tea. The girl smiled and, without saying a word, she turned to walk back inside.

When the waitress returned, Marie asked, "Excuse me, but I am on my way to help my sister move out of Dartmouth. Would you know just how much farther I need to travel?"

"Certainly. We are approximately seventeen kilometers up the Dart from Dartmouth. You can catch a ride on one of the fishing boats going down this evening or take the bus down."

"Where would the bus station be located?"

"You must have come in on the train. Just return to the station, and on the backside of the main terminal you will see the bus station. There are usually two buses per day that travel between Totnes and Dartmouth."

"Thank you so much. You have been very helpful." The girl attempted a weak smile, then turned and focused her attention on three soldiers walking by. Marie looked closely but tried not to stare. The three were American and the first she had seen that were not officers. The men were boisterous, laughing and making gestures with their arms and hands. The waitress acted as though she knew the men. Marie watched as one of the soldiers thrust his arm out, grabbing the young girl and pulling her onto his lap. She, in return, laughed and hugged him. After more laughter and words, which Marie could not hear, the girl rose and returned shortly with three pints of beer. Marie watched as the soldiers raised their pints in cheer. She continued to eat her fish, but when the waitress returned, Marie inquired, "The soldiers, are they American?"

Marie noticed the increased enthusiasm in the young girl's demeanor since the arrival of the three soldiers. The waitress said, "Yes. They are tenting over in the park. We have maybe 150 camping there. They are holding drills next door at the Great Hall."

"How long have they been here?"

"Since just before Christmas. They couldn't have come at a worse time, you know, with all the wet weather we have this time of year."

Marie looked at her and said, "I guess war doesn't wait for good weather."

***

As the name implied, Dartmouth sat at the mouth of the Dart River and had been used as a deep-water port as far back as the Crusades. Dartmouth sat within Lyme Bay, the largest bay in this area of England. Marie's bus came in along the waterfront road, and it was there that she caught her first sight of warships. The ships were British, moving in groups of four. Each group consisted of one large ship surrounded by three smaller ones. The smaller ships were heavily armed and moving much more quickly. She surmised the larger ships were either cargo or troop transports, while the smaller boats were acting as cover. All the convoys were moving in the same direction and probably docking near Dartmouth. The convoys were a good sign of military activity in the area and only reinforced what Catherine had mentioned earlier of troops in the region.

Marie also learned Dartmouth was the home of the Britannia Royal Naval College. There would be a high presence of British naval officers in the area, coupled with the presence of American enlisted men. She knew the American army was close by. Marie exited the bus, picked up her bag and walked away in search of lodging.

CHAPTER TWENTY-NINE

"**H**ow did everything go last night, Sergeant?" Paul asked Coffey, as the latter walked up with two coffees in hand.

Handing one of the cups to Paul, he replied, "Fine, sir. I think the men enjoyed themselves, behaved and are probably suffering a little as a result of the liquids consumed."

"Did you find that sweet Irish lass for O'Shea?"

"We did, sir. O'Shea was quite the happy soldier to be kissed by such a beautiful one at that."

"And how was your evening, Sergeant?" Paul smiled as he asked because a couple of the men had already spilled the news to Paul about the Hare and the Hound, Charly Rice and Coffey's obvious infatuation with her.

"My evening was fine, sir," noticing Paul's smirk he continued, "but I'm not certain that is the complete answer you're looking for, sir."

Paul stood, "Oh nothing, Sergeant. I just wanted to make sure you didn't feel as though your entire night was wasted babysitting a bunch of drunken soldiers." Paul blew on his coffee while placing his hand around Coffey's neck and pulling him closer. "The men already told me about this Charly Rice, John. Is she as pretty as they said?"

"Yes, sir. She was just about perfect, sir. The only thing is. . ."

"I know, John. She left abruptly and didn't return. They also said you looked like you'd been kicked by a horse."

Coffey was somewhat surprised by the Lieutenant's demeanor. He turned his head to make a comment when Paul said, "It's okay, John.

We will try to get back there as soon as possible. Next time I may even join you to see her for myself."

Just then a corporal came up, saluted and said, "Lieutenant, Captain Griffey wants to see you, sir. He is over at HQ."

Paul returned the salute, "Thank you, Corporal. Tell the Captain I am on my way."

***

Paul returned from HQ and found the platoon cleaning their gear. "Men, gather around. We have new orders. We leave this afternoon for Totnes. It is a village about an hour southeast of here. We will set up as part of the encampment outside town. Engineers have been down there since mid-December building the camp."

Dicatto broke in, "Lieutenant, would that be complete with saloons, gambling parlors and working girls?"

"I don't think it will be quite that lavish, Private, but I'm certain we will make the best of it. This is it men. We are going down there for final training exercises. I don't know when the call will come. But when the army feels we are ready, we are going to Europe."

Paul watched the men fidget, looking at each other and at the weapons they were cleaning. Some men reached into their pockets, pulled out packages of cigarettes and lit up. They had been together a long time. They signed up to train and to take the fight back to Hitler and the Nazis. Paul realized that their training was going to escalate. Although no one spoke of upcoming events, he wondered just how much each man thought about the weeks ahead. So far it had been easy marches, equipment checks and firing practice. Soon this would change! Paul looked at each man. No one was willing to make direct eye contact with another man. Thoughts jumped through Paul's head, *who will die first? How many of these men can I safely get back home?* No one spoke. Nervously, they took long, slow drags on their cigarettes, quietly finished their work and rose to pack up.

CHAPTER THIRTY

Marie found a house two streets over from the town's center with a "Rooms Available" sign in the window. Before going to the door, Marie closely evaluated the surroundings. The home was on a corner lot. By turning the corner, she viewed a small fence enclosing a garden behind the house. It was a two-story home with a front door and back door. The upstairs windows looked down onto the garden. At the back of the property, there was a weatherworn wooden shed. The shed did not look very sturdy; it was probably a tool shed. The property behind the fence was barren. Marie considered everything and decided to approach, talk to the owner and survey the inside of the house.

Marie knocked. A slightly overweight, matronly woman opened the door wearing a wrinkled, black housedress and a kerchief tied in her hair. "Good morning, Ma'am," Marie said. "I saw your sign in the window and would like to inquire about the available room."

The woman smiled and opened the door wider, saying, "Do come in, my dear." As Marie walked inside, she could see the woman's face was pale and chalky with bright purple spider veins across her cheeks and nose. The woman motioned for Marie to take a seat in a front parlor room. The room was small, dark, filled mostly with old furniture and had a couple portraits of people on the wall. Marie assumed the portraits were of relatives.

The woman brought in some tea. After an hour of conversation, Marie found out the woman's name was Margaret Sawyer. Mrs. Sawyer was a widow and had lived in the house for over thirty years, the last ten alone since her husband's death. She did not state her age, but she looked to be in her sixties. There were two rooms available. Mrs. Sawyer said many people were moving through Dartmouth from the surrounding villages of Blackpool Sands, Slapton Sands and Blackawton. Most were on their way out of Devon toward London, Bristol or Birmingham. She had not had a renter in more than six months and was in need of the additional income. Marie was pleased that, due to the need for income, Mrs. Sawyer inquired little about why Marie was in Dartmouth. More importantly, Mrs. Sawyer never inquired why a young woman would be traveling alone, looking for a place to live, and have no luggage to speak of. Mrs. Sawyer told Marie she could choose either of the two rooms facing the backyard. Marie thanked Mrs. Sawyer, paid her the first month's rent and went upstairs.

Marie spent the next few days walking the streets of Dartmouth. She worked diligently memorizing everything she could regarding street locations, bus travel schedules and boat transport times on the Dart River. It took some time, but finally Marie was comfortable with two separate escape routes out of Dartmouth.

While walking around the city, Marie also carefully watched the soldiers and sailors hurrying about. Most of the men in uniform were sailors, an equal number of British and American. The Naval College certainly would account for many of the men, and the harbor was bustling with ships. She spent time near the docks but found security there was extremely tight. Sentry guards stopped everyone on foot, on a bike or in an auto.

Marie decided to stay away from the entrance roads and found a bike path winding its way around the harbor and up to a small hillside. From this point, Marie could not directly see the harbor. She could, however, see just outside the inlet and clearly out into Lyme Bay. She counted more than twenty ships anchored in its waters. The ships were equally split between British and American. Marie took out a small notepad and pencil. In code she began to write down information about the ships in her view: type of ship, identification numbers, and number of visible guns. Marie used names of various types of vegetables to delineate ships. The larger transport ships were identified as large vegetables, descending down to the smaller sized ships represented as small vegetables. If anyone happened to see her notes, she would explain that she was helping Mrs. Sawyer plan a victory garden for spring.

The final part of her plan was to find a job that might bring her into constant contact with soldiers or sailors. After her time in London, she realized a pub was the best place for making contact and for finding men in a position of vulnerability. She would search the pubs until she ran into a tavern-keeper like Harry back in London, a friendly, unsuspecting man who might become enamored enough with a beautiful young woman and find a job for her at the tavern. *Two weeks*, she thought. *I need some information within two weeks. Then I can get back to London and relay what information I have back to Heinrich.*

CHAPTER THIRTY-ONE

The platoon was in its second week at the encampment outside Dartmouth. The weather was still wet and cold. February was proving to be just as wretched as December and January. Most of the locals said that by March the weather would become slightly warmer, but the rain . . . well the rain never lets up. "Get use to it you whimpering, bloody Yanks," they laughed.

Sergeant Coffey ordered the platoon to load into the back of one of the transports. Today, the entire company, some three hundred soldiers, was traveling down to Slapton Sands Beach. Slapton was the practice landing site. Word spread that some colonels from Eisenhower's command would be at the beach, and each man knew that their presence meant 'no screw-ups'. The truck bounced along road A379 past Dartmouth toward Slapton Sands Beach. The convoy of trucks spread out for more than a mile, and each truck had one of the ten platoons involved in today's exercise. Coffey told his men they were going to be the third platoon just off the left flank. After leaving the transport, the platoon would take up a position on the beachhead. When all the platoons were in place, cannon fire would commence from ships anchored just off shore. The ships would fire live rounds for fifteen minutes. When the firing ceased, the entire company would move off the beach toward Slapton Ley. The Ley was a natural water reserve, situated just beyond the road, approximately two hundred yards from the water's edge. O'Shea asked, "Sarge, how deep is this Ley?"

"I don't really know, but we are to get through the water and up to the high ground above the beach."

The Lieutenant said, "Today, we are expected to move slowly, getting a feel for what it will be like walking through wet, soggy mud. If the Ley is deep, we may find ourselves swimming a bit."

Coffey concluded, "With each exercise, we will be expected to move more quickly through the water and up to our target."

Dicatto hollered, "Hey Sarge, why this place? Couldn't HQ find somewhere else to practice?"

"My understanding is that the final landing zone is going to have a series of canals and marshes sitting just behind the beachhead, and we need to practice getting through it," Coffey said. "Let's make the best of it. Listen to orders and move as quickly as you can. We regroup on the far side of the Ley."

No one said anything in return, but Coffey could surmise what was going through their heads, as men glanced at the pack between his feet. *How am I going to swim through this water, keeping my weapon dry and my gear intact?* Mercifully, the answer to that question came when the truck stopped, and Lieutenant Schaefer came around to the back. "We're here. Men, leave your packs in the truck. Today you are going to work with only your rifle, full magazine belt and canteen. Load up and assemble on Sergeant Coffey, down near the water." Paul went back up to the front of the truck and pulled out his rifle, belt and canteen as well. Before walking back to where Coffey was waving and giving orders, Paul took one more glance up at the hills beyond the Ley.

*****

Three hundred men lay on the sand as ships offshore pummeled the hillside. The sound was deafening, piercing the morning stillness. Hillsides seemed to be caving to the power of each blast. Soil, shrubs and trees exploded and rained down debris on the Ley. This was a small exercise, a sort of get acquainted to the landscape exercise, Lieutenant Schaefer had said last night. However, as the topography ahead dramatically changed with each blast, soldiers soberly stared straight ahead. Fifteen minutes seemed like an eternity as the bombardment continued. When it finally ceased, orders were given to rise and move toward the watery reserve facing them. The troops shook off remnants of the fallen landscape, dusted debris off their uniforms, rubbed their eyes and picked at their ears. Some madly shook their heads, attempting to get the ringing to stop. They began to make their way over downed tree limbs, rocks and assorted rubble strewn over the beach. The Ley turned out to be only waist-deep, but the trudge through it was arduous. Many slipped and fell into the murky water. Groans, moans and profanity could be heard throughout the platoon. Private Dicatto, wading next to Sergeant Coffey, said, "If this is what we are going to pass through in France, those fucking Krauts are going to have an easy time of it."

Coffey said, "Dicatto, just focus on getting out of here as quickly as you can."

"I'm with you on that, Sarge."

It took more than an hour for the three hundred men to make it off the beach, through the Ley and to the assembly area. Orders were given to inventory their equipment and to fire their weapons. Each sergeant took a detailed report of equipment losses and weapon malfunctions. The reports were given to the lieutenants for compilation by Major Poder's staff.

***

Lieutenant Schaefer assembled with the other officers at 1900 hours and grabbed a cup of coffee as he walked into the room. The officers were standing around drinking coffee and smoking. It quickly became apparent to Lieutenant Schaefer that everyone was quite unhappy about the day's exercise. Maybe it was the drastic change in environment from the states or possibly just being homesick that had affected the men's performance. Most likely, it was the realization that this was going to be difficult. Soon men were going to die, and that was certain.

Major Poder walked in, and everyone came to attention. "At ease, gentlemen. Take a seat." Poder began his address, "Today was just our first exercise, and I must say not a very good start. We cannot move that slowly again. At that speed, estimates are a seventy percent casualty rate. We also either lost or could not fire five percent of the weapons. Remember, we worked without packs today. Next time your men will be carrying close to fifteen more pounds of equipment. We need to get across the low ground more quickly. Each minute means increased casualties. Are there any questions or suggestions for increasing our speed and efficiency?"

Lieutenant Rogers rose to speak. Rogers was a big man, standing over six foot five and weighing close to two hundred and fifty pounds. He had struggled in the Ley today, once becoming so bogged down in the mud that it took three of his men to pull and push him out. "Major, do you know from reconnaissance if we are going to face a muddy swamp similar to this in France? If so, are we searching for more than one landing site, maybe something less murky and deep?"

"I understand your frustration, Lieutenant, but the answer is we don't know. I understand from command they are looking at multiple sites, and that Slapton represents the closest we can come to mirroring the French topography. The answer is not to look for an easier route. The answer is to train over this terrain and to become more efficient."

Lieutenant Rogers said, "Yes, sir. I understand, but looking at a beachhead causing seventy percent casualties is not acceptable either."

Poder saw and heard other lieutenants nod and mumble in agreement with Rogers. Lieutenant Schaefer spoke up, "Sir, what about a collapsible bridge that could be thrown over the deeper areas?"

"Our engineers are looking into those structures as well, Lieutenant. Bridges, however, create a funneling effect and could increase our casualties. German machine guns will focus on those bridges and cut us down as we move across. Command still believes the safest way to get to high ground is by moving quickly, staying low in the water and spreading out over a large area."

Major Poder finished with, "Men, I know today was not easy for your troops. God knows I wish I could find a better way, but the reality is we have to work with this for now. Go back and tell your men to get a good night's sleep. Tomorrow we are back on the beach, and they will carry their packs. All weapons should be in working order. Your sergeants can pick up replacement weapons for those lost or not functional in the morning. Tomorrow, we leave for Slapton at 0600. That is all."

Everyone stood as Major Poder left the room. As Paul turned to leave, he overheard one of the lieutenants, "Fucking command! I hope they aren't getting cold and wet up at HQ." Paul walked back to his platoon knowing they were not going to be happy about returning tomorrow morning. But orders were orders, and the reality was that tomorrow they would be back on that beachhead.

CHAPTER THIRTY-TWO

The second time up the beach wasn't much easier. The extra fifteen pounds felt more like one hundred and fifteen. The platoons stayed in the same positions as the previous day, hopefully to give the men a slight feeling of security and comfort. Sarge, considering that old adage "misery loves company," had the men pair up while they crossed the Ley. The men worked better in teams, and the crossing was made within the same time limit as the day before. That gave Coffey encouragement that the crossing was successful, considering the additional weight each man carried. Unfortunately, this time the weapons check showed a ten percent weapons' malfunction. The loss of balance by the increased weight caused the men to lower their rifles more often, just to keep themselves upright. This action caused the rifles to become submerged in the murky mud, thus rendering the weapons unusable without cleaning.

Paul returned from the debriefing meeting and Coffey detected a somewhat defeated look on Paul's face. "Another disappointing meeting, Lieutenant?"

"I guess the best news would be that Major Poder wasn't here today. He sent Captain Grossman to observe."

"And?"

"Accounting for the additional weight, the Captain was pleased with the speed in which everyone made it across the terrain. However, we need to find a way to keep the rifles out of the mud and water, or we're going to be throwing stones at the Germans once we reach them."

Coffey asked, "How were our numbers compared to the other platoons?"

Paul said, "We fell somewhere in the middle. The platoons at each end of the Ley made it through at close to one hundred percent efficiency. Those like us in the middle suffered higher rates. One platoon found fifty percent unusable weapons."

Coffey said, "Lieutenant, what we need is some wrap to go over each rifle up to the gun butt. The wrap needs to be pulled tight to slow the mud's penetration. If some water seeps through it will be okay; the mud is causing the problem. The men aren't going to be firing their weapons as they move onto the beach anyway. Their focus will be on getting to the assembly area as quickly as possible. Then they can discard the wrap and be ready to fire."

"Not a bad idea, Sergeant. I will bring it up with Major Poder at the next meeting. Meantime, get the men loaded into the transports. We go back to the barracks now. Have each man go through his gear and clean his rifle. I don't know for certain, but have the men ready to go again tomorrow."

As Coffey rolled his eyes and shook his head, he said, "Will do, Lieutenant. I'm sure the men can't wait to put these muddy uniforms back on three days in a row."

***

Paul came back from his nightly briefing meeting and found Coffey sipping some warm tea. "You're becoming quite the Englishman, I see."

"Never liked the taste of coffee, but most of the time it is all you can find. So yeah, I guess I fit right in here," Coffey replied. "What's the plan for tomorrow, Lieutenant?"

"Well, first I brought up your idea about something to cover the rifles."

"And?"

"There was great support among the other lieutenants. Major Poder said he would carry the idea up the chain of command and see what happens, although he didn't sound too positive."

"I guess that's because he doesn't have to make the crossing and then try to fight them Nazis."

"I believe you're correct, but we can't do anything about it right now. What we can do is improvise for ourselves. Sergeant, have each of the men take two of their wool socks out. Cut the toe out of one and have them slide it down over the firing mechanism. Then take the second sock, pull it over the barrel and find something to tie it off. That might just keep enough mud out to improve our efficiency tomorrow."

"Tomorrow?"

"Yes, Sarge. Tell the men to be ready to leave again at 0600. Command shuffled the numbers. Tomorrow we are number eight. I don't know if that will make it better or worse, but it is our position in the line."

Coffey took one more sip of tea and said, "Yes, sir."

As he turned to leave, Paul said, "Oh, and Sarge, tell the men the top two groups tomorrow with the highest efficiency in combined speed and weapon reliability get a six-hour pass for town. That might make a difference."

Coffey smiled, "You know it will, but I'm not so certain this type of competition is what we need right now."

"I agree with you, but command is willing to try anything at this point."

"I'll tell them about the socks and get them ready, sir."

***

Each man lay on the beach, head down, and waited for the bombardment to cease. By day three, some men were resorting to plugging their ears with pieces cut from blankets or pillows. At the morning assembly area, each of Paul's men had his rifle partially encased with wool socks. Coffey saw no other group with socks or anything else covering the barrel or hinge mechanism of their rifles. He hoped this simple idea might be enough to make a difference.

The bombardment stopped, and the men rose quickly to move across the beach. Unlike the previous two days, no one took time to shake off the debris. Time was of the essence. This was now a competition, if not for survival, at least for rest, recreation and female companionship. The reward was not lost on anyone. Each platoon quickly made their way across the sandy beach and into the Ley. Paul and Coffey were making good time when they heard a yell from their right.

"O'Shea!"

Paul turned to see Corporal Johnson reaching down into the muddy water. O'Shea had tripped and was now completely submerged. Paul yelled at Johnson, "Corporal, toss me your rifle and get him up." Corporal Johnson was the man Paul had grabbed and threatened on the transport ship. After that encounter, however, Johnson had become one of the best members of the platoon. He worked well with each and every member. Corporal Johnson tossed the rifle to Paul and reached down, grabbing O'Shea's pack. O'Shea came up, helmet skewed to the side, his face black and dripping muddy water. Corporal Johnson said, "You stupid Irishman, we're not swimming across today."

Someone else hollered at O'Shea, "You better make sure your fucking rifle works when we get up there!" O'Shea adjusted his helmet and continued to move forward.

"I wrenched my knee when I went down," O'Shea moaned at Johnson.

Quickly, Johnson took his rifle back from Paul and reached under O'Shea's arm. "Put your arm over my shoulder. We will move forward together."

Paul looked at Johnson and O'Shea moving together as one unit, O'Shea hobbling some as they waded on. Coffey smiled at the two and said to Paul, "Good men, sir."

"They are, Sarge. Now let's get them out of here." Paul and Coffey continued forward out of the turbid water.

***

They were the third group to the assembly area. Not bad, considering their position in the line. The water today was waist-deep just as the last two days had been, although the mud did not seem quite as penetrable. Except for O'Shea, everyone made it through without falling or getting his rifle wet. When it came time to fire his weapon, each man successfully got off a firing round. O'Shea waited until last. He took the socks off both portions of his rifle, pointed the rifle toward the target area and slowly squeezed the trigger. The gun recoiled into his shoulder, and the cheers of the platoon muffled the sound of the report. They all hoped their one hundred percent efficiency rating with a third place time would be enough to secure one of the six-hour passes.

CHAPTER THIRTY-THREE

"**L**et's go! Hurry up! Those ladies have been waiting their whole lives to meet someone like me," Corporal Johnson said as the men made their way to the truck. Word got around quickly that Johnson had saved the day by pulling O'Shea up out of the water and then almost carrying him the remainder of the way.

Coffey and Paul jumped up into the back of the truck. Paul slammed his hand down on the back tailgate, a signal for the driver to move out. Each man was dressed in his only uniform that was not wet or muddy. Due to a liberal use of after-shave, the back of the truck smelled like a cheap whorehouse. Many of the men let their lit cigarettes hang from their lips. Paul stood up and grabbed one of the metal braces holding the truck's canopy in place. "We have six hours tonight and—"

Before he could continue, the truck erupted in cheers.

Coffey hollered, "Quiet down! The Lieutenant's speaking!" Suddenly, talking ceased, and each man looked at Paul. Those who were smoking squeezed the cigarettes between their fingers and took a long drag.

"This is the first leave HQ has given out since we got here. If we screw this up, there won't be any future leaves. Enjoy yourselves. You've earned it. But no one, and I mean no one, ends up meeting an MP or the local police. And everyone is back here on time. Do I make myself clear?"

Each man nodded but immediately returned to their conversations or jostling each other like a bunch of giddy, teenage boys on the prowl. Paul thought, *I hope to God these guys can behave themselves for six hours.*

***

Paul and Coffey left the men at the drop-off and pick-up point. Once again Paul said, "Don't be late and no trouble!"

The men all nodded, some saying "no problem," . . . "don't worry about us," . . . "you be safe too," and making other sounds as they drifted away from the truck in small groups.

Paul looked at Coffey and said, "Where to, John?" Coffey smiled. He was happy. Away from the men, Paul easily addressed him as John instead of Sarge or Coffey. Over these past months, Coffey realized just how close the two men had actually become. They were from two separate areas of the country, two completely different lifestyles, but somehow they had developed a bond.

"I think we go this way, Lieutenant, pointing in a direction completely opposite the direction the others had just walked."

"Look, John, cut the Lieutenant. Tonight it's just John and Paul, two guys out enjoying the evening. Like we were back home before this bloody war even started. Paul finished with a smile, "That's an order, Sergeant."

"Yes, Paul," John said as they stopped in front of a pub called The Golden Hinde, in reference to Sir Francis Drake's famous ship.

Paul and John noticed the nautical theme within the pub's interior; ship netting, anchors, and reproductions of old sea charts littered the walls. The bar was full, as were most of the tables. It was loud, with an equal number of men and women lost in relaxing diversions of conversation and amorous groping. Paul said, "This looks like as good a place as any. Let's grab that one empty table," pointing toward a table near the back of the room.

As the two walked toward the table, Paul caught a glimpse of one of the bartenders. She looked younger than him and was slim but athletic. Her hair was either a light auburn or dirty blonde. With the dim light, Paul couldn't be certain. What Paul noticed most was her smile. It was wide and inviting. A patron on the stool in front of her must have made a pass, because Paul saw her slap the man's hand away.

The slap, however, was playful. All the while she continued talking and laughing with the men. *It has been a while since I've seen anyone as lovely as you,* he thought. Not paying attention to anyone but the woman at the bar, Paul ran into the back of John as the two arrived at the empty table. "Sorry, John."

"See someone interesting?"

"That girl at the bar."

"Which one? There must be five or six women at the bar, and they all look like they have enough courtiers at the present time."

"No, not the women at the bar. The woman behind the bar."

"Well, maybe you should go over and place our order there. I'll still be here when you get back."

"No, that's okay. I'll order here right now. She looks rather busy. Maybe later."

"Suit yourself. Let's find someone to get us some pints."

Paul pointed behind John. "Right behind you."

John turned around in his chair and saw the backside of a waitress. She was just sliding three pints off her tray onto the table behind them. John placed his hand on the small of her back and said, "Excuse me, miss." Before he could say any more, the waitress turned around. John's jaw dropped, as his eyes caught and made contact with those of his waitress. "Charly!"

"John?" she said, questioning how this could be. "What are you doing here?"

"I should ask you the same thing. We shipped down here from Taunton. Why are you here?"

"Most of the troops moved away, as your group did, and work became scarce. I heard many groups were in Devon. I came down to see if I could find a place to work and to perhaps perform."

Paul nudged the table into John's stomach. Embarrassed and surprised, John said, "Excuse me. Charly, this is my friend, Lieutenant Paul Schaefer. Lieutenant, this is Charly Rice. I met Charly when we took leave in Taunton."

Charly offered her hand, "Nice to meet you, Lieutenant Schaefer."

Paul took her hand and said, "Pleasure to meet you, Charly. Please, it's just Paul tonight. I believe John mentioned your name before." Paul looked over at John and smiled, although John did not see it. He was concentrating solely on Charly.

Charly placed her hand on John's shoulder and said, "Let me get you two some beer. I get a break shortly, and I will come back and sit."

John sat silently. Paul said, "Great, Charly. Thanks." With that, Charly turned and walked toward the bar.

"Paul, she's here. She's the girl. . ."

"I figured that out, John. Get hold of yourself. Just talk to her, John."

"But last time she just left and didn't return."

"Well, she seems to have returned now. She even remembered your name," Paul said while turning to look at the woman behind the bar.

"She has. She did."

Charly returned with the beers and placed them on the table. "Give me just a minute and I'll be on break. I'll be right back."

John spoke up, "Charly, any chance the woman behind the bar might be taking a break as well? My buddy here would love to meet her."

Charly said, "Her name is Marie. She works here on weekends. She just moved here from London. Her apartment was taken over by the government and is being used by the military for something. She came here because of her cousin, I think. I'll see if she can come over." Paul watched as Charly returned to the bar and leaned into Marie's ear. Paul tried to act calm as Charly pointed toward Paul's table, watching to see if Marie gave any sign that she might be interested in coming over.

"Hey buddy, what a night. Wow, you remember me mentioning Charly. She's here, wow!"

Paul raised his glass. "To this evening. Charly is as beautiful as the men said. I got to see her and didn't even have to return to Taunton."

John raised his glass. "She is something, isn't she, sir? Maybe her friend will find her way over as well." They clanged pints, smiled and downed half of the amber contents.

Both men stood when Charly arrived back at the table. John pulled out a chair for Charly. "Thank you, John," Charly said as she took a seat. Then turning to Paul, "Marie is just finishing up at the bar. She is off the rest of the night and said she would love to join us for a while." Paul smiled and turned back to take another look at Marie who was just walking from the bar back toward the loo.

"Charly," John began. "What happened to you that night? You sang *I'll Be Seeing You* and looked over at us. I thought you would come back out. I . . ." John abruptly stopped. "I'm sorry, Charly. I shouldn't have brought that up. Please forgive me."

Charly leaned forward, "No, John. It's fine. I'm sorry I didn't return to say goodbye to you and the others. I was flattered by the attention you all gave to me and was a little embarrassed by my feelings for your group. When I finished the song and left the stage, I went to the back room to grab my things. I was on my way back to the bar when the fellow I had been seeing walked in."

"Oh, I didn't know. So you have a guy you're with?" John asked somberly.

"At that time, yes," Charly said. "We are not together any longer. He was one of the reasons I came here. I needed to get away and thought this would give me a chance to work and maybe find–"

Before Charly could finish, Marie walked up and broke the tension created by John and Charly's interlude.

Both men dutifully stood again. Marie had four pints, two in each hand, and placed them on the table. "From the bar it looked as though this table could use another round, and I hate to drink alone." Marie turned to Paul, reaching her hand out and said, "Hi Paul, my name is Marie." Paul immediately noticed Marie's accent was not English. He heard intonations of continental Europe.

Paul reached out his hand, "Hi Marie. I'm glad you could join us." Paul pulled the chair out for Marie and watched her closely as she sat down. Up close, Marie was even more alluring. Even in the dim, smoky light, Marie's eyes were sparkling blue and her smile was engaging.

Marie whispered to Paul, "I hope I'm not the first British girl you have met, or that wide grin will not mean nearly as much to me."

Paul lied. "Not at all, Marie. My grin is certainly sincere." Paul was energized by Marie's unreserved personality.

As everyone took their seats, John raised his beer for a toast. "Here's to meeting up once again and to meeting for the first time." The four of them raised their mugs, clanged them together and said, "To meetings." Paul and John smiled at the ladies and then nodded to each other.

***

For the next fifteen minutes, two independent conversations took place at their table. Both couples were focused on singular interests. Paul continued to find Marie engaging, learning she was actually from France and only recently a refugee to England. She lived for a time in London, but her apartment was close to Westminster and had been requisitioned by the government for military officers. Forced to move, she decided to contact a cousin living in Devon. Marie said her cousin did not have room for her, but she knew of places to rent and that there was work in Devon because of the increase in military operations within the area.

Paul told Marie he was from Pennsylvania. One brother had enlisted. The third brother, however, was still at home. Anthony was a Marine fighting in the Pacific. He was a lieutenant assigned to an infantry group that would land on European shores sometime in the future. Marie asked what America was like and said she desired to see it. "When all this cruelty ends," she said. Paul described the Gettysburg countryside with its lush, rolling hillsides and teeming dairy herds.

Paul and Marie's conversation was interrupted when Charly rose from the table. "My break is over. I need to go freshen up just a bit before I go up onstage and sing for the crowd."

John rose from his seat and said, "Paul, wait till you hear her! She can really sing!"

Charly looked at Paul and said, "Everyone sounds good after a few drinks in this place. The owner says it does help sales though, and I love to sing." Charly turned to John, placed her hands on his shoulders, leaned in and kissed his cheek. "It was good to see you again. I hope you get more leave before you ship out of here." Charly said goodbye to Paul and hugged Marie, whispering to her, "Enjoy the evening."

Charly left the group and passed by the bar before exiting toward the back of the pub. Returning a short time later, she walked to a small raised stage area. Immediately, John began to clap, and soon the entire pub welcomed Charly. "Thank you," she said. "I would like to sing a very special song. It is an American tune, just recently published, called *A Lovely Way to Spend an Evening.*" A young boy sat in the back corner of the stage and began to finger the keys of the piano while Charly's tranquilizing voice engulfed the room.

Paul stood and reached for Marie's hand, "Is it okay to dance in here? I haven't danced in years."

Marie rose. "Certainly we can." She pointed toward the right side of the stage. "Over there we will find room." Paul and Marie made their way to the area just off the stage. John stayed in his seat, intently focusing on Charly. Paul took Marie's right hand and gently placed his right hand on the small of her back. Pulling her toward him, Paul breathed in, enjoying the scent of a woman for the first time in a long while. He dated some in college, but since working in Washington, Paul had become too busy for leisurely pursuits. Now dancing with Marie, Paul realized just how much he had missed. He couldn't describe the feeling in any way other than comfortable.

Marie's left hand lightly rubbed across Paul's shoulder and neck. Paul moved closer, his breathing slow and rhythmic. She knew the effect she was having on Paul, while at the same time she was conflicted. She hadn't held a man since Hans, and dancing with Paul felt good. Marie, however, also knew she was here for a purpose. Heinrich needed information and soon. Next week, Marie needed to return to

London and send a report. Paul was the highest-ranking soldier she had met thus far. She needed more time with him in order to find out what she could of his training and any plans on a landing location. As Charly's melodic voice serenaded the audience with *I want to save all my nights and spend them with you,* Marie placed her head on Paul's shoulder. Marie closed her eyes and thought, *Inga, what happens next?*

CHAPTER THIRTY-FOUR

Everyone in the platoon was moving sluggishly the next morning. All the men had arrived back to the truck on time and without incident, but there was not a sober man among them. Even John and Paul were feeling a bit dazed by the end of the evening. When Charly finished her set of songs, she went back to waiting tables. To get Charly over to his table more often, John finished pints as quickly as possible. Paul and Marie came back to the table from dancing when Charly finished, but they didn't stay long. Marie asked Paul if he wanted to get away from the noisy chatter and walk outside. Paul and Marie excused themselves and left John to his voyeuristic venture. Paul did not return to the bar but met up with the men at the rendezvous point. Neither man spoke about the remainder of the evening's events.

Paul came back from the morning briefing and approached John. "No landings today, Sarge. We move out in an hour. We will begin our training today from the inland side of the Ley, working our way up the hillside to the top of the ridge. Full packs and equipment." John was amazed at how Paul easily switched from the relaxed, almost civilian personality of last night to the professional military mannerisms of this morning.

"Yes, sir. We will be ready to move on your orders. I will let the men know, sir."

***

186

Five platoons made their way from Slapton Ley up the hills toward the leading ridge. The entire time, British QF 17 Pounders from the top of the ridge were firing live rounds over their heads. The sound was deafening, and many of the men had constant ringing in their ears. Browning machine gun rounds struck rocks and ground just behind their location. Paul huddled with the platoon behind a crop of boulders. "See the building at the top of the ridge? It's just a couple hundred yards up the ravine." John nodded his head in acknowledgment. "We will split into two groups. I will lead a group to the left, and you will take a group up this section in front of us and come from the right side."

Sergeant Coffey counted off eight men and motioned for them to pass him and move closer to Lieutenant Schaefer. Just before John moved out, Paul said, "Sergeant, on my signal, you and your group lay some ground fire up this hill. My group will move out to the left and find cover in the copse of trees just beyond the clearing. We will then lay fire for your advancement."

Coffey said, "Make sure to stay low, Lieutenant. Those guys up there aren't firing those live rounds much above our heads."

"Will do, Sergeant. You and your group do the same. We'll see you at the top." With that, Coffey moved back to his group. Paul gave a three, two, one sign and Coffey and his men rose up, laying ground fire up the hill. Paul and his eight men stayed low and charged toward the trees. Each man hit a tree and braced himself against the backside. Paul hollered, "Fire!" Each man rolled around the side of the tree and let loose with his M1. As Paul's group fired, Coffey and his men dashed up the hill toward another rocky section and found cover. Immediately, Coffey's group opened fire on the building. Rounds struck the siding of the building with alarming force causing wood chips to fly. Dicatto slapped his Browning Automatic Rifle's bipod on a flat rock and opened up on the building. As Dicatto fired, Paul's group made their way further up the hill, now just twenty to thirty feet off to the building's left. Paul hollered at his group, "Grenades out! We are going to throw these just over the backside of the building. That will signal the trainers at the top to cease-fire. Everyone with me?" Each man acknowledged Paul's order. "Ready three…two…one…now!" Each threw a grenade, and from behind the building came a series of explosions.

Coffey's group moved up to the right side of the building as the explosions reverberated over the sound of gunfire. Within minutes of the grenade explosions, the trainers' gunfire ceased. A sudden calm overtook the area. Gunfire could still be heard off in the distance where another platoon was attempting to reach their target.

Lieutenant Schafer walked over to Coffey. "Nice work, Sergeant. Let's get everyone up and moving. We have a three mile walk out of here to the road where our transport should be waiting."

"Yes, sir." Sergeant Coffey gave the orders to the platoon to fall in and to move up the road.

***

Coffey walked over to Paul as the men began the walk up the road. "Hey, Lieutenant. I don't want to pry. You can tell me to back off if you want, but how was last night? Both our gals are pretty great, don't you think?"

"Our gals?" Paul looked quizzically at John.

"Well, I'm not saying it like we own 'em. I mean, it was something to find Charly and for you to meet Marie and all."

"I know what you're saying, Sarge. Marie is beautiful, articulate and wonderful. I don't think I have met anyone like her, certainly not any American girls that I have known. And for you to meet Charly again, well. . ."

"I know, Lieutenant. Isn't she something? Do you think we will get more leave time? I told Charly that we would be back soon."

"Might be wishful thinking, Sarge, but who knows what command has in mind. I know the lieutenants that did not get leave last night were grumbling something awful in the meeting this morning. Maybe HQ will give everyone a night off again later in the week. I'll let you know as soon as I hear anything."

"Thank you, sir."

Paul grabbed John's shoulder and turned him back so that their faces were close. Paul whispered, "John, I want to return to the bar just as badly as you do, but let's not get our hopes up."

Coffey smiled, turned around and caught up to the men.

CHAPTER THIRTY-FIVE

It was 0200. The spring rain that seemed to always be falling had progressed from a damp shower to a deluge. Lieutenant Schaefer's men were huddled together, ponchos tightly pulled over their clothing and rifles. Water was running off helmets like small cascading waterfalls. Occasionally, a man would look up at the ridge spreading out above them. This was the same ridge they had practiced on just two days earlier, but that was dry, cloudy daylight.

"Men," Lieutenant Schaefer began, "command wants us to make a similar attack as before but obviously under different conditions."

"No shit!" someone yelled from the middle of the huddled bodies.

Schaefer ignored the outburst and continued, "We will attack using the same grouping as before. My group will once again move to the left. Sergeant Coffey's will move right. We will alternate laying suppression fire as the other group moves forward. My men assemble on me and be ready to move."

As men shifted to their respective places, Johnson moved close to the Lieutenant. "Sir, in this darkness and rain, we can't even see that fucking copse of trees. We are running up this ridge blind."

"In two minutes they're going to open up with live rounds from that ridge. We're moving forward whether we can see the trees right now or not."

"Yes, sir"

"Give the order down the line to stay close and move quickly." Schaefer spoke into his radio, "Sergeant, are you in position?"

A crackling reply came back. "Ready to fire on your go."

"Fire now!" The sound of rain was muffled by the powerful sound of automatic weapons' fire. Dicatto's Browning rounds raced up the ridge. Mixed in with regular rounds were tracer rounds that lit up the dark, wet morning.

Schaefer reached back striking Johnson. "Let's move now! Stay low behind me."

Schaefer raced forward. Incoming rounds bounced off boulders from the area they had just left. After moving twenty yards, Schaefer stopped and hollered into his radio. "Get ready to move, Sarge."

Schaefer signaled for his men to prepare to lay ground suppression fire. "Fire!" Schaefer's men fired toward the top of the ridge. Through the radio, Schaefer heard Coffey yell for his group to move.

Assessing elapsed time in his head, Schaefer continued to fire but knew Coffey should have already signaled for his group's turn to lay ground fire. Schaefer hollered for his men to continue firing while he rolled to his back. "Sergeant, are you near position? Over."

"No sir, two of our men slipped moving up the hill. One has a broken leg, and we stopped to splint it."

"Get moving now! Your guys need to be laying fire, understood?"

"Yes, sir."

Schaefer turned back over and yelled to his men, "Ready to move in ten!"

Just as Schaefer rose to move forward, three mortar rounds landed within yards of their location. Tree limbs, dirt and rocks rained down on them. The concussion was deafening. He heard men yelling. Schaefer hollered down his line, "Everyone okay?"

Only one response came back. "Lieutenant, we need to fucking move. Those rounds are falling on us." Just then, another two rounds struck off to their left. More debris rained down on them.

Still nothing from Coffey, but Schaefer yelled to his men, "Move now!"

While moving past the copse, Schaefer heard Coffey's group open fire once again. He could see Dicatto's Browning tracers firing up over the ridge. After another twenty-five yards, Schaefer signaled for his men to stop and fire. Then he hollered into his radio, "Move, Sergeant!"

***

It took another thirty minutes to reach the top and locate the building. Schaefer and Johnson each took a grenade out. "On my three, we toss these over the building."

"Yes, sir." Johnson pulled the pin and readied to throw.

"Three . . . two . . . one . . . now!" Each man threw his grenade over the building.

Schaefer lay on the ground waiting for the signal that ended the assault. Rain was still pummeling the area. He realized the adrenaline had made him less aware of the rain while they were moving, but now he could feel himself shivering in the cold, wet darkness.

Firing from the trainers' guns continued for another ten minutes. Someone yelled out, "Fucking assholes. Stop already."

Johnson said to Schaefer, "They just want us to stay wet and miserable for as long as possible."

Schaefer said, "I think you're right."

***

Lieutenant Schaefer rode up front on the transport back. From his position, it seemed very quiet in the back. Darkness was just beginning to give way to morning light, but the downpour continued. Once out of the truck, Sergeant Coffey ordered two men to assist Private Murphy to medical to have his leg looked at. Coffey asked, "Lieutenant, what do you want us to do?"

"Have the men change out of their wet clothes and grab some grub. We will reassemble in one hour."

"Yes, sir."

Coffey gave orders and Schaefer stood in the dampness, watching the men. They were dividing into their two assault groups, not speaking to those in the opposing group. Schaefer's men were visibly angry, throwing belts and backpacks down against the wall. He could hear mumblings in disgruntled tones but could not make out anything specific. He and his group were lucky. Those live mortars could easily have killed them all. He knew it, they knew it, and from the looks of it, they were going to make certain Coffey's group knew it.

Schaefer waited for Coffey to step back outside. "Sergeant, grab your food. Get me some coffee and toast and meet me back here. We need to talk before I meet with everyone."

Coffey could sense the tension from the platoon and now from the Lieutenant. "Yes, sir. I will be right back."

By the time Coffey returned, Schaefer was out of his wet gear and was sitting at his desk. Coffey knocked. "Come in, Sergeant."

Coffey opened the door and entered, handing the coffee and toast to Schaefer. "Sir, I screwed up. We should have moved faster. I did not realize how close you and your guys came to being hit because of my delay."

Schaefer motioned for Coffey to sit. "Why did everyone stop when Murphy and Lewis went down?"

"We were cold, wet, and it was dark. In the darkness, I was confused as to our reference point. When Lewis hollered, everyone stopped. Lewis said he thought Murphy broke his leg. Dicatto stayed where he was and positioned the Browning to fire if need be, but everyone else assembled around Murphy. We splinted his leg, and that's when you called."

Schaefer stood and walked over to Coffey. Standing over the seated Sergeant, he said, "Sergeant, you will never halt another assault. You may have injured or dead men from your command around you, but you will continue to move forward toward the objective. If you wait, we all wait, and that may kill us all!" Looking down at Coffey, making

193

certain that their eyes met, he said, "Are we clear on that, Sergeant?" This was the first time Schaefer could recall being angry at Coffey as a soldier or as a man.

"When the men return, I want to review our mistakes this morning. I am going to ask command to place us in a new location and to make us train, once again, during the darkness of early morning."

"Yes, sir. I understand and agree. Lieutenant, we should also reinforce that the injured or dead may be one of us."

Schaefer hesitated a moment while that realization found its way into his reality. "You're right, Sergeant. You or I could be the first to die out there. That's a sobering thought."

Coffey and Schaefer could hear the men returning and went out to pull their platoon back together.

***

The next four days were spent working on equipment repairs, practicing at the firing range and running in full gear. Slowly things were getting back to the way they were before "that shit hole of a morning" as it was now known. Once again, the sarcastic belittling and childish pranks remerged. The platoon was again mingling between groups.

"Hey, Sarge, Hitler already had his Olympics. I think now we can walk into Germany and kick the shit out of him," hollered Dicatto.

"General Eisenhower wants you to be in the best shape of your life. He wants us to make a good impression on the French when we land. We can go soft after we start eating good French cuisine," Coffey hollered back.

"I understand good shape, Sarge, but Jesus, three miles in full gear? I doubt if any beachhead is three miles long."

"We're going to run right past them Gerrys straight to Berlin," O'Shea yelled out.

"Murphy is one lucky son of a bitch. He breaks a leg, misses all this shit and joins us when it counts."

The platoon left camp early by truck, being dropped off outside of Blackpool along the A379 road. Their run was along A379 that paralleled the beachhead they'd been using as their training beach. At Sands Road, the group made a right turn and ran up the hill toward the village of Slapton. At the top of the hill, the men dropped onto a small grassy patch. Canteens were quickly opened, and everyone was soaking up the liquid when Lieutenant Schaefer's jeep came around the corner. Before the men could stand, Paul said, "At ease, men. Drink up."

Sergeant Coffey came over to Lieutenant Schaefer and said, "Lieutenant, I didn't think we would see you until we were back at the transport in Slapton."

"I have some good news to deliver and thought if I came personally to deliver it, the men might be inspired to get to Slapton sooner."

"I don't know about that, Lieutenant. It was a long run today and that hill was . . ."

Before Coffey could finish, Paul said, "HQ just gave everyone a pass for tonight. As soon as we can get back and unload, we are out of there and back in town." Paul saw Coffey's eyes open, and a big grin engulfed his face. Paul leaned in close. "I don't need to tell you what that means. Your . . . our prayers have been answered."

Paul turned and addressed the men who were all still lying on their backs breathing hard.

"Men, I came out to tell you that we need to get to the transport in Slapton as quickly as possible." The men immediately groaned in unison. "One more thing. HQ has given us all a pass for this evening. It starts as soon as we are back and unloaded."

Every man jumped up and screwed the top on his canteen. O'Shea said, "Jesus, Lieutenant. Why didn't you say something sooner? You've been here close to five minutes already!"

Men took off down the road like cattle in a stampede. Paul jumped back into the jeep. "Sarge, I better get this jeep back before some captain misses it. See you at the transport."

"We'll be there shortly," Coffey said with a smile.

***

Lieutenant Schaefer walked over to the platoon. The men were already loaded into the back of the transport vehicle and ready to leave. Schaefer began, "Let me explain the impromptu decision by HQ to give us another leave so soon."

Someone in the group shouted, "It doesn't matter, LT, as long as we are getting out of here and into town."

The Lieutenant continued, "I agree regarding the leave, but there is more."

"Aww, isn't there always something more with the army?"

"Usually," Paul said. "Everyone is getting leave tonight, so I will make this brief. I want us into town earlier than the rest, so you can make headway before your competition shows up."

"We understand that goes for you too, Lieutenant." The men laughed and Paul blushed slightly.

"Yes, even me." Paul continued, "Seriously though, we are taking leave because beginning tomorrow, we are on a two week intensive training schedule. We will be taking our first trip out to sea and coming ashore on swift-moving landing craft. This will be the first of three training exercises. With each exercise, they will add men and equipment. The last exercise will more closely resemble the actual landing in Europe."

Everyone became quiet until O'Shea asked, "What about that second early morning assault you mentioned?"

"Command turned down my request. No time they say." Paul finished with, "I can tell by the sudden silence that you understand the significance of this news. We are almost there, but tonight let's enjoy ourselves."

Someone shouted, "You and Sarge have one hell of a good night too, Lieutenant."

Coffey finally responded, "We plan to. Remember, the MP's bring no one back, and everyone makes the curfew truck."

The men began laughing and jostling around on the bench seats.

***

Paul and John walked into The Golden Hinde. Coffey spotted Charly serving drinks to a table of four civilians. He glanced back at Paul as Paul said, "Go ahead, John. I'll find us a table."

John took off toward Charly, and Paul walked past the bar and found a table close to the stage area. He figured John would want to be as close to Charly as he could if she performed again tonight. Paul watched as Charly and John embraced, and Charly gave John a kiss on the cheek. Charly whispered something in John's ear and then walked back through the door behind the bar. John walked over to Paul's table and took a seat.

"That seemed like a warm hello," Paul said as John sat down.

John's broad smile couldn't hide his excitement. "Wow, Paul! I just wish I was seeing her somewhere other than in this bar, if you know what I mean."

"I do, John." Then Paul said, "I didn't see Marie in here. Did Charly happen to mention her?"

"She did. There is a phone in the room behind the bar, and Charly went to ring Marie. She isn't working tonight. Charly hoped she would find her at home." Paul looked down and frowned. Just as Paul began to say something else, Charly walked up.

"Paul, I phoned Marie. She was just having supper with Mrs. Sawyer, her landlady. She was planning on spending the evening playing some board games with Mrs. Sawyer." Paul looked more dejected as Charly continued. "When I told her that you were here with John, I thought she was going to come through the phone. Marie said that as soon as she finished supper and helped with the dishes, she would apologize to Mrs. Sawyer regarding the games and be right here."

Paul sat up straighter and smiled. "Charly, get us a round of drinks. I'm buying." Paul touched Charly's arm and quietly said, "Thanks, Charly."

Charly bent forward, placing her hands on Paul's cheeks. "I have to look after my men, don't I?" She proceeded to give John another kiss, this time on the lips, and then quickly made her way to the bar.

***

Paul and John were on their second round when Marie walked in. She spotted them and started toward the table. The men stood as Marie approached, and Paul pulled out the chair next to his. Marie gave him a hug and a kiss on the cheek, similar to the one he observed Charly give John when they first arrived. Marie turned to John, who was on the other side of the table, and said hello.

Marie was wearing a light grey, plaid skirt with a dark blue blouse and a grey sweater. Her hair was pulled back. Even in the dim light of the bar, Paul could see Marie had spent some time putting on eyeliner and lipstick to accentuate her features. When Marie slipped off her sweater, Paul noticed that the color of the blouse matched her stunning blue eyes. Paul stared at her. Marie gazed back at Paul, placing her hand on his, and asked, "What are we drinking this evening?"

Caught within his trance, Paul replied, "Oh, I'm sorry. Let me get you a beer." Just as Paul stood up, Charly walked over with a pint and placed it in front of Marie. Then Charly bent forward and gave Marie a hug.

"Coming here on your day off. What are we going to do with you, girl?" Charly said, "Enjoy the evening and don't spend all your time in this place. Maybe find a quieter place." Charly turned to John. "Give me thirty more minutes and then I'm off. Maybe we can find a quieter place as well, soldier."

Marie asked Paul how much time he had before he needed to be back at the truck. "We assemble at 2300 hours, so I guess we have close to four hours left."

Marie picked up her pint and, in one long drink, finished the beer. "We probably should get out of here. I can show you a little of the town, my home and the room I rent."

Paul and Marie looked over at John who was still looking around for Charly. John caught Paul's eye. Before Paul could say anything, John said, "You two get out of here. Charly will be back soon." John gave Paul a stern glare and, with everything he could muster, said, "Lieutenant, make sure you are back on time!" As the three rose from the table, John leaned in and said to Paul, "This may be our last night out for a long while, so make certain that you have as much fun as I plan to have this evening."

Marie grabbed her sweater, and Paul helped her place it back over her shoulders. Moving out onto the street, the evening chill hit both of them. Paul placed his arm around Marie and pulled her close. "It's cool, but at least the bloody rain has stopped."

Marie smiled, "Bloody? You are adapting quite well to the mother language, I see. If you stay here much longer, you just might become a true English gentleman."

"I doubt that will happen, and I doubt we will be here much longer."

Marie perked up and squeezed Paul's waist, "Are you shipping out soon? Where will you be going?" Marie tried to sound as concerned as possible, but she surprised herself. She was truly concerned for Paul.

At the end of the street, Paul stopped for a moment and turned Marie toward him. He cupped her chin in both hands and softly kissed her lips. Paul said, "Marie, I was ready to sign up for this war and to go off and defend my country, and now–"

Marie leaned in and kissed Paul, more passionately this time. "Paul, war pulls strangers together. We have only a little time, and we must enjoy every second of it. My house is just down this street. I will introduce you to Mrs. Sawyer. I also want to show you some things."

Paul and Marie hurried on down the street. "We're here," Marie said as they approached the house. They walked up the stairs and Marie unlocked the door. "Mrs. Sawyer, it's Marie. I have brought a friend with me." Paul held the door, and Marie walked into the foyer.

All the lights were off with the exception of a small light on a table just inside the foyer. Marie looked at the table and saw a note. She picked it up and walked into a small parlor just off the foyer. Turning on a lamp, Marie read the note from Mrs. Sawyer.

Marie,

It was good that you cancelled our evening together, as my niece called just after you left. She is going into labor with her first child, and her husband is stationed up in Scotland. She asked if I would take her to the hospital and stay with her. I will call or return home tomorrow.

Mrs. Sawyer

Paul asked, "Is everything okay?"

"Yes, Mrs. Sawyer's niece is having a baby, and she called for some help. Mrs. Sawyer said she would be back tomorrow sometime."

Paul said, "Isn't it wonderful, Marie? Amid all this hardship and negativity, here are two people that love each other and want to create life rather than end it."

Marie smiled, "You're such the romantic. Have a seat. I am going to get us something to drink." When Marie returned, she gave Paul a glass of wine and raised hers saying, "To Mrs. Sawyer's niece's baby. May he or she find peace and not war." Paul toasted with his glass and took a sip. Marie undraped her sweater from her shoulders, and Paul took off his jacket. They sat in the old, overstuffed chairs in the parlor room, and Marie asked again about Paul's comment regarding leaving England soon.

Paul said, "We have not received any specific orders, but our training has become longer and more involved. Also, the two leaves granted by headquarters lead me to believe there won't be many leaves in the near future."

Marie asked, "Have they told you where in Europe you will land?" Marie was hoping Paul might have been given specific information regarding a landing site.

"We have no information on a landing site. I'm certain officers higher up probably know. As for when, nothing definite has been said. There are rumors that next month there will be a full-scale training, complete with gun support and a full convoy of ships. If it happens, I doubt the real thing is too far off. There aren't enough explosives and ammunition to waste on training."

"That's true." Marie wrote something on the back of Mrs. Sawyer's note and handed it to Paul. "This is my address here. If you have no more leave, will you still write to me?" Marie took Paul's hand, "You can get letters out, can't you?"

"Yes," said Paul. "I will write to you as much as I can."

Marie finished her wine and set her glass on the table. Reaching for Paul's hand, she said, "Come, let me show you my room."

Paul rose and followed Marie upstairs and to the back of the house. He walked through the doorway to her room and glanced around. The room was sparsely decorated. A small single bed and end table sat on the far wall. There was a chest of drawers on the right side and a small rocker on the left. On top of the chest of drawers was a photo. Paul walked over and picked up the photo that showed a young man and woman.

"My parents, from before I was born," Marie said. "The photo was outdoors in the mountains. They were standing on a platform over-looking a lush Alpine valley."

"They look happy."

"They were. They loved each other very much." Lying, she continued, "Unfortunately, my mother died shortly after I was born, so I don't have many memories of her. But my father spoke lovingly of her often. He wanted me to know all about her."

As Paul was returning the picture to the top of the chest, he turned it over. On the back there were words written in German. It said, *My dear, may we always be this happy.*

Paul said, "Marie, I thought you were French. This is written in German."

Instinctively, Marie thought of a response, "My father was French. My mother was German, but she lived in France. She wrote that on the back." Hoping to change Paul's tone, Marie continued, "Before I was born, my parents traveled back and forth between my grandparents' homes in France and Germany. After my mother died, my father and I never returned to Germany, but he wanted to honor my mother's memory by keeping some German items." Marie asked, "How did you know it was German? Does the army provide language lessons?"

"No. My great-grandfather came to the United States from Germany in the mid 1800's. My family spoke German and English as I was growing up. In fact, we still speak primarily German around the house."

"My parents spoke French and German at home, and I learned English in school. There are still many English words that give me problems. Paul, you come from German ancestry. Does it burden you to be asked to kill Germans?"

Paul glanced at the picture again. "No. I am first an American and will fight as an American anywhere my government asks me to. Second, I believe the German people are not the ones wanting war. Hitler's Nazi party is the driving force behind the savagery currently witnessed throughout Europe. In time, the German people will see the evil behind Hitler's regime and will work with us to destroy Hitler and his party."

Marie hesitated for a brief moment, remembering she was playing a part. "Let's stop talking about war and killing. Tonight is about love and happiness." Paul reached his arms around Marie's waist and pulled her close, saying, "*Lassen Sie mich lieben sie.*"

As Marie moved her lips up to Paul's, she replied, "I will let you love me. Come to my bed."

CHAPTER THIRTY-SIX

Paul and Marie lay together in their nakedness, arms and legs entwined, exchanging stories of their youth. Paul told Marie of his German family, their political views and their farming background. "My family members have always been pacifists, predominantly for religious reasons, but this war is different."

"How so?" Marie interrupted.

"First, there was the Japanese attack on Pearl Harbor. It was a definite act of war we needed to respond to. After Germany aligned with Japan and declared war on us, well, we had no choice but to respond."

Marie asked, "Do you mean to say that without Japan's attack at Pearl Harbor, Germany and the United States might not have gone to war?"

"Not necessarily," Paul said. "I think eventually the United States would have come to the aid of the French and British people anyway. The world could not allow Hitler and the Nazis to continue their barbaric takeover of Europe."

Marie momentarily forgot where she was and with whom she was speaking and said, "What about the atrocious demands forced on Germany by the Allies after the last war? Don't you think England and France's hostility toward Germany influenced current conditions and gave rise to Hitler's party?"

Paul rolled over and looked closely into Marie's eyes. "Marie, I'm surprised! You sound as if you're defending the German cause."

Marie didn't show any alarm but realized the mistake she had just made. "No, no! Not at all. In fact, remember I am a refugee as a result of what the Germans did to my father and me. But also remember that my mother was German."

Marie saw that her words had a calming effect on Paul. His muscles relaxed and he leaned in and kissed her forehead. "I understand," he said. "Remember I'm German as well. I believe most Germans are good and very much want to live peaceful lives. But the Nazi regime is evil, and we are going to stop them."

Marie changed the subject. "Why didn't your brother, Anthony, sign up to fight Germans and use his German language skills as well?"

Paul answered, "Anthony was really angry after Pearl, and he was younger, just out of high school. He couldn't become an officer. He wanted to get into the fight quickly, so he joined the Marines. He has already been in battles out in the Pacific."

"Is he safe?"

"I sure hope so. I haven't heard from him in a while. I hope to get a letter before we ship out of here."

Marie wanted Paul to get back to discussing his training and possibly divulge information she might be able to relay to Heinrich. "Tell me again. How much time do we have before you ship out?"

"I don't know, but my guess would be not much, maybe May or early June. Everyone is tired of rehearsals and practice. I know command has one or two big exercises scheduled soon, probably within the next couple weeks. If those are successful, then maybe we ship out sooner."

"Where do these rehearsals take place?"

Paul responded, "That I can't talk about. I don't know much anyway, but all of our practice areas and just what we are doing is secretive. If anyone found out that I spoke about it, I could be arrested."

Although Marie did not mind deceiving Paul, she also felt a fondness for him. The attraction and chemistry was stronger than she remembered having for Hans.

Marie realized that no new information would be forthcoming. She rolled over on top of Paul and pressed her warm, naked breasts onto his chest. "I don't want you arrested, but I do want to see more of you. I hope you are able to get at least one more leave before your big rehearsal." Marie passionately kissed Paul and she felt him rise. "In case you don't get another leave, make love to me once more before you go."

Paul smiled and rolled Marie over, kissing her as deeply as he could ever remember kissing a girl. Marie wrapped her feet and legs around Paul and the two moved with romantic passion.

***

At quarter till eleven, Paul exited Mrs. Sawyer's house and began a swift jog back to the assembly area. Approaching the truck, Paul saw many of the men sitting along the street, smoking and engaging in animated conversations. Dicatto spoke first, "Hey, Lieutenant. How's it that we beat you back here? Did you get lost, or did you find a British waif to befriend?" All the men erupted into howls of laughter.

"Private, I did, in fact, meet a very nice young woman. She just happens to be a French refugee. She also wanted me to know just how grateful she was for our help in liberating her country."

Paul was unaware of Sergeant Coffey's presence behind him as the men began to hoot and holler. "Lieutenant, are you telling the men about saving French mademoiselles one beauty at a time?"

Paul turned to Coffey, "Yes, Sergeant, I was. But I see you are the last to arrive. Maybe you might enlighten us on your evening. Did you get some of those private singing lessons you were hoping for?"

The men began to roar with laughter again as Coffey said, "Maybe we will discuss singing some other time." Coffey turned to the men sitting on the curb. "Up we go. Everyone in. It's back to army life for us." As the men began to climb into the back of the truck, Coffey quietly said to Paul, "We can talk later."

Paul whispered, "Fine, John, but the next time you dress quickly, try to align the buttons on the shirt. It looks more military." Paul turned and walked toward the truck cab's passenger door, leaving Sergeant Coffey to fix his shirt buttons.

CHAPTER THIRTY-SEVEN

After Paul left, Marie washed herself using a warm water basin in the bathroom. Information and plans were racing through her head as she dressed in her nightclothes. *I need to get back to London and get a message to Heinrich,* she thought. *Tomorrow morning I will leave a message for Mrs. Sawyer telling her that I had a few days off and will use the days traveling up to Bath.* Marie also needed to let Mr. Donaldson, the Hinde's owner, and Charly know that she would be gone for a few days. She could not afford for anyone to become suspicious of her absence.

Marie took out her small bag and packed a few things. Reaching to the back of the top dresser drawer, Marie slid out the thin, six-inch, double-edged knife and placed it in a holder on the underside of her carry-bag. It was a small, yet lethal, weapon to use and easy to deploy if needed. Now almost midnight, Marie needed sleep. She would rise early the next morning and go to Charly's, The Golden Hinde and to the bus station to get a ticket to Totnes.

The vision of Paul continued to invade her mind. For the first time, she was thinking of another man, someone other than Hans. Making love with Paul was easy and so pleasing to her. Hans had been loving but rough and somewhat overpowering. Paul was tender. Marie's skin still tingled. As she lay in the bed she had just shared with Paul, Marie imagined his presence on top of her and began to once again rhythmically move her hips. *After this ugly war, can I find someone that will please me the way you did tonight?* With those thoughts playing in her head, Marie simply fell off to sleep.

***

Mrs. Sawyer had not returned by the time Marie left the house. She placed a note in the same spot Mrs. Sawyer had used the previous evening. Bag in hand, Marie's first stop was Charly's.

When Marie arrived, Charly was eating breakfast and having a cup of coffee. Charly noticed the bag and said, "Where you off to? Did Paul do something wrong last night?"

"Paul did something wonderful last night, but that's not why I'm here," Marie excitedly said.

"Well, tell me!"

"I don't have time right now, Charly." Marie recited the story she had practiced last night. "I need to go back to London for a couple days to take care of my flat and to talk to the people subletting. I thought I would go now, because its not likely Paul will get another leave soon. I don't want to be gone if he comes back to town."

"I thought you said the British military was using your flat, and that's the reason you came down here."

"They do have use of my flat, and I need to make certain they are going to remain," Marie replied. "You know the military. They just might leave without so much as a letter, and I might be responsible for payments. I am going to speak with the landlord and arrange the end of my lease."

Charly seemed okay with Marie's explanation and said, "So what about last night?"

"Paul and I went back to my home. By luck, Mrs. Sawyer was out for the evening. We had a lovely time sitting, just talking. He told me of his family and why he signed up for the army. Did you know he has a brother in the Marines fighting in the Pacific?"

Charly acted as though she did not even hear the end of Marie's repartee, "You just sat and talked?"

Marie smiled and coyly said, "Well no, that's not all we did. Paul is so caring and loving."

"Caring and loving. These are difficult times, my dear. Did he please you?"

"He most certainly did!" Marie remarked excitedly. "How about John? How was your evening?"

"We came back here, and believe it nor not, he asked me to sing for him. Well, I told him get your clothes off soldier, and I'll make us both sing!" Marie and Charly both laughed.

"I must go to the Hinde and let Mr. Donaldson know I will be gone for a few days. I'm not scheduled to work, but just in case I am slightly longer, I don't want to jeopardize my job."

Charly said, "Good idea. Mr. Donaldson can be a twit sometimes." Marie and Charly gave each other a hug and kiss, and Marie made her way out the door, walking toward the Hinde.

***

Mr. Donaldson was in the storeroom stacking boxes of beer when Marie entered. "Good morning, Mr. Donaldson."

"Good morning, Marie. What brings you here on your day off?"

Marie explained, "Mr. Donaldson, I received a telegram yesterday from the War Department regarding the use of my flat in London. They asked if I could return to London for a few days to transfer my lease over to them entirely. I don't know why we could not take care of this by mail or telegram, but they insisted I come to London."

"I don't see any problem with you being gone for a few days. We probably won't be busy until the yanks get another leave. From what I hear, that might not be too soon."

Mr. Donaldson's comment piqued Marie's interest. She asked, "Just what have you heard, Mr. Donaldson?"

"The missus and I had dinner last night with two of the town's aldermen. Some British and American officers were at the dinner as well. They couldn't say too much, you know, but they did say the troops were going through the last stages of practice. They even said Monty and General Eisenhower would be down here within the month to watch a full dress rehearsal."

"A full rehearsal? What does that mean?" Marie inquired.

"I'm not certain, but whatever it is, they said twenty thousand strong. Anyway, they said after the exercise it was off to France."

"They told you the landing would be in France?"

"Correct, they said France. That should make you happy. Maybe you can get home sooner."

Marie thought about the information Mr. Donaldson had just unwittingly relayed to her. "That would be nice, Mr. Donaldson. I mean getting home sooner."

Mr. Donaldson finished stacking the last box. "Go ahead, my dear. Take the week off. Let me know when you return, and say hello to Monty for me if you see him."

Marie stepped forward and gave Mr. Donaldson a hug. "Thank you, Mr. Donaldson. I will return as soon as possible." As Marie reached the storeroom door, she turned and said, "I'll give Monty your best."

***

The final stop was the Dartmouth bus station. Walking to the station, Marie noticed increased military activity, especially for the early morning. There was not much of an increase in lower level military personnel but certainly a greater presence of military officers, cars and jeeps. One of the roads leading into the town center came from the area of the British Naval College. Marie had learned the college was headquarters for the British Naval escort ships used in the training exercises. There was a steady stream of cars moving along that particular roadway.

At the station, Marie purchased her ticket to Totnes. Just to be safe, she would wait to buy a train ticket back to London's Paddington Station once in Totnes. Her timing turned out to be very good. There were only two buses between Totnes and Dartmouth, and her bus was going to be boarding in fifteen minutes. As Marie sat on the wooden bench awaiting the bus, she felt for the knife on the underside of her carry bag. Her fingers slid inside the slit where she felt the cold steel of her double-edged knife. Marie knew she was secure.

CHAPTER THIRTY-EIGHT

"**G**entlemen, welcome aboard." The address came from the Lieutenant Commander aboard LST 507. LST stood for Landing Ship, Tanks. LSTs were large ships that could be driven up on a beach. Dropping the front allowed tanks, trucks and men to disembark. Close to three hundred men, in full gear, sat on the deck of the LST507. It was a beautiful morning. The normal damp, windy, overcast skies had given way to brilliant sunshine. Lieutenant Schaefer looked in both directions and saw four other LSTs anchored, each with men on their decks and Higgins Boats moored to the sides. Higgins were beach landing craft named for Andrew Higgins, the creator. Crafted after swamp boats, Higgins Boats sat shallowly in the water and ran at 9 knots. Each boat held up to thirty-six men. When the briefing was concluded, men would climb over the side the LST and ride the Higgins to the beachhead.

The officer continued, "Within the hour, you will hear three bells sound. At that time, each platoon assigned to Attack-One will climb down and assemble in their launch boat. Once loaded, the boats will push away. Attack-Two will depart thirty minutes behind Attack-One. You will travel at full speed to the beachhead. One hundred yards from the beachhead, your driver will holler a command of "READY", and an orange light located in the front, right corner will begin to flash. At twenty-five yards, the light will go to green. Within seconds, the driver will cut the engine and the door will drop. You will hear a "GO" command, the green light will flash, and everyone will exit as quickly as possible. The door will be open for thirty seconds. The driver will then place the craft in reverse, pulling away from the beach." Men were looking around, checking their gear and nervously fidgeting with their helmets and uniforms.

The officer continued, "While riding out, you have certainly become aware that these boats do not provide the utmost in protection. Get out of the boat, into the water, and up the beach as fast as possible."

"No shit!" said Johnson. "These sides are made of plywood. What the hell is plywood going to stop?"

O'Shea spoke up. "Maybe the Germans are low on weapons and are going to use BB guns."

Johnson retorted, "Don't be an asshole, O'Shea."

Everyone laughed and began to stand and stretch, while the last piece of information was relayed by the officer, "Oh and remember, guns from shore will be firing live ammunition over your head, so stay low."

Dicatto said, "Geez, more live ammo. What's with all the live ammo? They got that much to waste?"

O'Shea hollered, "Hey, save some of those live rounds for the Krauts, why don't ya."

Thirty minutes later, three bells began to ring. Hundreds of men, on five separate LSTs began the process of climbing down the ropes and stacking like sardines in their plywood coffin boats. The day's exercise had more than a thousand troops landing in two waves on Slapton Sands Beach.

Once assembled, Lieutenant Schaefer hollered out to his men, "We are in Attack-Two. Once the first boats pull away, we will wait twenty minutes and then move over the side. Let's get up the beach to our rendezvous point."

The first boats pulled away. "Twenty minutes," Coffey said. A sober atmosphere descended on the Higgins Boat. No one spoke after Coffey. Dicatto squatted in the back corner of the Higgins, concentrating on getting out of the boat and up the beach. He knew, as they all knew, this exercise was extremely dangerous.

***

By the time they moved toward the beach, heavy machine gun fire from the mounts simulating German guns was heard over the whine of the Higgins' engines. Between the machine gun fire and the sound from the Higgins' engines, Coffey found it impossible to even hear Johnson who was standing next to him.

Men could not see over the sides of the Higgins, but by the increasing sound of the machine gun reports and the reverberation caused by so many boats traveling in such a small space, exit anxieties mounted. The orange light came on. "READY!" The boat moved quickly. Seemingly within seconds, the light went green, then flashing, and the front dropped. "GO!" Lieutenant Schaefer, Sergeant Coffey and Corporal Johnson jumped forward into the water and away from the opening. Platoon members followed in quick succession behind as each safely exited the boat and began wading toward shore. Bullets whizzed overhead, landing with a sucking thud as the water boiled behind them.

The platoon, already divided into separate rifle teams, used a cover-fire leapfrog technique to move up the beach to the Ley. Once in the Ley, members partnered as they had done in earlier practice sessions, helping each other remain upright as they slogged through the muddy water. It only took Lieutenant Schaefer and his men twenty minutes to move from the Higgins to the base of the hill. Lying against the hillside, men were gasping for breath and looking back toward the beach. Other less fortunate platoons were still working to get to their end point. "FUBAR," one man said. Then others, between pants, began to repeat, "FUBAR."

***

It was dusk by the time they pulled back into camp. Orders were to proceed immediately to the mess area for chow. Officers were told to grab their food and assemble in the conference room. Paul was just setting his food down when Major Poder walked up onto the raised stage. "At ease, men. Everyone quiet down and take a seat. Those without food, for now, please take a seat." Groans could be heard from those still without food. Major Poder continued, "Overall, today's exercise was very successful. The majority of boats were unloaded within our time allowance, and most units made it across the Ley and up to the hillside faster than anticipated." Applause erupted from the floor. The noise level rose substantially and men were seen slapping each other on the backs.

Major Poder interrupted the celebration. "Hold up just a minute!" The Major waited as the noise abated. "We did have one negative incident that I need you to understand and to also relay to your men. Our machine gun fire strafed three Attack-Two boats on the west end of the line. The gun placements did not adjust for the changing tides; therefore, the line of fire was too low."

Before Major Poder could continue, someone inquired, "Casualties, sir?"

Another hollered, "How could they fuck it up, Major?"

Major Poder sensed the agitation of his lieutenants. "Yes. Eight killed and twelve wounded. One of those killed was Lieutenant Wilkinson." Everyone in the room was silent until the Major continued, "After you eat, you will all return to your units. Reinforce that these are dangerous exercises. It is tragic these men died today, but anything can happen in training. Tell your men that this event will not deter our timetable. There will be no exercises tomorrow. We will assemble at 0600 for a service for the deceased. No one will mention this outside of the area."

Someone near the back stood up. "Sir, have Lieutenant Wilkinson's family and the families of the others been notified?"

"Not at this time. The men will be buried here, and after the invasion, command will decide just when to notify their families. I expect you to control your units and remind them that all mail is censored. Tell them to be ready for our next exercise. That is all."

Officers stood as Major Poder walked out, but the Major saw by their expressions they were troubled with the announcement.

CHAPTER THIRTY-NINE

Marie arrived back at London's Paddington Station just past 5:00 p.m. She was tired from the journey and wanted to get back to her flat. Tonight she needed to spend the evening reviewing the notes she had written while in Dartmouth. Marie considered going back to Hotspur's the next day to see if she could find others with information regarding the training, departure date or landing location of the Allies. She knew something important was taking place in Devon although Paul did not talk about anything specific. Marie sensed whatever was going to happen would happen soon. Marie decided she would go to Hotspur's the next evening and then wire up her transmitter to send all the information back to Heinrich.

The streets were bustling with activity. Men dressed in work suits and carrying briefcases walked home from a day at work. Women, many wearing overalls, scurried along the streets. Most of the men and women carried cloth bags full of ingredients for the evening meal. Although hurrying along, most took a moment to smile and nod at each other as they made their way. Some even stopped and chatted for a brief moment.

The streets were full of litter. Some spilled out into the gutters, mixing with foul-smelling water. Mice and rats scurried about, scavenging the piles for morsels of food.

Marie stopped at a small park just up the street from her flat. Although cold, it had not rained for days, and children were taking advantage of their extended stay outside. It was dark. The park was only lit by two lamps at the gate entrance. She watched the children playing a game of tag and smiled when she noticed one girl who was obviously much faster and more agile than her male counterparts. Marie listened to the boys curse in frustration as they failed to catch their female adversary. *Good for you, my child. Don't ever forget that you are the equal of any boy. . . or man, for that matter.*

As Marie approached her building, she glanced toward three men standing across the street. She first noticed the men a couple doors back, but now their stares became worrisome to her. Something inside Marie's brain told her to keep walking. *Go past the flat. Just keep on walking and see if they follow.* It was probably a waste of her time. She was tired and hungry. Anyway, she had been gone for a while. For all she knew, these three men might now live across the street. As she slowed and reached for the stair rail of her building, the jolt within her brain struck again. Marie let the bag slip out of her hand, making it look as though the slip was her reason for stopping. She bent down and picked up the bag with her right hand, using her left to slide the knife from its holder. Keeping her body between her hand and the men across the street, she slid the knife into her coat pocket. Marie continued down the block and waited to see if anyone followed. If they did follow, she would take care of them. If they did not follow, she would return by another street and make her way to the flat via the back of the building.

At the end of the block, Marie turned right and hurriedly crossed the street. Spying a small vegetable store, she entered. She turned back toward the window and pretended to be looking over the produce, all the while looking back at the corner. No one turned the corner. After ten minutes of watching the street, Marie turned to find a store employee giving her the eye. The clerk most likely believed Marie was going to steal some of the produce and place it in her bag. He looked ready to pounce. "Oh, I'm sorry, sir. I must have been daydreaming. I'm so exhausted from work today."

The clerk walked over. "Miss, may I help you find something?"

"I was looking for two or three potatoes to go with this squash," Marie said as she picked up a yellow butternut from the bin.

"The potatoes are over here," said the clerk as he pointed to a bin against the sidewall. "Did you say three?" he asked as his hand reached into the bin.

"Yes, that would be wonderful. Thank you so much." Marie walked away from the window. Placing the squash on the counter, she asked, "Sorry about blanking out for a minute. I have been working too many long hours, and I'm exhausted. How much do I owe you?"

The clerk smiled. "I understand. Everyone has been exhausted and stressed since the bombings started. We are all doing our best to overcome each adversity. That will be thirty pence, Miss."

Marie took her coin purse from her pocket and found thirty pence. After handing the money to the clerk, Marie picked up the potatoes and squash and placed them in her bag. "Thank you, sir," Marie said as she turned to leave.

"Excuse me, but I don't think I have seen you in here before. I know most of the residents around here. Are you new to the area?"

Marie responded, "I don't live around here. I'm just visiting a friend and told her that I would bring some vegetables for this evening's stew." Before the clerk could inquire any further, Marie said, "Thank you again." With that, Marie turned and hustled out of the store.

As she reentered the street, Marie surveyed the area, searching the doorways and alcoves for the three men she had seen earlier. Satisfied they were not around, Marie still turned and walked further away from her building. She decided to go up one more block before eventually returning back to her flat from the next street over. She purposely had selected her building because of the second entrance door in back. Once inside, a small hallway led to the foyer and the staircase ascending to her floor.

Slowly approaching the back of her building, she saw no one. Once inside, Marie walked to the foyer. The front door to the building had a small window inset. She looked out to see if the three men were still there and breathed a slight sigh of relief to see they were gone. *They were probably just three unemployed men who were not fit for military duty and wasting time before going to a local pub to get their fill of a liquid diet.*

Marie did, however, spend a bit of extra time examining her flat door. When everything about the door passed her thorough inspection, she placed a key in the lock and entered.

***

Other than the vegetables just purchased, there was nothing in the room to eat. She boiled water, cut up the squash and potatoes, and placed them in the pot. The vegetables would be enough for her to eat. There was also a bottle of unopened wine sitting on the counter. The wine had been a gift from Harry. As she ate, Marie made plans for the following day. She would spend the day walking around the Whitehall area since most of the military and government officials worked there. She planned to eat lunch somewhere in the area, hoping to find possible contacts. If she was unable to gather useful information, her backup plan would be to try Hotspur's again. There were always military men in Hotspur's at night. At the very least, Harry or his daughter might have information they might unknowingly pass on to her.

***

Lunch was a failure. The evening was darkening, and sporadic rain showers were returning. Just as she had imagined, Hotspur's was full, loud and teeming with activity. None of that, however, stopped Harry from noticing Marie as she entered. Walking up to Marie, Harry said, "My dear, Marie, welcome back." Harry gave her a hug and kissed her on the cheek. "I thought something most dreaded must have happened to you. It has been months since you were here. You have brightened my day, young lady, and made an old man glad to be alive in this damp, dreary city."

Marie returned the hug and kiss. "Harry, you're such the charmer, and you always make me feel so welcome." Making up a quick lie, Marie said, "I could not find new employment in London and heard of work in Bristol. I left abruptly, but I did send you a note. It must have been lost in transit since you obviously did not receive it."

Sadly Harry said, "I did not, my dear."

Marie took Harry's hand in hers. "I'm here now, at least for a short time. I missed the city and had some days free so I decided to come back to see you and Catherine."

"Do you have a place to stay? If not, I can find some room in my small apartment," Harry said with a smile.

Marie returned his smile and said, "Thank you for your offer, Harry, but I am staying with a friend." Changing the subject, Marie asked, "Is Catherine around? I would like to say hello to her as well."

"She is. She's probably just in the kitchen getting an order. Come over and sit at my table. I will tell her you're here. I will have her bring you a pint."

Marie sat at Harry's table, giving off the aura of importance while searching for someone who might help her with information. Catherine arrived with two pints in hand and placed them on the table, sliding into the chair next to Marie. "Harry surprised me with the announcement of your arrival. It is so good to see you again."

"It is good to see you as well. It's good to be back, if even for just a short stay. How are your husband and your family?"

"Thank you for asking. My husband is still somewhere in Northern Africa, making sure the Germans do not return. I think he is finally safe for the time being. The little one and Harry keep me busy. What about you? Did you find some work?"

"I did, but it is in Bristol. I am back in London for just a few days."

Catherine reached for Marie's hand. "Bristol! Oh, I should introduce you to Colonel Thompson. He comes in most evenings when in London. He is attached to General Montgomery's staff and is headquartered in Bristol. He has been Montgomery's eyes and ears during the training in Devonshire."

Catherine smiled, "He's single and not so bad looking either."

Marie was excited. Colonel Thompson would be the highest-ranking officer she had met thus far. Working with Montgomery, he would have information regarding the training exercises and the possible landing date of the European invasion. "Catherine, thank you so much. I would love to meet him. I have not met many people as yet, especially good looking military men."

Catherine stood up from the table and searched the pub. Sitting back down, she said, "I don't see him yet, but I would expect him soon. He comes in most evenings on his way from meetings."

Marie asked, "Has he said anything about how the training is going or when we can expect troops to invade Europe?"

"He stated the training was going more slowly than the general hoped, and the troops were becoming tired and bored with the pace as well. Most of the time he says he can't talk about it, but he has made it sound as though the invasion would be soon."

Marie was listening to Catherine and, at the same time, trying to determine the best way to get Colonel Thompson alone. It was also possible the Colonel might have more information back at his flat. Marie eagerly anticipated meeting Colonel Thompson. She began scheming how she could get herself invited to his place so she could see just what information could be found.

Marie was finishing her pint when Catherine gave a wave to someone behind her. "He just walked in! I think he saw me. He is on his way over." Catherine stood when the Colonel arrived at the table. Thompson gave Catherine a hug and kiss on the cheek. Before he could say anything, Catherine made the introductions. "Marie, this is Colonel Lynn Thompson. Colonel, this is my friend, Marie Monin. She is visiting from Bristol."

Colonel Thompson turned to Marie and took her hand, "Good evening, Miss Monin. It is a pleasure to meet you." Thompson was well over six feet but not heavy. His hands were large and felt like the hands of someone who worked outside.

Marie smiled and said, "It is very nice to meet you as well, Colonel Thompson."

Thompson immediately said, "Please, just Lynn."

"Then please call me Marie," she said with another smile.

Catherine said, "Colonel, take my chair. I have to get back to work. I will bring you a pint and another for Marie." Catherine cleared the two glasses from the table, turned and walked back toward the bar.

Lynn sat. "Catherine said you were visiting from Bristol, but your accent. . ."

Before he could finish, Marie said, "You are very perceptive, Colonel. Excuse me, Lynn." Lying, she continued, "I am currently living in Bristol, but I am a refugee from France. I have been in England for almost a year now. Your country was most gracious to take me in when I lost my family."

Lynn leaned forward, showing concern, "Lost your family? How tragic."

Marie hesitated for a moment. Lynn was certainly astute. She was impressed by how well he picked up little things. He was not going to be fooled easily. She playfully reached for Lynn's hand as he gripped his pint. "Not as tragic as it may seem. My mother died when I was a little girl, and my father recently died of natural causes. I had no one left. With the war being fought in my country, I decided to start over in yours."

Lynn smiled, obviously pleased with Marie's physical contact. "I am glad you were not a victim of Nazi atrocities. I was at Dunkirk, you know, and I saw first hand just how bloody ruthless these Nazi bastards can be."

Marie saw Lynn's pleasant reaction to her touch. She reached out with her other hand, grasping Lynn's hand between hers. "That truly must have been horrendous. I am sure you lost many good friends there." Trying to draw Lynn out of the past and into the present, Marie asked, "What are your duties now, here in England? Are you working to get back to Europe and take your revenge on the Nazis?"

"I am doing just that. I have been assigned to General Montgomery's staff. He is working with the American, General Eisenhower, to devise an invasion plan. Prime Minister Churchill is very eager to get our troops to Europe and eventually to Germany."

Hoping for some crucial information, Marie continued, "The sooner we can defeat the Germans, the better for all of Europe. When will the invasion take place?"

"Oh, I am not certain. I can't really talk much about what preparations are being made, but you can be certain we are going to do everything possible to defeat Hitler and the Nazis, and soon." Just as Lynn was finishing his comment, another soldier slammed into the back of his chair, spilling beer onto the table.

The young and slightly inebriated soldier said, "Excuse me, sir." Noticing Thompson's uniform and rank, the soldier rose quickly to attention and said again, "Colonel, sir! Excuse my awkwardness, sir! May I buy you another drink, sir?"

Lynn stood and said quietly to the soldier, "Everything is fine, Corporal. No harm done, but you might want to slow down the drinking just a wee bit."

"Yes, sir! I will, sir! I will leave now! Again, my sincere apologies to you and your lovely lady." Marie politely smiled as the young soldier turned to walk away.

"Marie, I would love to continue our conversation over dinner. Harry's place might be a bit too clamorous for quiet conversation. Would you care to join me at a smaller, more intimate dinner establishment?"

Marie was encouraged. Just a slight forwardness on her part was enough to get Colonel Thompson to soften up and, hopefully, to give her the advantage in controlling the evening. Marie stood and smiled while softly slipping her hand on Thompson's elbow. She whispered, "I would love to find a quiet place to continue our conversation."

CHAPTER FORTY

After eating, Paul returned to find Coffey sitting on the end of his bunk cleaning his rifle. "Sergeant, please have the entire platoon assemble."

"Yes, sir. Should I tell them what it's about?"

"Just tell them I need to discuss our next training exercise."

It took Coffey fifteen minutes to find everyone. The entire platoon now sat in front of Lieutenant Schaefer, and by their expressions, he could tell they knew something was amiss.

Lieutenant Schaefer began, "I want to first say how proud I was of all of you today. You stayed calm, worked together and moved quickly from the beach to the ridge. I know it was only an exercise, but these are as close to the real thing as we will encounter. Getting this down perfectly just might save more of us when the real day comes."

Johnson said, "Thanks, Lieutenant. You did real good as well, but we've heard. . ."

Paul stopped him. "I think I know what you heard, Corporal." Paul waited a moment before continuing. "There were some casualties today. The live fire hit the Higgins that Dog Company was in. Lieutenant Wilkinson and seven others died. Twelve more were injured." Before anyone could speak up, Paul continued, "It is a sad, terrible event, but we all knew with using live ammo there could be casualties. Command needs to make these training exercises as real as possible in order to save lives when it really counts."

Johnson spoke up again, "We know, Lieutenant, but it still sucks."

"I hear you, Corporal. Tomorrow morning there will be a service for the dead. No practice tomorrow. We will continue exercises the following day. Command wants me to remind you that none of this is to be mentioned outside our group. Nothing will be said in letters home or to civilians outside." Prior to dismissing the men, Paul said, "Once again, I want you to know I am proud of just how far we have come as a unit. I am proud to be able to serve with all of you. Dismissed."

Before anyone moved, Sergeant Coffey asked, "Lieutenant, has command given any consideration to the safety of these Higgins?" Coffey continued, "Without trying to hit anyone, those gunners caused eighteen casualties. The Germans are going to be aiming at us as we exit those things. I'm worried about our survival rate. I hope command is as well."

Paul surveyed the men. They were nodding in agreement with Coffey. "I agree with you, Sergeant, but there will be no changes at this late date. We are riding those boats to the beach."

Everyone rose from where they were seated. Sergeant Coffey came up to Paul. "That was tough, Lieutenant, but as you said, these guys are a good group. They will get through this okay. I will keep an ear open anyway." Coffey finished speaking, "We will all be ready day after tomorrow."

"I know, Sergeant. Thanks. I am going to retire to my quarters. If you need me, you can find me there."

Just as Coffey turned back toward the unit he said, "See you tomorrow, Lieutenant, 0600."

***

Paul sat on his cot with writing paper and a clipboard on his lap. He knew he could not mention today's events but needed to write something to his parents and to Anthony. He paused for a moment and thought of Marie, realizing he missed her. He wanted another chance to hold her, maybe for the last time. He wanted to tell her about the dangers of training and about the impending invasion, but he knew that he couldn't. Really, he wanted to bolt out of camp, go to her, hold her and tell her he was falling in love with her. Just as Paul began his first letter, Sergeant Coffey knocked.

"Lieutenant, do you have a minute?" Coffey asked as he stood in the doorway.

"Certainly, Sergeant. Come in and have a seat. What's on your mind?"

"It's Private Dicatto, sir. We had an incident you should know about."

"Go on, Sergeant."

"All the guys were sitting around after chow, talking about today's events. Some of the guys were close to Wilkinson's men you know. Well, all of a sudden, Dicatto grabs his sidearm and points it around and then to his head. He's yelling that he might as well end it now. He says if he takes his own life at least he knows who pulled the trigger. Then he starts yelling about losing his brother."

Paul stood up and walked toward Coffey. "His brother?"

Coffey answered. "Yeah, no one even knew he had a brother, but something happened to his brother. He then lowered his weapon and started crying. Johnson was sitting next to him and grabbed the gun from his hand."

"Where is Dicatto now?"

"He got up and walked outside. Some of the guys went after him. You know, to make sure he didn't do something stupid. I thought you should know, sir, although I don't think you should be too hard on him. We were the last group at chow, so no one else saw the commotion. It doesn't need to go any higher, does it? I think this training and waiting is just getting to everyone."

"I agree, Sergeant. Nothing will be said about this to anyone up the chain. Go find Dicatto and have him come see me."

"Yes, sir. Thank you, sir," Coffey said and then walked out.

***

Minutes later, Coffey and Dicatto knocked on Paul's door. Coffey said, "Sir, Private Dicatto is here."

Paul walked toward the door. "Thanks, Sergeant. You may go." Paul motioned toward a chair. "Private, please have a seat."

Dicatto sat down and immediately said, "Lieutenant, sorry about all the fuss, but I am fine now. I just needed to get out of there for a bit, sir." Dicatto then asked, "Am I in trouble, sir? I sure hope not, sir. I have been training with these guys for a long time, and I don't want to leave."

Paul reassured him, "No, Private. You're not in trouble. Nothing is going to be said to anyone else. This issue will stay with our guys."

Dicatto looked visibly relieved. "Thank you, sir. That means a lot."

"What's this I hear about a brother? Sergeant Coffey said no one even knew you had a brother."

"He's was older than me. He left home at sixteen. I was only twelve. I haven't seen him since then, close to nine years now."

Paul interjected, "But the Sergeant said you mentioned that you lost him. Nine years is a long time to bring it up now."

Dicatto continued. "No, sir. I didn't lose him before. He just left. He joined the army at some point. Just before I enlisted, my folks got a letter from him. He said he was sorry that he left the way he did. He said he was doing okay and was in the army. He had switched from infantry to airborne and was in Africa. He was part of the 82nd Airborne."

"Did you or your parents get some recent information regarding him?"

"Yes, sir. He died in January. My parents got the visit and the telegram. He died jumping in at Anzio. Gets hung up in his chute and lands in a tree. A fucking tree kills him, sir. A fucking tree! Then you guys almost get it by mortars and those guys get shot up today by our own people. I just lost it. Won't happen again, sir. I am sorry I caused you any problems."

Paul replied, using Dicatto's first name, "Anthony, I'm sorry for your loss." Paul continued, "You know, Private, my brother's name is Anthony as well."

Dicatto looked up at Paul. "Really, sir? I didn't know that. In fact, I didn't know you had a brother either!"

"I guess we all have secrets we've kept from each other. Anyway, I have a brother, Anthony. He's a Marine somewhere in the Pacific. I haven't heard from him in a while. In fact, he hasn't heard from me either."

"I hope he's okay, sir."

"I do as well, Private. This training is getting to everyone. We all know men are going to die during the fight, but we are not prepared for men dying while preparing to fight." Paul's voice changed. "I need you. You're a good soldier, Anthony. You've shown that during our preparations. We are almost done here, and soon we will be in Europe. Go back to your bunk, Private. Get some sleep and in the morning, be ready to finish this job."

Private Dicatto rose and stood at attention. "Yes, sir, and thank you again for not saying anything. I don't want to leave. These guys are my family, sir."

Paul said with a smile, "Even Corporal Johnson, the Georgian redneck you wanted to take out on the crossing here, is family?"

A wide grin showed on Dicatto's face, "Yeah, even that rebel, sir. Thanks again, Lieutenant."

Paul pulled the door open. "Now get out of here, Private."

CHAPTER FORTY-ONE

Marie and Lynn walked further away from the Whitehall district. "The farther you get away from the government area the easier it is to find quiet places to eat."

"Do you know this area well?" asked Marie.

"I do. I have a flat not far from here. I use it on the nights when I am in London."

"How often do you travel between Bristol and London?"

"That depends on General Montgomery and our training exercises. Usually I am here for two to three days and then back in Bristol for a week or more. I am scheduled to leave tomorrow evening." Lynn continued. "When do you return to Bristol, Marie? Maybe we could travel back together."

Marie looked up at Lynn, "I would have loved traveling back with you, but I've already promised someone I would stay at least until the end of the week."

Lynn looked disappointed and asked, "Is this someone a male friend? Are you seeing someone?"

Marie smiled and took Lynn's hand. "Oh no! My friend is female. I am not seeing anyone. This war has taken most of the available single men." Marie gave a coy smile, "Or hadn't you noticed?"

Lynn squeezed Marie's hand. "Great! I am free until tomorrow evening. Let's begin with that quiet dinner." Lynn and Marie were standing in front of a small restaurant called The Cellar. "This restaurant is quiet, but the food is rather marginal."

"With all of the rationing taking place, all restaurant food is marginal. If it is quiet, it will be fine. I would like to hear more about you and your work with General Montgomery."

"And I would like to hear about you as well." Lynn opened the door to The Cellar for Marie, "Shall we?" The entry was a small, dimly lit landing, with a staircase descending to the restaurant below. As they negotiated the stairs, Lynn said, "This was actually the wine cellar for the large building on the corner. Back in its day, I hear the building was an exclusive hotel with an elaborate restaurant, and this cellar was connected to it."

"What happened to the hotel?" asked Marie.

"The owner's son died in the last war, and the owner lost his mind. Eventually, he lost the hotel and restaurant. A group bought the building and turned the rooms into apartments. The restaurant was divided up as well, and those rooms were also for let on a weekly basis. Later this restaurant opened up in the old wine cellar, hence the name."

Marie asked, "How do you know so much about it?"

Lynn smiled, "Well, to be quite honest, Marie, my apartment is in the old hotel."

Marie returned the smile, "Well, maybe we should take our after-dinner drinks in the leisure of your apartment. That is, unless you share the apartment with someone."

Lynn grinned widely, "That would be a wonderful idea, as I don't share the apartment with anyone. . . at the moment."

Hand in hand the two made their way into the darkness of The Cellar.

Lynn and Marie found a small booth in one of the three alcove rooms. They were the only patrons seated within the section. Marie sat and Lynn moved in next to her. "How long have you been with General Montgomery?"

"I was assigned to his staff just after his return from North Africa. We have been working closely with our American Allies in the preparation for an European invasion."

Marie asked, "Aren't the Allies already in Europe? I read about an Italian invasion."

"We are. This will be the Western invasion, and it will be larger and more powerful than the Italian invasion."

Marie sat up, pretending to be overly excited, "Will you be landing and liberating my homeland first?"

Lynn paused a moment and then said, "I can't give you any details, but feel safe knowing France will soon find itself free of German control."

Marie placed her hand on Lynn's thigh. She saw an immediate response to her gesture. "Certainly you must know a great deal of information regarding the invasion. You fill a very important post within General Montgomery's staff." Then softly she whispered, "Being French, I am just hoping the invasion will come before the start of summer. Can you tell me that much?"

"Let's just settle with the weather for a crossing is better before fall sets in again."

Marie reached over and turned Lynn's face down toward hers. With a pouting expression she said, "Well, if you can't tell me more, then I will have to settle on the fact I may be home in time for Christmas." Marie tilted her head up and kissed Lynn's cheek.

Lynn placed his arm around Marie and pulled her closer saying, "I was beginning to hope we might be able to spend Christmas together here in England."

Marie kissed Lynn's cheek again and said, "We shall see."

Throughout dinner, Marie continually attempted to steer the conversation toward the impending invasion and the exercises in Devonshire. Lynn vaguely answered a few questions but largely avoided saying any more about his work. Frustrated, Marie realized no more information would be forthcoming during their time in The Cellar. Marie's plan moved to thoughts of Lynn's apartment. Odds were good that Lynn carried information in a satchel which might be in the apartment.

Marie said, "I need to freshen my lipstick and use the facilities. I was hoping your loo would be more sanitary than the one here. That is, if you still want to have after-dinner drinks in your flat."

Lynn slid over and stood up. "That sounds delightful. I was hoping you would still consider drinks in my flat a possibility." Lynn paid the bill, and they left the restaurant walking toward the corner.

***

Once inside the building, Marie surveyed the surroundings. The entrance must have been the hotel's foyer at one time. Off to one side was a hallway that probably had led to the old restaurant but was now made up of smaller rooms. Lynn placed his hand on Marie's back and guided her toward the stairway to the left. As she moved to the stairs, Marie realized the front door was, most likely, the only way in or out of the building. It was not the best option for escape, but unfortunately, the only option.

Lynn's apartment was on the third floor. Marie thought, *too high for jumping out a window.* Whatever happened within the next hours, Marie understood she needed to be quiet, and exiting through the front door was going to be mandatory. As they approached Lynn's third-floor door, she was grateful they had not contacted any other patrons or visitors. In fact, only the waiter from The Cellar could place her with Colonel Thompson. Of course, Catherine would know about their meeting, but Catherine had not seen the two leave together. It would be difficult to tie The Cellar dinner back to introductions at Hotspur's.

Lynn turned on some lights. "The loo is just down the hallway to your right," Lynn said as he closed the door.

"Thank you so much. I will just be a minute."

"Take your time. I will get us some drinks." Lynn continued, "Scotch or some coffee with amaretto?"

Marie smiled and said, "Let's have the scotch. I am not ready for coffee."

Lynn returned the smile. "Good choice. Some Glenfiddich it will be."

Marie did need to use the loo, but while sitting she used the time to consider her options. Lynn's apartment was small. The kitchen was just an extension of the living room. The loo was five steps down the hall, and another three steps led to Lynn's bedroom. If Lynn had additional materials in the apartment, most likely they'd be in the bedroom. He carried no satchel this evening, and she did not see one in the living room. Marie needed to get into the bedroom without Lynn noticing.

When she returned, Lynn was sitting on the sofa. He stood as Marie came toward him, handing her one of the glasses of Glenfiddich. "To Catherine and our fortunate meeting this evening!"

Marie raised her glass. "And to the liberation of my country sometime soon."

After a few sips of scotch, Marie said, "Lynn, will you please excuse me again? Either the dinner or the scotch is making me feel a little nauseous. I am so sorry." Marie patted Lynn's hand. "I will only be a few moments."

"I warned you the food was not the best in London."

"You did. I do not hold you responsible." As Marie rose from the sofa, she said, "I see a radio on the table. Maybe you could find some soothing music to play. I hope I won't be long."

Marie proceeded down the hall as Lynn rose to find the music. After turning on the sink's water, she made her way to Lynn's bedroom. The room was small. A single bed protruded from the wall opposite the door, and a dresser was situated under the window on her right. Looking behind the door to the left, she saw a corner desk. She closed the door and went to the desk.

On top of the desk lay a leather satchel probably used by Lynn when traveling. Also on the desk was a pen, pencil and letter opener. Before looking in the satchel, Marie went back to the door and carefully listened. Music was playing softly. She thought about hollering to

Lynn, but reconsidered that option. *Hollering might bring his unwanted attention.* Back at the desk, she opened the satchel.

Marie dumped out the contents. There were three folders, each containing various sheets of papers. Quickly, she scanned the first. The papers were meeting notes and requisitions for equipment and supplies. There was nothing regarding training dates, landing dates, or landing areas. The second folder was empty. The third had tide and weather charts. The words May and June were written in the margin. There were two other papers in the folder. One sheet had the letters 'BIGOT' printed at the top and below a list of officers' names. The second paper was a memo from Eisenhower to Montgomery stating he would be arriving in the Devon area on 24, April.

She was not certain what all of the information meant, but it had to be important. She folded the pages from the third folder and placed them in her undergarments. Just as she was turning to leave, she heard Lynn's voice behind her. "Marie, what are you doing?"

Startled, Marie turned her head toward Lynn. "I am sorry, but after I was done, the loo had a stench. I needed some air and decided to use your room to freshen up. I hope that was acceptable."

Lynn retorted, "The water in the sink was still running. I didn't smell anything when I turned the water off." Lynn's eyes turned to the desk, "My satchel's opened! What were you looking for?"

Marie turned her head back to the desk and placed her hand on the letter opener. "I don't know. When I sat at the desk, maybe I moved the satchel. I'm sorry." Marie smiled and said, "Let's go back to the other room, sit on the couch with our drinks and listen to the beautiful music."

Lynn moved closer. Anger showed on his face. "I'm not sure what you were doing, but we are not going to be listening to music this evening. Marie, I need to take you back to my office. Our staff will question you. This is extremely disturbing to me. I must report this at once." Lynn reached for Marie's arm. "Please come with me."

In one swift motion, Marie drove the letter opener into Lynn's left elbow joint. The effect was optimal. As he screamed, Lynn's left arm fell limply to his side and his right hand reached for the opener. Swiftly, Marie kicked her right foot up into Lynn's groin. Lynn was able to turn slightly diffusing some of the kick's impact, but off balance, he fell back onto the bed.

Marie knew the room was too small for any successful altercation. In the room she would be trapped. Lynn was far too big to fight in a small space. Marie swung the satchel at him and rushed down the hall.

In the living room, she saw her coat and bag sitting on the chair ahead. Lynn appeared as Marie was pulling her knife out of her bag. She turned toward him. His left arm was still hanging at his side, the opener in his right hand. If he was still holding the opener, Marie thought, he must not have retrieved a gun in the bedroom. He was bent forward and limping slightly. There was hatred in his eyes like a wounded animal fighting to survive. Lynn was considerably larger and certainly much more powerful than Marie. If Lynn was able to grab her or corner her, she was finished. She hoped the combination of pain and anger would dull Lynn's ability to rationally defend himself.

"Who are you? What do you want?" Lynn questioned as he slowly moved toward her.

"It doesn't matter now who I am. You are hurt. Do you want to sit down?" Marie knew Lynn would never sit, but she believed by restating his injury he might subconsciously focus more on his wounds than on her. This needed to end soon. Someone walking by or in another apartment might hear the altercation and call for help.

Lynn continued moving further into the living room. "I don't want to sit down, but you can sit in that chair if you wish, pointing toward the chair holding her bag and coat. Then you can tell me what you were looking for. All the questions about the trainings and landings. You were trying to get information." Lynn continued limping forward. "You are not a French refugee are you, Marie? In fact, I imagine your name isn't even Marie." He asked, "Ist es Marie, Fräulein?"

"Very good German, Colonel." Marie backed further into the kitchen space. Spying a broom in the corner, she grabbed it with her left hand. Still holding the knife in her right hand, she moved forward toward Lynn. The broom could help her with distance control, but it was really just a prop. Lynn might have a gun in this room, so she could not let him dictate where she went. Taking the offensive, she moved toward him. Marie jabbed the broom toward Lynn's left side, and he instinctively raised his hand to grab it. When he did, he winced in pain. As Lynn dropped the broom, Marie lunged forward. Lynn swung the letter opener, but Marie blocked his attempt with her left arm and drove the knife into Lynn's left side.

Speedily, she backed away again. Lynn dropped the opener and grabbed his side. Blood was seeping out making a bright red pattern on his shirt. Marie achieved her goal. Lynn was in a rage. Breathing heavily, he lumbered toward her. *Stay in open spaces. Keep moving. Don't let him corner you.* Marie still held her knife, moving always to Lynn's left.

At the table, she picked up the bottle of scotch and smashed it down on the wood tabletop. The liquid spattered across the table. She now had two weapons, the knife and a six-inch jagged bottle. Just as she raised the bottle, Lynn came at her. Pulling his hand from his side, he grabbed for the bottle. Marie was able to turn the bottle enough to stick his hand with the jagged end. At the same time, she dropped low and swung the knife.

She stabbed, driving the knife into Lynn's thigh and then retracted it. Lynn tried to trap Marie by falling on top of her, but she was too fast. She jumped back and Lynn crashed down on the table, breaking two of the legs off as he went to the floor. Marie was behind him before he could rise to his knees. She plunged the knife into his back hoping to strike the heart from the rear. It was enough. Lynn let out a gasp as his face fell silently to the floor.

Marie pulled the knife from his back. He did not move, and she could see no signs indicating breathing. Searching the room, she found her shoes that she had kicked off in order to ease her movements. Marie placed the knife back its holder and also pulled the papers from under her clothing. She put on her coat and placed the papers in her coat pocket.

Marie was shaking and breathing hard. The fight had drained her energy. She wished she had been able to just steal the information and disappear without killing him. Closing the door, Marie saw no one in the hallway and prayed she would see no one on the way out of the old hotel.

CHAPTER FORTY-TWO

I t took more than an hour for Marie to make her way back to her flat. It was almost 2:00 a.m. and she was exhausted, but she knew she needed to leave immediately. Lynn said his plan was to leave for Bristol in the evening, but he might still have planned to go back to his London office first. If he did not show up at his London office, someone would certainly be sent to find him.

Pulling the papers from her coat, Marie placed them on the table. She discarded the BIGOT paper as the names of officers gave her no pertinent information. The only names she recognized were Montgomery, Eisenhower, and Colonel Lynn Thompson. The communiqué from Eisenhower spoke of April and his visit to Devon. She recalled Paul had previously mentioned Eisenhower and Montgomery coming to their base. The letter may just be referring to another meeting or it could possibly be the time for a major training prior to an European assault. An April training would make sense if the actual landing was going to be in May or June. May and June were the months written in the margin of the tidal charts.

Whatever this was, she needed to pass the information to Heinrich. Marie retrieved the wireless and placed it on the table. With Colonel Thompson's death, Marie considered that the Allies might change their plans completely. Although making considerable changes at this point would likely be far too costly for the Allied war effort, most probably major changes would be dismissed. Security, however, would certainly be increased in the area around Devon. Weighing these issues was not her concern. Her assignment was to gather the information and pass it on.

She cranked up the wireless and began to transmit.

Major training sometime in April, in Devon, near Dartmouth.
Eisenhower and Montgomery to be present.
Possible invasion May or June.
Location of invasion uncertain.
U.S. Colonel dead.
Leaving London immediately.

Marie placed the wireless back into its hiding place and at the same time, gathered another hundred pounds. She decided to sleep for a few hours and then take a train back to Dartmouth. She would stay in Dartmouth for one more week. Even if Marie was tied to Colonel Thompson, it would take at least a week to find Catherine and Harry and connect Marie to Dartmouth. Just as Marie was lying down on her bed, she was surprised by a knock at the door.

CHAPTER FORTY-THREE

Marie moved off the bed and onto the floor, slipped her hand under the bed and grabbed her suitcase. From within the suitcase, she snatched the Beretta. A second knock. The door had no eyehole to look through. It was nearly three in the morning. Marie could not think of anyone she knew having a reason to come to her apartment at this hour. She had been away for more than two months and had returned only two days ago.

Two possible scenarios filtered through Marie's mind. First, someone might have followed her from Colonel Thompson's apartment. If so, the person or persons probably would not knock. The second possibility was that it was British Intelligence, the SOE. She thought it was possible they had uncovered information on her and had been waiting for her to return. She remembered the three men who had been standing across the street on the first day she arrived. They could have been watching for her and were checking to see if she, in fact, had returned.

In the end, Marie decided the best decision was to remain quiet and wait to see if the person at the door entered or left. Taking no chances, Marie stayed on her knees behind the bed with the Beretta pointing toward the door. No third knock broke the morning silence. A few hours of sleep were now out of the question. Staying here was no longer an option. Marie rose from her knees and opened the suitcase. After gathering the remainder of the money, she closed the suitcase.

One other thought now emerged. Could someone have picked up the signal from her wireless? She couldn't take a chance. The suitcase and the wireless needed to be destroyed. Destroying the wireless meant she no longer would have contact with Heinrich or with the people arranging her escape from England. She knew the escape route was through the port city of Ramsgate, just north of Dover. *One week in Dartmouth and then escape through Ramsgate.*

Marie slipped on her coat, placing the knife in her coat pocket. Next, she lifted a cloth travel bag over her head, letting it hang against her left hip. With her left hand, she slid the suitcase off the bed and walked over to the door. Holding the Beretta in her right hand, she set the suitcase down and used her left hand to unlatch the door and turn the knob. The hallway was clear. If someone was watching her apartment, both exits would be compromised, but the rear provided the best opportunity. The back door had a window that would allow Marie to scan the back alley. She saw no movement, but it was still dark. Morning daylight was still more than an hour away.

Waiting around was not a good option. Hesitantly, she opened the back door and crept out into the early morning London cold. Although almost a month into spring, the morning dampness still chilled her face and hands. The gun was in her right hand, hanging at her hip. Within the first few steps off the porch, Marie felt she was ill prepared to defend herself carrying both a suitcase and travel bag. Fortunately, no one approached. Exiting the alley, Marie made her way out to Dorscher Road, the street behind the apartment. At this time of morning, the street was empty of pedestrians. The last time she was in London, she had noticed a vacant alley just a block over.

Finding a suitable location in the alley, Marie set the suitcase down. Lowering herself between some old boxes, she looked down the alley. No one was following her. She relaxed just a bit. Picking up the suitcase, she continued on. At various locations within the alley, Marie found piles of trash. At each location, she took some clothing items out of her suitcase and mixed them with rubbish already littering the alley. The last stop was the back of an auto repair garage. Mixed within the garbage were dirty rags. She could smell oil and gasoline on the rags. Opening the suitcase, she stuffed it with the dirty rags.

By now there were lights on in some of the buildings, but she encountered no one in the alley or along the street. The vacant lot she was in was overgrown with weeds and had more trash scattered about. Marie took a few minutes gathering paper from the lot and burying the suitcase in a combination of oily rags and paper. Marie placed the transmitter in the middle of the rags. She struck a match on her Beretta and dropped it on the rag and paper pile. The oil and gas ignited and engulfed the suitcase in an inferno of black, sooty smoke and flames. Marie slipped the travel bag back over her head and exited the lot. Marie waited one block over and watched the smoke continue to rise. By the time she heard anyone make noise regarding the fire, the suitcase and the surrounding lot were fully engulfed.

CHAPTER FORTY-FOUR

The service for the dead soldiers began at 0800. General Walters, from General Eisenhower's staff, expressed his condolences on behalf of The General. "These men died preparing for the greatest invasion in the history of military engagements. Dying in preparation is no different than dying in battle. These men are heroes to our cause. We will remember them for their courage under fire. They are and will remain our brothers. We will carry on their fight and we will win this war."

A bugler began the playing of taps that was followed by a rifle salute. There were no coffins and no one knew what had happened to the bodies. Paul doubted the remains would be shipped home anytime soon, if at all. In fact, Paul believed command would not even notify the families of their deaths until after the invasion.

Some men stayed around for additional Sunday services while others returned to their barracks. A meeting for officers was scheduled for 1030 hours. As Paul approached the barracks, Coffey and Dicatto stood up. "At ease," said the Lieutenant.

"Sir," began Dicatto. "What happens now? More practice? When do you think we will move out to the mainland?"

"I'm am no more certain about a time than you are. Officers are having a meeting in about an hour. I hope to know more at that time. For now, just relax. Once this thing starts for good, you are going to be wishing for days like this."

"Yeah, probably so, Lieutenant," Dicatto said as he sat back down on the bench.

Paul turned toward Coffey. "Sergeant, have the men all gathered at 1130 hours. I don't think this meeting will last an hour, but whatever information I get, I will pass on to them at that time."

"Will do, Lieutenant." Paul opened the door and walked to his room while Coffey sat back down next to Dicatto.

Dicatto took out a cigarette and lit it. "What do you think, Sarge? Will command stop risking our lives practicing and get us into what we signed up for?"

Coffey answered, "Yeah, I think everyone has had enough, but command is not going to let this practice be the last one. I'm guessing we have another big one coming before we ship out. Let's see what the Lieutenant has to say later." Coffey leaned back and closed his eyes.

***

Major Poder approached the podium and all the officers took their seats. "Gentlemen, it is time to look ahead. This training has not been easy, but it has been necessary. Each platoon has worked hard and sacrificed a great deal to get us to this point. I know everyone, including me, is ready to end this and move out for Europe." Low murmurs and shuffling sounds were heard throughout the room.

The Major continued. "Let's quiet down. I want to answer the question on everyone's mind. When do we ship out? Unfortunately, I cannot answer that. Currently command is looking at tides and weather, but I can tell you it will happen before the end of June." The noise grew louder as Major Poder finished drinking a glass of water. Major Poder pounded the glass on the podium. The room quieted once again.

"In two weeks we will be conducting Exercise Tiger, most likely our last training exercise. Tiger will involve all branches of service in a combined assault."

Someone in the front stood and asked, "Can you give us the details of Tiger, sir?"

"I am about to do that," retorted Poder in a gruff tone. "On April 22, you will be taken to an assembly area near Plymouth. You will receive additional supplies and boarding assignments. You will be divided into two groups. The first will board transports on the 25th. The second group will board the 26th. Ships will set out for Lyme Bay. The navy has been ordered to take a long, looping route to Slapton Beach. This is to help you get accustomed to the travel time at sea crossing the English Channel." The room turned deadly quiet. The Major continued. "The exercise will commence with air bombardment of the hillsides and beyond followed by ship bombardment of the beachhead. Airborne troops will parachute in early on the 26th. While the ships are firing, the first wave will descend into their Higgins. Just as in the previous practice, there will be two waves of beach assaults. You will be informed which wave number you are in later. Troops will make their way up the beach to assigned rendezvous locations."

Someone asked, "What about those leaving Plymouth on the 26th?"

Major Poder answered, "The second group will stay on the LSTs and will come ashore with the tanks when the LSTs beach."

Paul stood. "Will there be live firing again, sir?"

"Yes, Lieutenant, there will, but we will monitor the tides more carefully."

Another lieutenant rose. "What information can we take back to our men, sir?"

Major Poder answered, "You can let them know of the training. You should also tell them you will be moving to new quarters in a few days. Gentlemen, this is it. Generals Eisenhower and Bradley will be here. If they are satisfied, we take it next to Hitler."

The officers began to stir again. "One more item," interrupted Major Poder. "As mentioned, there are two departure groups. Your departure information is tacked on the wall. See it as you exit. Remember, no one is to mention our movement or training outside this base." Major Poder ended with, "That is all."

There wasn't much chitchat by the officers as they funneled out the door, stopping only long enough to check their departure date. Everyone was surprised and maybe shocked at the thought of ending training. One more practice and then off to France or wherever the landing site would be. Officers hurried out of the room, anxious to relay information to their platoons.

It was only 1115 hours, but the entire platoon was waiting outside the barracks when Lieutenant Schaefer walked up. Smiling, Lieutenant Schaefer said, "I have very good news. After more than three months, this training is about to end!" Shouts went up from the group.

"When do we head out, sir?"

Schaefer continued, "Settle down! We have one more training, codename Exercise Tiger. In four days, we will move our location to somewhere outside Plymouth. We board a transport on the 26th. Our part in the exercise begins sometime early on April 27 with a beach landing commencing the morning of April 28. Exercise Tiger will be a full dress rehearsal. The LSTs will simulate the Channel crossing by taking a long, looping route to the target zone. While in transit, we will hear air and naval bombardments."

Lieutenant Schaefer stopped for a moment watching his men's expressions. Most were fidgety, but all eyes still focused on him. "There has been a change in our position. Being a part of the second departure group means we will not land in Higgins Boats. We will stay onboard the LST and land with the tanks coming ashore."

Johnson asked, "How come, Lieutenant? We were one of the top groups each time. Why aren't we with the first groups landing?"

Paul looked at Johnson, "We weren't just one of the best; we were the best! However, orders are orders, and we will follow them without question." No one looked happy about the change in orders. Looking at their faces, Paul said, "Actually, I wasn't looking forward to riding in one of those flimsy, wooden death boats." Many of the men nodded in agreement. "If General Eisenhower is satisfied with both landings, we may move to Europe by June."

Johnson spoke again, "What do we do for the next few days, sir?"

"You get your gear in order. Check everything out. Anything not functioning gets either fixed or replaced." Paul hesitated then added, "Oh, and on Wednesday of this week, we have a six-hour pass to town." Paul smiled and ended with, "Enjoy."

Sergeant Coffey walked over to Schaefer. "Will you be coming with us on Wednesday night, sir?"

Paul grinned, "That depends, Sergeant. Would you be considering drinking and dining at the Hinde?"

Sergeant Coffey said, "Lieutenant, I can't think of any better place to spend the evening."

Both men smiled. Coffey ended the conversation, "Sir, I will make sure all the equipment is in top working condition."

"Thank you, Sergeant, and remember to tell the men nothing is to be said about the training outside of this area." Paul opened the door to his quarters and entered.

PART III

EXERCISE TIGER

CHAPTER FORTY-FIVE

England, 1944

The train and bus rides to Dartmouth were both uneventful. There were very few passengers, and no one seemed to take much notice of Marie sitting near the back of the car. The earlier door knock still bothered her, however. *What were the chances of someone being up that early in the morning and knocking on my door by mistake?* Marie realized that the likelihood of a mistaken knock was remote. It was more likely someone would be back to search her room and could possibly be following her even at this moment. Although, if she was being followed, why did they let her burn the suitcase in the empty lot? The best answer was whoever was watching wanted to find her contact.

The events of yesterday and today were certainly troubling, but they did not alter her current plans. She would stay one week in Dartmouth, find out anything further and get to Ramsgate. Her contact in Ramsgate would have a wireless to relay any new information to Heinrich. If someone were, in fact, following her, she would silence them as well.

Marie walked up the steps to Mrs. Sawyer's home. The trip from the bus station normally took fifteen minutes. Today, Marie took almost two hours stopping in a number of retail establishments, pretending to be shopping but always looking back out through the windows. No one caught her eye, but she still felt something inside that alarmed her. The front door was unlocked, and as she entered, she heard

Mrs. Sawyer in the kitchen. Marie hollered, "Mrs. Sawyer, it's Marie. I am back from London."

Mrs. Sawyer came out as she was wiping her hands on her apron. She approached Marie, gave her a hug and said, "Welcome back, dear. I hope that all went well in London with the apartment and all."

Marie returned the hug. "Yes, yes. Everything is fine."

"Good. I am just making some supper. There is certainly enough for two. Come and join me. You can tell me all about London."

"And you can tell me about your niece's new baby," Marie continued. "Let me just put my coat and bag in my room. I'll be right out."

Marie closed the bedroom door behind her. She took the knife and Beretta out of her coat pockets and hung up her coat. To her knowledge, Mrs. Sawyer had never been nosy or even entered her room without permission. Taking a chance that her room was still private and secure, Marie placed the knife back in the top dresser drawer and the gun in the nightstand. As she was walking back out, Marie stopped for a moment at the dresser and held the picture of her father and mother. Whispering, she said, "Papa, what have we all become? What have I become?" Marie set the picture back down and walked out to the kitchen.

Two settings were on the table, and Mrs. Sawyer was dishing something from the stove. "Please have a seat, dear. Pour us some wine, would you, dear?"

Marie poured the wine and sat down. Mrs. Sawyer placed the two bowls of lamb stew on the table and proceeded to sit. "Marie, is something wrong? You look somewhat out of sorts if I may say so."

Marie said, "No. No. It is nothing. I'm just tired from travel. It is so good to be back." She smiled and continued, "Mrs. Sawyer, you have been so nice to me from the first day I walked up to your home. I never told you, but my mother died when I was quite young, and then it was only my father and me. Being with you has made me realize just how much I've missed by not having time with my mother."

A tear came to Mrs. Sawyer's eye. "And I never told you that my late husband and I never were able to have children, only nieces and nephews. You have been like the daughter I never had."

Marie raised her glass, "To family then."

Mrs. Sawyer raised her glass as well, "To family."

Marie took a sip of wine. Setting her glass down she asked, "So, do you have a new great-niece or great-nephew?"

"Great-nephew. It was a long labor for my niece, almost 22 hours. In the end, everything worked out fine. His name is George, and he looks very much like his father. I made extra stew to take to my niece's tomorrow. If you have time, maybe you would like to join me."

Marie paused for a moment as she thought of just how little time she had to gather any new information. Reconsidering, Marie said, "I would love to join you. I will have an hour in the morning before I go back over to check in with Mr. Donaldson at the Hinde."

"Very well. We will plan to leave at eight tomorrow. You can be back over to the Hinde before the afternoon crowd arrives." Mrs. Sawyer blew softly on her stew and said, "Now tell me all about London."

CHAPTER FORTY-SIX

It was eleven when Marie walked into the Hinde. Mr. Donaldson was working behind the bar. The bar was full, but the restaurant area was nearly empty. Donaldson looked up and caught Marie's eyes. "Marie! Welcome back."

Before Donaldson could say more, Marie responded, "Hello, Mr. Donaldson. Monty sends his best and says you need to be ready for the call."

Donaldson laughed. "Maybe in the last one, my dear, but I don't have much to offer Monty anymore."

"You are much too hard on yourself, Mr. Donaldson. I bet you could fight with the best of them."

"Maybe so, Marie, but let's hope we can end this bloody war before they need me."

Marie came behind the bar and offered to fill an empty pint for a thirsty patron. "I came by today to let you know that I am back and available to work whenever you need me. I see you are not too busy now. Maybe later in the week?"

Donaldson walked over to Marie. "Actually, if you have time, I could use you right now for a couple of hours. My ears at City Hall tell me the entire base will be taking leave Tuesday or Wednesday evening."

Marie was elated and responded, "I'll be glad to help out for as long as you need me today." Then she asked, "What else have you heard about the training?"

Donaldson motioned for Marie to follow him. Stopping in the hallway just off the bar, Donaldson turned to Marie. "Something big is about to happen. My friend told me this will be the soldiers' last leave. After Wednesday they all head for Plymouth. There is going to be a big training exercise at the end of the month. They say the invasion will take place sometime before the middle of June."

Marie showed surprise and happiness. "That is wonderful news! The war may finally be ending soon!" The information Donaldson reported coincided with the information Marie garnered from Colonel Thompson. Mr. Donaldson told Marie he would be back as soon as possible. Then he walked down the hallway, past the loo and out the back door. Marie returned to the bar. As she worked, Marie mentally made plans to leave Dartmouth after Wednesday night.

She was delighted to hear the information already transmitted to Heinrich was accurate. No further information would be gained here. Staying away from London for a couple more days might be wise.

The next couple of hours were routine. The bar remained busy with mostly the regular local group of older working-class men from around the tavern. It was good to be back. Marie liked the work and engaging in lively banter with locals. As she worked, however, Marie kept an eye out for new patrons or for anyone taking a prodigious interest in her.

Donaldson returned to the pub from the rear. Two employees walked in just behind him. The tables were beginning to fill, and soon patrons would be ordering supper. Marie said to Donaldson as he walked up, "I can stay longer if you need me."

"I think we can handle the crowd tonight, Marie. My wife is on her way right now. She and I will handle the cooking, and I think two servers and a bartender will be enough. I will need you tomorrow and Wednesday night, however."

Marie finished wiping up some moisture from the bar and said, "I'm off then. I'll see you tomorrow evening." She questioned, "Tomorrow, same time as usual, half past three?"

"Make it three," said Donaldson. "Might take slightly longer to get enough food prepared for the anticipated crowd."

"Will do." Marie turned at the door, "Say, Mr. Donaldson, has Charly been working? Will she be in tomorrow as well?"

"It's been light for the past few days, but Charly has worked some afternoons. She will be here tomorrow and again on Wednesday."

"Thanks again, Mr. Donaldson. I will see you tomorrow." Marie closed the door behind her and began to walk back toward Mrs. Sawyer's.

Three blocks from home, Marie had a prescient feeling. She doubted she had been traced back here from London, but the feeling was overpowering. Instead of going home, Marie turned down by the Dart. The river was beautiful during the spring as it ran swiftly over the landscape and out to Lyme Bay. While sitting at the river's edge, Marie continually scanned the area for pedestrians taking a lingering interest in her.

Her uneasiness persisted. Marie wasn't satisfied she had not been followed. She stayed longer and waited until dusk before walking home. Taking a circuitous route, Marie backtracked at various points and stopped to observe those walking behind her. It was after 7:00 p.m. when she opened the door. Mrs. Sawyer was asleep in front of the radio with the music playing softly. Marie locked the front door and quietly ascended the stairs to her room. Keeping the lights off and closing the bedroom door, Marie made her way to the wall beside the back window. Slightly parting the drapery, Marie searched the backyard and surrounding area for movement. Satisfied that no one was watching, Marie changed into nightclothes and fell onto her bed, exhausted.

CHAPTER FORTY-SEVEN

Tuesday was long and arduous for the 557th. Groups taking leave that evening were anxious in anticipation. Those taking leave on Wednesday were just trying to get through Tuesday and on to Wednesday. Coffey's men were haltingly checking weapons and supplies and sorting items to be used in Exercise Tiger.

Coffey was absent most of the morning. He returned just prior to lunch carrying a cardboard box. Johnson was sitting outside the barrack door smoking a cigarette. As he approached, Coffey said, "Private, grab as many of the guys as you can. I have some extra supplies for everyone." Johnson jumped up, stuck his head inside the barracks and hollered for the men to assemble.

Most of the men were inside, sitting on their cots. Coffey laid the box down. "I found some wool socks and wool sweaters. Cut these up and use them again as protection for the rifles. Everyone make sure they have two socks. If your partner is not here, grab a pair for him as well."

Men began rummaging through the box while Coffey continued giving additional information. "After lunch we will assemble back here. We're getting our delivery of life vests. Someone is supposed to deliver the vests and explain, once again, how to properly wear them."

Dicatto spoke up, "Gee, Sarge, how hard can it be? It's a life vest."

Coffey said, "I don't know, but the navy wants us to get the instructions. All of you, including Dicatto, will be here after lunch."

Sergeant Coffey bent down and picked up one sweater and two socks. "I will see you all back here later."

***

Each man was given a life vest and told to sit. Everyone listened, although somewhat hesitantly, while the petty officer explained the proper use of the M1926 lifebelt. "This unit is the M1926 lifebelt although it works like a vest and not a belt. It attaches around your chest under your armpits. The belts can either be blown up by the CO_2 cartridges attached or manually by mouth."

O'Shea shouted, "Then why call them belts?" Murmuring to those around him, "Fucking navy imbeciles."

Just as the petty officer was about to answer, Dicatto lifted his head and opened his eyes. "With these on, we will be floating ducks for those Gerry machine gun mounts. It will be like a fucking arcade game for them."

Johnson spoke as well, "If we find ourselves in the water, sir, why can't we just swim to shore? It can't be that far."

The petty officer looked annoyed. "Two reasons. First, you may be onboard a ship at sea when you find yourself in the water. Second, the water will be extremely cold. Most of you will become incapacitated within minutes of hitting water of this temperature."

Now under his breath, Dicatto said, "Jesus, fucking navy is afraid that they can't even get us to the landing site."

The petty officer continued with the explanation. "The common mistake is to consider these as belts. Remember, to perform as designed, they need to be worn up under the armpits. When properly placed, the belt will keep your head above water should you blackout or become unable to swim." The petty officer finished with, "If there are no questions, I will be continuing to the next group. Good luck. Let's hope no one needs to rely on these."

CHAPTER FORTY-EIGHT

By Wednesday at 1600 hours, everyone was showered, shaved, doused with cologne and ready to get to town. The thought that this would be their last leave before shipping out to Europe was not lost on anyone. As Sergeant Coffey and Lieutenant Schaefer approached the platoon, everyone stood at attention. Lieutenant Schaefer immediately responded, "As you were." The lieutenant continued, "Last night, men. Everyone is on their best behavior. We can not afford to have anyone in the brig or in the Dartmouth jail tonight." Lieutenant Schaefer finished, "Have a good time and be back at 2200 hours sharp. Remember no discussions about the training. Everyone load up."

Men laughed and jostled each other as they piled into the back of the transport. Someone hollered from the back, "Sergeant, you and the Lieutenant make sure you behave yourselves. We can't afford to have you taken in by the local officials or MP's either." A loud roar of laughter followed. Smiling, Sergeant Coffey jumped into the back and gave two solid fist pounds on the back gate. Sluggishly, the truck rolled down the camp road toward town.

***

Paul and John opened the door to the Hinde and noticed a smaller crowd than expected. Marie was working at the bar, and Charly was out on the floor wiping up a table. As the two walked in, Charly looked up and waved for them to come over. She gave each man a hug and kissed John. "Where is everyone tonight?" asked John.

"It's still early, but business has been slow the past week. Last night's crew and your guys are the majority of our business right now." Charly sadly continued, "And we hear that this may be your last night."

John gave Charly a hug and said, "Maybe so, but we have six hours tonight!" John kissed Charly again. While still holding her closely, John asked, "Any chance you might get a little time off this evening?"

Charly said, "I can leave after my performance around nine." Then she asked, "What time are you due back?"

"The truck comes at 10. It gives us one hour alone."

"Good. We can go back to my place."

Paul pushed the chair into John's legs. "Excuse me, Sergeant. Would you ask the lady if a soldier might get a drink sometime before we ship out?"

Charly pulled away from John. "Sorry, Paul. I will get you a beer and make certain Marie knows you came in."

As he sat down, Paul smiled and said, "Thanks, Charly."

Marie came over with the two pints. As she approached, Paul stood. After setting down the drinks, Marie reached her arms around Paul's neck and kissed him. "I missed you!"

Paul kissed her again. "I missed you as well. Charly told John she has some time free tonight. Any chance you do as well?"

"Not as of now, but I will check later. I do have some breaks. I will let you know when I am free." Marie took Paul's chin in her soft hand, gently kissed his lips and said again, "I missed you."

Paul and John spent the next three hours drinking and waiting for the few moments that Charly or Marie were able to break away and sit with them. Paul found out that Marie had returned to London and released her flat to the military. "I guess Dartmouth will be home for a while now. Charly and I are considering finding a house to rent together."

John said, "Great!"

Marie replied, "I think so as well. It will help us pass the time while you two are gone. We will be able to share your letters and support each other while eagerly awaiting your safe return."

Paul took Marie's hand. "I hope it will not be for long."

Marie placed her hand on Paul's, "It will always be too long." Just as she said it, she looked away from Paul. She withdrew her hand while her eyes opened wider.

Seeing the concern in her face, Paul asked, "Marie, what is it?"

Marie, realizing that she was shaken, responded, "I'm not certain. The man that just walked in and sat at the end of the bar looks like a cousin I haven't seen since I left France."

Paul turned to look. "Let's go over and see."

Marie immediately grabbed Paul's hand and said, "No! No! If it is not, I don't want to make a fool of myself. Let me just stay here while Charly performs. I will consider approaching him when Charly is done."

The man at the bar was one of the three men Marie had seen standing outside her London apartment. It would be too much of a coincidence to think he just showed up in Dartmouth. *How did he find me here?* It made no difference how. He was here now, and his two friends most likely were here as well. They probably divided up and were hitting all of the bars searching for her. He looked around while drinking his beer. Thus far, he showed no sign he had seen her. She needed time to come up with a plan.

It was good that John was lost in Charly's performance, but Paul continued to talk. Marie tried to listen while at the same time she was making plans to either escape or confront the man at the bar. Charly finished her singing and waved for John. John excused himself. "Sorry guys, but I have about an hour with Charly until we leave." John said to Paul, "I will see you back at the truck, Lieutenant."

Somewhat angered, Paul said, "Look, Marie, you've stayed here long enough. You should have already gone back to work, and you certainly have not paid much attention to anything that I have said. Just go over and see if it is your cousin."

Marie said, "You're right. I have acted poorly. I will go see." She leaned in and kissed him. "I'm sorry. I should have been more attentive to you. Let me take care of this and see if I can get away."

Marie stood and walked to the far end of the bar, grabbing the arm of another waitress on the way. Paul watched as Marie spoke to the waitress. At the bar, Marie wrote something on a paper and handed it to the waitress. Surprising Paul, Marie did not approach the man at the bar. Instead, she walked through the back toward the loo and out the back door.

CHAPTER FORTY-NINE

The patron opened the note the waitress had just placed in front of him. *I want to turn myself in. I have information that can help you. I don't want my employer to know. I will wait out back for you.* He closed the note, placed it in his coat pocket and threw two quid on the bar.

Marie saw the back door open slowly, a revolver leading through the opening. The man quickly stepped out and to his right as Marie stood across from him with her arms slightly raised. "No need for a gun. I'll not cause any problems. I'm tired of running."

"Good for you. Now turn around and place your hands behind you." With the gun still pointing at Marie, he walked slowly forward.

Marie turned, but as she did, she used her right arm to sweep a stack of wooden crates over. The movement worked. The crates fell forward. For an instant, the man took his eyes off Marie. Instantly, she drove her left foot up into the man's gun hand, dislodging it and sending it flying back toward the doorway. Without hesitating, Marie dropped her left foot back down and spun. Her right foot found his knee. The man screamed with pain and lurched forward grabbing the knee. Marie sensed he was not trained for combat as all his moves were defensive ones. He must have believed the gun would be enough to subdue her. He was gravely mistaken.

As he bent down to grab his injured knee once again, Marie brought the palm of her right hand crashing forward into his nose. She felt the cartilage give under the force. He dropped to his knees and then fell facedown on the hard dirt. Marie moved to retrieve the gun from the ground. As she reached to pick up the gun, Marie glanced back to make certain her assailant was still down.

Although a skilled fighter, Marie had made one mistake. She had focused only on the assailant and, therefore, did not hear a second man coming down the alley. Just as her hand found the revolver, the second man dove into her. Marie fell sideways as the second assailant grabbed for her arms. On top of her, he used a knee to pin her left arm, and his left hand struggled to control the gun in her right hand. A powerful fist smashed into her cheek. She tried hard to focus on holding the gun as a second right punch found her face.

Suddenly, a third man flew through the air and pounced on her assailant. They both spun to the side with their arms and legs swinging wildly. Still clutching the gun, Marie sat up. She tried to clear her head, which throbbed, and her left eye was closing from the punch. Blood seeped from her nose. Glancing back, Marie observed that the first assailant was still down and the two other men continued their battle. The third man was under the second and was taking a beating similar to hers. Marie now realized that the third man was Paul. He must have come out when he saw the patron follow her out the back door.

Marie raised the gun and fired. The round's impact knocked the assailant off Paul, and he collapsed on the hard ground. Paul rose slowly and looked at the bleeding man and then at Marie. She stood, still holding the gun on her assailant. Before Paul spoke, Marie said, "I came out back to get away from the man at the bar, but he had some-one waiting out back. They attacked me."

"Why? Why would these men want to hurt you? You had that wait-ress give him a note. I watched you."

Marie cried. "Paul, these men attacked me when I was in London. I was able to escape from them, but they followed me here. I don't know why they are trying to hurt me."

Paul stood and Marie rushed toward him, throwing her arms around his neck. "We must call the police, Marie."

"No! No! Paul, you cannot become involved in this. If the police or MP's find you here they will take you in for questioning. You will be removed from your men while the police investigate. You must leave here, now! Go! I will call the police after you have gone."

Clutching Marie, Paul said, "Marie, I can't just leave you here. I must tell the police what happened. I will tell them you were attacked and were defending yourself. I can support your story and let the authorities know the man you shot was on top of you and assaulting you."

Marie pulled back slightly and held Paul's face in her hands. She kissed him, waited a moment and kissed him again. "Paul, you know that I am right. You must go now before anyone sees you here." Tears and blood were mixing together and rolling down her face.

A flash of Major Poder's stern words that any further issues with Coffey or Paul would result in a court martial caused Paul to reconsider. Paul touched Marie's bruised eye and bloody cheek. Sliding his hand from her cheek, Paul cupped Marie's chin and softly kissed her. "I love you. I don't want to leave you like this. I want to help you."

"I want that too, but now is not that time. You have already saved my life. Now you must go."

Paul and Marie hugged each other. "I will write as soon as I can. Let me know as soon as possible that you are safe. I love you."

Marie said, "I know you do. Now go!"

Paul turned and ran out of the alley.

***

Finding an unlocked storage room behind another of the buildings in the alley, Marie worked rapidly. She went to the first assailant and found a faint pulse. She dragged him into the room and found some rope to tie him up. The second assailant was dead. Blood had stopped seeping from his body, but there was a significant amount pooled under his body. She dragged him into the room as well and did her best to cover the blood with dirt.

She must leave Dartmouth now! By morning, the two men would be found if not sooner. She thought of the third man out there somewhere. He was most likely watching either her house or the bus station. This was not the way Marie had planned to exit Dartmouth, but her training had prepared her for making abrupt changes. Hans had always said, *"Being able to make changes quickly keeps you alive."*

She spent a half hour circling the house and making certain that it was not being watched. Up in her room, Marie packed her travel bag. She slid the knife into the holder and placed the revolver she had taken from the assailant in the alley into her bag. The Beretta, retrieved from the nightstand, was placed in her coat pocket. No need for secrets. Anyone that confronted her now would die. Marie wrote two letters. One was to Mrs. Sawyer. She apologized for leaving so abruptly, and in the envelope she left some money.

She also asked Mrs. Sawyer to hold the second letter and to give it to an American serviceman that might come looking for her. On the outside of the second envelope she wrote the words "Lieutenant Paul Schaefer". Marie placed the two envelopes on the table in the foyer as she quietly left.

It was now well after midnight and too late for buses. The earliest bus was, most likely, a morning bus. She hoped to catch it before the two bodies were found.

As she had done at the boarding house, Marie took time to search the surrounding area looking for the third man. She found him across the street and down two buildings from the bus station. He was sitting alone at a table, sipping tea. Marie walked further down the street and crossed safely out of distance. Fortunately, these businesses had back alleys similar to the one at the Hinde. She found the cafe's back door. Marie walked quietly inside. There were very few customers or workers to be seen at this late hour. One worker did approach, however, and Marie said that she was meeting the gentleman sitting near the front. The worker nodded, and Marie made her way to the table.

Marie came up behind the man and pulled out a chair. "Good evening," Marie said as she sat down. She pulled enough of the revolver out of her coat pocket for the man to see. Looking directly into his

eyes, Marie coldly said, "You don't want to die right here, right now."
Marie continued. "Smile for the waitress when she comes over. Tell her
that your friend would like some tea as well." She finished by saying,
"Also, you will want to continue to keep both of your hands above the
table."

The waitress came over and received the order for tea. When the
waitress was gone, the man began to ask, "How did . . ."

Marie stopped him. "Your friends found me, but it did not end
well for them. If you cooperate, you live. If you don't, you die. It is
rather simple. I may be captured, but will live my days in a cell. You, my
friend, will not see another English sunrise."

Marie watched him as she spoke. He was scared. She hoped to use
his fear to her advantage. When the tea came, Marie took the cup in
her left hand, always keeping her right hand in her coat pocket. "Why
were you watching my London flat?"

"You did not return to re-register. In researching your paperwork,
there were some discrepancies noticed. We traced you to the flat but
could not locate you. My directors feared that you might be a spy."

"And how did you find me here?"

"Colonel Thompson was found dead."

Marie stopped him. It was as she figured. They traced her back
through Thompson and Hotspur's.

Marie finished her tea. She had not eaten all evening and was hungry as well, but the tea would have to be enough. "We are going now.
Leave enough money on the table. Then you will get up, and we will
leave by the front. If you don't do exactly as I say . . ." She paused.
"Well, you will, because you don't want to die for this."

They both rose and walked out into the early morning darkness. "To
your right, please. Let's walk down the street." Marie had him walk just
in front of her as they moved away from the bus station. They walked
three blocks over to the river. At this hour, Dartmouth was deserted.
They had not seen another person while walking the three blocks.

The river's edge was just as deserted. Boats were tied up all along
the river. Marie stopped alongside one of the boats. There were coils

of rope stacked on deck. "Let's climb onboard this boat. Be careful now."

The man climbed up, followed closely by Marie. "Pick up the rope and open the hatch to go below."

"Why are we going down there?"

"Just do as you're told. Move now!"

He grabbed the rope, and they both descended the stairs. They were standing inside a small compartment. There was a bench and table to their right, and in the front was a small stove. The compartment was for cooking, eating and sleeping. The bench probably doubled as a bed. Marie said, "Sit on the floor."

She pointed to the rope. "Use the rope and tie your feet and legs together. Make certain it is tight." When she was satisfied with his progress, she said, "Now roll over on your stomach and place your hands behind you." Once again, he complied. He started to turn his head to the side, and Marie said sternly, "Keep your face looking down at the floor!" He turned his head back with his nose touching the wood plank.

Marie bent down and swung the gun at his head, smashing it into the back of his skull. He let out a soft sound as his arms and head went limp. She felt his neck and found a pulse. Marie knelt beside him and tied his arms behind him. She also checked to make certain that his feet were indeed secure. When she was satisfied he was not going to be a problem for the next few hours, Marie curled up on the bench and fell asleep.

CHAPTER FIFTY

Marie woke to find daylight breaking. She sat up and looked at her foe. He was still out, but every now and again she saw his body twitch. He was making occasional moaning sounds. She checked to ensure the gag and ties were tightly secured and then went out the hatch to the deck above.

People were commencing to move along the river's edge. She waited until it looked clear enough and then moved down off the boat. She hoped no one would be using the boat anytime soon, but there was no way to know.

Swiftly, she made her way to the bus station and found an employee working the ticket counter. The most likely escape route was through Totnes, back to London, and then to the coast.

Stepping up to the counter, Marie said, "One ticket to Bristol, please." She decided that a longer, more indirect route might actually be the safest. Bristol was northwest while London was to the east.

The clerk handed her the ticket and said, "That bus will be leaving in one hour, Miss."

Marie picked up the ticket, handing the clerk three pounds. "Thank you so much." Marie walked across the street to wait the hour in a small cafe. She chose a different cafe than the one she had visited the previous night.

She had not eaten since early evening the night before, and she was in need of food and drink. Once she was seated, Marie ordered tea, eggs and a muffin. While consuming her simple foodstuff, Marie began to think about her escape through Bristol and Birmingham to

Ramsgate. *Yes, the best way to the coast is through the midlands. They will be looking for me to leave quickly. It will be safer for me to move slowly and take my time.*

She sipped the hot tea and also took a bite of muffin that was generously smeared with marmalade. All she needed to do now was wait for her bus and hope that her luck would not run out.

CHAPTER FIFTY-ONE

Paul sat on the edge of his cot. Six days had passed since the incident at the Hinde, and he still could not shake it from his thoughts. He desperately wanted to know if Marie was all right and if the police believed her account of the assault. Surely, they would see her face was swollen and bruised, but how would they account for a young woman successfully defending herself against two men? Unfortunately, there was also the gun. Paul had tried to secure information about the incident before they left for Plymouth, but he was unsuccessful.

The 557th, now in Plymouth, waited for their boarding orders. Paul had attended a briefing the previous night regarding Exercise Tiger, the third full training exercise for American troops. Each successive exercise increased the numbers of participants and equipment. It seemed so long ago that Operation Duck, the first exercise, had been conducted, followed by the disaster of Operation Beaver in March. Operation Tiger would be the third and, hopefully, final exercise.

Officers were told that two convoys of LSTs would leave Plymouth heading for Lyme Bay and the beaches of Slapton Sands. The first convoy would be leaving on April 25 and landing on April 27 while the second convoy would leave on the 26th and land the morning of the 28th. The lengthy travel from Plymouth to Slapton would simulate transport through the Channel and the crossing to Europe.

Once the first LSTs were in place, air and naval bombardment would commence, and the airborne of the 82nd and 101st would drop behind the target lines. That would be followed by the army's assault of the beachhead. Each lieutenant was given orders that showed their group's assignment. Paul's orders still showed his men would be landing on the beach in LSTs with the second phase of the attack. The LST would beach itself and his men would depart alongside the tanks.

Officers were informed Generals Eisenhower and Bradley as well as Air Marshall Sir Arthur Tedder would be present. If pleased with the exercise, they would give the final okay to make the European landing.

After the briefing, Paul found Major Poder and inquired as to the reason for his men's position in group two. "Sir, if I may speak freely."

"By all means, Lieutenant."

"I see my orders show that my platoon is still in group two. My men have worked hard and performed well from the very start. I know that they would like to take a leading role in the landing, sir."

"I agree, Lieutenant. Your platoon has performed better than most. It was your group that showed us the need to protect our weapons from water and mud."

"Then I don't understand, sir."

"Lieutenant Schaefer, you are very important to us. You speak German. You will be needed to interrogate prisoners and to decipher notes, maps and any other German documents that we find. Command made the decision to move you to a safer position in the line, Lieutenant. Now, go back and let your men know."

"Yes, sir." Paul saluted Major Poder.

***

Paul's meeting the previous night with Major Poder left him feeling unsettled. He had not relayed the information to his men. Paul wasn't quite sure how to tell them the reason they would not be leading the assault. Did command not think his men were too important, but because he could speak a different language, he was too important? The bottom line was orders were orders, and they would abide by them without question.

There was a knock at his door. "Come in."

A young corporal entered whom Paul had not seen before. "Sir, there will be a meeting of all officers at 0800 hours. That is just over an hour from now, sir."

"Thank you, Corporal." The corporal turned and left the room. Paul got up from the cot and walked outside. It was late April, but the weather still had not changed much over the past months. It was always damp with a slight chill in the air. Paul pulled his coat collar up around his neck and went to find Sergeant Coffey.

✳✳✳

After the 0800 meeting, Paul returned to find Coffey and the platoon sitting outside the barracks, just as he had ordered Coffey earlier. "This is it, men. Exercise Tiger begins for us today. We board at 1600 hours."

Johnson spoke, "Sir, some of the other platoons have already boarded, and their ships left dock this morning. What's going on?"

Schaefer continued, "We are still with the second landing group."

Men started moaning and shuffling. A couple of men angrily stomped on discarded cigarettes. "What happened? Why didn't we move up to the first launch group? We worked our asses off to be with the lead groups."

Paul decided not to say anything about his conversation with Major Poder. "Orders are orders. I'm sure command has their reasons. We're going to be the best platoon this army has, and there will be plenty of time to prove it. Now listen up and say no more!"

The men settled down. Some lit new cigarettes, but everyone was silent. "As I said before, we board at 1600 hours. The convoy will move out to sea in a looping pattern. We will be at sea on the 27th when the first shelling will be heard. The first landings will take place sometime on the 27th. We will then move toward our target at Slapton Beach. Our orders have us landing early in the morning of the 28th. Make certain you check all of your gear again and be ready to move out on Sergeant Coffey's word." Paul finished, "Anything else?"

Dicatto asked, "Sir, some of us have letters to send out. Can we take them down to the mail room?"

"Yes." Paul replied. "It would not be a bad idea for everyone to write home today, but remember, mention nothing in the letter about the exercise."

Paul turned toward Coffey. "Sergeant, make sure everyone is ready to go by 1500 hours." He then opened the door to his room. Once inside, he pulled out paper and began to write his own letters to his parents, brothers, and one to the address Marie had given him.

CHAPTER FIFTY-TWO

A messenger ran along the docks in Cherbourg, France. Finding a German sailor, the young messenger said, "I am looking for Kapitan zur see Petersen."

The sailor pointed, "Over there. His attaché will take whatever you have." The messenger proceeded, handing the message over to the attaché. The message was an order to make preparations to patrol the waters off Lyme Bay.

Kapitan zur see Rudolf Petersen was the Führer des Schnellboote in charge of the German S-boats stationed along the French coast. S-boats, or Schnell Boats meaning "fast boats", were swift-moving torpedo boats, 35 meters in length, with a crew of 21. The boats moved at 35 to 40 knots. Each boat was equipped with two 21-inch torpedo tubes, holding up to six torpedoes, and two 20mm cannons on deck. Petersen read the message. Addressing his attaché, Petersen said, "Have the officers prepare their boats for a search this evening. We leave at 2200 hours."

The attaché snapped his boots and saluted, "Heil Hitler!"

***

The British regularly patrolled the Channel, attempting to intercept S-boats or other German ships moving toward Great Britain. The British and American military designated S-boats as E-boats, or "enemy" boats. By 2300 hours, however, the nine E-boats commanded by Petersen's men slipped past British patrols. Close to midnight on April 27, the

E-boats were in sight of Southern England. One of the Oberleutnant's in the 9th Flotilla was Gunther Rabe, a 26-year-old naval officer. He gave the command for his men to be on close watch for signs of a British or American convoy. The sea was dark as ebony and the air was as soft as a mother's loving whisper. Rabe opened the door to the bridge breathing in the cool, salt air. "We have word there may very well be enemy transports in these waters tonight. Keep glasses to your eyes and your ears open to the sounds of the sea." His men saluted and followed orders, turning their attention to the open waters.

Rabe's first report of British and American ships in the area came just before 0200. Radio communications were made between the S-boats of the 9th and 5th Flotilla Groups. All the sailors proceeded to their battle stations and torpedoes were loaded into each bay. Rabe thought to himself, *Kapitan Petersen was correct with his prediction of British ships in these waters tonight.*

***

The convoy had left Plymouth with only one escort ship, a corvette, the HMS *Azalea.* A second British destroyer, the HMS *Scimitar,* had been scheduled to escort the convoy as well, but the *Scimitar* had been involved in a minor collision the day before and was unavailable. British naval command had decided that one escort ship was sufficient.

The men of the second assault group were now in the midst of their night at sea. Just after midnight, naval command gave orders for the convoy to turn the line toward the beaches of Slapton.

The eight LSTs and the HMS *Azalea* made their final turn toward Lyme Bay. The ships were traveling in a single line. Sailors were performing their nightly tasks while rotating soldiers stood watch on deck. All of Lieutenant Schafer's men were asleep below deck when the first torpedo struck LST 507. The ship shook under the explosion. Private Jessup, from California, fell out of his bunk and said, "Wow! Earthquakes in Britain!"

O'Shea picked Jessup up off the floor. "No way! They don't have those things here. I think we've been hit."

Dicatto hollered, "Everyone up! Get your gear." As Dicatto was speaking, the alarm sounded.

Sergeant Coffey yelled, "Everyone up on deck, full gear! Make sure to grab your lifebelts!"

By the time the platoon made it on top, cannon fire could be heard from somewhere in the vast darkness of Lyme Bay. Sailors from the 507 were firing as well. Tracers from the ship's cannons periodically lit the darkness. Cannon and engine noise made communication between soldiers nearly impossible. Dicatto moved toward the edge of the ship when machine gun fire strafed the surrounding area, forcing Dicatto to dive to the deck and scramble away from the ship's side. "Jesus, those fuckers are firing at us." Then he yelled at Coffey. "Sergeant, what the hell are we suppose to do?"

Sergeant Coffey yelled over the noise. "Everyone stay low and assemble on me, now!"

The 507 was the last in line and all the men on deck could see gunfire coming from the LSTs in front of them. It was evident that the 507 had been hit by a torpedo, and a second explosion, probably from the engine room, sent flames up through the hatches.

Forward of their position, Lieutenant Schaefer saw another LST explode. Lieutenant Schaefer turned to Sergeant Coffey, "Sergeant, let's get our guys moving toward one of the lifeboats." Coffey gave the order and each man made his way to the stern lifeboat area.

A sailor met the men. Addressing Lieutenant Schaefer, the sailor hollered, "Sir, we have not received orders to abandon ship as yet. Please wait in this area, and if we receive word, your group is third in line."

Schaefer acknowledged the sailor and told his men to remain where they were and to stay low. He then said, "Make certain your gear and lifebelts are properly fastened."

Johnson hit O'Shea in the arm. Pointing toward soldiers in front of them, he scoffed, "Look at those idiots. They have their lifebelts tied around their waists. Fucking idiots."

Another explosion rocked LST 507, and O'Shea said to Johnson, "We need to get off this fucking ship, and soon!"

***

Racing around the convoy at close to 40 knots, Rabe's men continued to fire their 20mm cannons. Rabe already had fired two of his torpedoes and was in the process of loading the next two into the tubes. Reports between the S-boats confirmed two LSTs had been hit, with one already sinking.

Rabe gave the order for his boat, S-130, to turn out toward the open ocean. After a few moments, he turned back facing the convoy. Rabe gave the command to fire. Two torpedoes left their tubes, slicing through the waters toward yet another LST. At his distance from the convoy, Rabe saw three distinct fires. Three of the LSTs were either sinking or listing badly. Out of torpedoes, with only the 20mm cannons in use, Rabe was considering his next maneuver. Just as he was about to give orders to pull back, command radioed for all the S-boats to escape the area.

Rabe thought the order was a good one. As of now, there had been little return fire from the British or American ships, but certainly there were warships in the area that would respond. With little offensive weaponry left, the order to vacate was the correct one.

***

Finally, the message to abandon ship was received on LST 507. The first two groups of soldiers boarded the lifeboats and began to lower to the sea. The 507 lurched, and one of the two lines lowering a lifeboat turned, throwing everyone onboard into the cold waters below. With the fire spreading out over the top deck, Lieutenant Schaefer ordered his men to the side of the boat. "We are not waiting any longer. Just as we practiced. We are going over the side."

Sergeant Coffey hollered to the platoon, "Remove your helmet, fold your arms across your chest, check below and jump. Hit the water with your boots, inflate your lifebelts and swim away from the ship!" In groups of four, the platoon plunged over the side. The long, dark fall of some twenty to thirty feet was quick, but submerging in the cold, black abyss of the Atlantic seemed to take forever. There was no way to assemble now. Every man was on his own.

The frigid water was less than 50 degrees, and within minutes, numbness began to invade each man that survived the jump. Coffey was in the process of swimming away when he swam into a dead soldier. Treading water, he could not see the soldier's face. The dead soldier had his lifebelt around his waist, thus making only the middle section buoyant. His head was submerged. Coffey knew that all of his men had properly fitted their belts. He pushed the dead soldier away and continued to swim toward the sound of men yelling in the distant darkness.

Johnson and O'Shea jumped into the water holding onto each other. Johnson admitted to O'Shea that he was not a very strong swimmer, so O'Shea told him to hang on as they swam away from the damaged ship. Oil and gasoline, floating on top of the water, was on fire. Twice Johnson and O'Shea beat flames away as they swam.

Lieutenant Schaefer cleared the ship and began to swim away from the sinking LST. Immediately, Schaefer ran into an unconscious soldier who was floating with his head just above the water. In the flickering of the fires behind him, the lieutenant could barely see the face of the unconscious soldier. "Dicatto! Dicatto, are you okay?"

Dicatto gave no response. Paul felt for the carotid artery. He had a pulse although it was weak. Schaefer grabbed the back of Dicatto's lifebelt and began to sidekick further away from the doomed LST.

***

Lieutenant Schaefer and Dicatto reached one of the life rafts. Paul looked up and saw maybe ten men leaning over the side and five or six men clinging to ropes that dangled into the water. "Help us! I have an injured soldier here! He needs to be lifted onboard!"

One of the soldiers in the water let go of the rope with one hand and reached for Dicatto. He pulled Dicatto toward the raft while Schaefer grabbed for another hanging rope. Together they held Dicatto's head and shoulders out of the water. Once again, Schaefer yelled to the men onboard the raft. "This is Lieutenant Schaefer! You need to lift this injured man into the raft!"

Two soldiers leaned over the side. "There is no room in the raft, Sir. You need to just hang on."

Paul yelled back, "You lean over and grab this man, NOW!"

"Sir, there is no more room!"

Letting go of Dicatto for a moment, Paul reached down into the cold water and found his sidearm. Bringing the revolver up out of the water, Paul pulled the trigger. To his surprise and to the surprise of the men on the raft, the gun fired. Shocked by what had just happened, one of the men on the raft leaned over and yelled, "Jesus, Lieutenant! What the hell!"

"Soldier, you either lift this injured man onboard or I'll make room by firing the next shots into this raft!"

Two soldiers leaned over the side of the raft. "Okay, Okay! We got him." Both men grabbed a part of Dicatto's vest and pulled him onboard.

Schaefer placed the revolver back in his holster and grabbed for the rope with both hands.

***

Coffey was still swimming alone in the water. His limbs were heavy, he could feel he was becoming lethargic, and hypothermia was overtaking him. Rolling over onto his back, he began to float in the oily water. He tried to keep his eyes open, but the cold was defeating him. The last vision Coffey remembered were of flames dancing above the water and the sight of LST 507 slipping quietly below the waters of Lyme Bay.

CHAPTER FIFTY-THREE

Foggy mist fell over Lyme Bay as darkness gave way to light. Almost five hours had passed since the German torpedo attack. Three LSTs were struck, two had sunk, and one had been badly damaged and limped toward port. After receiving the alarm, the remaining five LSTs and rescue ships were slowly dragging the waters looking for survivors. Sadly, there were as many dead, floating lifeless in the cold water, as there were living.

A rescue boat sent out from LST 511 picked up Johnson and O'Shea. Earlier, they had swum to a capsized lifeboat and had been holding on with eleven other soldiers. When Johnson and O'Shea were pulled from the water, only one other soldier was still clinging to its side. The three were taken onboard and given blankets and coffee. O'Shea was shaking so badly that he spilled the entire cup, so a sailor came over and sat beside him. "Here, let me hold the cup for you. Take small sips." O'Shea looked at the sailor and smiled, opened his trembling lips and drank.

Another sailor walked by and Johnson asked, "Would you have any smokes?" The sailor placed a cigarette between his lips, lit it, and passed the cigarette to Johnson. Johnson barely could whisper, "Thanks."

Lieutenant Schaefer was still holding on when a rescue boat found them. Men onboard the life raft said Dicatto had regained consciousness for a short time, but later had slipped back just before the rescue boat arrived. Paul made certain a medic aboard the ship was looking after Dicatto. Returning to the top deck, Paul approached an ensign. The ensign said, "We will get you to dock as soon as possible, sir."

Paul looked at the ensign, "Not until you have found as many survivors as your ship will carry."

"Yes, sir. Have a seat inside, sir, and grab some coffee."

Paul took a blanket and wrapped it around his shoulders. "If it's okay with you, I will stay out on deck and look for survivors in the water. Some of the men out there are mine, and I'm not leaving here until we find them."

The ensign said, "Yes, sir. I understand."

***

It was April 30th, two days since Lieutenant Schaefer had been pulled out of the frigid Atlantic. More than 700 soldiers or sailors were dead or missing and another 300 injured. Three men from his platoon were known dead. Dicatto and Coffey were in the hospital fighting for their lives.

Schaefer was in the officer mess area when Captain Rickles came in. "Lieutenant, may I have a word with you?"

Paul looked at the Captain and replied, "Of course, sir. What is it?"

"Lieutenant, you reported that you fired your revolver while in the water."

"Yes, sir. That is correct. Soldiers on the life raft were probably in shock, and I needed to get their attention. I needed to get them to help me with a wounded soldier, sir."

"Well, Lieutenant. I have interviewed every man listed on that raft, and no one can remember hearing any shot fired. Maybe you were just hallucinating in the cold water."

Paul paused for a moment, "I don't think so, sir."

"Well, it's over, Lieutenant. I have filed my report. No shots were fired."

Paul gave the captain a salute. "Yes, sir. I understand, sir."

"Good. One more thing, Lieutenant. I need three men to drive to Dartmouth and gather six doctors that will be coming out to help us with the injured. I want an officer to travel with the men into

Dartmouth. Take two of your men, grab three jeeps and get those doctors. On your way out, see Captain Nichols. He has the address of the
pickup location."

"Yes, sir. I'll leave right now." Paul turned and went to find Johnson
and O'Shea.

***

It took almost an hour to get to Dartmouth. They arrived in town from
the west on Townstal Road. All three jeeps stopped at the junction of
Townstal and Church Road. Paul turned to Johnson and O'Shea. "You
both continue down Townstal to Coombe Road. The doctors are waiting for us at the junction of Coombe and North Embankment."

O'Shea asked, "What about you, Lieutenant? Where are you
going?"

"This is between only the three of us. I am going to find Charly and
let her know about Sergeant Coffey. We are to pick up the doctors at
0900. We have some time. I won't be late. Just get there and wait for
me."

They both responded, "Yes, sir. We'll see you at North Embankment."
O'Shea and Johnson continued down Townstal while Paul made haste
down Church Road.

Paul pulled up outside Mrs. Sawyer's home. He wanted to see
Marie and to have her accompany him to give Charly the news regarding John. Racing up the stairs, he punched the doorbell. Mrs. Sawyer
came to the door. "Mrs. Sawyer, you don't know me. My name is Paul
Schaefer. Maybe Marie mentioned my name."

Mrs. Sawyer said, "Why yes, she did, young man. Please come in."

Without hesitation, Paul said, "I'm sorry, Mrs. Sawyer. I'm in town
on important business, and I am running late. Is Marie here? It's
important. I need to see her."

Mrs. Sawyer looked away, picked up an envelope and turned back
to Paul. "I'm sorry, Mr. Schaefer. Marie has gone. She left me a note

saying that she had to leave and that if a soldier came, to give him this. I assume it was meant for you. It has your name on the envelope."

"Gone! What do you mean, gone?"

"That's all I know. Here is the envelope. I'm sorry."

Paul took the envelope, turned and walked back to the jeep. Sitting in the jeep, Paul opened the envelope. Holding his emotions in check, he began to read.

Paul,

You know I have gone. I never wanted to hurt you. I wish that we had met in another time. I once told you that I was clairvoyant. I pray that I am now. I believe that we will meet again, maybe in a time of less death and sorrow. Know that I never thought of you as my enemy. Please find a way to forgive me.

Marie.

Paul's eyes began to water and slowly a tear found its way down his cheek. "Enemy." Paul's thoughts turned to the men in the alley. He recalled the picture on Marie's dresser with words written in German. *She's German, a Nazi. Those men were trying to capture her, and I helped her to escape?* Suddenly, thoughts of his nightmare, Exercise Tiger, draped him like a scene from Stoker's *Dracula*. Did he unwittingly give Marie information that led to the assault? He tried to think about what he might have said to her over the past months. Slumping forward, he rested his head and arms on the jeep's steering wheel. *Did these men, my men, die because of me?* Speaking to no one but himself, "Marie, how could you?" Raising his head, he squeezed the steering wheel. Anger overwhelmed him. "God damn you, Marie! You used me, you bitch! I am coming to Europe to kill Nazis, including you, Marie!"

CHAPTER FIFTY-FOUR

Twelve men sat around the table at Camp Griffiss, Bushy Park, London, England. All were high-ranking officers with the Supreme Headquarters of the Allied Expeditionary Force. Each man nervously awaited General Eisenhower's arrival. It had been just nine days since the disaster of Exercise Tiger, and today's meeting had been called to review past events and update plans for future trainings. Rumors had spread that the General was also going to have a message from President Roosevelt.

General Eisenhower entered the smoky catacomb used as the conference room. All assembled swiftly rose and stood at attention. General Eisenhower addressed the room. "As you were, gentlemen. Please sit." The General took the chair at the head of the table. "Paul, why don't you begin with the latest information from the site?"

Lieutenant Colonel Paul Thompson was head of the assault training. He was a 1929 graduate of West Point and the man responsible for the various training exercises at Slapton Sands. Paul began, "General, as of yesterday, we have six hundred and ninety confirmed dead, three hundred injured, and another seventy still missing."

General Eisenhower interrupted, "I knew the casualty number was high, but I was unaware just how high." Others at the table looked shocked at the casualty numbers presented. The General continued, "I am concerned with the high number still missing. Do you have any ideas? Is there a chance we will find more survivors?"

Lt. Col. Thompson responded, "Sir, I doubt we will find more survivors. We have been sweeping the waters daily. Bodies, however, are still washing up onshore. We have MP's down on the beaches working to keep civilians away, but it has been difficult. The tides have washed some of the bodies outside our quarantine area. Some of the missing soldiers are likely still encased in the two sunken ships. We are doing everything we can to find all of the missing soldiers."

General Eisenhower brought his hand to his chin and frowned. "Lieutenant Colonel, quarantine a larger area of beach, place more MP's on duty and do not, I repeat, do not let any civilians near the area. We need to keep a lid on this." Eisenhower added, "Is there any chance that some of these missing soldiers could have been picked up by the German boats? Do any of the missing officers have BIGOT status?"

Thompson avoided General Eisenhower's stare and looked down at a piece of paper on the table. "Thankfully, sir, all of the BIGOTs have been accounted for. Unfortunately, prisoners are a possibility. We will keep looking for the missing. We are attempting to send divers down to investigate the sunken ships as well. I will keep you updated, sir, each day as to our count. Finally, we have been in contact with Colonel Donovan's office. His European agents have heard nothing from German communications within France."

"Thank you, Paul. This is not your fault, but we cannot afford any of this to leak out. We can only pray that none of the missing are prisoners."

Lieutenant General Douglas spoke up. "General, if I may ask, whose fault is it? How did German boats get into our training and cause this to happen?"

"I don't have those answers as yet," General Eisenhower responded. "British intelligence said that all German spies had either been caught or turned. The British said that there is no chance that a spy compromised our training."

Lieutenant General Avery spoke up. "I don't believe that German boats were there by coincidence, General. Those British bastards aren't going to admit they fucked up! This is on the British, sir. First, their agents let a German spy get through, and then the British escort ships fuck up our protection."

"That may be true, General, but right now we need to contain this information, find the missing and plan for the future." General Eisenhower's aide passed out a file folder to each man at the table. "Gentlemen, please open your folder. First, you will see a communiqué from President Roosevelt. He is aware of the situation and has consulted with Prime Minister Churchill. Until we can account for all the soldiers involved in Exercise Tiger, no notification will be made to the family members of the deceased. All of the dead will be buried here. After a successful invasion, decisions will be made on notification and the return of bodies to their families." Everyone at the table was quiet.

General Eisenhower continued, "As for the invasion, we must conclude that the Germans may know that they interrupted a training exercise. No BIGOTed officer is reported in the missing, so the invasion target and dates should still be secure. We cannot, however, be certain that important information has not leaked out, and we cannot afford to lose more men during training. Our planned execution date during the first week in June remains in place. If the weather and tides continue to hold as believed, we will launch on June 5 or 6. Look over the remainder of the training files within your folder." General Eisenhower stood. "Remain seated. That is all." The General turned and walked out of the room.

Officers closed their file folders, reached for cigarettes or pipes and began to stand to leave the conference room.

CHAPTER FIFTY-FIVE

After almost a month of traversing through the English midlands, Marie was finally in Ramsgate. It was early. Fog lay heavy on the wharf. Scattered street lamps were failing to illuminate the damp environment, and Marie struggled to see the boats tied to their moorings. A week ago, Marie had mailed a coded letter to an address in Ramsgate. The letter gave the date of her arrival and the need to exit immediately.

There were three full docks of boats gently swaying to the tidal movement. Marie stood in front of the first dock. Thick fog made it impossible to identify her escape boat, the *Mariana*. Carrying her bag and with her gun in her coat pocket, Marie walked down the dock and back. No *Mariana*. As she moved to the second dock, she heard a voice.

"Surely, you don't want to die right here, right now." Using the same greeting she had used in Dartmouth, Marie turned to see the third man, the one she had left tied on the boat. "We meet again although this time I have the opportunity to make the surprise entrance."

Marie slowly placed her bag on the wet dock. "My mistake was to let you see another English sunrise."

"I thank you for that, and I will return the favor by not shooting you now although revenge for my friends seems to call for it."

Marie acknowledged him by nodding while slowly sliding her hand into her coat pocket.

"You will want to remove your hand from your coat pocket just as slowly as you placed it in. And, please, don't be holding a gun. I would like to end this encounter without harm to either of us."

Marie smiled and withdrew her hand. "How did you find me?"

"Unfortunately for you, the boat's owner came by shortly after you left and found me. Although I suffered with an extreme headache, but of course you would know that, I realized your most likely escape would be by bus. I found the agent that sold you the ticket to Bristol."

"I'm not quite as good as I thought at covering my plans."

"You were very good. We were always just slightly behind you, but in the end, no, Germans are not quite as good as they think they are. British stubbornness always prevails. Now it is your turn to lay on the ground, face down. I'm sorry this may cause you to soil your dress, but the alternative would be to shoot you standing where you are."

Marie placed her knee on the ground and began to bend forward. As she did, a shot broke the early morning silence. Her adversary clutched at his chest while reflexively firing his gun. His bullet struck Marie as she had begun to stand. Both now fell forward onto the wet ground.

Coming up from the dock, the man that had fired the shot bent down to assist Marie. "Come, my dear. We must get you to the boat."

Marie held her right side just above her breast with her left hand. Blood was seeping through her fingers. The boat captain lifted her off the ground, cradling her in his arms. He looked once more at her assailant whose lifeless body was face down on the ground, his blood mixing with watery soil.

The captain carried Marie down into the boat's galley. Laying her on a bench, he threw wood into the stove's furnace.

Marie opened her eyes. The physical pain was greater than anything she had ever known. She tried to speak, but it came out more as a whisper. "Please, help me. Take off my coat and blouse."

The captain came over to her. "My name is Fredrick. I don't know. . ."

Before he could finish, Marie repeated, "Just take my coat and blouse off. And hurry! Next, find some rags and boil them in water on your stove. I need to try to stop this bleeding."

Fredrick did as instructed. Coming back to Marie he said, "I must now get us out of here. Those shots certainly would have awakened people. Soon the police will be arriving."

Marie gathered some energy and sat up. "Yes, yes. Get us moving now. When we are out of the harbor, come back down and help me secure the bandages." Fredrick swiftly moved up the stairs. Within minutes, Marie heard the engines whine, and the boat moved out into the harbor.

***

Fredrick returned and grabbed three more pieces of wood, throwing them into the stove. The light inside was weak, but Fredrick could see that Marie's wound was still bleeding. Using a wooden spoon, Fredrick retrieved the boiling rags from the pot and placed them on the table. "Give them a moment to cool," he said.

From a first aid kit, Fredrick grabbed some gauze and a bottle of alcohol. He brought them over to the table placing them next to the wet rags. "The alcohol will hurt, but it may help to clean the wound. You know that the bullet is still in there."

Marie said, "Yes, but we cannot risk taking it out now. Pour the alcohol on one of the boiled rags and press it into the wound."

Just before pressing the rag to Marie's body, he said, "This is going to cause you great pain. I am so sorry."

"Just do it quickly," she said. Marie screamed and instinctively grabbed for Fredrick's arm as the wet rag made contact with her wound. Fredrick used his free hand to stop her. Then Marie passed out on the bench. Fredrick tightly wrapped the gauze around Marie's chest. Blood was still seeping out through the gauze, but it seemed to be slowing. When finished, he rose and went back up top to make certain the boat was on course for France.

***

An hour later, Fredrick returned to find Marie awake. "Please help me to sit," she said.

Fredrick assisted Marie. "My boat is old and slow. It will take us a few more hours to reach port."

Marie asked, "Do you have a working radio on board?"

"Yes. It is upstairs."

"Good. Use your transmitter and make contact with those picking me up in France. Tell them to have a doctor meet us." Marie then asked, "Would you have some paper and something to write with?"

"Yes." Fredrick retrieved paper and a pencil from the cupboard next to the table. As he placed the paper and pencil on the table, he looked closely at Marie's face. She was white and her eyelids were drooping. If the bleeding kept up, she most likely would not make it to France alive. "Can I make you some tea?" he asked.

"Thank you. That would be nice."

"I have some bread as well." Fredrick placed the teapot on the stove and the bread next to the paper on the table. "I must now go back upstairs. I will be back to get your tea shortly."

Marie smiled. "Thank you again for helping me. You saved my life."

Fredrick returned the smile. "I hope so, my dear."

When Fredrick was gone, Marie took the paper and pencil. *Dear Paul.* She began to compose another letter to Paul. *You may have returned to Mrs. Sawyer's and now know that I deceived you. Yes, I meant to, but I never would harm you. The time we spent in my bed was as a man and woman, not as soldiers and enemies. I have left England, but not before suffering a severe wound that may, unfortunately, take my life. My greatest regret is that, if I die, I will do so without seeing you or holding you again.*

By the time Fredrick came back down, Marie had finished her letter to Paul. In it, she told him of her true life and, once again, asked Paul for his forgiveness. Fredrick placed the cup of tea next to the bread. Marie was eating a piece of bread, and Fredrick pulled off a piece for himself. Marie gave the folded paper to Fredrick asking, "May I ask one more favor from you, Fredrick?"

"Certainly, my dear. What is it?"

"Show these pages to no one. When you return to England, place them in an envelope and send them to the address I have written on this paper. Will you do this for me?"

Fredrick took the papers, looking at the address. "This is to an American serviceman. Are you certain you want me to do this?"

Marie tried to reach for Fredrick and he grabbed her hand. "Fredrick, I might die tonight or, if not tonight, soon. Surely, you can see this." Squeezing his hand as tightly as she could, Marie said, "I promise you that I have not betrayed the Fürher, Germany, or my duty. This is personal. I need you to promise you will do this for me."

Fredrick bent forward and kissed Marie's hand. "I will. I promise. Now close your eyes and rest. We will be there shortly."

***

A truck was waiting at the dock as Fredrick shut down his engine, and the boat bumped the dock's siding. He threw ropes to two men standing on the wooden platform before going below. Marie was lying on the bench, covered by a blanket. A man spoke to Fredrick from the door hatch. "Captain, I am Dr. Gereau. May I come down?"

Fredrick looked up as the doctor proceeded down the ladder. "Doctor, she is over here. I fear she is not doing well. She is unconscious and has been for a while now."

Gereau moved in front of Fredrick and felt Marie's head. "She has a fever, and the wound looks to still be bleeding. Help me get her up on top. My men have a cot for her. We will take her to my home."

They placed Marie on the cot. Dr. Gereau listened with his stethoscope. Turning to Fredrick he said, "She is still alive, but barely. You did a good job cleaning the wound and keeping the bandage tight, Captain. Unfortunately, it may not be enough. We will take her now."

"Yes, doctor. I, too, must be getting back to England. I have some work to finish there. When I return, I will check with you to see how she is doing."

Dr. Gereau gave the captain a piece of paper. "This is my home address. Please come by upon your return. Good evening." The two men with Dr. Gereau had already placed Marie in the truck. Dr. Gereau opened the passenger door. "I will see you upon your return."

Fredrick walked back down the dock, unlashed the boat from the mooring plates and prepared for the return across the Channel.

CHAPTER FIFTY-SIX

June 1, 1944

"**L**ieutenant Schaefer, Major Poder would like to see you in his office immediately, sir." The messenger was a young private that Lieutenant Schaefer did not recognize.

"Do you know what the Major wants?" asked Paul.

"No, sir, but Colonel Erickson is in the Major's office. A third man in civilian clothes is in the office as well, sir."

Paul was concerned and confused by the request. "Thank you, Private. Tell the Major I will be right along."

"I'm sorry, sir, but I was given orders to escort you there immediately, sir."

Paul rose from his desk. "Okay, Private. Let's go."

Paul walked outside his hut. Two MPs were standing at attention, one on each side of the door. Paul asked the MP to his right, "Is there a problem? Am I under arrest for something?"

The MP remained silent. Paul walked forward, behind the private and in front of the two MPs. Paul was trying to understand what was happening when he remembered the alley. *This must be about the shooting in the alley. Marie must have been questioned.*

Sergeant Coffey walked up. He was returning from his checkup in the infirmary. Coffey suffered from hypothermia and had been hospitalized for two weeks. He had just returned to the unit and needed to be rechecked once again. His feet were still giving him some trouble. "Sir, what's going on?"

Paul turned toward Coffey and said, "I don't know, Sergeant. Just look after the men until I return."

"Yes, sir. I will." Perplexed, Coffey watched as Paul was led away.

***

The private knocked on Major Poder's door. "Come in."

Paul and the two MPs entered the Major's office. Major Poder addressed the MPs. "You may wait outside."

Then to Paul, Major Poder said, "Lieutenant, please take a chair."

Paul sat in the only unoccupied chair in the room. Major Poder said, "Lieutenant, this is Colonel Erickson and Mr. Cooke. Mr. Cooke is from British intelligence." Cooke was a small, thin man, about forty, wearing a crisp, grey suit. Under his thin mustache, Mr. Cooke was scowling at Paul.

Paul nodded at each of the men but said nothing to them. Addressing Major Poder, Paul asked, "Sir, may I inquire as to why I am here and why there are MPs outside the door?"

"Lieutenant, our censors reviewed a letter that was sent to you. It arrived two days ago."

Paul asked, "A letter from whom, sir?"

"There was no return address, and the letter is not signed. The writer, Mr. Cooke believes, is a German agent."

Paul sat quietly, expressionless. Finally, he spoke, "Sir, may I see the letter?"

Mr. Cooke interrupted, "Lieutenant, you are German and you were conspiring with a German agent."

"Mr. Cooke," Paul immediately snapped, "I am an American citizen. It is true my family is from Germany, but I have never been anything but American, sir."

Major Poder attempted to ease some of the hostility brewing within the room. "Lieutenant, tell us about the writer of this letter."

Paul began, "I met a young woman in Dartmouth. Her name is Marie, and she worked at one of the pubs, the Hinde. I met her while we were given leave." Paul spent the next hour explaining all he knew about Marie. He told everyone that she misled him as well, but that he never revealed any information regarding training plans or schedules.

At one point, Mr. Cooke broke in asking, "What can you tell us about a shooting and beating that took place behind the Hinde?"

Paul paused. He had never made a report regarding the shooting. "I thought this young woman, Marie, was being attacked by two men. One man was on top of her, striking her in the face. I knocked him off, and there was a struggle. The next thing I know, there's a shot, and the man falls. Marie shot him."

"That man was one of mine," Cooke shouted in a captious tone. "You conspired with a German agent to kill a British intelligence officer. Actually, she killed a second agent just a couple of weeks ago while making her escape."

Colonel Erickson finally spoke, "We believe she also killed a British Colonel in London."

Paul was overwhelmed by all of this information. He thought, how could Marie, a woman he thought he was falling in love with, do all of the things they were saying? In the end, all Paul said was, "I am sorry for the loss of your officer, Mr. Cooke, and for the British Colonel as well. Had I known she was an agent, I would have told someone. I would have brought her in myself." Once again, Paul reiterated, "I am an American officer. I was recruited because of my German ancestry and knowledge of Germany. I would do nothing to harm America or its allies."

Colonel Erickson stood. Paul rose and stood at attention. "Lieutenant Schaefer, these are serious charges against you, but we are under a very difficult time constraint. Major Poder will discuss with you where we go from here."

Paul looked at the Colonel. "Yes sir, I understand."

Colonel Erickson turned to Major Poder. "I leave this to you now." Both men saluted the Colonel, and Erickson opened the door and left. Cooke rose, looking as though he had lost a fight, said nothing and left the room.

Major Poder told Paul to sit. When he did, Paul asked, "Sir, what is going to happen to me? To my platoon?" Paul continued, "Sir, this may not be the right thing to ask, but may I see the letter?"

"Lieutenant, those men want you incarcerated until after the war. Mr. Cooke would like you shot as a traitor."

Paul attempted to speak again. Poder abruptly raised his hand. "Say nothing, Lieutenant. As the Colonel said, time is the issue now. We are going to Europe within the week."

Paul responded, "Within the week?"

"Yes, Lieutenant, and that is not enough time to move your men around or to find another lieutenant with your capabilities." Poder relaxed. "Lieutenant, we need you. Yes, you are an American. I never doubted that, but you made some critical mistakes. The bottom line is that we need your German expertise. General Eisenhower made the final call on this. We need you interrogating prisoners and interpreting German communiqués and maps."

"I will do whatever you ask, Major."

"As for the letter, Lieutenant, I will let you read it. If there is anything in there that may help us determine if this Marie is still in England or if she has any information on our landing time or site, we need to know. And now! Do you understand?"

"Yes sir, I understand." Major Poder reached over and handed the pages to Paul. He noticed small smears of brown stain on the first page. It looked to be dried blood. He began to read, *Dear Paul,* . . . ."

ACKNOWLEDGEMENT

Although this book is historical in its context, it is a work of fiction. All historical inaccuracies are mine, and any connection of fictional characters to real people is coincidental.

Eisenhower, Montgomery, Hitler, Himmler, Heydrich and many others were obviously real people, and I tried to place them accurately within the context of their war functions. Marie and Paul, as well as Paul's company, are purely fictional characters.

With that being stated, Exercise Tiger, unfortunately, did take place along the Southern Coast of England at Slapton Sands in April 1944. German S boats did torpedo American ships as they were making way to the practice area. Approximately 750 sailors and soldiers died in the waters of Lyme Bay when three LSTs were hit by German fire. More Americans died during this practice than perished on Utah Beach on D-Day. The number of American casualties for Utah Beach was roughly 200 dead. However, the number for Omaha Beach was much higher.

How did the German navy know of the practice schedule and location? After the war, the British SOE, Special Operations Executive, said they had either arrested or turned every German spy located in Great Britain. In National Geographic, June 2002, Thomas Allen wrote that there were significant breaches of BIGOT security during the training exercises. One such breach included a weekly crossword puzzle published in the London *Daily Telegraph* which used puzzle answers of Utah, Omaha, Mulberry, and Neptune. Each word was associated directly with the D-Day landings.

The fact remains that somehow, either by coincidence or by some other means, German S boats found and sank American LSTs. Both American and British authorities kept the disaster at Slapton Sands a secret. There were two reasons for this. First, the authorities did not want Hitler to know that his navy had disrupted a landing practice and that the landing practice was taking place in Southern England. Second, American military leaders did not want to inform families that their loved ones died during a practice session. Notification to American families took place after June 6, 1944.

I first heard of Exercise Tiger and the displacement of British citizens from the area of Devon from a British friend, John Allison, while visiting in Bath, England. I was curious as to why this episode is seldom, if ever, mentioned in U.S. history books.

I began my research in England by visiting Slapton Sands. Later, I reviewed the work of Ken Small, a man that spent his life uncovering information and artifacts surrounding the events of April 1944. I read Small's book, *The Forgotten Dead*. Two other books helped me understand spies and British life during this time: *The Oral History of Special Operations in World War II,* by Russell Miller and *The Magic Army,* by Leslie Thomas, respectively. It was after this research that I decided to write a work of fiction and to create my own scenario for the events leading up to Exercise Tiger.

I would like to thank Joyce Allison, John's wife, for her care and kindness while visiting England. Without the Allison's support and friendship, my book would not have been written. This book is dedicated in memory of John Allison.

Thanks also to Diane Sawdon, Rae Roisman, Harry Gordon, and Lynn Aase, friends and colleagues that took time to read some of these pages and give me valuable insight and critiques. A special thanks goes to James Seckington, a valued critic; without his help and refinement, this book would not have been completed.

Most importantly, thanks to my wife Karen for her support and assistance throughout this entire project. I could not have done this without you.

Made in the USA
San Bernardino, CA
18 August 2014